the Vintage Wren

Volume 1

Chautona Havig

ISBN-13: 9781544930299
ISBN-10: 1544930291

Chautona Havig lives in a small, remote town in California's Mojave Desert with her husband and eight of her nine children. When not writing, she enjoys paper crafting, sewing, and trying to get the rest of her children educated so that she can retire from home education.

Fonts: Times New Roman, Alex Brush, California FBold Pro, Bickham Script Pro.
Cover photos: ValuaVitaly/thinkstock.com and bobbidog/istockphoto.com
Cover Art: Chautona Havig
Edited by: "Jillow"

The events and people in this book, aside from any caveats that may appear on the next page, are purely fictional, and any resemblance to actual people is purely coincidental. I'd love to meet them!

Connect with Me Online:
Twitter: https://twitter.com/Chautona
Facebook: https://www.facebook.com/justthewriteescape
Instagram: https://instagram.com/ChautonaHavig
My blog: http://chautona.com/blog/
Goodreads: https://twitter.com/Chautona
BookBub: https://www.bookbub.com/authors/chautona-havig
Amazon Author Page: https://www.amazon.com/Chautona-Havig/e/B0032191W2
YouTube: https://www.youtube.com/user/chautona/videos
My newsletter (sign up for news of FREE eBook offers): http://chautona.com/newsletter

All Scripture references are from the NASB. NASB passages are taken from the NEW AMERICAN STANDARD BIBLE (registered), Copyright 1960, 1962, 1963, 1968, 1971, 1972, 1973, 1975, 1977, 1995 by The Lockman Foundation

Fiction / Christian / Contemporary

Dedication

To Challice and Braelyn—my eco-girls. I'll never be a Cassie, but you both inspired me to write this book, and as I've researched, I've learned enough to make more changes than I could have imagined I would.

I love you girls more than you'll ever know. I'm crazy proud of you both, and I can't wait to see what the Lord has in store for you.

January
prologue
the Challenge

Saturday, December 26—

Over the din of screeching children still on Christmas overload, teenagers laughing loud enough to hide their awkwardness, and songs on the sound system that occasionally drifted back into Christmas as if not willing to allow the season to end, a voice broke through the intercom announcing a seventy percent off sale on all gold and silver in jew-ler-ee department. Cassie Wren paused before a display of acrylic champagne flutes on display for the exorbitant price of eighty-eight cents and stared at her friend. "C'mon, Lauren. I dare you. Go get in one last plea for proper pronunciation."

"I'm so tempted. That's almost as bad as real-a-tor—no, it's worse. I'm surprised the Jewish community hasn't decided it's offensive."

"There you go!" As she spoke, Cassie made a decision—*definitely these. For less than thirty bucks, I don't have to wash or pick up glass shards. Totally worth every penny.* She grabbed four at a time and piled them in the bottom of her cart. "Just see if you can get them on board. These days, the best way to get people to stop using any term is to make it offensive instead of just inaccurate."

Lauren stood still, staring at the cart as if still trying to make up her mind. Cassie nudged her as she placed the last two flutes in the cart. "Go ahead. You know you want to."

"Actually, I'm trying to figure out why a woman with at least fifty vintage crystal champagne flutes is buying thirty more—in *acrylic* no less."

"I decided I didn't want to risk breaking any. You know how the parties get. Everyone is packed in my little place, and I have that heavy porcelain sink. I lost four last year and it would have been more if I hadn't spent half the night rescuing them from ending up ground into the carpet. I'm not doing it again. I want to *enjoy* this party."

With a nod of concession, Lauren consulted the shopping list. "I suppose you want those heavy-duty silver plastic forks?"

"Yeah. And those heavy-duty plates, too. I'll have the party cleaned up inside twenty minutes. Better grab some more lawn trash bags. One fell swoop—almost no dishes."

This time, Lauren folded her arms over her chest and glared at Cassie. "Except for thirty champagne flutes, fifty ramekins—"

"Both disposable... this year, I got smart. Almost everything is disposable. Sweep everything into the trash and *done.* All the fun for half the work."

"But—" Lauren stared as Cassie whipped around a corner and began dumping plastic forks, knives, and spoons into her cart. "Those glasses aren't disposable, Cass!"

She heard it—that tone in Lauren's voice. "Lauren, I don't want to wash them, and at that price..." Cassie grabbed several packages of paper plates, towels, napkins, and zip-lock bags in almost one fluid movement. "I can afford to save myself the work. And..." She winked as a new idea hit her. "It's saving a ton of water. Eco-friendly!"

That did it. Lauren went from incredulous to indignant in half a second flat. "That is the *furthest* from eco-friendly. Those stupid flutes will be there sitting half-covered in dirt when this world is consumed by fire. You can't *do* that, Cassie. That's excessive even for you!"

"Fine. I'll dump 'em in a bag and drop them off at the thrift store."

Lauren pounced on that faster than even Cassie could have expected. "So why not just go get some at the thrift store? Cheaper, maybe, and you're not buying *new* stuff you're just going to toss? You can take them back."

"Oh, no! I don't have the time to go searching through half a dozen thrift stores for enough plastic flutes. Who donates those anyway?"

"Apparently, you do. Thirty bucks, Cass—*thirty* dollars. That's over an hour of your wages down the drain—or in the landfill, anyway."

"No... in the thrift store bin, thanks to you and your guilt trips." As they passed the display again, Cassie snagged ten more. "Just in case. I would hate not to have enough..." A look at Lauren's indignant expression prompted her to add by way of concession, "But I'll return the ones I don't use. How's that?"

"But that's forty dollars! *Two* hours of work. *Two!*"

Cassie didn't flinch. "It's worth it to me. I'll save so much time, and my time is worth something. I'll toss everything into garbage bags and be done with it in minutes. I don't want to start the New Year with a dirty house. That's just dumb."

"It's filling the landfill."

"Helping it fulfill its purpose. After all, it's called the landfill." When Lauren didn't look amused at her, albeit weak, attempt at a joke, Cassie went for logic. "Besides. It's already been made. It's not like I can do anything about that.

Lauren winced as Cassie turned another corner and reached for a box of black garbage bags. "Do you realize you've got over a hundred dollars of stuff in there—a hundred dollars of stuff you are going to send to the landfill? Why don't you just skip the party and toss the cash in the trash?"

A snicker escaped before Cassie could repress it. "Because all of our friends would kill you for even suggesting it?"

Lauren's protest fizzled before the second syllable could reach her throat. "Yeah... you're right. Maybe you could have an after party—a cleanup thing. Everyone comes over, eats pizza, and helps clean up. Save you money and save the planet."

"Sounds tacky to me." Cassie cocked her head as she watched her friend. "So, what's with you and the sudden burst of eco-consciousness?"

"You know I'm no fanatic, but um... C'mon. Look at that. The cart is overflowing with stuff that is destined for the landfill. Doesn't that bother you even a little?"

"Nope." Cassie grabbed a box of aluminum foil and another of plastic wrap.

They made it halfway across the store—almost to the checkout lines—before Lauren spoke again. "So... don't you ever think about just how much money you throw away? I mean, we both know I'm not a tree hugger or anything, but sometimes I make the eco-friendly choice just to keep from throwing away my money. You—forgive me, but it's true— seem to look for ways to load up the landfills."

"I don't think much of it. I mean, if I needed to save money, sure. It would probably be the easiest way to do it, but..."

"Easy? You think it's easy? Ha!" As they pulled into one of a dozen over-loaded lines, Lauren eyed Cassie's cart. "All that money just to avoid washing a few dishes. You know, you should try it at least once just to see if it's as much work as you think it is. I'll bet you'd be surprised. I mean, most would fit in that dishwasher you *never* use. How much work could it be?"

Visions of her mother standing at the sink for hours, washing spoon after spoon, plate after plate, and what felt like an endless line of glasses and cups. "How much time it took my mom... she spent *all day* in that tiny kitchen just trying to keep up with the constant washing because Dad was too cheap to buy a 'water guzzling' dishwasher. I doubt I'd use enough dishes in a week to fill mine. So, I use paper plates. It's fine."

Cassie's eyes took in the cart before her. She inched it forward as the person in front of her moved up to the conveyor belt and began unloading everything from crayons to dog food. Two bras piled on top of a bath rug, and she couldn't help but wonder at the randomness of the contents of that cart.

She has a bit of a point. But I'm rarely home. Why waste perfectly good water to avoid paper plates? Lauren cleared her throat in a wordless attempt to reiterate her question. Cassie sighed. "It's not hard at all, actually. I'm just more into *water* conservation than land conservation. That's all."

"You're into *Cassie* conservation, and that's about it."

She started to protest—to insist there was little to no truth in that at all. *It's just a matter of needs versus wants. I want convenience and don't* need *to save the money or the planet for that matter.* But before the words could cross her lips, Lauren brought out the big guns—so unfair.

"Look. I know you better than yourself sometimes. Your love of convenience is an *addiction*, not convenience. And it's a good thing you have that option, because you wouldn't make it a ye—week living green. You probably wouldn't even know where to start."

Indignation, frosted with a liberal application of amusement, filled Cassie. "Oh, come on. I could if I had to. I just don't *have* to."

"If you say so."

This time, the words prompted no amusement at all. As she presented her "case," Cassie sorted items in the cart with slow, deliberate movements. "The news, the Internet, every magazine on the stands—they're full of the latest so-called 'green' fad. They change nearly every week. One week we buy artificial Christmas trees once and use them for a lifetime; so don't buy pre-lit ones. The next week it's all about buying real trees because they're compostable and it ensures forestation continues."

Lauren's eyes rolled as she nudged the cart forward. "Whatever. I still say you couldn't do it. Just *consider* washing a dish now and then. Why'd you even buy them if you never use them?"

"Just because I don't wash dishes doesn't mean I *couldn't*. You're being ridiculous." Frustration mounted as Cassie realized she'd allowed her temper to get the better of her again. *You should consider that for your New Year's Resolutions. "Learn to do XYZ to control your temper."*

She sensed it—Lauren backing down. *Five... four... three...*

"Yeah, you're probably right. We can all do more than we think we can."

That's true. And, I know you're not trying to be obnoxious. Everyone gets a little... intense near the end of the year.

From the fringes of her consciousness, Cassie heard Lauren's next words and all rationality left her. "I'm just teasing you, anyway—hyperbole."

"Argh! Why do you do that? What the heck is hyperbole again? Is it like spoonerism or onomasomething?"

"Sorry... just exaggerated for effect." Lauren tried to change the subject, asking if they needed more ice while they stood reasonably close to the machines.

Cassie didn't bite. "So why not just say, 'I was exaggerating.' Why do you *do* that? The reason people graduate from school is so they don't have to remember that stuff anymore."

"This from you, the would-be writer." Lauren tried to laugh and shrug it off. "Look, I said I'm sorry. So, what about the ice?"

Even as she loaded her cart full of disposable paper and

plastic products onto the conveyor belt, with three bags of ice thanks to Lauren, Cassie turned her friend's words over and over in her mind. *She started to say year. Year! She didn't even downgrade to month. No, she doesn't think I can make it a week. I'm soooo tempted to do it and prove her wrong. So tempted.*

Thursday, December 31—

The counter resembled an explosion in a restaurant kitchen. Cassie grabbed a garbage bag and swooped everything into it that could possibly be tossed before shoving it into the storage bin just outside her back door. She dug under the sink for her bottle of 409 and sprayed every surface not inhabited by food with a liberal hand. Paper towel roll under one arm, she worked her way from the fridge to the sink to the stove, and across the island she'd created from a sideboard she'd found at a garage sale back in October. "You, my pretty, are going to save me so much serving hassles!"

The tempered glass top gleamed after a few squirts of Windex and a few swipes of a fresh paper towel. That's when her genius idea to remove the garbage bag proved not so genius after all. She snatched a plastic grocery bag from a wastepaper basket under the sink and shoved the towels inside. "There. Clean and out of the way." A faint twinge unsettled her subconscious as she slammed the door to her bin shut once more. *That's a lot of garbage just for prep. Lauren would have fits.*

Of course, she still had trays to assemble and such, but with the messy hors d'oeuvres finished, she could get ready. A glance at the clock told her she had exactly forty-five minutes— max. "Okay... straight hair tonight. Faster than taming the frizzies into curls."

But despite her limited time, Cassie stood in the shower, allowing the hot, steamy water to beat the kinks out of her neck and shoulder muscles. "I wish I had time for a good soak, too. If only..."

The water grew cool, and as it did, she stared at the movement in the bottom of her tub as it swirled and disappeared down the drain. Guilt drove her to jerk off the faucet and reach for her towel. "Lauren is going to pay for this. I think I'll buy her a subscription to that hippie magazine that composts toilet waste or something."

The long, tedious task of drying and straightening her hair kept her from dwelling too long on the unexpected discomfiture that came with what should have been a satisfying shower. She retrieved her larger makeup bag and laid out the items she'd decided to wear on the counter before her. "Special occasions require special attention to details." A glance at the gold charmeuse dress hanging behind her prompted her to reach for her golden glitter eyeshadow. "I almost threw you away, too. But with that dress... perfect."

If she'd had time to do big Marilyn Monroe hair, she would have. Instead, Cassie pulled back the sides in combs that created semi-poofy wings, and allowed it to curl loosely around her shoulders. "Would've looked stupid to go all Marilyn for big band anyway. And she was a platinum blonde. 'Chestnut' doesn't come close."

Winged eyeliner, heavy black mascara, glitzy eyeshadow, and perfectly shaped, slightly thicker brows, thanks to a eyebrow pencil—perfect. That left lipstick. "Go for bold vermilion or understated, pale pink?" She held two lip stain wands up to her face and the verdict became clear. "Red. Definitely."

It took almost as long to clean up her prep mess as it did to get ready, but with sling-back heels in one hand, and her phone in another, Cassie dashed through the house and into the kitchen just as the timer beeped. "Perfect!"

She ripped a few giant lengths of aluminum foil from the roll, stashed the box, and began creating warming tents for stuffed rolls, mini-quiches and mini lasagnas. *That is a lot of aluminum foil...* But the thought fizzled before it could bubble over and make a more permanent stain on her conscience. *And aluminum comes in nature anyway. It'll be fine in a nice landfill— putting it back where we got it, so to speak.*

Despite her defensive arguments, Cassie couldn't help one last wince at the array of things she'd planned to dispose of before dawn.

Cassie surveyed the room with satisfaction. People mingled, laughed, joked, and even made bumbling attempts at swing dancing as a playlist of big band hits filled her duplex. A friend's date bopped past with an acrylic flute in each hand overhead. "Great party, Cass. Love the theme. Jeremy said last year it was Beach Boys."

Actually, it was 80's pop, but who's being picky? "Glad you're enjoying yourself. Be sure to try the mini lasagnas!" *And what they have to do with big band, I have no idea. But it works.*

The doorbell rang—hardly audible over the din of laughter, music, and incessant conversation. Cassie hurried to open it and grinned at the sight of Lauren standing there with a man she'd never met. "Lauren! Since when do you ring?"

"Since my cousin arrived last minute and I was *trying* to hide my lack of manners before he tells Aunt Joyce about it? Thanks a lot!" She pulled the man Cassie had taken for her date forward. "Remember how I said my cousin might be moving here? Well... here he is!"

The man offered a hand just as Cassie beckoned them inside. "Evan Robinson. So nice to meet you. Lauren insisted on bringing me, but—"

"Of course! I'd be furious with her if she left someone new in town alone on New Year's Eve." Something about her words, or perhaps their delivery, sounded excessively effusive, even to her ears, but Cassie ignored it. "Cassie Wren."

Jeremy passed again as if on another mission for drinks. "Well there's a friendship for the birds."

And there's proof you were listening in.

Lauren blinked in confusion, but Evan grinned—a wide, open, friendly grin that took a handsome face and made it interesting. "Nice to meet a fellow ornith." His eyes surveyed the room. "Looks like a cool party—great music."

When Lauren disappeared into the room, Cassie had no idea. She led Evan to the island, suggested the mini-lasagnas and the stuffed rolls. "—sausage, cream cheese, and basil. So, good. I'll gain ten pounds just being in the same room with them, but it's worth it. New Year's only comes..." She flushed. "And, of course, that's not a ridiculous observation at all. Ignore me. I'm suffering from whatever malady gets you out of socially awkward situations this week."

Cassie beckoned a couple of friends nearby to their side and began introducing him. "Silvie and Amy, this is Lauren's cousin, Evan."

A voice called to her from across the room, so she left the trio munching on snacks and wove through dancing guests to the opposite corner. *Note to self: Next year, the chair goes out for the party, too. It doesn't provide enough seating for the space it consumes.*

"Hey, did you get Glenn Miller's 'Little Brown Jug?' It's my favorite. Mom used to make me watch that old movie about him all the time as a kid. That's the only one I remember from it."

The title didn't sound familiar but Cassie assured Jeremy—of course, it *would* be him—that she'd have it on in a jiffy. "Give this song a chance to end... maybe one more."

"You're the best! That's why everyone works hard to stay on your guest lists." A glance toward the island hinted at his next question. "Amy doing okay tonight?"

"Probably just waiting to see if you'll dance with her..."

That's all it took. Jeremy skirted the room and joined half a dozen people lounging around the island with Evan. *You can do it, Jeremy.*

━ ♫ ━ ♫ ━ ♫ ━

No one knew when trombones and clarinets gave way to electric guitars and drums, but Cassie's living room pulsated with the beat of a new indie rock band just as midnight neared. Cassie inched her way to the sound system she'd borrowed from her brother and got prepared to switch it to "Auld Lang Syne" by Guy Lombardo's band. She'd auditioned half a dozen different ones, but that one had been her favorite.

A voice beside her almost made her jump from her skin. "Have you seen Evan?"

So... Silvie finally shows some interest in a guy. Won't your mother be relieved? Aloud, Cassie suggested the carport. "I saw several go out there for a moment of fresh air. Grab a coat, though. It's so cold."

"It is a bit stuffy in here..."

Ooooh... you really are interested. That's a fascinating development. Wait'll Lauren hears. The sight of her friend watching them from across the room amended that thought. *Or have you already? I wonder if you can tell what your cousin thinks of her...*

Cassie turned to suggest Silvie hurry only to find the young woman already heading out the front door—sans coat, of course. She sent a silent plea to Lauren who retrieved a coat from a pile in the coat closet and hurried outside with it.

Half-empty and empty disposable ramekins littered almost every surface. Paper plates, forks, napkins—everywhere the eye could see. Cassie ached to grab a trash bag, but the clock on the wall gave her less than ten minutes until midnight. She shouted for someone to start pouring drinks. Amy and Jeremy stopped dancing and rushed to the kitchen. A minute later, Jeremy appeared at her side. "Amy sent me to run this. I spilled two of

17

the drinks. Sorry."

"I tried... to let you stay with her, that is. I'll send her back to make sure you don't 'mess this up.'"

With a wink and a self-conscious smile, Jeremy turned all his attention to a stop and a play button. Charged with matchmaking, Cassie hurried to the kitchen. She found Amy scrubbing at the floor with her dishcloth and tried not to gag. "Poor Jeremy. He's so embarrassed."

"If I hadn't been pouring the expensive stuff, I wouldn't have cared so much, but..." She stared at the bottle. "How many are going to want real champagne?"

"I usually go with a third of the guests. It's a decent guess. I'll get the non-alcoholic stuff." As Cassie poured, she watched the clock. "Can you call everyone in and then get over there— make sure Jeremy doesn't destroy the system somehow?"

Amy giggled as she wiped a few drops from the counter. "He is a bit of a klutz, isn't he?"

The opportunity presented itself, so Cassie took it. "Only when you're around."

A rosy pink darkened Amy's blush and made her look a bit overheated. "Really?"

"Yep."

"He has never asked me out. I've almost asked him a couple of times, but..."

Cassie leaned close and whispered, "Now's your chance. But we're going to be late if you don't hurry."

Guests strolled through the kitchen, picking up their drinks as they filled her dining and living rooms in anticipation of the countdown. A glance at the couple by the speakers told her that Amy had asked. Jeremy's red ears gave him away every time. *That's cool. One good thing for the New Year. Yeah!*

A voice—one so close it almost made Cassie yelp— preceded a hand covering hers in an attempt to keep her from spilling glasses. "Almost time."

"Hey, Joel. Haven't even gotten to say hi tonight!"

"You're busy." He grabbed a few glasses. "I'll go pass these out to those who didn't get any yet—real or non-alchie?"

"Those are non." Cassie gave him a smile that would likely be too encouraging, but for once, she didn't care. "And thanks. We've only got... ninety seconds or so."

The music quieted at fifteen seconds til. Amy called out the countdown. "And... Go!"

The room erupted in shouts of "...*ten... nine... four... two... one!*" "Auld Lang Syne" filled the room, and all around her, Cassie's friends hugged or kissed. A voice behind her startled her. "I'd kiss you, but since we don't know each other, how about a 'best wishes for the New Year' instead?"

She turned and smiled at Evan. "Having fun? Happy New Year, to you, too." Cassie surprised herself as much as Evan as she kissed his cheek. "It's Scriptural, isn't it?" Those words churned in her stomach. *And if you're not a Christian, I've probably just insulted you. Great.*

"Good point." He nodded his head in the direction of the corner where Jeremy and Amy stood lip-locked in a sweet, but lingering embrace. "Don't suppose that counts as 'holy' does it?"

Before she could reply, Cassie caught Joel's eye. *Oh, great. He's hurt. He'll never admit it, try never to show it, but man... I can read you, buddy.* All she could do was offer a reassuring smile and turn back to Evan. "Yeah. Not happening."

"Glad to hear it. I wouldn't like to think of people who didn't know each other being quite so... chummy." He raised one eyebrow—just one. Cassie wanted to smack it off his head.

Why can't I do that? It drives me nuts. So not fair.

"—you could go out with me... maybe get coffee?"

Wait. That was a lead-in for a line? Great. She might have said yes. In fact, her mouth opened to ask when he had in mind, when Silvie came into view. *I can give her a shot. I mean, he's a nice guy, but I don't know him. And she obviously likes him. I've never seen her so intrigued.*

19

"Sorry... it's not a good week for me."

"Maybe some other time, then.

Her conscience berated her for doing it, but Cassie found herself agreeing. "Maybe. Why don't you see if you can talk Silvie or Lauren into dancing? I don't think I've seen either of them dance all night."

Guilt dissolved as she saw Evan speaking to Silvie. *And that's all it takes.*

⚞ ⚞ ⚞

A group of five—her four best friends and Evan—tramped down her steps, calling goodnight and wishing her a Happy New Year. Again. Michaela called out, "What time do you want to meet tomorrow—today—whatever?"

Cold, exhausted, and aching to get out of her heels, Cassie protested. "I don't even want my eyes *open* before one o'clock. Let's do... lunner. Or dunch—whatever you call the brunch of the evening. Maybe... three o'clock?"

"Sounds great," Lauren agreed. "We'll eat around three-thirty or four, and then we can snack if we're hungry later."

Evan called back as he followed the group of gabbing females to their cars. "Nice meeting you. I'll call about that coffee again sometime."

She wanted to urge him to do just that, but the slight stumble Silvie took was enough to leave her goodbye at an echoed, "Nice to meet you, too!"

Inside, she surveyed her trashed rooms with the practiced eye of a woman who knows her parties. "Better than last year, but still pretty pathetic. So glad I spent the money on disposable."

With a trash bag in hand, she made short work of the living room mess. Dining room—equally easy. The kitchen took longer, but with only half a dozen dirty dishes and the need for a mop and a counter wipe down, it really wasn't *too* bad. One phone, two sweaters, and a set of keys. "Who didn't get their *keys?* That's weird."

"Mine..." Joel's voice from the doorway nearly sent the bag of garbage flying all over her kitchen.

"What are you—oh. I forgot. The table." Cassie kicked off her shoes. "I'm so tired, I can hardly think straight."

As they retrieved her coffee table, an end table, and a couple of lamps, Cassie yawned, dragged her feet, and tried *not* to whine. Once the lamps were in place, Joel, with hands on her shoulders, steered her to her bedroom. "I switched out your comforter. Someone set a mini-lasagna on the bed—probably while waiting for the bathroom—and then someone else set something on it—all squished."

So that's how I got half the house clean before I knew you were here. Cassie gave him a quick hug as she thanked him. "You're the best. I should finish up out there, but you're right. I just need to sleep."

"I've got it. You did most of it anyway. See you Sunday if not before."

As much as Cassie knew she should protest—at least *pretend* to protest, anyway—she couldn't bring herself to do it. She closed the door, stripped out of the dress, and pulled on her comfiest sleep pants and long-sleeved t-shirt. A face wipe removed her makeup, and eye pads removed her mascara. Teeth, brushed hair, and a rinsed face—ready for bed. She didn't even take the time to pick up her dress from the floor before climbing under the covers and snapping off the light.

In the kitchen, the faint sounds of someone moving around told her Joel still worked to make it perfect. *Lord, if we could just find him someone really special—you know, someone not me—that'd be awesome. Maybe that should be my New Year's Resolution. Find Joel a girlfriend.*

That idea gave way to others—the blog she might start. A book overwrote the blog idea. She'd always wanted to write one. Why not now? *If I wait until the time is perfect, it'll never happen. Oh, and volunteering somewhere. I want to do that. And really, maybe this is the year for an instrument. I put it down every year, and every year I cross it off. Maybe...* The idea of a week of green inched its way into her thoughts, crowding out others.

It's too easy. Just wash a dish or two. Don't buy stuff you throw away again. Anyone could do it. I should do it for a week... show Lauren that she's overcomplicating things.

Visions of fresh fruits and veggies in her refrigerator, an empty trash can on trash day, and the surprised expressions on all her friends' faces when she carried a bag of recycling to the center filled her with warm fuzzies until dreams took over and turned her fledgling thoughts into a fully-formed, eco-conscious, Utopian dream.

Week 1: Paper

Friday, January 1—

"The best part of New Year's Day—no schedule dictating your every move. It's better than a weekend, any day."

Her leather tote bag lay half-abandoned on her bed. As Cassie found notebooks, pens, and lists, she shoved them in the bag. Finding all her annual goal-setting paraphernalia proved easier than choosing an outfit. "Don't I have anything super cute that is also comfy? Why don't velour jogging suits look amazingly adorable?"

She settled for knit "jeggings" and a sweater dress softer than anything she'd ever owned. "It's a bit over-dressed, but it's comfy and cute. No makeup and a ponytail. That'll dress it down..."

Cassie flopped between picking up little things, putting them away, and getting ready. By the time she left her room, she'd made the bed, put away clothes, and stuffed her dress in a bag for the dry cleaners. As she made her way to the kitchen, she ran through a mental list of resolution ideas. "Is this really the year for a business? Maybe more research. Location...that's the killer. Maybe it's a qualified goal. If I can find the right spot..."

She stopped still as she entered the kitchen. Every dish she'd washed—put away. The bag of champagne flutes—gone. "Did you toss 'em or wash 'em?" A glance through her cupboards and the dumpster didn't answer the question, but her back car windows showed the answer. "There... how'd he know? Dumb question. He always knows."

Living room—there were vacuum tracks on her area rug.

"Okay, that's pathetic. How did I not hear that?"

She reached into the fridge to grab a container of yogurt and smiled at the neat rows of leftover lasagnas. "Probably should freeze those. Thanks, Joel." Those words sent her in search of her phone. Cassie typed out a text of gratitude and promised to take him out for ice cream in the next couple of weeks. IT'S THE LEAST I CAN DO.

Six bites—that's all it took to polish off the little cone of yogurt. Six bites. Cassie dumped the cone and the plastic spoon in her garbage and went to brush her teeth. But as she reached for a Dixie cup to rinse her mouth, Cassie gagged. "Oh, ew! Do people actually leave washable cups in the *bathroom?* That is so gross. Another reason I'll never 'go green.' Ew. No. Way."

Her more rational side insisted you could just grab one from the kitchen each day, but her emotions held firm. "How anyone can drink out of a cup that's been sitting in the bathroom all day. Ew!"

If that revelation wasn't enough, as Cassie dropped the cup in the wastepaper basket, she saw the toilet paper roll hanging half-askew and gagged again. "Surely people don't cut out *toilet* paper. Washable TP? No way. Not even going there. Washable butt wipes. That's... oh that's nasty. How do people do this stuff?" The answer came quickly enough. "Well, they don't. That's just the problem. They only do the parts that aren't too much of a hassle. I'll never do this. No idea why Lauren even got to me, but I won't do something half-way just to look good, and I'm not doing *that.*"

With a sigh of relief that should have warned her of impending doom, Cassie grabbed her tote bag from her bed, retrieved her coat from the front closet, and snatched up her keys and phone. "Onto *realistic* goal setting. And a normal life. Gotta love normal lives."

Country music blasted at her all the way to Lauren's apartment. As much as she would have loved to flip to a different station, the twang, the maudlin' lyrics, and her general dislike for the sound kept thoughts of washable toilet wipes at bay. So, by the time she entered Lauren's apartment, her mind pulsated with promises of "...kickin' off those boots and hangin' up the truck keys cause her baby's got time to please." *I don't even know what that means. And I hope it stays that way.*

"Hey, Cass! We were wondering if you'd make it. You looked wiped out last night." Despite Silvie's cheerful greeting, Cassie heard just the faintest hint of a sharp edge to it.

He didn't ask you out. And you heard his invitation for coffee. Great.

"Yeah... I piddled around a bit. I was just worn out." She dropped her bag next to an empty chair and went to grab a bottle of water from Lauren's fridge. "How's everyone doing? Any contenders for the most exciting? The most likely to flop? The most likely to succeed?"

"Well, I think Amy's got the most exciting..." Lauren winked at Amy, and Cassie turned just in time to see it.

"Yeah?"

Amy shoved a notebook at her as Cassie seated herself and grinned. "How's that?"

"'Get Jeremy to ask me out before Valentine's Day.'" Cassie nodded and pushed the book back. "Nice..."

"No fair *telling* him to. He'll do whatever you say, but that's not *him* doing it. I want a date for Valentine's Day this year— with *him.*" Amy flipped a page back and slid it over to Cassie again. "What do you think of those?"

And so, the annual Goal Fest began. As she listened to the others, Cassie flipped through the pages of notes she'd spent all week making, and as she did, she wrote her short list on the first page of the year's official "Goals and Resolutions" notebook.

Open a store if I can find the right location.

Silvie broke through her thoughts. "Oh, hey, Cassie. Question."

"Shoot."

"Someone said you were donating all those champagne flutes to the thrift store. If you wash them, then what's the point of buying them?"

A sickening foreboding she couldn't identify washed over her. The answer would only start a debate. Still, Cassie wrote her next idea before answering. "I'm not washing them. If they want them, they can do it themselves."

"Ew, gross. I wouldn't want to be them."

"I wouldn't either. They can throw them away, for all I care. I'm only donating them because Lauren pitched a fit about me tossing them."

Michaela spoke up before Lauren could protest. "Hey, can I have them? I love that they're not glass—no glass shards ground into my carpet to shred my feet later. Perfect."

Yesss! Oh, yeah. Despite her inner cheering, Cassie just nodded. "Where are your keys? I'll go put them in your car right now."

It took less than five minutes to go down to the parking lot, move the bag of glasses to Michaela's beast of a Buick, and jog back upstairs again. She burst through the door just in time to hear Amy say, "—never give up water bottles. Not happening. I like sports tops and I hate washing them. Every time I buy one to fill at home, I can taste that it's not clean. So gross."

"Yeah... I can't see Cass giving up her water bottles either." Lauren glanced at Cassie. "Do you like refillable bottles? I've never seen you with one."

Despite the hint of a jab the question felt like, Cassie shrugged and answered as if it hadn't bothered her at all. "Don't care either way. I just like my water cold, and the filter isn't cold enough."

"Hey, who decided to do the fifty-two weeks of organization? Anyone?" Amy tapped her pen on the page. "I can't decide if I'd keep up with it. Didn't it seem a bit much?"

Michaela shook her head. "I know I'll never do it. It's supposed to take an hour. The last thing I read that said that took me a minimum of four every week—in a chunk, no less. I still can't believe I made it three whole weeks!" She shoved a book to the middle of the table. "I was going to do the 365 days of gratitude, but Mom got me this for Christmas. So, I think I'll just do it instead. I can make most of the entries be about gratitude, but it'll be a bit more realistic if I have a day where everything went wrong and I'm not scrambling with some contrived thing like, 'Grateful for having a water heater to blow up and destroy my bathroom wall' or whatever."

"I found an app for the five-year journal. It's so cool." Amy tapped Michaela's journal. "Just like that book, but instead of writing on paper, you put it in the app. Then, at the end of each year, it spits out a pretty PDF for you."

"That sounds perfect for me," Cassie agreed. "You can just do it whenever you have the time that way—don't have to be home." She dug for her phone and asked for the app name. "I think I might do that." As she waited for Amy to find it, Cassie scrawled *Five Year Journal App* on the page.

Something Amy said jerked her from her thoughts. "—have thought she'd be more of a paper person. She always has the most notebooks at this thing." Her eyes met Cassie's. "They have some really pretty ones at the bookstore on Fifth..."

"I can find the app. It's fine." *And then maybe you'll shut up about my addiction to the evil paper monster. Sheesh.*

"Well, I am definitely doing the seventeen habits thing." Lauren sent Cassie a reassuring smile—a smile that only served as another dig, despite the intention.

"Is that the twenty-one-day thing?" Cassie stared at her page. "I don't know if I want to do seventeen new habits."

Lauren turned a bit green as Michaela suggested that a few of Cassie's could be eco-friendlier choices. "You know, just a little less paper or something. How many bags of trash *did* you take out last night?"

"Oh, come on. It was a party. Who wants to start the new year with a houseful of dishes to wash?" Lauren winked at

Cassie and murmured, "See, I do listen. And you have a point. It wasn't about the landfill, honestly. It was a money thing. I shouldn't have projected on you like that."

But the words that were meant to soothe only festered more. Amy jumped on that and ran with it. "That's a great idea. Less in the landfill is still less!"

The conversation drifted to other goals and resolutions. Fitness, books to read, travel, foreign languages...Amy even debated the idea of trying out for a community theater play. And all the while, Cassie added the things she most wanted to do to her list.

Next to the business idea, she wrote, *The Vintage Wren*.

Below the five-year app, she added, *Learn guitar*.

Plan and save for road trip for next year.

Volunteer at the mission

And then—though when she wrote it, Cassie couldn't have said—she saw it. *365 days of green*.

Her notes captivated her full concentration, or she might have thought to cover the words. Silvie's giggle pulled her from her choices of Bible reading plans. "What?"

But Silvie just pointed and turned to the others. "Can you imagine Cassie doing *365 days of green?* Really? Couldn't happen."

Amy chimed it. "Sure, she could." The soothing confidence turned into yet another sharp needle jab as Amy added, "Just wash a fork every day instead of using a plastic one. Voila! Green."

‡‡‡‡‡‡

When Cassie didn't protest, Lauren's heart sank. *She's getting ticked. And really, I can't blame her. We're all teasing her, but it's not like any of us are exactly eco-responsible ourselves.* When a new round of jokes began, Lauren tried to head off what she expected to be a full blow-up. *Cassie's temper—legendary. Her ability not to lash out at people while* past the boiling point—impressive. But everyone had their limits. Cassie looked close to passing hers.

"Oh, come on." The others looked at Lauren as she spoke—all but Cassie. "She's not like that, and you know it. If she did choose to do something like that, she'd really do it. Just leave her alone. Sheesh."

As more seconds ticked past without Cassie responding, Lauren's heart sank further into the pit of her stomach. Oh, boy. She's gone from ticked to ticking time bomb. Now what do I do. Lauren tried to change the subject, but when Cassie struck out, "Learn the guitar," a cold, clammy feeling washed over her. Lord, help!"

"Hey, you said you really wanted to do that!" Amy's protest increased as Cassie struck out on finding the five-year app. "I said I'd get it. Hang on."

"It's fine."

Those two words, cold, silent... Lauren swallowed hard. Dare I think it? Deadly. She's about to do something she'll regret, and I don't know how to stop it.

Volunteering at the Mission got a strike through just a minute or two later. This time, Lauren couldn't help but argue. "Oh, no. I wanted to do that one with you. You made it sound so important."

"Do it yourself."

One after the other, Cassie struck out all the plans she'd made—all but the 365 days of green. The table grew quiet as the others seemed to sense just how far things had gotten.

Then it happened. She circled it. Lauren caught her breath. Silvie almost whimpered. But Amy tried reason. "You don't have to do that. Just break it down into habits. Do it for one of your seventeen habits. Twenty-one days is so much more manageable."

You just ensured she did it. Thanks a lot, Amy!

Cassie's voice, so low and emotionless, it was difficult to understand, barely reached Lauren's ears. "Nope. I'm going to prove to myself and everyone else that I can do it." Her eyes rose and met the gaze of every woman there. "Besides. I've had it. I'm sick of it. So here I go. One goal. It's just a big one. We've always talked about that. I'll let you know how it goes next January.

After that, the planning party fizzled. Lauren watched as her friends slowly gathered their things and inched toward the door. Cassie stayed until everyone else had gone. Then she shoved her things in her tote bag and hoisted it over one shoulder. "I may need help—lots of it."

"Just call anytime." At the door, Lauren couldn't help but add, "And you know... you don't have—"

"Don't say it. Just don't." Cassie gave her a weak smile. "But... I won't refuse prayers. I'm starting to wonder just what I got myself into."

Saturday, January 2—

The day loomed before her with that kind of foreboding, ominous tenacity that brooks no refusal. Escape is futile, resistance impossible. Cassie sat at her kitchen table with a double-sided piece of lined paper and her erasable pens. Green for "definitely." Brown for "probably." Pink for "under great protest." Red for "over my dead body." She rearranged the pens, putting brown for the dead body option, and then moved it back again.

"Red means stop more than brown signifies death. Yeah..." Again, she stared at the little legend she'd created at the top right of the page. "Guess I actually have to write things down."

No paper products.

The words unnerved her. She added a word. No paper products-UNNECESSARY *paper products.* "That's better. I am *not* doing butt wipes."

But even before she could write down her idea for no *unnecessary* plastic, Cassie ordered her phone to call Lauren. Familiar, comforting, almost dulcet tones filled her ears moments later. "I've been waiting for your call. What is thwarting your fledgling efforts today?"

"I'm coming up with a list…" Cassie grabbed a legal notepad, winced at the realization that it's *paper,* and began writing things as she thought of them. "Okay first let's talk Kleenex. Do I *have* to do handkerchiefs? I can't imagine owning enough to get me through a bad cold. That's just gross. And a purse full of nasty handkerchiefs? I'm gonna need a bigger purse!"

"Well, I don't see how the spread of disease is any greener than not using Kleenex, so I'd stick with them for illness, for sure. Maybe a little cosmetic case to hold used handkerchiefs for daily use, though?" When Cassie couldn't bring herself to reply, Lauren's words filled the room again. "And at home, you could always just burn them—kill germs and reduce landfill waste."

Despite her best efforts, Cassie couldn't hide the relief in her voice. "So that's not cheating?"

"Reducing isn't the *only* way to be green, Cass. You have to consider full environmental impact, and people's health counts, too."

A new thought produced a nervous giggle. "And maybe if I ask for cases of Kleenex for my birthday…" With great reluctance, she added "buy handkerchiefs from a thrift store" onto her shopping list. Then she shuddered. "I think I'm doomed. Already I'm grossed out. I can't buy new ones—that flies in the point of not buying unnecessary stuff so they stop producing it." Cassie hesitated. "That *is* why you don't buy new stuff, right? It's so that companies eventually produce less?"

"That's what I always thought." A beep blared through the phone. "Hang on. I've got brownies in the oven—boss' birthday tomorrow. Be right back."

Cassie hardly noticed her absence. Her list of things to consider purchasing grew. Her list of things to avoid—even longer. Frustration mounted, hooked its feet in stirrups, and rode wildly across the plain of her panic-stricken conscience. *I am so out of my depth. Why do I do this stuff to myself? I either have to do it or give up now.*

As she thought, she wandered through her house, looking at all paper products she could cut out. "Towels, plates, napkins, dusters—oh, man! I love those things. Sticky notes, notepads, notebooks..." As the list grew, so did her panic. By the time she reached the bathroom, she'd refused to even look under the sink where her stock of triple-ply Charmin waited to, as a commercial for another company always proudly announced, "do its duty to your booty."

On the little shelf to the right of her sink, Cassie's skincare basket beckoned. She knew, even without looking inside, what would have to go, and her heart sank a little lower into her chest. "Lauren?"

"Yeah, I'm back."

"Help."

"Oh, no... what'd you find now?"

"Face wipes."

Lauren's snicker should have annoyed her, but Cassie had ridden far past pride and galloped headlong into utter despair. "Just use a washcloth, Cass."

"I don't *own* washcloths. What's the point if you don't *use* them?"

"Then get an old towel, cut it up, and you've done the 'make it over' part of that old saying. It's perfect." Cassie formed a retort, but Lauren's excited voice drowned her out. "You could probably even get an empty baby wipe container from someone at church. Take a bunch of those cloths, mix up some face cleanser in it, soak, 'em, and voila. Just as convenient on the daily front, anyway. You'd just have to wash them and mix up a new batch of cleanser two or three times a month."

Cassie's pen scribbled feverishly as she tried to get down all she wanted of Lauren's suggestions. Despite her previous arguments, she had to ask. "So... why not just buy washcloths? Don't we want to encourage people to buy "good" stuff? Eco-friendly stuff?"

It took Lauren a moment to answer, but when she did, she spoke in strong, clear sentences. "I don't think you should—at least not in the beginning. You don't want to get in the habit of buying new stuff to create a green life. It's counterproductive. Now, if you can buy used ones somewhere, sure! So, me, I wouldn't. I don't think it would be wrong but I think if you don't at least in the beginning, it'll help you stick to your plan."

"I hate it when your logic interferes with my preferences." A box on the middle shelf of her hall closet brought a smile to more than Cassie's lips. "Aha! Eureka. Mom's annual towel and dishcloth stocking stuffers! I swear, she should just stop doing stockings for me. But no, she likes the fat things up there."

"And," Lauren agreed, "It gives you washcloths for face wipes! Perfect. You just have to find ways to have conveniences you like without being wasteful. Be creative. Find a balance."

A fresh determination filled her. Cassie strode back to the bathroom and glared at the wall beside the toilet. "Okay. So, let's talk toilet paper."

Laughter so loud it hurt her ear filled the phone. Cassie punched speaker again and listened with growing relief as Lauren insisted that she was going a little overboard. "Buy the stinkin' TP."

"Right? I can't do it. I mean, I'd have to wash them, and then wash the washing machine after I was done. That's a waste, too. I just *can't*. I can't."

"See, that's where I think you're going wrong with this whole thing. You buy the TP. You just go with one that's only one or two ply instead of three. *Less* paper is still improvement."

Petulance is never pretty. Cassie looked up and saw her reflection in the mirror as she whined, "But I like my Charmin!" Oh, how she hated the ugly way it wrinkled her nose. And made her look like someone attempting to audition for "Cruella deVille."

"You know, try it, okay?" Lauren encouraged her with the vim and vigor of someone trying to convince a kindergartner to allow him to rip out a loose tooth. "Just buy one roll of the one ply stuff and see how it works. If you still hate it when the roll is gone, then go back to your super-soft stuff."

"Uh..." Cassie examined her teeth as she tried to find a legitimate reason *not* to switch to public bathroom stall fare. When they didn't produce some sort of sign, she moved to eyebrows and reached for the tweezers at the sight of a new rogue hair. "Well..."

"Fine." Lauren sounded as if she'd gone from wheedling mama to authoritative dad. "Then just pay *attention* when you use TP in public—at church or the store. See if it's *really* that bad. Can you reduce your toilet paper usage for the planet or not?"

She tried not to—really. But Cassie just huffed and agreed to consider it. "So, I've got a bit stockpiled—you know, winter weather stock-ups and stuff. I get to keep this, right? I can use up whatever I bought?"

Lauren tried not to laugh—Cassie heard it in her voice. With a pat to the little roll of Charmin swinging carefree from the holder, she almost skipped from the room while Lauren reassured her. "It's just a waste if you don't. I mean, it all ends up in the same place if you use them or don't. Using it up at least saves water."

Relieved, Cassie sauntered back down her short hall to the living room and collapsed on the couch. "I'll consider this later. Thanks, Lauren. I owe you."

"Call anytime. It's why I gave you that lifetime free pass to Lauren's Counseling Service. Otherwise, you'd be my indentured servant for life by now."

⊩⊩⊩⊩⊩⊩

Her phone blipped an obnoxious tune, alerting her to a text. Her eyes flew open, and she scanned the room in a dread-filled stupor. Toilet paper did *not* hang from or cover every surface. "It was a dream—nightmare. Wow. Ugh." Cassie sat bolt upright and stretched. "Maybe I should reconsider my toilet paper. If that kind of dream is going to haunt me until I do..."

The power of suggestion drove her to the bathroom where she sat and stared at the roll lost in frustrated indecision. "I *could* see if it makes a difference. Count how many squares—oh, that's ridiculous." Only the memory of her phone still lying on the coffee table kept her from calling Lauren to hash out this new idea. "But if I could prove that it only takes say... five squares of Charmin to every twenty of that one-ply junk..." Again, she stared at the roll. "How many squares do I use each time, anyway?"

She pulled a length off that looked normal and counted. "Eleven... that would be... thirty-three? No way. I know I don't pull that much off at church. Ugh."

Shouts from her neighbor and his buddies outside her bathroom window sent Cassie's thoughts inward. *The last thing I need is for them to hear me talking to myself—about* toilet paper. *What kind of stupidity is that?*

Just as Cassie wadded up the ball, she tore it in half and stared at five squares. *Is it enough?* She laid the strip over the roll of toilet paper and tore the other strip in half. Three squares. *No way...*

Then she decided she couldn't do it. Three. Her hand reached for the strip of five. It reached for the other three. *If I can even cut my consumption—maybe in half. Then it's only like I'm using 1.5 ply. That's fabulous.*

Five minutes later, three of which she spent scrubbing her

35

hands, Cassie sent a text message to Lauren. IN CASE YOU WERE CURIOUS. THREE SQUARES OF TP IS NOT ENOUGH!!!!!!

She flipped the screen back to the text message that had awakened her. Joel. HEY. JUST CHECKING IN ON YOU. SOMEONE SAID SOMETHING ABOUT YOU GOING GREEN. I THOUGHT THEY MEANT YOU WERE SICK, BUT THEN I REMEMBERED YOUR GOAL PARTY. SO, WHICH IS IT? ECO OR BARFO?

A slow smile formed as Cassie's fingers swyped across the screen. ECO. YOU'RE SAFE FROM MAKING ME CHICKEN NOODLE SOUP—AND SO AM I. ;)

The sun dipped behind clouds and the room instantly felt cooler. Cassie jumped up to turn up the furnace and almost stopped herself. "No way. Nuh uh. I'll deal with that on energy week. This is paper. One thing at a time. Combine their twenty-one days with my three-sixty-five. Perfect." Her subconscious suggested that she might not want to work on a new one each week, but Cassie pooh-poohed that idea. "Three new habits at a time is *not* too much. Not when I've had practice at two of them before starting a third.

Alas, habit is a harsh taskmaster. As her stomach growled, Cassie jumped up to make herself a "cup of soup" and stared at the paper-wrapped Styrofoam container. "Ugh. How will I have soup?" A glance in her cupboard showed plastic and paper wrapped packets of other soup mixes, cocoa mixes, boxed meals—the works. "I am so going to starve. You can't buy *anything* that isn't covered in paper."

Lauren's timing couldn't have been better—or worse, depending on how she took it. The text arrived just as she absentmindedly grabbed a plastic spoon and dug it into the cup of steaming ramen noodles.

LOL.

Sunday, January 3—

Despite the thermostat bumped to seventy-five, Cassie shivered in her double fuzzy-socked feet, fleece sleep pants, thermal sleep top, and warmest sweater. She held icy fingers over the toaster as it gave her pale bread a nice tan and then bumped it up to "bronze" just to be able to hold her fingers there for another minute. "Overdone toast is worth the defrosting qualities of that toaster." It may have been her imagination, but Cassie thought she heard her teeth chatter—twice.

As the toast popped up, Cassie's arm shot out to tear a paper towel from the roll and fumbled when her hand hit air. "Wha—oh."

Her eyes glared at the open space where a roll of absorbent papery goodness should hang. "You know, I didn't think my crossroads would arrive quite so quickly or over something so stupid. But seriously? I want to give up. I like my paper towels!"

Yep. Right there—chatter. Her stupid teeth actually chattered. Cassie snatched a plate from the cupboard—washable, since the paper ones now resided in a tote in her overloaded storage bin—and plunked the toast on the plate. Butter, honey, in seconds the plate waited with inviting simplicity. "Well... plates *are* prettier, anyway. That's something."

With a throw blanket over her shoulders and another over her legs, she curled up on the couch with her coffee mug warming her hands. She eyed the cuffs of her shirt pulled down over her fingers and sighed. "Aaaand... there goes another shirt—stretched out beyond recognition. Oh. Goodie."

The verse of the day app buzzed just as she took her first sip of coffee. With less enthusiasm than her spirit suggested she should have for minor things like the Word of the Most High God, Cassie told her phone to read it to her. "'Whatever your hand finds to do, do it with all your might; for there is no activity or planning or knowledge or wisdom in Sheol where you are going.'"

Cassie blinked. "Um... isn't Sheol another word for hell? Did the Bible just tell me that I'm going to hell? Or is this God's way of hinting at what is to come with this stupid little 'experiment' of mine?" She ordered the phone to give a definition of Sheol and felt little encouragement when it informed her that the Hebrews believed it to be little more than a mass family grave. "Yep. Proof right there. I'm going green, and it'll be the death of me."

Her toast sat abandoned on the coffee table. "Totally gross, now. Almost burned *and* cold. Wonder what else..." The words trailed off in a wisp of conscience. The fact that it was paper week did little to alleviate the guilt that formed as the temptation to toss the bread rose. "It *is* biodegradable." Still, the plastic bag she'd extracted the bread *from* prodded at her conscience until Cassie couldn't stand it. She jerked the plate from the table and devoured both pieces in much less time than it should have taken before chasing it with a gulp of now lukewarm coffee. "Ugh. Nasty breakfast."

The alarm on her phone drove her into the kitchen. "No time to wash the plate. It's only one—well, and the mug. But I've got to hurry. I'll wash 'em later."

As she stepped into her bedroom, over-warm air blasted her from the heating vents. "Ugh! Why is it so...?" A suspicion grew. Cassie dashed down the hall and stared at the heating vent nearest the kitchen. "Closed. Probably someone at the party. Great. Just wasted all that extra warmth for nothing. Sheesh."

⚓⚓⚓

The morning's Bible study lesson—the lilies of the field. The sparrows. God's provision. Stewardship. Cassie managed *not* to bawl. A few knowing looks from her friends told her that the news had already spread through the church. *Lord...*

She squirmed in her seat through the whole lesson *and* the

sermon. Whether because it was the first Sunday of the new year, or because it just *happened* to be the next verses in their regular study, she couldn't tell, but timing couldn't have been worse.

Only the way Joel slipped out of his seat and came to sit next to her hinted that her misery must have shown on her face. He pulled out a Tic-Tac box and gave it a muffled shake in a silent offer of one. Cassie snatched it and poured half into her hand before passing it back and whispering, "Thanks..."

By the time the service ended and the last prayer for wisdom and strength for the coming week had been prayed—quite apropos, she thought—Cassie felt reinvigorated. "I can do this."

Joel's one raised brow did little to daunt her. "Why do you think that?"

"Because I can do all things—even live without paper towels—through Christ Who strengthens me... or however that goes. It's going to be great. I'll learn what I want to make a permanent change in my life and what is just excessive."

With a quick hug and a half two-step shuffle, Cassie wove around groups of chatting friends and strangers as she hustled to the bathroom. She'd reminded herself half a dozen times since waking. *Make sure you pay attention to the TP.* However, she hadn't remembered little things like toilet seat covers. "Oh, no! Really, Lord? Really?!"

A voice from the stall next to her startled her. "What's wrong? Are you okay?"

"Toilet seat covers. What do you consider the environmental impact of them to be?"

"Um... negligible? It's a tiny and thin piece of paper that dissolves in water, isn't it?"

Who am I kidding? There's no way I'm going without it. I'll use two fewer squares to make up for it. Aloud, she merely thanked the woman. "Gotta have my covers. There are just some things not worth the hassle."

"Um... okay. Hope you're feeling better."

Three minutes passed. Still Cassie sat there staring at a length of one-ply toilet paper. *No way is five squares gonna cut it. No way. I have to cut two, and that means three. Not. Happening. Six... still, four? Nope. So, seven?* Cassie half-balled it up and sighed. *Nine minimum.*

And that's when the reality of what she was doing hit her full-force. *I am sitting in the church bathroom with my pants resting nicely on the germ-riddled floor, using a seat cover that is now useless because of my stupid pants, counting TP squares in a futile attempt to reduce paper waste. Who am I and what happened to my rational brain?*

She jerked a few more squares from the roll and exited as quickly as possible. As she washed her hands, Cassie berated herself for her stupidity. "You are pathetic. Total sucker. Just wait'll you have to make a serious decision. You're sunk."

⸭ ⸭ ⸭

When lunch became a repeat performance for breakfast—right down to the fumbling attempt to snag a paper towel, Cassie plopped her sandwich on a plate, grabbed one of the paper napkins she'd saved for guests, and called Lauren on her way to the couch. "Okay. We need to talk paper towels."

"Kitchen towels, Cass. It's not a difficult concept. Your mom bought—"

"I know! I mean, my brain knows what I need to do, but do you know how frustrating it is to want one and not have it? I'm going nuts! I mean, what if I spill something *nasty* like oil or spaghetti sauce?"

She heard it—a cough-covered snicker. "Um, Cass? Dishcloths or towels. Like I said, you know this."

"But that's disgusting! If it's the floor—"

"You use it, rinse it out, and toss in the wash."

So, she sounded ridiculous. Cassie knew it. She protested a bit too much, and wouldn't even attempt to deny it. But the

40

words flowed unbidden anyway. "And then I just waste a bunch of water! How is that better? We have great gaping gobs of this country that is totally uninhabited—probably will be forever. Water—you can't make more. You can't bundle it up and fly it up to the moon or shoot it off to the sun to be consumed there. So...."

Exasperation—Lauren didn't bother to hide it anymore. "Look *you* made this commitment, not me. You're only on what, day three? Just stop now before you stress yourself out anymore. No one is going to blame you." After a moment of utter silence, she added. "And it's not like you can't reduce anyway. Just go for it—go green*er* instead of trying to overhaul your life overnight.

"Nope. I'm doing this. I said I would and I will."

"Uh oh."

Cassie stared at her phone, waiting to hear that some horrible thing had happened... like Lauren had dropped an entire roll of toilet paper into the toilet or a roll of paper towels into the sink. When she didn't continue, Cassie asked the obvious. "What?"

"I just know that tone. I won't bother trying to talk you out of it. So, did we solve your towel dilemma?"

"I suppose." Cassie stared at the paper napkin beside her untouched sandwich and closed her eyes. The obvious answer presented itself, but she prayed for an out. *If You could just prompt her to point out that buying stuff isn't very eco-friendly either... that'd be nice.* She swallowed a chug of water and dove in. "Okay... let's talk napkins."

Lauren sounded strangled. Was it laughter or concern? Cassie couldn't decide and couldn't bring herself to ask. It took two repeats before her words became comprehensible. "You just need more washcloths or towels. Cut them up, buy them at the thrift store... even ask for them for your birthday, but you'll need something to get you through until April."

"I'll never make it. I think I need a boyfriend yesterday. He

41

can bring me bouquets of washcloth roses wrapped in kitchen towels before dates and on Valentine's Day. Two dozen washcloths beats roses that'll wilt any day."

"You don't belie—"

But Cassie interrupted with a swiftness and sincerity that surprised even her. "I do *too!* I never imagined it. Roses are just amazing, but when you can't use a stupid paper towel and have mayo on the counter, you *want* more washcloths. Now napkins. I can't stand the idea of used washcloths. I wish I didn't convince myself that buying new was a bad idea. I'd totally go for it."

"Restaurants don't use terry. They work well enough."

She closed her eyes and tried to imagine wiping her face with the napkins. The result felt inconclusive. *I'm always careful not to get makeup on them if I can. Hate the idea of staining their stuff.* A groan escaped. "I wish I could just buy some on Amazon. Get them here by Wednesday, and be done with it, but I feel like I should be using what is already out there."

"You could cut up one of your vintage sheets or maybe an old flannel shirt or two—maybe your thinner jeans that you don't wear anymore?" Lauren even suggested putting a call for flannel on the local swap page on Facebook. "But I have to say, I like the idea of cute denim napkins. It'd be like watching your brother rub his hands on his jeans... but at least this would be deliberate. Get creative."

"I—" Creativity felt like a precious commodity sold on the black market at that moment. "Okay. I'm going to go see what I've got. I need something before dinner. Talk atcha later. And hey, Lauren?"

"Yeah?"

"Thanks for putting up with me—for not laughing at me."

Lauren's tone shifted. "Anytime, Cass. If it counts for anything, I'm crazy proud of you. I know I goaded you into this. I didn't mean to, but I did."

She didn't want to admit it—fought against it for several

long seconds—but Cassie managed to confess her own culpability. "I'm a big girl. I inferred a dare where you didn't mean one. But I'm going to do it. I'll learn something—even if it's not to be so rash."

Cassie's duplex felt empty and cold as soon as she disconnected with Lauren. She started at one end of the kitchen and looked into every cupboard and drawer. From there she ransacked her living room, all closets, and her bedroom. In the spare room, in a box full of decor for her annual Fourth of July parties, she found two royal blue tablecloths she'd purchased in desperation and kept, "just in case." The white lines of the plaid unsettled her a bit. They might end up looking pretty seedy quickly, but she couldn't think of anything else. "Okay. You'll work—never did like the color. Should've been navy."

She carried it back to the kitchen, ripped the plastic cover from it, winced, and tossed the plastic in the trash. "Next week. I can freak out next week.

With the fabric laid out on her "island," Cassie went in search of her paper scissors, which were not, of course, in the drawer of her living room table where they belonged. The longer it took her to find them, the more careless she became. Drawers stood half-open, doors didn't close. Baskets looked rumpled. But at last, she found them in a bag of party decor—used to open it, of course. "Sometimes, I think I'd lose my mind if I could afford to be without it long enough to look for it." She blinked. "That makes no sense. Whatever. Maybe it just proves my point."

Measuring out the napkins—not easy. She finally dug through the bin outside and pulled a paper towel from the roll. *I like this size. It works.* Cassie shivered her way back into the house and laid the paper towel atop the fabric as a pattern. "Okay... here we go."

Four hacks later, she threw the scissors halfway across the room. "I swear, there's an unwritten cosmic law that says, 'If it is eco-friendly, it must be frustrating enough to inspire profanity and a deep, abiding desire to use an entire roll of paper towels all at once.'"

She stared at the offensive and useless scissors for the better part of a minute before an alternative idea sent her scurrying for the kitchen shears that hadn't left the knife block since the day she'd unpacked it from the box of stuff donated to her by her mom. "Ha! Now I have a use for you."

They might not have sliced through the tablecloth "like butter" but they did make short work of hacking out a couple of dozen napkins. The latter bunch even had semi-straight edges and looked moderately presentable. With shears raised overhead like the Statue of Liberty's torch, Cassie declared, "Give me your trash, your plastic, your stacks of napkins yearning to break free from landfills and even more. Send these, the renewable, the recyclable to me. I lift my sheers in defiance of the pursuit of more!"

As her voice reverberated around her in the little kitchen, she shrugged. "Not good, but hey... can't believe I remembered that much."

With the satisfaction of a job well-done, Cassie folded each napkin and shoved them in a drawer that held coupons—probably expired—and a bunch of receipts she knew she'd never look at again. Her nose wrinkled. "As soon as I figure out how to recycle you guys, you're outta there. Meanwhile..." She smoothed her napkins, shut the drawer, and leaned against it, folding her arms over her chest as she did. "Yep... that'll work."

Monday, January 4—

The third time Cassie reached to tear a sheet from her note cube, she dumped the whole thing in the bottom of her purse. *I can use it up later—after I've changed habits.* Instead, she pulled up the document on her computer and added to her half a dozen previous notes of the morning.

Ten minutes later, she pulled it back out again and added a personal note to a stack of papers she snatched from the paper tray of the office printer. Binder clips held the stack together until her boss approved them. She knocked on the door. "I have the contracts and notes for the Dempsey case. Did you want them before I go to lunch?"

The salt-and-pepper beard that still looked half-grown after six months—she'd never get used to it. But a lawyer like Doug Sylmer could get away with it. With his success rate, he could wear burlap and not bathe for a week before each case and probably still manage to make a decent living. *And as long as you do, I do. Win-win.*

"I'll take them now. I think I'm going to go over to my club for lunch before the meeting. I can look them over then. You have a nice lunch, Cassandra."

"I hope... thanks. Will you be in later today or...?" His steely eyes met hers and held for one of those uncomfortable moments that always left her unsettled and uncertain. *Man, I wouldn't want to be trying to bilk someone with exaggerations while you are cross-examining me. I'd totally bomb it.*

"I don't think so. Just try to get those letters to people on last week's dockets out today. Oh, and try to reschedule Mrs. Kothari for later this week. She'll go with us if we can get her back in here before anyone else does."

With her assurances that she'd make that appointment, Cassie closed the door behind her and snatched her purse from beneath her desk. *Aaaand I'm outta here. Starving. What'll I have?*

The cacophony of midday traffic assaulted her senses as she stepped through the double glass doors that separated the Steele Building from downtown Rockland. A taxi pulled up in front of the building, and without thinking twice, Cassie hurried to claim it. The occupant, a woman in a suit that likely cost more than her paycheck, stepped out and brushed past with the impatience of a woman on a mission. Either that, or eager to get out of the open air before it began raining and she drowned. *Upturned noses have that tendency.*

With the door shut and the driver's eyes on her, waiting for directions, Cassie realized she needed to think fast—to decide fast. "Do you have a lunch recommendation? I'm starving."

"You must be new to Rockland, miss." The man's heavily accented voice made understanding him difficult, but she sighed in relief as he smiled at her. "You should say, 'I need a good restaurant somewhere in a four-block radius. I'm starving and am on a tight schedule.'"

"Let's pretend I said that. What do you recommend? If you find somewhere I can get it to go and they're fast, I'll call and order and have you wait for me."

He suggested several places, but Cassie chose a sandwich shop three blocks over. "I haven't been there since summer, I think! Great idea. They always have what I want in the case, too. Win-win."

And they did. Caesar salad with a turkey sandwich. Her hand reached for her favorite water brand and hesitated. The label—paper. Frustrated, she shifted and snagged Aquafina. "At least it's plastic... I have a whole week to figure that one out."

"Huh?"

The voice behind her sent a rush of heat to her face. *Gotta stop talking out loud! It's getting embarrassing.* Without even a glance over her shoulder, Cassie muttered, "Just thinking out loud. Sorry."

"How about I buy that lunch and you tell me all about it? Most people *avoid* all the plastic they can. I'm intrigued."

Cassie dropped her choices on the counter and fished for her wallet. "Very nice of you, but I'm in a rush."

A business card slid across the front of the counter. "Maybe another time."

Cassie pushed it back. "Maybe not." She passed her card to the girl behind the register and smiled at the irony of paying for her meals with plastic next week. "Have a nice day..."

At the door, she glanced back and found the man behind her still watching. *Man, I'm glad I didn't see those eyes before I said no. I might have done something totally stupid.* Cassie waved and called out, "Thanks for the invitation. It made my day."

"Just wish you'd made mine."

Warm fuzzies kept her from freezing all the way back to the taxi. "Thanks for waiting."

"Back to the Steele Building?"

"Yep. I think I'll go eat in the lounge. Warm, nice view— perfect."

If she'd only known...

⸙ ⸙ ⸙

She made it to the lounge, found a table, and spread out a napkin for a placemat. And that's when her stomach flopped and not in the way she liked. Cute guys making eyes at her equaled lovely flops. Failure equaled miserable ones. This... this was the latter. *Of course.*

Cassie stared as she pulled a paper-wrapped sandwich from a plastic bag. Her hand actually shook as she withdrew the plastic bowl holding a salad she'd salivated over for four blocks and ten floors. The bleak January skyline shown from the windows beside her did little to brighten her spirits. The plastic she could justify—*this week.* But that paper wrapping filled her with unexpected and annoying shame. *Lord, please...*

The intern at Roth, Jothikumar, and Sylmer pulled out a chair next to her and peered at her with evident curiosity. "Not hungry after all?"

"No. Just praying." *Well, it's technically true.*

"Sorry."

It may have been her imagination, but Cassie got the distinct feeling that he leaned away from her and when he inched his chair forward, he also dragged it a little to the left. A smile filled her heart and reached her lips. "Having a nice day?"

"They've got me researching precedent for manslaughter

47

of a fetus."

As opposed to homicide in an abortion clinic? Don't say it, Cassie. Don't say it. You aren't paid to voice your opinions. Do. Not. Say. It. Self-recriminations notwithstanding, Cassie heard herself say, "I never understood why a man *inside* an abortion clinic could ensure the 'early birth' of a baby..." *There... that was tactful, wasn't it?* "But someone outside it tries to hurt a woman and accidentally kills her child and *that* is considered a separate crime to the assault. I probably don't have a legal mind or something."

It worked, too. Cassie got her opinion stated, albeit in a circuitous way, and now intern Mike could rattle off his knowledge of law for her. Perfect distraction while she plowed through a sandwich and salad ensconced in wrappings that would then wind up in the trash. Once in a while, she asked if he'd tried Google or Bing. The amused glances Mike sent her hinted that he found her supposed lack of law knowledge "cute."

Just the way I like it.

"—get drinks sometime?"

She blinked twice at the assortment of chicken, mozzarella, and lettuce on her fork before the man's words registered. "Um... what?"

From the red slowly creeping up his neck, Cassie realized that she had *not* misheard him. "I just thought it might be fun to get drinks sometime..."

Oh, boy. Cassie's reputation as an easy let down failed her. She shook her head with a little too much fervor and fumbled to cover it. "Sorry. Big chunk. Um, I really appreciate it, but I don't drink." *And the fact that I just decided that has nothing to do with the truth of it.*

It wasn't the first time in recent weeks she's arranged her decisions to play fast and loose with the truth. Cassie filed a mental reminder to examine her heart on the issue of truth and kicked into "easy let down" mode. "But I know that Jennie at

Faber and Foyle always checks her makeup when you walk into the lounge."

Unbelievably, it worked. Mike's attention slid to the other side of the room and checked out the leggy blonde with an interested eye. "Hey, thanks. Sorry. Didn't mean to offend you. Religious thing?"

"Sort of. It's new, too. I just can't give up on my resolutions before I've had a chance to keep them. Glad you understand."

His attention shifted back to her, and she sensed another shift as well. *Drat. Went too far.* Before he could open his mouth—ask her out for coffee, if her guess were correct—Cassie jumped up. "Better go talk to her before Bernstein gets to her." With that, she bolted from the table, pausing only long enough to dump much too much garbage for her comfort. *Tonight's goal: Plan tomorrow's lunch better.*

Tuesday, January 5—

As snow dumped on Rockland with enough force to trap her at home the next day, Cassie burst through her back door and dumped her coat, bag, and store bags on the floor. "Oh, it's cold! Could be colder, but that snow just adds mess and city-wide nightmares to the mix!"

The tantalizing scent of loaded baked potato soup filled the little kitchen, but Cassie forced herself to ignore it in favor of a long, leisurely dinner without guilt. As if in protest to the cold, her furnace kicked on. Routine kicked in as she moved through the duplex and settled in for the night. She pulled fleece sleep pants, fuzzy socks, a long-sleeved t-shirt, and her slouchy cardigan from her drawers and closet before dumping her clothes in the hamper. "Full. Great."

A load of jeans and dark flannel shirts filled the washer—right where she'd left them before she dashed out the door that morning. Cassie scooped it all up and tossed it in the dryer. One dryer sheet later, she set the timer at seventy minutes and slowly sorted the rest of her clothes into the washer or its appropriate basket. She dumped the rest of the "brights" into the washer, shifted it down to medium, and poured her favorite detergent into the stream of water filling the tub. Lid cup rinsed, she twisted it back onto the jug and slid it onto the shelf as she closed the washer lid. An unease filled her as she stared at that enormous plastic jug.

"It lasts forever. That has to count for something, doesn't it? I can't buy stuff in a box. That's paper. I *have* to have soap!" Logic said she could only reduce what she could live without. Laundry soap wasn't an option. People had been washing clothes for centuries. It ruined fabric fibers not to get the dirt out. Everyone knew that. "I'll research it, but I'm not ruining my clothes to save a bit of plastic. I'll switch to a box if I have to. It's *more* biodegradable than plastic, anyway. Weird that on week one, the week where I have to cut back on paper, I'm already switching to something *with* more paper."

Cassie snapped off the light and made it halfway down the hall before something new assaulted her thoughts. With force enough to knock her into a wall—and it did—she whirled in place and strode back into the tiny laundry room. There on the shelf above the dryer, she stared at the box of dryer sheets.

"I didn't even think twice. Now what do I do? Isn't fabric softener bad for washing machines and fibers? Seems like I read that. Ugh. Still, though. Box over plastic bottle... for now, I stick with these, I guess. Maybe I'll do like Mom does and use each one twice." She glared at the box. "Well, I'll try it anyway. I am not living with static. No. Way."

That decision made, Cassie hurried into the kitchen for a bowl of soup. She lifted the lid and stared into the pot, certain it would be a nightmarish mess of disgusting proportions. Instead, after a couple of stirs with the spoon, she nearly danced to the cupboard for a bowl. "This is *cool*. I mean, c'mon. No cooking? That's easier than going out."

She snatched up her purse to retrieve her phone and reached for a paper towel to dry off the outside. Instead, her hand connected with the kitchen towel she'd hung over the jury-rigged towel rack she'd put in the holder. "Ha! Towel. Right. Of course, man... this means a lot of laundry. Bet I double my washer usage with all this. Ugh."

Undaunted, Cassie ordered her phone to call Lauren and pulled out the little baggies of bacon, cheese, and chopped onions she'd prepared. "Hey, Lauren. It's me. You're not going to believe how easy dinner is when you make it while you're at work."

"Um... you knew this. You've done it before."

Cassie ignored the prosaic dismissal of her epiphany and continued with her rhapsodies in potato. "I just put all the ingredients in the crockpot, turned it on low, and voila. Walked in to the most *amazing* smells—scents—whatever. My stomach is doing a happy dance even before I take a bite."

"You've got issues, Cass. You say this every time you do it. Maybe if you just did it more often..."

The temptation—too perfect to pass up. "What, and turn something beautiful into something redundant?" Though she ached to say, "Never!" Cassie couldn't do it. She'd have to now. "But seriously, I have to do this. Did you know that you can't buy a stupid *sandwich* without it being loaded with refuse?"

"I assume you mean *packaging*?" If you eat in, there's less usually. Nicer restaurants—"

"Would devour what little extra I have in my budget inside three days." Cassie sighed. "I have to start carrying lunch to work. And I have to do it without using plastic baggies."

"Get containers and take them. It's fine. Maybe one of those cute bento boxes!" Lauren raved about compartmentalized lunch boxes perfect for a working girl on the go. Just as Cassie opened her mouth to insist it couldn't happen—that she couldn't start buying stuff like that yet—Lauren stomped on her objections. "And you could find a used one on eBay or something. It's perfect!"

Okay, so that's really not a bad idea. I could do that. As she described her day to Lauren, Cassie settled herself on her couch, took a bite of the steaming soup—burning her tongue, of course—and pulled out her iPad. Her fingers flew across the keyboard as she tried to search for bento boxes on eBay.

"So, is this Mike the guy you thought was going to ask you out last month?"

"Yep. I think going out is his New Year's resolution. Oh, and that reminds me. I've noticed a new habit of ensuring what I want to be true *is* true... after the fact. Probably not what the Lord would consider honest, eh?"

Lauren's silence sent unpleasant shivers down her spine. But before she could assure her friend that she fully intended to repent of this newly discovered flaw, Lauren sighed. "Man... I think I do that. I'd never thought of it. I suppose it is dishonest, even if you make sure it ends up being the truth. Deceptive. Ouch." A weak hint of playfulness entered her tone. "Thanks a *lot* for the conviction, Cass. This is supposed to be about *you*, and your change. Not me."

"Semicolon/end-parentheses?"

This time, Lauren's laughter reset the happy balance of their friendship. "Yep. Exactly."

Cassie went to scoop another spoonful of soup and found an empty bowl. She jumped up and made her way back to the crockpot. "I ate it all—without even noticing. I'm definitely going back for seconds. Wish you were here. Gotta run!"

"You can do this, Cass. I have total faith in you."

As she stared at a sink half-full of dirty dishes, Cassie sighed. "Well, that makes one of us."

⚏ ⚏ ⚏

The dryer buzzed just as Cassie finished washing up the dishes. She stared at her hands—at the raw, redness of her knuckles—and made a decision. "If this much washing does this

52

much damage already, I'm buying gloves." She eyed the dishwasher. "Or, maybe I can stop running it empty every other week and run it full every other day. That might work."

She dried off her hands and reached for the lotion, but the memory of wet clothes in the washer stopped her. "After the laundry. Yeah."

Her monologue with herself—strangled at the sight that greeted her when she opened the dryer. Jeans, shirts, and what had once been napkins jumbled together in a still-damp ball of threads and twisted fabric. "Oh, come on! Lord, I tried. You saw me. Can't a girl get a little help here? Ugh!"

Cassie dumped the wadded mess in her laundry basket and carried it to the living room. As she worked to extricate her clothes from the web of strings holding them captive, she ordered the phone to get her mother "stat." It called with regular speed and obnoxiously allowed the call to go to voice mail.

"Mom. I need you. Semi-emergency. No blood. No broken anything. No one in danger—no one but my sanity and my favorite parts of my wardrobe. Save me."

Voice mail—her mother's call screening process. Leave a message with exactly what you want to discuss, and Marla Wren might just return that call. On a good day. And if you were her kid. As much as she hated to admit it, Cassie knew that was her one saving grace—that lovely bond of sharing the same body, childbirth, potty training, and "the talk."

Her mother's ring tone barely had a chance to play before Cassie tapped the screen. "Help!"

"If you tell me you've dyed your hair or—"

"Napkins."

That shut her up—for at least two and a half seconds, too. "Napkins?"

"Cloth ones. I cut them from a tablecloth. Then I didn't like how they felt when I used them, so I washed them with my jeans and flannel shirts—the darker ones, anyway. Whatever.

53

The point is, now I have a huge ball of hog-tied jeans and shirts!"

"Oh, brother. I take it this means you didn't hem them."

Cassie closed her eyes and took several long, slow, cleansing breaths. People didn't use the word "hem" in her presence. *How could you do that to me, Mom?!* Once the wave of panic ebbed a bit, she tried speaking. "Um... remember the pillowcase I made? *Remember?* I lost half that thing to the hem. It barely fit a travel pillow by the time I got done. And that dress—the one you said, 'Oh, it'll be a snap to shorten that'? Remember? It was a snap all right. Turned into a mini-dress inside ten hours flat."

"Okay... well, at least, you should sew around the outside—straightish lines. Zig zags. Even those scissors that make the zig-zag cuts. Drat. What are they called? Those work to stop unraveling, I think."

The scissors sounded amazing, but she didn't have time to find someone who owned a pair she could borrow or buy. "Okay, but without those scissors, what's the best option for me?"

"Um... well, I'd just sew around them—maybe half an inch inside the edge or so. You'll lose a few threads the first time or two, maybe. But thin it'll be fine. Actually, you should get a nice fringe."

Before she asked the next, and most obvious question, Cassie stared out into the street. *It's reasonably clear. Snowing stopped. Maybe the big storm isn't coming after all.* Resolved, Cassie put the next question to her mother. "Okay, so can I borrow your sewing machine?"

"Huh?"

"I need to do this. I need these things."

Silence. Cassie waited with the patience that comes after a lifetime of knowing someone. "Cassie, why do you need cloth napkins? You're the paper queen."

"Well, I'm going to be the 'green queen' for this year. So that means no paper. And I didn't buy fabric," she hastened to add. "I used something I already owned. So there."

Despite knowing it couldn't be possible, Cassie heard her mother scribbling. She heard the pen scratch across the page, the pause, the continued, feverish writing. And then the words came. Words that Cassie mouthed as her mother's voice filled the living room. "I'll be praying for you, Cassandra." A second later she added, "And sure. Come get the machine."

It took ten minutes of debate, watching the weather monitors to see if the expected blizzard would pass by or be just a light snowstorm. Rockland weather reports—notoriously inaccurate. But in minutes, she warmed her car, climbed in, and took off through the streets of her decaying neighborhood to the outskirts of Westbury and her parents' lovely old, established, and increasingly revitalized sub-division. She managed to avoid considering the environmental impact of instant gratification in the quest to reduce her impact on said environment.

However, with machine in tow, Cassie spent the entire drive home calculating exactly how much gas and oil she'd used to retrieve the machine, doubled it, and tried to compare it with the transportation costs of easily several dozen rolls of paper towels over the life of her new napkins. "If they can be saved, anyway. Surely this is significantly less. It's a lot less on my budget."

Despite the positive pep talk, Cassie watched the miles add up and considered the time the car had spent idling as she warmed it and then again as she dashed inside the house to retrieve the machine. "Not to mention fifteen minutes of trying to explain to Mom that I haven't gone hippie." A slow smile overwrote the grimace at the memory. "Then again, I should have let her think it—hinted at considering the concept of 'free love.' That would have gotten me out of there." She pulled into her driveway and jerked the car into park with more force than her mechanic would appreciate. "Then again, I would have heard about it over the phone for weeks. Better that I deny all."

By the time she set up the machine, threaded it, and stared at the Chinese puzzle that had turned her "threads" into threads, Cassie doubted again. So, while she muttered about the incongruity of being able to thread a sewing machine without difficulty but unable to fold a narrow strip of fabric and sew it down, Cassie retrieved her phone and called Lauren.

"Okay, here's the deal." She ripped one square from the ball, trimmed off the threads, and tried to measure a straight line from the "edge" of the fabric. "So, I made those napkins, right?"

"Yeah..."

"Didn't hem them. Washed them. You can imagine from there. What was I not thinking?"

Lauren's laughter—an unexpected balm to her raw emotions. "Oh, Cassie. I love you. So, what's the solution. You could hem—never mind. Bad idea."

"Right? But I did go get the machine. Mom says if I sew around them, it'll stop the raveling and create a nice little fringe."

"I think cutting the corners off will do that, too. My aunt quilts, you know. That's what she does when she pre-washes the fabric she buys. Says it keeps the fabric from becoming a mess."

"I'll do both, then." Even as she spoke, Cassie grabbed the kitchen shears and lobbed off the first four corners. "But I had to go to Mom's. You know, to get the machine. So I'm curious. Did I just negate any napkin waste prevention by burning gas and oil to go get this stupid, energy sucking machine? I used up at least a gallon of gas—so not eco-friendly. So, what should I have done? And if you say hand-sew the stupid things, I'll PT your condo."

Lauren's eruption of mirth made it a little difficult to understand her, but Cassie thought she asked, "Don't you mean TP?"

"No way. That stuff is gold. Paper towels, however—*PT*—I

am not allowed to use, so I might as well get some fun out of."

Again—laughter and in every form. Chortles, chuckles, giggles, guffaws. She sounded like an audible thesaurus. "This—" she wheezed. "This is some seriously great stuff. You've got to turn this project of yours into a blog or a vlog or *something*. People would totally get into your insights. Call it 52 Weeks of Green or 365 Days of Green."

"Really?" Despite her intention to demur, the idea grew on Lauren immediately. "Do you think people really want to read the frustrated rantings of an unconvinced environmentalist?"

Lauren's confidence only grew. "See! Right there. Make that your tagline! I'm serious. You are so funny, and it's a real issue for people brought up in an instant lifestyle. We were taught to be consumers and then bam—almost overnight, we're supposed to give up our previous way of life for this new 'eco-friendly' one. We're supposed to be the generation who saves the planet, but sometimes we just want to save a little time and borrow against tomorrow."

Cassie hopped up from the table and bolted for a notebook. She scrawled down Lauren's ideas as they spoke, her project abandoned on her little dining table. As Lauren excused herself for a moment, Cassie surveyed her notes with a curious eye. *I could do this... maybe. Wonder if anyone would read it. Might be an experiment for that book idea...*

"Hey, Cass!" Lauren's voice exploded through the phone as she returned. "I have a great idea! You could even set up challenges for people. I mean, think about it. If one person doesn't use napkins for a day—no real environmental impact. But if you had readers who did it—and each one say didn't use three a day. And maybe you had a thousand readers. That's *three thousand napkins!* Then you're not in it alone, and you're helping make a significant impact without expecting everyone to change their whole lives."

Lost in thought, Cassie didn't respond until Lauren shouted her name again. "Wha—oh! Yeah! That would be kind of cool. I could keep track for the year. See just how much difference one person can make by herself *and* by influencing others. And you know..." She waited until Lauren urged her to continue. "I did originally have writing a blog or a book on my goals list. I had planned to go with book because I thought it was better, but this could be like fodder for one or something."

"So, you'll do it? C'mon. Say you'll do it. You're so funny and it'll lighten up an otherwise kind of intense subject. At the end of the year, you can look back and see how far you've come."

She nodded—as if Lauren could see her agreement—as she listened. "I bet I'm surprised at what frustrated me then and what I thought would be easy but wasn't."

The brainstorming session flew past, the napkin project forgotten, and excitement building with every new idea. "You can make them short," Lauren insisted. "People have short attention spans anyway—bite-sized blurbs that don't take a million scrolls on a phone, you know? I mean, no one wants to read a treatise on the evils of buying newspapers. They just want to hear that you can get along fine without them."

"Nooooooooooooo. do. not. say. that. I need newspapers— for my system. I can manage in winter—there aren't that many sales to go to, but when garage sale season starts up..." She dropped her head to the sewing machine, hardly noticing the way her head cracked against the metal, and moaned. "I can't do this. I *can't*. I *need* my newspapers."

"You'll figure it out," Lauren assured her. "I'll help you. Oh! Oh!" Cassie waited with classic impatience. But just as she opened her mouth to demand her friend continue after that exuberant prelude, Lauren zipped a link to her. "You could do like this chick. Look, she never actually *writes* an article. She just does a picture with a caption or a super short video. You could even do just a Periscope of it."

"I want a written record, or I'd totally go with Periscope. But for once in a while, it would be fun."

Before Cassie could ask her next question, Lauren cleared her throat in what could only mean one thing—impending rebuke or purposeful teasing. "Um, Cass?"

"Yeah?"

"I don't hear the sewing machine."

She dropped her head back to the machine. "I'll send you pics in a minute. You won't believe this."

"Take good ones—put them on the blog. People will love it." At Cassie's groan, Lauren laughed, insisted on receiving a link the minute she had the blog set up. "But napkins first. And don't forget to take some to work with you!"

"In *what?* Am I really going to carry dirty napkins in my purse? I can't use Ziploc bags, and—"

But Lauren interrupted before she could get on a roll. "Just use one of those cosmetic cases your mom is always giving you. Didn't you get a new one for Christmas or something? It looks pretty in the purse, but they'll hold the dirty ones—just like your handkerchiefs if you ever do those. Win-win. Now bye!"

Sewing the napkins proved more time consuming than she'd expected. Half of them, she forgot to backstitch and had to go over them again. Then she liked the idea of double-stitching, so she did on the rest as well.

She snipped a hole in her favorite flannel shirt in a desperate and futile attempt to separate it from a napkin and legs from two different pairs of jeans. That, of course, meant she'd have to mend—not likely on the middle of the back of a shirt—or turn it into handkerchiefs. She opted for the latter.

Then she had to prevent fraying on them, too.

Unfortunately, that didn't touch the next injustice. Despite constant smoothing, each of the napkins curled in a wrinkled ball. Cassie eyed the hall closet with disdain dripping from her eyelashes. "I do *not* have time to iron what I'm going to wipe my face with! This is ridiculous!" That thought prompted her to pull out her phone and take a picture of the ironing process. "At least I can turn it into a blog post—tomorrow's after I use them at work. We'll see. Dumb things. Paper is so much better."

⫱ ⫱ ⫱

The antique mantel clock that sat atop her armoire—the one that always gained a minute a week—chimed the three-quarter mark. Midnight in twenty minutes. "Gotta reset the time on that thing."

But even with the reminder that morning would arrive long before she was ready for it, Cassie continued to tweak the blog style, the categories—everything. Just as it chimed midnight, she sat back. Satisfied.

"There. My journal of this journey is ready to go." That idea sparked her first post. Despite every intention of making the first one about her napkin fiasco and how she'd overcome, Cassie found herself writing a short piece on twenty-first century journals.

The Eco-Journey Journal

It starts here. It starts with a weird reality. This blog is basically my journey of a year of eco-conscious decisions and actions. It's an e-journal—a paperless record of my reduction of excess paper in my life.

There seems a strange sort of irony to it, but there's no contradiction. Isn't that what irony has to have? I'll have to ask my friend, Lauren about that. Perhaps I should call it a fortuitous coincidence. There, Lauren. I used one of your words. Be proud.

But despite that, this method of recording my year means that there's less waste! And with my notebook addiction, it could mean a serious hit to the logging industry. I hope I don't put any lumberjacks out of business. Maybe they could design a blog platform that doesn't require a computer science degree to understand.

See you tomorrow, blog world. I'll have fascinating, riveting tales of napkins. Try not to lose sleep due to the anticipation.

Wednesday, January 6—

Cassie's assumption that she'd tackled the napkin problem and kicked it out of the game came to the test on Wednesday at lunch. From a tote bag she'd received as a "free gift" for spending sixty-dollars at the cosmetic counter at Macy's, Cassie pulled a plastic bowl of salad. She fumbled for a fork, the small plastic container of dressing, and her separate crouton container—designed to ensure they stayed nice and crispy. Fork, bottled water that she dreaded giving up the following week, and... Her mind whirled to try to remember what she'd missed. A minute later, she dashed from the lounge, rode the elevator to her floor, snagged her purse, and rushed back.

By then, one of the silver-haired financial planners had seated himself at the other end of her table. "Sorry... I thought the table was empty—or would be when maintenance goes through."

"No worries. Just forgot my purse." With just a little pride—more than she'd ever have imagined—Cassie pulled her little cosmetic bag from the purse, retrieved one of her napkins, and set it in her lap. *There. Not that hard, really. Why did I think it would be such a big deal?*

The man—his name, one she couldn't remember—watched her over the top of what looked like a chicken or turkey wrap. Cassie ignored him in favor of her phone and watching the ever-stagnant stats on her fledgling blog. *Four views. Four. I wonder how long it takes for there to be someone who has never heard of you? A week? Six? Ten years?* A new question formed as she dunked her fork in the dressing. *Do I want people to read it? I could make it private. That would work.*

But to her surprise, the idea of no one reading, cheering her on, laughing with her—it discouraged her. *I'll keep it public for now anyway. What's the point of putting it online—oh.*

Paperless. But still, I could have done Google docs if I didn't want people to read it.

"May I ask a question?"

The words jerked her from her internal debate. "Um, sure."

"Why do you bring cloth napkins in your purse? Don't they get your purse dirty when you get done with them?"

Without a word, Cassie fished out both cosmetic bags—a cloth plaid version and a clear plastic. "I have one for clean ones and one for dirty?"

"Isn't that a bit excessive?"

Mike passed and stopped mid-stride. "What are you doing?"

Defensiveness welled up in her. She ignored Mike to answer the older gentleman's question. "I wanted to see if it really was harder—" Conviction hit hard. It was the least true of her creative honesty attempts, and it shamed her. "Well, it's deeper than that, really. I'm trying this for a year—no waste I can do without. This is week one, and I had to make these things..." She waved her napkin like a surrender flag. "Just so I wouldn't have to use a paper napkin."

"Why not just use a napkin. It's biodegradable. I tried it in my backyard to prove to my nephew. Bury it, keep the area reasonably moist, and in a year or so, you can't even find where it was."

Arguments, ones she'd heard for years, welled up inside her—arguments about how packed together in landfills there wasn't enough dirt and moisture to properly break things down or how in plastic trash bags, nothing broke down properly. However, thanks to the previous evening's excursion to procure the means to *make* said napkins actually washable, a new idea formed. "I think it's about more than what happens when we dispose of it. I think we need to consider the production and distribution impacts on the environment. The fuel, manufacturing—all of it. If it were *just* about post-use, I might agree, but I think an environmentalist could destroy that reasoning."

She wiped her lips and stared at the napkin. "They still feel weird, though. I love my paper. But I can't say that paper is way easier if I'm not even willing to *try* something else. One year won't kill me." Under her breath, Cassie whispered, "I hope."

"I think you've lost your mind. Radicals like you end up making things worse for the rest of us. Some states have actually *banned* plastic grocery bags. Have you *tried* to carry a couple of brown paper bags full of stuff home? Ruins them." Mike turned to the other man. "Right?"

"He has a point."

"But cloth bags have the advantage of plastic, but your sharp-cornered lunch meat isn't going to rip out the side and send everything sprawling across the sidewalk on your way home from the subway."

It felt a little déjà vu-ish—saying the very words she'd mocked oh, so recently. Was it even right to argue in favor of something she hadn't convinced herself of yet? Did that fall under the same dishonesty as her recent habit of playing fast and loose with the truth?

The man stood and rolled his wrappings in a ball—tight as he could. Something in the movement made her wince. *Surely, that makes it harder for it to decompose...* The thought sent her mind reeling at how quickly she changed her thoughts. *Whoa...* So lost was she in her own mental rabbit trails, she missed most of what he said.

"—you luck. You seem happy with it. That's what matters. Follow your heart. It won't lead you wrong."

She tried not to wince. Oh, the sermon her father would preach if he heard it. The inside of her lip grew a large blister as she bit back her words. "Thank you."

Mike followed her to the door, tossing the remains of his lunch as they passed the garbage. Cassie hardly noticed the movement, but Mike pointed it out. "What, no lecture? No self-righteous tirade against the evils of not recycling?"

Eyes blinked. Her breathing slowed as she stared at him, trying to calm herself. "What are you talking about?"

"I just tossed a Coke bottle, and you didn't even notice. A bit hypocritical, don't you think?"

Her eyes met his—stared. She opened her mouth to protest and snapped it shut again. *Ridiculous. It doesn't deserve an answer. Just get out of here.* As she sank into her office chair and dropped her lunch bag and purse under the desk. *Won't Lauren just love that.*

Mike's words—the financial guy's words—they taunted her, mocked her. "Man, I was that person—probably still am. Wow. So rude. I can't believe I did—do, whatever—that. I *have* to stop thinking that just because I have the right to my opinion means I need to express it."

⫘ ⫘ ⫘

The cursor blinked at the last word as Cassie read the day's entry. Her pictures—if she did say so herself—looked great. She'd even tucked a few of her ironed napkins in the remaining balls of clothes she still hadn't managed to fully separate and showed a bit of what it looked like with a disclaimer worthy of any reality show: *Some images may be recreated to demonstrate just how ridiculous things are.*

Napkins or Nemesis

I like napkins. Or rather, if I want to be completely honest, I like paper towels. I use them in place of napkins usually. Of course, that wouldn't work. And did you know you can't eat out on a budget without getting a paper napkin? It seems obvious, but until you're staring down a paper napkin under your sandwich—your *paper-wrapped sandwich*—you have no idea just how many things you had no idea you just use without thinking about them. Mine—napkins.

I did what every eco-conscious person would do. I hope, anyway. I found a fabric tablecloth in my cupboard, pulled it out, cut it up, and voila. Napkins. I should tell you that my paper scissors refused to cut that tablecloth, so I used kitchen shears. In case you wonder, they cut through cloth like butter—probably since they're made to hack through a slice of beef an inch or two thick.

Did you know they put some kind of gross finish on fabric? Yeah. Ugh. Wiped my mouth with one of those things and it was:

1. Ineffectual.
2. Gross.

So, I washed them with my jeans and shirts. *note: here is where you might want to grab a box of Kleenex or better yet, a handkerchief or three. As you can see from the recreated photo (which, I assure you, is not half as bad as the original mess), I kind of missed a step.

And this is where I realized just how much *work* this stupid project is going to be. I had to get a sewing machine. Sew those things. Trim them. The works. And then, since they'd been balled up in the dryer for over an hour, I had to *iron* the ridiculous things.

Tell me how using gas and electricity to create something from something else and make it functional is an eco-conscious decision again? No, don't. I might find a way to get out of it next time if I don't request help for the dark side.

There's only one flaw in the napkin plan. People. Reminds me of a movie where someone asked what was wrong with people and the one guy says, "They're people." Yeah. That. Did you know people think it's their business to try to shoot down why you're doing something—even if you didn't volunteer that you were doing it until they dragged it out of you?

I didn't. Until I heard them. Then I realized that I do it all the time. So, I'm going green in my opinions, too. I'm going to *reduce* the number of un-asked for opinions I share, *reuse* ones that others have made so at least I'm not pretending to be an expert on everything, and *recycle* the age-old, "If you don't have something nice to say..."

Tomorrow marks the end of the week. Stay tuned for the tally on refuse reduction. If pounds were only as easy to shed as the number of napkins and paper towels one uses.

Thursday, January 7—

A week's worth of tally marks on a large legal pad. With

phone in hand, she transferred her notes to the legal pad and tried to ignore the incongruity of writing about paper reduction on a piece of paper. She failed. The moment Cassie wrote her last mark and deleted the note, she called Lauren. "I'm doing a balance sheet for the week and it's on a legal notepad. And, I have to admit, I'm feeling a little sick at realizing that I've only used the top quarter of the page, and I want to tear it off and toss it once I've got it in my computer."

"Deep breath. Why not just use your phone?"

"I did—away from home. But you know how things click better for me if I write them. What'm I going to do?"

Lauren didn't answer for several long, torturous seconds—seconds in which Cassie imagined all kinds of ridiculous things—sand tables to write in, using the margins of grocery ads, and keeping a stack of junk mail envelopes to write her shopping lists on. *Just like Grammy. Ugh.*

"Hey. I got it. Those Boogie Boards that Michele at church uses to keep her kids quiet in church. Go on Facebook and post in one of the swap forums. Get two or three, even. Surely some moms bought them and their kids don't use them like they thought."

Notepad abandoned, Cassie made half a dozen posts in as many minutes, and returned to her calculations. "I think I reduced the equivalent of a full roll of paper towels if you combine the face wipes, paper plates, Dixie cups, and the rest of it—not bad, really."

"That's *great!* And really, it's better than that, because you avoided some things that you didn't have to yet. You were conscious about your energy usage—"

A cough erupted before Cassie could stop it. "Except that my consciousness of it was because I *used* it when I shouldn't have."

"Well, go figure it out. I'll stalk the blog, but you have to hurry. I have an early morning tomorrow. Amy called me on my lack of commitment to my health, so gym at five a.m."

"Gotcha. Okay. I'm off to tally it up and post." At that moment, she realized just how often she'd called Lauren in the space of one week—more than she had since her last boyfriend seemed ready to dump her and she needed consistent counseling to determine the best course of action. "Hey, Lauren?"

"Yeah?"

She swallowed an emotional lump and sighed. "Thanks for helping me through this."

"Hey, it's nice to help you for a change. I haven't had a chance to call for purchase justification all week. You kept me entertained without needing to shop or anything." Lauren's giggle sounded near hysterics. "Do you even see the ridiculousness of you going green because I made fun of your shopping—and I'm the one who needs 'Shoppers Anonymous' meetings?"

"I'll take you shopping on Saturday and you can spend my savings for the week."

Lauren's giggles kicked up to past hysteria. "Spend—cost—paper towels—what, buck and a half? Mmmmaaahahaha!"

After half a minute of Lauren's uncontrollable giggles, Cassie shook her head and signed off. "Goodbye, Lauren. Goodnight. Get some sleep and read it at work tomorrow or something."

Cassie dragged out her iPad, and her fingers flew across the keyboard as she called up the URL for her blog. With the tally marks for reference, she laid out the week's totals.

One Week of Green

Tonight, is the last night of the first week of this little experiment. Now, technically I didn't do much on the first, but I think just the *decision* to do all of this should count for something, so I'm sticking to natural weeks so I don't have to try to keep everything straight.

Follow the calendar and all that jazz. So, this is what I've figured out for the week.

I reduced:

Paper towels
Napkins
Paper and plastic cups (including Dixie cups)
Packaging (even labels on some water bottles have paper! I used plastic while I can. *blush*
Face wipes
Sticky notes/notepads
Dryer sheets (MUST FIND ALTERNATIVE—static isn't an option. I tried. Blech.)
Notebook paper (several days' worth for this journal for one thing!)
Catalogs (technically I got them in the mail, but I did cancel them with the companies—four of them. I figure that counts, right? I NEVER order from a catalog. Why do I get these things?)
Kleenex (well, a couple. For blowing, I still haven't done it, but I did wipe a bit of a run with one of my flannel-shirt-turned-Kleenex handkerchiefs, and it wasn't too bad.

I increased:

Laundry
Water in the kitchen (Dad swears that dishwashers use more than washing by hand. I proved him wrong. Next week, the dishwasher)
Gas (for getting the sewing machine for the napkins)
Plastic (just a couple of times but in the interest of full disclosure...)

Neutral:

Junk mail (I have so much. I usually just toss it. There has to be a better way. I didn't ask for it, though, so I'm not counting against me)
Newspaper (because I don't get one Monday-Thursday. Only Friday, Saturday, and Sunday. I want to cry when this comes tomorrow. Totally cry.)

You know what? I'm calling this a good week. I mean, I saw so many things I'd never considered before. And even defending my choices helped me see other sides of this ecological coin. I worked hard to focus only on paper stuff, but I did reduce more. I started to take my mom's sewing machine back on Wednesday, but then I heard she was coming my way to buy something at the Container Store, so I asked her to grab it while she was just a few blocks away. Win/win. For her, me, and the environment.

I do need to buy my own sewing machine, though. I need more handkerchiefs, and I'm looking at plastic for tomorrow. Gulp. Let's just say I have a feeling that I'm going to need it—fast.

Still, no one is going to take away my sense of accomplishment. I made it through one week, and I survived with only about twenty-three calls to my best friend. I did it with probably a net profit of a dollar-fifty. A lot more if you count making the napkins. If you add that and the handkerchiefs, I probably saved thirty bucks. That's pretty good.

Going green can be expensive if you buy all kinds of new things to make it easy. Ask me how I know. You have no idea how much I just want to do *that*. I'd still be reducing. But I'm not doing it. Why? Because I want to look back on this year next January and know that I didn't do a snow job of this thing. I want to give it everything I have. I want to be authentic.

One week of much less paper... *check!* A week of plastic reduction coming up! Stay tuned.

Week 2: Plastic

Friday, January 8—

Cold, crisp air blasted Cassie as she stepped out of her car. She snatched her purse from the passenger seat, slammed the door shut, and locked it. A patch of ice nearly sent her sliding into a guy and his girlfriend as they strolled arm-in-arm to the door of the pub. *So help me, I'm going to kill someone in these boots.*

A second slide as she passed them prompted the guy to reach out and grab her arm. "You okay?"

"Yeah. Sorry. Thanks."

Mortified, she rushed to the door, waited until they neared, and opened it for them. The guy tried to take it from her, but she shook her head. "Gives me something to hold on to. Go for it while you're safe!"

Once inside, she slipped around them and scurried to the table where Lauren, Amy, and Silvie sat waiting for her, menus in hand, drinks at hand, and giving her a hand as she appeared. Cassie bowed, slid up on the bistro styled chair and shrugged. "So, what's with the applause?"

"You made it a week! And you did great!" Amy's eyes swept the circle of friends. "Right? I mean, I'm not the only one following her blog, am I? I'm totally impressed."

Lauren offered a thumbs-up and added, "Dinner's on me tonight."

"I actually saved money this week, so why—"

But the others protested before she could finish. Silvie waved her hands and glared at Cassie. "No way. Not happening. She beat me to dibs. I was totally going to take it."

A week's worth of self-denial, trial and error, and consistent stress culminated in one happy, warm-fuzzy moment as Cassie's friends gave her genuine praise for her efforts. "You guys are the best. So, what's the special tonight? I'm starved."

Lauren's eyebrows drew together as she thought. "Pot roast melt with Swiss, I think."

"No, it's the fish and chips." Silvie winced. "Sorry. That sounded kind of rude. Remember, I asked what he recommended..."

"Right. Special is fish and chips, recommended was the pot roast melt. Oh, and he said their turkey club is really good right now. Something about great avocados...?" Lauren nudged her menu. "Get a steak. You totally deserve it."

Tempting as it was, Cassie nixed the idea. *If you're buying my dinner, then I'm totally* not *choosing the most expensive thing on the menu!* "I was leaning toward the fish..."

Just as she said it, a server passed with a basket—a *paper lined* basket—of fish and chips. "Ugh."

The trio stared at her with what seemed a bit too captivated interest and spoke in unison. "What?"

"How do you think the sandwiches come... on a plate?" She winced even as she heard herself.

But Lauren just shook her head and told her to relax. "Get what you want. I bet they'd put anything on a plate if you asked. Just ask."

Desperate to change the subject, Cassie turned to Silvie. "So... Are you going to call Evan?"

If she could have said anything worse, the look on Sivie's face denied it. "I doubt it. He probably wouldn't do it anyway."

It worked. The entire table switched to the subject of Silvie and Evan Robinson. Lauren's expression hinted that she'd assumed Cassie had decided against him if he asked again. Cassie zipped a text to her. IF SHE'S NOT GOING TO, I MIGHT.

With the impatient air of an overworked server at the busiest time of the night, a guy appeared, check book in hand

and pen poised. "Is everyone ready to order or..."

Everyone looked at Cassie, but protested. "Save me to last. Then he won't hate you guys. The guy tossed her a quizzical expression before turning to Amy. "What can we get for you?"

Two fish and chips—and a pot roast melt. When he finally turned to her, Cassie winced as she dove into her rehearsed speech. "Don't hate me, but I need a special favor."

"If we can..."

"I want the fish and chips, too. But can you put it on a plate, please? No paper-lined baskets or anything?" Each word she spoke sounded worse than the last. "I know it's a lot of trouble, but—"

He snapped his book shut and slowly backed away. "No, we can do it. I just..."

"She dared herself," Lauren explained in a rush. "No wasted paper."

"Gotcha." But despite his claim, the man clearly didn't "get" anything.

When an awkward silence settled over the table, Lauren leaned forward and "whispered" as loudly as she could over the bad 80's pop blasting through the pub. "So, guess who has a date tomorrow night."

All eyes turned to Cassie, but she threw up her hands. "I got no date—got no prospe—"

"Oh, give it up, Cass." Silvie's tone had a note of uncharacteristic spite. "You know you could go out with Joel anytime you wanted. You're just too blind to see him."

With a roll of her eyes she didn't even try to hide, Cassie shook her head. "Um, no... I am not blind to him. I'm just not interested."

"But he's so in love with you!" Silvie's voice rose a notch. "Anyone can see it. I'm surprised he hasn't—"

Determined to stop the discussion of her dating life *before* it got rolling, Cassie leaned back in her chair, folded her arms over her chest, and leveled a look designed to quell any further queries. "He's told me *exactly* how he feels. I've told him *exactly* how I feel. And he chose to stay friends. If that's hard on him, I'm sorry. I really am. But I'm not going to pretend to like a guy I don't just because I care about him in every other way." She frowned. "That sounds so junior high." Cassie's voice rose a notch and took on a pathetic attempt at "valley girl" style. "I'm not gonna like, you know, like him because like, he's not the guy I like. You know?"

"In junior high..." Amy's eyes swept the table. "I was there, I know this." She turned back to Cassie and grinned. "You totally *would* have gone out with him just because he liked you. You were a sucker for any guy who had the slightest interest in you."

Though she winced at the truth of it, Cassie couldn't help but protest. "You make me sound *desperate*."

"You were! Desperate to make the lonely guys happy. I, for one, am glad you got over that phase."

"Well, none of the relationships ever worked, did they?" The server arrived with their drinks, and after a sip of root beer, she finished her thought. "That's why I stopped. I always wanted one to care about making me as happy as I was trying, and they never did. They just didn't want to be alone."

"Well, no one has perfected the art of being contented and alone more than you." Lauren's forehead furrowed as she spoke. "Wait, that sounds wrong." As she apologized, Lauren pulled out her phone and finally read the text Cassie had sent. "You know what I mean." Even as she spoke, Lauren smiled and nodded.

A text buzzed in Cassie's phone moments later, but she didn't bother to open it. *It'll say, "Good." Or something like that.*

"I think we got off topic..." Cassie waited until the others looked her way before adding, "I think Lauren was hinting that she had a date? I want to hear all about this!"

Without bothering to hang up her coat or even change clothes, Cassie dropped to the couch, pulled the magazine she'd purchased at lunchtime from her purse, and flipped to the article on "52 Ways to Go Green." She hadn't been interested at first, but the subtitle, "...easy, fun, and great for the environment," caught her eye.

"Let's see if this can be 'fun.' I don't believe it."

A third of the way through the article—all on ridiculous things she couldn't imagine would make any kind of impact at all—Cassie dropped the magazine and stared at it in horror. "I bought *paper!*"

Without a second thought, she dug through her purse for her phone and tapped Lauren's face in her contacts list. "Lauren!"

"Is the house on fire?"

"Um... what?"

"Then don't shout. That 80's garbage gave me a headache—worse than your party last year. It's official. I'm allergic to 80's music."

Without a second thought, Cassie lowered her voice and began a tirade about her failures as an eco-conscious American. "I mean, c'mon! Who prints—*on paper*—an article about going eco-friendly. Isn't that kind of oxymoronic or ironic, or some other kind of 'onic'?"

Lauren tried to calm her, but Cassie had gotten herself so worked up she began pacing and ranting. "I don't think I can take it anymore. The restaurant guy looked at me like I was a freak of nature, I can't even buy a *magazine* without horrible guilt. How am I going to make it fifty-one more weeks? *Fifty-one!*"

"One day at a time. So, you bought a magazine. It's not a crime. I mean, the thing was already printed when you did. It's not like you ordered a subscription or anything. So just give it to the Mission, a doctor's office—even the *library*. Take it to your Grammy and let her give it to the senior's center. They make stuff with those, right?"

"I don't know... maybe. Grammy's mom used to make these ugly Santa Claus things—and snowmen, I think—out of old *Reader's Digests*."

"So, there you go. Donate it, get extra use out of it, and move on. You're going to make mistakes, Cassie."

"But so soon..."

This time, Lauren's voice sliced through the airwaves and into her heart. "Just shut up for a minute. Listen to me. How you handle these mistakes is what'll keep you from going nuts. You make a plan for next time and move on. But some things are going to happen—things that won't fit your plan. Sometimes you'll have to buy things you normally wouldn't. And you're going to have to deal with that."

Dread washed over her as she listened to Lauren talk. *I can't let myself do that! I can't! At least until it's a habit, I need to be careful. I need to.* But, when Lauren paused for breath—a brief interlude in her lecture mode—Cassie interjected a question. "Okay, how? What do you mean?"

"Um... okay, say you babysit for someone. Most people are going to have disposable diapers and wipes. So first, you have to *use* them. And second, if you run out, you'll have to buy—"

"What?" Visions of cloth diapers sporting smeared packages of grossness danced before her eyes. "Oh, no, no, no... I am never babysitting for anyone *ever* again." Another thought produced an addendum. "And I'm not having kids."

Lauren's laughter should have irritated her, but Cassie grew adamant. "No way. If I have to do cloth diapers, I am *not* having kids."

"Don't get pregnant this year, and it won't be an issue. You didn't sign up for life. You signed up for one year." One. Simple. Year."

Cassie flopped back on the couch, eyes closed, and exhaled every bit of air she could from her lungs. "You're right. You're absolutely right. One year. I'm not getting married in the next month or two so I'm safe."

"Cassie?"

She winced as she answered. "Yeah..."

"Go write your blog post. Everyone's waiting."

Great idea. I can vent there and stop bugging Lauren while she has a headache. "Okay. You're right. Get some ibuprofen and go veg out on Facebook or something. Thanks..."

But by the time she reached her room to retrieve her laptop, Cassie decided a few other things were a bit more important. Comfy clothes—face cleaned. She tossed a load of towels in the dryer and winced at the idea of hanging towels to reuse. Just as a new rant welled up in her, she stuffed it down again. "I can deal with that on water week. For now, I'm sticking to paper and plastic. That's it."

Fuzzy sleep pants and a silky soft knit t-shirt, hair brushed out and tied back with a headband, and one laptop in hand, Cassie strolled to the living room, made herself comfortable, turned on the TV, and punched the DVR recording of *The Blacklist*. "Okay, Reddington. Entertain me. I've got work to do."

The cursor blinked as she considered the day's post. But then everything flowed as if transcribing.

Week Two: Plastic

Yep. You got that right. It's already plastic week. Surprisingly, I didn't have too much trouble, today. I had a few hints of what might happen later, but I've decided *not* to deal with them until they arise. Why? Because I already flip out on my friend, Lauren, WAY too much.

Today's post isn't about plastic, though. I'm still having issues with paper. It started with an innocent trip to that great pub over on the east side just off the Loop? Yeah. Totally recommend their *food.* But their *presentation?* Got a problem there. Why? Because it turns out that almost everything they serve is in a plastic basket (washable so totally okay in my book) lined with… you guessed it, paper! I thought I'd have to order expensive stuff just to avoid the stupid paper thing. I mean, surely, they wouldn't serve their sirloin on paper, right? But my genius and aforementioned friend suggested asking for a plate. I see a long year of annoying restaurants by asking them to dirty more dishes to aid me in my quest for less in our landfills. Because say… a hundred pieces of waxed paper not used will make such a difference. Add to that the probability of the cook forgetting until the server sees it and makes them dump it onto the plate… ouch. But I did it. To be consistent with my commitment to reducing waste, I did it.

Then I came home, opened my purse, and what did I drag out of that thing? A *magazine!* Yep. I bought a stupid magazine. Oh, the irony of buying a stack of bound, glossy, biodegradable-less paper that is seventy-percent advertising—to learn how to reduce waste. Yep. The article was on going green. Note: It was a worthless article, too. There's nothing fun or helpful about using computer sticky notes instead of paper ones. Really? Fun? And then you have to be *at* your computer to see your reminder to floss—because that makes the most sense, right? Bathroom mirror—not helpful at all. Computer.

I freaked out at first, but Lauren talked me down. And I've been thinking about it since then. She's right. I'm going to make mistakes. I just have to learn from them. So… I think I'm going to give me a kind of "point system." I earn "cheater" points for those times when I really want something I have had to give up—like a bottle of nail polish or whatever. Or, I can save them up for a long time and have a whole, normal week! Wow. Wouldn't that be cool?

Yeah. I better make sure that the only week that would be possible in is the week after Christmas or something. Or, I'd totally do that. We all know it.

So, right now, I just want to confess that I failed in the magazine department, but otherwise, it was a good day. And, I want to thank my friends for cheering me on. I know they think I'm nuts. Forget that, *I* know I'm nuts. It's just nice to have someone rooting for you. Until tomorrow…

Saturday, January 9—

A steady, pulsing, ever-increasing... *noise*... reached her subconscious and ripped her from the cocoon of sleep. Cassie sat up and stared at the wall wide-eyed and panting. *Wha...* She scrambled for her phone and stared at the screen. *Saturday!*

Cassie threw off the covers and bolted into the bathroom. Cold water splashed her face and helped wipe away the remaining remnants of sleep. "Okay! Let's see who is bold enough to have a sale today..."

She half-walked, half-stumbled through the small duplex, and jerked open the front door. An arctic blast almost pushed her back inside and left the newspaper on the step. "Who, in their right or wrong mind, would go out in this? It's craziness!"

But, despite her protests, Cassie grabbed the paper and shivered back inside. She dropped it over the back of the couch and strode into the kitchen for coffee. And there, her world slammed to a screeching stop. Her Keurig stood ready—ready and waiting for her command. Her hands fumbled for her phone, but she couldn't find it. "Whe—oh. My room. And it's four-fifteen. I can't call Lauren at this time of morning over a plastic coffee crisis! Grow up!"

As if the need to torment herself overrode all reason and any hope of sense, Cassie pulled the cabinet door open and stared at the beautiful array of little K-cups waiting for her. "Italian roast... Krispy Kreme... Organic bold... Hawaiian..." A whimper escaped. "*Caribou...*"

Steady, pounding, ever-increasing... her head threatened to erupt like Mt. Vesuvius if she didn't inject herself with a shot of caffeinated deliciousness post haste. She grabbed the organic bold as if somehow the word "organic" overrode the plastic casing. "Great. I have to buy a regular coffee maker. And I have to buy my own beans and grind them so I can avoid the stupid packaging." Her eyes nearly crossed thinking of it. "Don't I?"

Determined *not* to let it get to her before she had the mental-boosting resources that only a great cup of coffee can provide, Cassie started the machine and glanced around her with a nervous eye. "Now what else do I have that I've forgotten about? Waiting until today was stupid. Really stupid."

Not for the first time, Cassie closed her eyes and tried to imagine talking to a dog instead of herself. "Not bad..." A cat— that was out. "He'd judge me. I know it."

Paper plates and cups had been painful. She'd never pretend otherwise. But as plastic wrap, utensils, "disposable" containers, and, of course, *Ziploc bags* filled her island, Cassie thought she'd choke. Only the scent of her quick and snappy cup of brewed perfection kept her with some semblance of sanity. She wrapped her hands around her insulated mug, inhaled the rich aroma of her bold organic roast and tried to quell the symptoms of Ziploc withdrawal.

She made it through half her cup of coffee before she swallowed hard and opened the cabinet under the sink and pulled out the plastic trashcan liners. Plastic cups over the sink. Plastic crockpot liners. The island overflowed with a slew of plastic products designed to make her life easier.

Her phone—she needed her phone. Cassie bolted for the living room, stared at the couch, the coffee table, back at the island. After a minute or two of lifting and setting down every item again, Cassie remembered her bed. "Didn't bring it out."

In minutes, a photo of her pile posted to Instagram with the caption: *PLASTI-GEDDON. Can I cry now?*

The Ziploc bags called to her. "Why not a selfie? I mean, if people can take them with their favorite nail polish..." She closed her eyes, shook herself, and ordered that thought away. "Scarlett O'Hara, Scarlett O'Hara, Scarlett O'Hara, *be* Scarlett O'Hara. Think about it tomorrow—or next month. Whenever."

Another photo followed the first—a pathetic-looking selfie

of her clinging to a box of Ziploc bags. The caption? *Can we maintain a long-distance relationship? Only 358 days until we can be together again, my love...*

In a move she'd regret later, Cassie slid another cup under the spigot of her Keurig, popped the cinnamon roll coffee cup in the machine, and punched start. "Gotta live it up while I can. Yep. Embracing the wild, eco-destructive side while I can."

Sixty-seconds... that's all it took for her to down the rest of her first cup, rinse it in the sink, and reach for the barely finished one as she moved into the living room. She reached for her stack of sticky notes and stared at them. "I haven't even begun and I'm already in a mess!"

Her phone read four-thirty—much too early to bother anyone with an opinion. Rebellion welled up in her and she pulled out a pen. "I have to do *something*! I can't just try to read those tiny prints while I'm driving..." She sighed. "I can't get the paper anymore anyway. I have to do a digital one. And I can't copy it. So..."

The letters on the front page of the newspaper swirled before her eyes. "What did Lauren say about using my phone...?"

At that point, Cassie threw the sticky note cube across the room. It landed with a satisfying splat on the opposite wall—right next to the window, of course—and broke in three pieces as it fell to the floor. "I'm not *stupid!* I know the answer to this! I can think. I can function. I don't have to rely on old ways to do things. I'm strong. I'm independent. I'm intelligent daaaaad burn it!"

The near lapse into a long-abandoned habit of using unsavory language shook her more than anything else could. "That's it. Fine."

She flipped open the paper and dug through it to find the classifieds. The second she found them, the rest piled beside her. A niggling sense of impending revelation began as she flipped through the classifieds for the sale sections. Two more pages landed atop the discard pile. A third. And there they were. Three estate sales—one on the highway to Ferndale. Two in the better residential areas of Rockland proper. *Yes! Three!*

Cassie read each with a keen eye, spotting the one that must be run by Gayle—the estate liquidator extraordinaire. "Key words, no extraneous nonsense. No appeal to sympathy. This stuff'll be priced high. Drat."

Still, Cassie stared at the ad, trying to decide what to do. Her phone buzzed with a notification. A glance at it showed a "heart" from Instagram and a comment: *You're nuts! I couldn't give up my Ziplocs! No. Way.*

Ignoring the message, she snatched up the phone and tapped the screen. With perfect focus, she snapped a picture of each of the sales and noted the times. It only took a moment to rearrange the pictures in the order she'd take them. The first insisted on "no early birds," which would mean she couldn't get there until seven o'clock. But changing up the route would be even worse.

"Argh! I need a critter to talk to. Don't they house train rabbits? Maybe that would work. A dog requires walking. Not doing it in this weather. No. Way." She frowned. "Do they make doggie treadmills?"

The full impact of her decision on her life hit hard and fast as she realized that even if she could find the space for one, it would probably be made of plastic and other forbidden items. "Unless I bought it used…"

With nearly two hours until departure for sales unknown, Cassie opted for a shower, a room cleaning, and maybe even a few minutes on her blog. However, when she stood, the stack of plastic "orphans" called to her, begging her to put them back in their homes. "Love me!" they cried. "Let me be useful!"

But instead, Cassie snagged one of the plastic trash bags, dumped everything she could fit in it, grabbed another, dumped the box of trash bags in it, and loaded it with the remaining items. Minutes later, her already stuffed storage shed groaned as she slammed the door shut and locked. "There."

Arms loaded with cloth napkins, vintage pillowcases, and a few vintage flat sheets, Cassie wove her way through the rooms of the old Victorian house—one of the oldest homes still standing—and swept each item for nuggets. A voice behind her, liquidator Gayle's, put Cassie on her guard. "Cassie! I thought you'd be here. Who could miss an estate sale at the Brown House!"

"The what?" Cassie knew she sounded disingenuous, but she had no idea what Gayle meant. She turned and smiled. "I found some things I think I want, but what brown house?"

"This one—Mayor Brown's house! *The* Mayor Brown? Longest running Mayor in Rockland history? Over twenty years in office. This is his house." Gayle peered at her when Cassie's eyes widened. "You really didn't know?"

"Nope."

Gayle tugged her sleeve. "C'mere. You're not going to believe the stuff in here that's *original* to the house. Like this desk." She led Cassie to a desk in one of the rear rooms. "This was Mayor Brown's study and that..." Gayle pointed to an enormous mahogany desk. "That was *his* desk. The city wanted it for the museum, but they wanted it *donated*."

Horrors! How terrible of them to hope that a piece of Rockland history could be donated so they won't be slammed for wasting taxpayer dollars on something like that. Really? Aloud, Cassie simply asked the price.

"They wanted three thousand, but I told them no one would pay more than twenty-two hundred."

"No one will pay that, Gayle, and you know it. These huge old desks are out. People don't want them anymore. They'll get a better return if they donate it to the city and take the three thousand in a tax write off." When Gayle balked, she nodded. "I see what you mean, though. No commission on donations."

Undaunted, Gayle led her to what had once been a dining room but now looked like a showroom for antique furniture. "See that rosewood dressing table? It once belonged to the mayor's daughter. No one wants it because it needs a few repairs, but I bet you could work your magic on it."

Cassie knew better than to look. *Don't do it... don't...* But one glance sent her senses swooning. "Well, maybe it's not the repairs... maybe you're asking too much?"

"Two fifty."

Cassie pulled out her phone and typed up a text. I'LL GIVE YOU ONE-FIFTY ANYTIME YOU NAME. She passed it to Gayle. "If you want a way to contact me, just put your number in there. I'll come get it anytime."

"That's a hundred dollars—"

"A hundred *fifty* more than you'll likely get if you keep trying to sell it at that crazy price. That leg isn't just damaged. It's *broken.* It'll take me *forever* to get it spliced and strong again, and you know it. So that's my offer. If you want a backup, put in your number and hit send. If not, I want to look at the kitchen stuff again and then I'll be done."

Three Wilendur tablecloths that had somehow escaped her notice landed in her arms just minutes later. "I'm getting sloppy. And this one is in *perfect* condition. Oh!" A Quaker lace tablecloth—still in the package, no less—caught her eye. She snatched it up, nearly losing the stuff already weighing down her arms, and hurried to the table by the front door. She unloaded everything and began counting it out. Gayle met her there just as she asked the price of the tablecloth.

The woman scribbling down each item glanced at it and muttered, "Twelve dollars."

"Oh, no Dot. That's still in the package. Fifty."

Cassie didn't hesitate. She picked it up, passed it to Gayle, and said, "Then you can keep it."

"Isn't that a bit pricey..." Dot stared at Gayle. "No one will pay that."

"She will. She knows what it's worth." Gayle eyed Cassie with the look of a woman who thinks she knows more than she does. "Don't you?"

"I do. I know every dime it's worth. And that's at least fifty dimes more—more like a hundred. But..." Oh, how she hated the concession. "I'll *pay* that fifty dollars if you sell me the rosewood for one twenty-five."

Gayle waved her phone. "I have an offer here—*from you, I might add*—for one-fifty."

"And if you want me to pay fifty bucks for the tablecloth, you have to knock off twenty-five from the table. But the only way I'm paying twenty-five for that tablecloth is if you give me the rosewood at twenty-five off. So, sell both or neither. It's up to you." With a smile and not another word, she turned back to "Dot." "Do you have a total for me?"

"Fifty-two, fifty."

"One seventy-seven, fifty," Gayle growled. "But you have to have that thing out of here by four o'clock."

Without a word, Cassie pulled out her phone and zipped a text to Joel. GOT ONE FOR YA. 12 BEAUMONT ST. OLD MAYOR'S HOUSE? "THE BROWN HOUSE". ROSEWOOD DRESSING TABLE WITH BROKEN LEG. MAKE SURE SHE GIVES YOU ALL PIECES. IT'S PAID FOR. SHE'LL TRY TO TELL YOU THAT IT'S A HUNDRED MORE. IGNORE AND SHOW THIS RECEIPT.

Cassie turned back to Gayle as the woman started back toward the office again. "Wait. I need a receipt for the rosewood."

"Really, Cassie?"

"I'm not the one picking it up. It'll benefit both of us. Trust me." She smiled. "I'm sending it to Joel the minute I get it."

The woman's flustered movements confirmed Cassie's suspicions. *You are not nearly as sly as you'd like to think. And you're going to get yourself fired if people complain.*

Receipt in hand and her arms full of linens and one Jadeite bowl, Cassie shuffled down the sidewalk to her car and piled her items inside. Regret filled her at the absence of the vintage desk fan on the back seat, and she turned to go back inside. "Should've bought the dumb thing while I was in there. She'll mark it up just because I want it."

⚊ ⚏ ⚏ ⚏ ⚊

The second sale—a total bust. Everything sounded great in the ad but total junk in reality. She made a sweep through the rooms looking for something—anything—that would make waiting on the drive to Ferndale worth it. Not even a twenty-five-cent paperback book tempted her. So, as she pulled into the drive at the farmhouse just five miles outside Ferndale, Cassie whispered a prayer for packrats with good taste and a tendency to save things for "special."

A familiar haircut that could only belong to her friend sent Cassie scurrying from her car. "Bentley!"

As the woman turned, Cassie waved and slid up the drive and to the back porch. "Hey! I hoped I'd see you here."

Hugs, laughter, compliments—the routine never failed to make a day of sale-ing go from frustrating to amazing. "I thought I'd missed you for sure." They stopped inside the door and Bentley pulled a water bottle from her purse. "Thirsty?"

"Always with the water bottles..." Cassie reached for it. "Thanks!"

"I'm the queen of hydration, but what can I say. Researchers tell me I'll have supple skin well into my eighties. They better not be lying."

Cassie began to reply when she spied a huge collection of granite ware. "Oh. Wow. All *red!*" A sharp pain in her side reminded Cassie to quell her excitement. "Thanks." She hissed the word even as she turned to find the person in charge. By the front door, a woman sat with a cash box and a legal pad. Cassie rushed up to her and jerked her thumb back toward the kitchen. "So, how much for the red and white tin stuff?"

"Oh..." The woman glanced through the doorways at the

86

stacks of plates, colanders, cups, bowls... "How about a dollar a piece. Just keep it easy that way. Cups aren't worth it, but it'll make up for things like that big bowl."

"Sold." Cassie glanced around her. "Got a box for me to put them in until I can transfer them to my car?"

The woman pointed over to a corner. "We put some there, but none are big enough..."

Bentley must have overheard enough of the conversation, because she began carrying in everything her arms could hold. "I have fifteen pieces here..."

It took five minutes to get them all, count them all, pay for them all—with an extra thirty dollars added on to soothe Cassie's conscience—and begin carting them to the car. Fifteen minutes later, she carried out two antique quilts, a coffee grinder, and a baby scale. Bentley walked out with a sewing basket on legs.

They stood outside in the cold, chatting. But when Cassie took her last swig of the water in the bottle, her world plummeted from granite ware high to plastic lows. "I just drank water out of a plastic bottle. Oh. Great."

"Wha—oh. Right. I saw that on Facebook—the eco thing." She gave an apologetic shrug. "Sorry..."

"My fault. It's my job to remember." Cassie stared at the bottle as if it would morph into something else—*anything else*—if she only stared at it long enough.

Undaunted—or determining to attempt to be—Cassie tossed it in the backseat and turned to go. But before she could hug her friend goodbye, Bentley shook her head. "I'd never make it. I just would *never* make it."

Cassie opened the car door and slid into the seat. "And you say that as if you're assuming I will."

<hr/>

Curled up on the couch, Cassie opened her laptop and began the day's blog post. After the fourth attempt at a title, not to mention a topic, Cassie stared at the template and wondered... "Do people even *read* blog posts anymore? Aren't blogs 'out' or something? They've been around like forever!"

The options lay before her. Plasti-geddon, Water bottle failure. Or the beauty of recycling old treasures for today's use. "That one is at least more positive than what I've been doing..."

Then it hit her. A memory. As if writing themselves, the words appeared on the screen.

<u>It's a Conspiracy</u>

Day 8. Just in case you were curious. Eight whole days. It began simply enough. Get up at four o'clock as usual. I think I'm probably the only person my age who gets up *earlier* on the weekend than during the week—at least the only one who does that and not so she can go running until her lungs freeze. Nope... here's the scene for ya.

Bolt out of bed because my stupid alarm scares the sleep right outta me. Shiver out the door to grab my *newspaper*. Yeah. Just gimme a second here. Go in the kitchen and start my *Keurig*... Yep. That thing. And eradicate all extraneous plastic from my cupboards and drawers. Here are a couple of pictures I uploaded to Instagram. Just in case you were curious about what abject misery at 4:30 a.m. looks like. That's it. Right there. For me anyway.

I got great stuff at today's sales, got to see a friend, downed a plastic bottle of water, headed home—you caught that, right? How weird is it that even with my entire life hyper-focused on eradicating paper and plastic from it, I can accept a bottle of water and drink the whole stupid thing before it hits me that it's *plastic?*"

But these are merely confessions—not today's post. I'm just keepin' it real. I'd call today a 95% flop. Yessir. Bust. Washout. Epic fail. All that stuff.

Anyway... Here's the scene. I'm driving away from Ferndale when I realize I probably need gas. So, I stop at that last station just before you get to the highway to Dolman. I get gas. It's about twenty degrees. So cold, but not "gonna freeze your butt off inside four seconds" cold. I go inside. I'm thirsty. It happens.

Have you ever tried to buy something to drink in a mini-mart that doesn't involve plastic or paper?

I think I just stood there staring at the case, spinning around and staring at the fountain drinks, back at the case, over at the coffee machine...everything. You go in for something so innocent as paying and getting a drink and nothing you can buy works. For the record, that store has ZERO cans. Zip. Nada. None. Zero. They also have NO GLASS. Nope. Not even one of those over-priced tea type drink things—can't remember the brand. You have two options there. Paper coffee cups, plastic fountain drink cups, or plastic bottles.

Look, I tried everything. But even the travel mugs they sell with country stars etched into the *metal* are all plastic on top. Maybe it's overkill—probably is—but I can't imagine giving up *that* quickly. Part of me just wanted to go and find another gas station. You know, one with glass or cans or something? I've got a couple of weeks before *those* are off limits. Instead, I figure I'll just stand there and make myself figure it out. But of course, if I did that, I'd dehydrate before I could even hope to. Picture it: there I am ten years from now, a desiccated corpse because I couldn't get a simple drink.

So, the way things are going, one of three things will happen. I'll either:

o   Become a hyper bunny from over-consumption of coffee since Starbucks allows me to refill my mug.

o   Have super strong arms and maybe abs from carting around a giant canteen of water everywhere.

o   Become agoraphobic because I fear what'll happen if I can't get to water.

Yes, I know 4 can happen. I could give up. But if all the things I am, I'm no quitter.

Anyway... I actually had to *waste* gas by going to another gas station to find a stupid drink? So now what do I have to do? I have to carry a stupid soda fountain everywhere I go. Yeah. That'll be a saver.

A slow smile formed as Cassie reread her post and punched "publish." A feeling of satisfaction washed over her... right up to the moment she saw the broken cube of sticky notes still lying on the floor where she'd left them. "I am *so* going to miss you guys."

Sunday, January 10—

Just as Cassie went to swipe her debit card at the checkout counter, the bagger—reaching for the plastic, no less—droned, "Paper or plastic?"

She waved her hand. "Sorry, I can't do pla—" And that's when grocery shopping went from her least favorite form of shopping to one of her least favorite things to do of all time. "I can't do paper either. Wha—" She frowned. "Just..." With a frantic glance around her, Cassie's eyes landed on the store's "reusable" bags. *But I don't want to buy more stuff. That defeats the purpose.*

"Um..." Even as she thought, Cassie keyed in her PIN number and punched the "no cash back" option. "Just put it back in the cart. I'll..." She started to say load and unload directly into the car, but the memory of fresh snow falling as she'd driven over to the store stopped that idea. "I'll be back in a few minutes. I've got to find something—"

"We have these bags..." The cashier hurried to a nearby display, but Cassie shook her head.

"Sorry. Can't do that either—weird challenge." Conscience insisted she'd stretched that truth a bit, but Cassie ignored it. "If I can just leave my cart right there for ten or fifteen minutes..."

The woman shrugged. "We can't be responsible for it, but I will try to keep my eye out. It's the best I can do."

"Great."

One by one, items slid off the conveyor belt and into the bagger's hands. Meanwhile, she put out a call on Facebook and Instagram. HELP. DOES ANYONE HAVE TOTE BAGS I CAN BORROW? I HAVE GROCERIES AND NOTHING I CAN PUT THEM IN.

Suggestions flooded her phone all the way to the car. Two people—the two friends living farthest from the store, of course, offered the use of their eco-friendly shopping bags. A third suggested doing without. "Oh, right," she muttered as she climbed behind the wheel of her car. "I'll just freeze to death going back and forth. No thanks."

At the first stoplight, she read the next messages—mostly unhelpful, but Amy suggested a box. "Well, that's true... a box would work. It's paper, but it's just using something I already have sitting around. That's *better* I suppose..."

Just as the light turned green, she saw another suggestion flash up on the screen. She hesitated, trying to read the words before moving, but a beep behind her sent her jerking forward into the intersection. A block down, she couldn't stand it any longer and made a sharp right into a parking lot. Another blare of the same car's horn hinted that perhaps she might be overreacting—just a little. Still, Cassie fumbled for the phone as she pulled into a parking space and winced as her bumper scraped on a concrete divider.

"Argh! Those things should be outlawed! What is wrong with people?" A glance at the screen is all it took. She saw one word, crates, posted a quick, "That's it! Thanks!" and zipped toward home. Triumph filled her. "Okay, you stupid 'green gods.' You can't beat me!" A wince followed. "Nope. Can't do that. Fine... 'green *demons!*'"

Thanks to streets filled with half-crazed fans from some sporting event—hockey, she suspected—it took ten minutes to make a five-minute drive, but Cassie burst through her door and dismantled her crate table. The decor she kept in each crate landed on the couch, the top leaned against the couch, and she stacked crates inside each other before dashing out the door again.

And it took until she pulled into the parking lot to realize that she had forgotten to lock her door. "Great. Gonna get robbed, too. It's just such a *wonderful* day."

It took two shopping carts to make the system work. One cart wouldn't hold all four—three, yes. Four... nope. So, while the checker and several baggers looked on with confusion, amusement, and a dash of dismay, Cassie packed cold stuff into one, cans and bottles into another, produce into the third, and everything else into the last.

"Need help out with that, miss?" The older gentleman bagger offered an encouraging smile and reached for the cart nearest him, but Cassie snatched at it. "I've got it, thanks."

Despite her rude and vehement protest, the man didn't waver. "C'mon... it'll make me look good with the boss. Wouldn't want these youngsters to outdo me. He'll think you said no because you don't think I can do it." When she still hesitated, he inched the cart forward. "My grandma was from back in the hills of West Virginia. She used to get all her groceries in crates like these. We'd drop 'em over the side of the old truck and hop in behind them. The fastest kids got to sit on the wheel well. Aaah... those were the days."

How it happened, she didn't know, but he talked her all the way out the door, across the parking lot, and had her groceries half-loaded before she could dump her purse on the front seat. "You have a good night, miss. And I don't know why you chose to bag 'em this way, but you get points for the planet and for originality. Not to mention, nostalgia for me."

The sense of success—of *beating*—an ideology that threatened to destroy her peace of mind filled her as she listened to him, but as she, once more, inched through the streets between cars of honking, swerving, lights-flashing revelers, that success dwindled into an overwhelming feeling that she'd lost all reason. "What am I doing? I just drove home, tore apart my coffee table, drove *back* to the store, and now I'm burning more fuel to drive home again to save, what? Six? Seven plastic bags? How is this helping anything?"

The feeling only intensified with each crate loaded onto her kitchen island. There they stood—four craft crates not designed to do more than sit somewhere and look cute. "I could at least have some cool antique crates. They'd be sturdier, too."

An illogical and ill-timed thought of needing to choose that house pet before talking to herself drove her partially insane, likely combined with her overreaction to yet another unexpected but predictable problem with her new life, precipitated a crying jag like she hadn't had since she didn't know when. With tears streaming down her face, she shoved vegetables and cheese in the fridge, meat in the freezer, and cans and bottles in the cupboard. By the time the crates had been emptied, the idea of actually putting them *back* sent fresh waves of despair over her.

So, as the only seemingly-rational thing she could think of, Cassie dumped the collection of clocks and books she kept in one crate on the floor, wrapped her arms around a bronze-casted reproduction of Rodin's *The Thinker*, curled up on the couch, and wept. Again.

Never had she felt such a tug—a *pull* to pray. Never had she found it so nearly impossible. Her thoughts, her heart—they spun on an endless cycle of repetition that made her doubt the efficacy of those prayers. *Isn't there something about "vain repetitions" in the Gospels?*

Cassie lay there ten minutes—an hour—when a knock at the back door jarred her from her dozing. Without even opening an eye, she called out for whomever it was to enter. *I know I didn't think to lock it. Hope it's not some creep.*

She waited, but despite feeling the blast of cold air when someone entered, her unexpected guest—or guests, she mused—didn't announce themselves. A moment later, she heard crates being arranged where her coffee table should sit. *Should have known it would be you.*

"Thanks, Joel."

His chuckle soothed the remaining ruffled feathers of her heart. "No problem. I saw Facebook and I figured. You sounded a little frantic"

At that, Cassie sat up, crisscrossed her legs, and hugged *The Thinker* to her chest. "I can't do this, Joel. I just don't think I can. I mean, look at this mess!" Her eyes swept the room and landed where Joel tried to arrange her books and clocks into some semblance of attractiveness. *I'm going to be under there like a mechanic, rearranging stuff before morning. I know it.*

"Cass..."

"No, really! I can't even buy stupid *groceries* with a crisis. And really, since when do I fall apart like Elsie Dinsmore over every stupid little thing?" She tossed the statue onto the couch and grabbed his shirtsleeve. "Come look at this." She flung open the freezer and showed the packages of meat. "Styrofoam and plastic. Plastic bags for fish and chicken strips." She slammed it shut with excessive force and jerked open the fridge. "Even my stupid *spinach* comes in a plastic *tub*. I could get it in a *bag,* but..."

Joel's head shook as she spoke. "No, no. You buy it in bunches. It—"

"But it's not *baby* spinach then. And the baby spinach is so much better. I love that stuff."

He said nothing as she jerked open cupboards, showed can after can. "Next week or the following I'll have to do metal. I think I'm going to stockpile my favorite stuff. Call me evil, but yeah. Man..."

Cassie whirled to look at him, certain he must be trying to stifle some kind of amusement at her expense, and threw up her hands. "I refuse to go so green that I die of starvation in some misguided attempt to save the planet! I swear, there's not a single thing that doesn't require some kind of stupid paper, plastic, glass, or metal packaging in that entire store."

"Apples?"

Cassie glared at him. "If it wouldn't be rude, you know, after you came over to help me in my time of distress, I'd slug you for that." Her eyes caught sight of her half-reassembled table. "Tell me how going back and forth, back and forth is 'eco-friendly'?"

But Joel stopped her before she could get enough steam to begin a new tirade. "But you're not worrying about that today. You're not doing gas. You're doing paper and plastic. You shouldn't even be *thinking* about anything else right now. You'll get way too overwhelmed."

"Yeah. Too late for that."

Joel dropped one arm over her shoulder and led her back to the living room. "C'mon. Cut yourself some slack. We'll work on little things—you know, thinking ahead." He gave her a gentle shove into the couch and dropped to the floor in front of her. "You can do this. I know you can. You're going to show them all." Nothing he could have said would have given her more peace, more confidence.

Cassie started to thank him when he turned to finish the coffee table. "Meanwhile, I brought you a present." He tossed her an inscrutable look and added, "It's in my car. I'll get it when I'm done with this."

Again, Cassie pulled her feet up onto the couch and sat cross-legged. "A present?" Her eyes narrowed. "What *kind* of present?"

"Well... it's the kind you *really* need, are *really* gonna hate, and are *really* gonna be glad I gave you—all at the same time."

Her lips twisted in a sardonic smile as her eyes narrowed even further. "So... what you're saying is that it's not a quart of ice cream...

But Joel shook his head as he wrestled the table top back in place. "Um... I don't think I can *buy* you a quart of ice cream... but I might could make you some..."

"What?"

"Well, the cartons are paper, right? Or plastic? Or both. That's not going to help you any. But I could make it—cream and sugar and—"

But Cassie interrupted. "All of which come in plastic or paper containers! Half what I bought tonight has paper. The rest—everything comes in something!"

"Mom's been buying stuff from that place over by Dolman—HearthLand? They have milk, butter, cheese, eggs, meat, and even stuff like sugar and flour and oil—all in big containers. You buy it by the pound or ounce or something. Just bring your container, choose how much you want, and voila!"

"That's great!" She inched forward and passed Joel the statue. "Except..." A sigh escaped. "Of course, that means an hour and a half of gas every time I run out of milk! How is that possibly better?"

Joel arranged Mr. Think-stuff in his crate, and the sight of it gave her an idea. "Actually, can you pull him out again? I think he's going to be my pet." Cassie took him, moved a tiny birdcage from her end table, and set him there. "Yeah... I like that."

"Looks good." Joel stood and inched his way to the door. "And you don't have to go every week even. You go once a month, stock up, freeze the extra milk, learn how to make eggs last—whatever."

"Yeah..." His words registered. "Wait... you can *freeze* milk?"

He nodded. "Yeah! Mom does it all the time. You just let it defrost in the fridge, shake it up, and it's good as it was the day it came home." She gave him a skeptical look, but Joel smiled down at her. "You can do this. Now what kind of ice cream do you want? I've got to go find the stuff—and a recipe. And—"

"You're nuts! You're totally nuts. You'll never find something in metal or glass. I love—that you'd do it for me, but..." *Don't get careless with your words. He doesn't deserve that.*

But even as she spoke, his expression changed. "I could get a cone! If I got it on a cone, that would be fine, right? I mean, you eat the cone, so no packaging equals no waste which equals eco-friendly."

Cassie jumped from the couch, grabbed her purse, pulled out her wallet, and threw it at him. "Go!"

Joel made it as far as the door before turning back again. "You know... do you have a quart jar? They sell them packed in quarts...." Even as he spoke, Joel scanned the kitchen for some sign of something marked "quart."

A dash for the cabinet beside her sink, a triumphant yell, and she plopped a case of twelve, quart-sized, wide-mouthed mason jars on the island. "Just bought them tonight," she growled as she tried to wrest one from the packaging. Joel managed to get it out first try, of course. "I saw this thing on Pinterest—you use them to make salads for the week. Everything stays fresh! So... it's better than plastic, right?" As she talked, she scrubbed out the jar, dried it, and handed it to him. "You're the best."

The words haunted her as she went to rearrange her clocks and books, her milk glass collection, and the birdcage in the crates. "Thinker, I have *no* business saying stuff like that to him. He deserves better than that. It's just a habit, you know? And..." A new thought kicked her in the gut—knocked the wind from her for a moment. "Should it *be* a habit to tell people they're 'the best' so often that I can't stop myself before saying it to Joel? I mean, not everyone can be 'the best.'"

For just a moment—a very short, brief, minuscule moment—Cassie considered making that a goal for the week. *No more useless, meaningless phrases—or using meaningful words until they're worthless.* But sanity overrode good intentions. "Yeah. Like I need one more thing to think about."

When forty-minutes passed, Cassie grew concerned. After an hour, she gave up and pulled out her laptop. "I think he went home, Thinker. He probably went everywhere and they said, 'We have to use our containers.'" She giggled at the snooty, schoolteacher voice she'd adopted. *He'll point to that word "quart" and insist they use it. Or worse...* Her eyes widened. "Thinker. He bought their quart, didn't he. He went home to repack it in the jar so I wouldn't know."

The day's blog headline eluded her at first. Everything sounded boring, trite, or too cutesy. Then it hit her. With fingers flying across the keyboard, the words—all two of them—

appeared.

I Cried.

But the words for the post wouldn't come. As seconds ticked into minutes and another quarter of an hour, Cassie gave up on Joel. "Probably gave up after no one would do it. I would have been fine with the cone..."

She jumped up, grabbed her phone, and zipped a text message. YOU OK?

No response.

Phone in hand, she called up a new note and began typing out everything she'd purchased that night and any alternative she could come up with. "Spaghetti sauce... I could make it, but that means cans... so..." A new thought wrenched her gut. "Or, I could buy *tomatoes* and... sauce them? Can you do that without like... special equipment?" A glance over her shoulder showed her new "pet" pondering the question. "You let me know what you come up with..."

Just as she conceded and wrote down "unpackaged produce—make your own salad," Joel burst through the back door. "I did it! I found a place that would do it!" He passed the jar to her with a triumphant flourish. "Salted caramel gelato." He winced. "Or have you found a new passion this week?"

Without a word, she scooped out a huge dollop, plopped it into a bowl, snagged a spoon, and slid it across the island. Minutes later, they sat opposite one another, not speaking, not even interacting—just *being.* Joel finished his, squeezed her shoulder, and murmured, "I'll go get your gift and leave it on the island. But I'm going before you get a chance to look at it and throw it at me or something."

She tried to protest, but as he walked through the back door again, gift in hand, her eyes narrowed and his words came back to her. "*—it's the kind you* really *need, are* really *gonna* hate, *and are* really *gonna be glad I gave you—all at the same* *time.*"

With eyes narrowed Cassie eyed it with utter disdain. "He was so right about you. If I could, I would have thrown you at him."

She didn't get up, didn't examine it. Instead, she pulled out her laptop, stared at the title, and left it. The words came now—quickly, almost feverishly.

I cried tonight. But before I did that, I did something stupid, and one of the best friends I'll ever have came to my rescue. He heard the panic in my tone and just came to the rescue. Because that's the kind of guy Joel is. Reassembling my coffee table because I turned it into shopping crates was huge, okay? It was. But driving all over Rockland in search of some place that would let him buy ice cream by the quart—and put it in my quart jar—that's a true friend. And he did it all without making fun of me. Usually, he would. Usually, I could take it. It just goes to show how well he can read me. I'm pretty impressed.
And he brought me a gift. I almost cried at that, too. But not because I was touched. No... because he's right. I need the stupid thing. What'd he bring me?
A sewing machine.
Guess who has to find a way to make tote bags so she can go shopping before she starves? He knew it. He got it. He's amazing. Thanks, Joel.
Until tomorrow...

Monday, January 11—

Thinker eyed her as she toyed with blog title ideas. However, no matter how many times she jerked her head over to him, trying to catch him in the act, he sat resolute, lost in apparent thought. "You're faster than a Weeping Angel—or whatever those creepy things are called. Well played, my friend. I sure wish you'd *answer* me, but if you did, I'd probably have to commit myself."

Those words did it. With a gleeful smile, she typed out her title.

Committed.

On all fronts. Yep. I should be, and I am. Kind of cool if you think about it. Anyway, today was "one of those days." It started out well enough. I made salads in my nifty new jars and I was early to work—even after stopping at Starbucks (with a line out the door, no less). Note: Starbucks is the coolest place for a girl in my position. I get all the caffieny (yes! That is a word! Or it is now. Deal with it) goodness and the planet gets no paper. Win. Win. Win.

Of course, lunch killed all that. I go downstairs with my eco-friendly jar of salad and my eco-friendly fork. I sit down. I open the jar—not so easy to stir jars of salad. And um, where do I put the dressing? Talk about gross. Some people actually put it right in the jar, but I didn't want to. Still, it has its advantages. I mean, I finally remembered to do that thing—you know, where you dip your fork in the dressing and then stab the salad? So, I'm going eco-body-friendly, too. Bully for me.

But water. Man, I think it's time to reconsider the evilness of plastic water bottles. You know those commercials that show how many bottles of water Americans drink every year? You know, like end to end they would fit around the globe a million times or something? (before anyone corrects me, that's called hyperbole)

Let's rethink this. What's the coolest planet out there? I mean, anytime you look at pictures of the planets in the sky, what do you see? Jupiter? It's okay. Mars? Whoopdeedoo. Neptune. *yawn*. But... *Saturn*. Now Saturn is cool. Right? I mean, c'mon. God loved it so much He put a *ring* on it! Eh??? More than one, right? (don't judge me for my rusty astronomy skills!)

Let's update Earth! Let's put a ring on HER. We'll just take all those bottles, create ring sections, hang them in space, and voila! Win-win for everyone! And before you get all negative about it, yes, we *would* need more and more. There's these things called meteors and asteroids—and I bet space winds or storms or something that totally mess up stuff. I mean, c'mon. They have to fix sturdy stuff like satellites. Surely, they'd have to fix these, too. And they could just let them fall into the earth's atmosphere. They'd burn up, right? Like the flames on the pods when astronauts come back? You know, *I Dream of Jeanie?* I've seen footage. Just incinerate that stuff before it hits our atmosphere. Gone! Win-win.

Now. Before anyone destroys my great idea with silly things like logic and science, just think about it. Earth. With rings. How cool is that?

Of course, until I convince the world of this great plan, I still need water. So, I'll be stuck staying hyped up on caffeinated bean juice and water oooor… *drum roll, please* I washed my Starbucks cup. Yes. Yes, I certainly did. Not only that, but I filled it up at the fountain. So not only did I not waste a whole plastic bottle, but I didn't waste the dollar-fifty it would have cost me. All I wasted was about twenty-minutes of agonizing over the stupid thing. Yeah. Genius—that's me!

But… that isn't what made today a fabulous day. If anyone doubts that green-living messes with brain cells and probably contributes to early-onset Alzheimer's, this will remove said doubt.

Did you know that the subway restrooms have SQUARELESS toilet paper? That's right, folks. You just tear where you want and voila! Guilt-free cleansing. Yes, there's a bit of irony in speaking of cleansing and the subway restrooms in one sentence, but man… I am so making a weekly or semi-weekly, or okay… fine. DAILY trips. Totally doing it. I mean, it's a short walk from the building and while our restrooms are cleaner, I know their cleaning schedule.

I never imagined I'd be positively giddy over the use of something that I've avoided all my life. Yeah. I was scarred by an overflow as a kid, okay? Thought that was what happened when you didn't go when you were told and had to use the SUBWAY BATHROOMS. Ahem.

Whatever. I'm over it. Rockland transportation department? You are my heroes. Never change. And where do I send next year's Christmas card?

Tuesday, January 12—

Onions sizzled on the stove as Cassie peered at her phone for the next step in the quest for amazing sandwich beef. "Take shredded beef and add to caramelized onions, add a quarter-cup Worcestershire sauce…" She blinked, reread it, and pulled her quarter cup measure from the drawer. "That's a lot of sauce…"

But the moment she grabbed it, the bottle slipped from her hands and crashed to the floor. The dark brown sauce splashed *everywhere*. Socks, drenched in sauce, threatened to carry the mess through the house, so Cassie hopped up onto the island, shed the socks, and flung herself as far into the living room as she could. "Whew!" A glance back at "Thinker" brought a smile to her face. "Thanks for the sympathy, bud. I'm sure you're upset about the mess, and not sayin' it's not a problem, but um... my *dinner?*"

As if to mock her, a trail of smoke began over the frying pan. Cassie dashed for her trainers, dashed back, moved the pan, and stared at the mess before her. "Crisis two averted. Time to clear crisis one and figure out three."

But before she could reach for the non-existent paper towels, or even a dishcloth, Cassie caught sight of the house across the street. Unlike the row of Craftsman bungalows-turned-duplexes on her side, the other houses stood unchopped by enterprising butchers who cared more for profit than restoring architectural art into the masterpieces they'd once been.

Cassie eyed her coat on the rack by the back door and sighed. Overkill—sure. A wool dress coat was *definitely* overkill, but at least she wouldn't have to crunch through the kitchen minefield of glass for her parka.

Mrs. Morrison's house—across the street and north one house—would be her best bet. "Mr. Chao might have soy sauce, but Worcestershire?"

The woman—easily in her seventies—opened the door just as Cassie put her foot on the first step. *And I doubted that you watch every move that people make on this street...*

"Cassie Wren! What brings you to my side of the street?"

"Disaster?" She shivered inside and rubbed her hands together as she tried to describe the mayhem she'd created in her kitchen. "I don't have a spare bottle of that stuff, but I'd better get one, I suppose—before I move to glass... "

The woman glanced back at Cassie—three times—as she went to retrieve the requested Worcestershire sauce. Mrs. Morrison's voice called out from the kitchen, "Will you get that?"

Cassie blinked. "Get what?"

"In about four seconds, Thomas is going to pound—" The front door shook with force indicative of a police battering ram. "On it."

"You're good, Mrs. M. You're really good."

"Nah... he's just really nosy." When the door rattled again, Mrs. Morrison called out, "Hurry! Before he destroys my original door! Do you know what those things cost? Clearly he doesn't."

Without another second of hesitation, Cassie jerked open the door and narrowly missed having her face rapped on by Mrs. Morrison's neighbor—the one Cassie's mother always called, "Mr. Miyagi."

"Sorry, Cassie. I saw you come over, and thought you might need help..." He hurried inside and shut the door. In an exaggerated whisper he added, "Better shut it or Bev'll whine about the two cents we just wasted."

"You can leave them on the hall table there, Thomas. I live on a fixed inco—"

"—come. We know. The whole town knows." He winked at Cassie, and this time he managed a genuine whisper as he added, "A 'fixed' annuity thanks to sound money decisions in her twenties. Learn from her, Cassie. Why, if I wasn't so determined to die a happy bachelor, I'd marry the old thing for her money."

She should have been shocked—probably would have been—if the old guy didn't say something similar every time the man stood within twenty feet of his penny-pinching neighbor. Instead, Cassie just shrugged. "Who says singleness is all that? I mean, most people my age are doing their best to get *out* of it."

"That's because you don't know how wonderful what you have *is*. It took two marriages and a near miss to teach me that lesson."

Mrs. Morrison appeared with a bottle—wrapped in a kitchen towel, no less—and passed it to Cassie. "Now tell me what *you* are doing with Worcestershire sauce. I happen to know you can't cook."

"I can cook just fine," Cassie protested. "People like my cooking, even. I just usually prefer not to."

"So why the sudden culinary foray—it's nowhere near Independence Day, and New Year's is over."

A dilemma lay before her. Resist as long as possible for some semblance of privacy or get the ordeal over with so she could move on with her new, unwanted, unlovable life. A sigh escaped before she could speak. "I made a commitment to 'go green' this year. So, my favorite foods—you know, frozen dinners or take out—it all comes in packaging I can't buy now. So, I have to start cooking." She shook the towel-wrapped bottle. "That's why I need to buy a couple more of these before glass week, or I'll have to make my own or something." She frowned at the thought. "Can you *make* Worcestershire sauce?"

Cassie unwrapped the bottle and tried to read the ingredients, but Bev's hands tucked the towel around it again. "We wouldn't want a repeat in here. Now get home and clean that stuff off your floor before it stains." Bev patted Cassie's cheek. "I'll come over and hear all about this 'green' thing in a day or two. Seems right up your alley with all that thrifting you do."

Mr. Chao listened to the exchange but blocked the doorway as she tried to leave. "Smart thing you're doing there, young girl. I wish there were more like you."

She snickered. "Um, there are more than you'd think. I'm a holdout. I like my convenience. I like paper towels." Cassie winced at the whine in her voice. "I have to go home and clean up my mess without the glorious ease and protection of a nice wad of paper towels."

Bev disappeared and returned with a handful. "It's my New Year's gift to you. Use it to get the glass up at least. Worcestershire sauce in a cut—ouch!"

Why she did it—what *possessed* her to do something so out of character—Cassie couldn't say. She hugged the woman with a ferocity that surprised even her and whispered, "You are so good to me. Thanks!"

As she slipped past Mr. Chao, she kissed the old man's cheek and promised to give him an update. "I even started a blog. It's 3-6-5-days-of-green-dot-blog. I even have a cool tag line that Lauren gave me. 'The frustrated rantings of an unconvinced environmentalist'"

Thomas Chao pulled out an iPhone and tapped the URL into it. He showed her the screen. "That it?"

"Yep! Happy reading. At least it's good for a laugh."

Just as the door closed behind her, Cassie heard Mrs. Morrison snap, "Let me see that. Three-sixty-five days of green... hmm... you know; we could give her pointers."

⚓ ⚓ ⚓

Her kitchen hadn't been so clean since before the party—and probably wouldn't be again until December thirtieth rolled around again. "But it looks good, doesn't it, Think?" A slow smile formed. "Oh, yeah. You are totally 'Think.' It's like 'Tink' from *Peter Pan*. Love it."

Think sat in serious contemplation over his new moniker.

A list that would take several scrolls to finish filled her phone—a list of things she needed to plan for. Cassie stared at it and frowned. "I hate this. Where's that Boogie Board post? I need to bump it." She stared at Think. "You know; I've learned one solid thing about myself already. I am a paper girl. I think better on paper—when I write it down." The memory of her goal planning session—complete with a cool new notebook that now lay languishing with only one decision made in it—sent her back to her spare room and in minutes she sat curled up on the couch beside Think all ready to plan out her next projects. "I need something for shopping—actually, I need a few somethings.

Tote bags for groceries
Mesh bags for fruits and vegetables
Something washable for meats

Washable Ziploc style bags

Other items followed, but her eyes kept sliding up the list to those. Determined, she wandered through her house in search of something—anything—to make tote bags out of. "They are most important; I suppose…" When nothing sturdy presented itself, she glared at her collection of vintage tablecloths and linens. "Why don't they make tablecloths out of outdoor canvas or something? Those things would survive anything—even a shopping trip with me."

That left a single question—whom to call. Cassie curled back up on the couch and leveled an inquiring gaze at Think. "Lauren or Mom?"

Cassie could have sworn his toe curled a bit more. "You're right. Lauren. Mom would flip. And then bring me five hundred premade bags. Kind of defeats the purpose."

Lauren picked up first ring. "Where've you been? I feel utterly unneeded. You've replaced me, haven't you?"

Laughter bubbled over as Cassie imagined the ridiculous expressions on her friend's face. "I needed that tonight. And yeah… sorta. You know my reproduction Rodin?"

"*The Thinker?*"

"Yep. He's now up on my end table and I call him 'Think.' He's my new buddy so I don't feel stupid talking to myself all the time."

Silence hovered in the airwaves and Cassie swallowed hard. When Lauren still didn't speak a moment later, she snapped, "What?"

"Gotcha."

"You are so dead."

With a giggle, Lauren demanded to know the latest crisis. "What can't you live without now?"

"Well, it's not new, but it's time to deal with it. I need tote bags for groceries. But if I buy—"

"Right. Gotcha. So, make them. I read about Joel's gift."

Don't do it. Don't go there. Please. I don't want to deal with it tonight. In an attempt to stave off another lecture, Cassie tried to focus the conversation on the real problem. "I just don't have anything that I can use. It's not like I have a hidden supply of canvas." She giggled. "Dad better be glad I gave him back his drop cloths. I so would be cutting them up right now."

"Speaking of cutting up. Don't you need scissors and stuff? I mean, kitchen shears work, but don't you want good scissors?"

Cassie stamped down frustration. Of course, she wanted good scissors and a nice box of notions—whatever those were—to make this new project as easy and fun as possible, but that wasn't going to happen. "Well, I have to use what I have. Maybe I'll find a sewing kit at an estate sale."

"Great idea. Okay, so cloth. You need something for cloth. Something sturdy... old curtains?" Lauren's snicker hinted at what she'd say next, and Cassie said it with her.

"It worked for Maria von Trapp."

As tempting an idea as it was, Cassie shook her head. "Sure wish I could use these ugly things, but they're not mine, and I still haven't found what I want." A new thought prompted a groan. "Man, I just got rid of that stained shower curtain. It was sturdy sorta-canvassy stuff. It would have been great."

Lauren murmured something. It sounded familiar, so Cassie asked her to repeat. "I just was trying to remember that old thing they said in the depression. 'Use it up—you don't have anything to use up. No cloth. Wear it out—well, that's not going to help you. Make do... or is it make it over? Make it over...'" Lauren sent her to her room. "Tell me what's in your closet, your drawers, everything. Your get *rid* of bag. Just everything."

"I think you said everything. But okay. I have a couple of dresses that would absolutely not work even if I was willing to give them up. There's that corduroy skirt that I love—and hate. Maybe it would be better as a bag. Can you make a bag from a skirt?"

Even through the airwaves, Cassie could swear she *heard* Lauren's shrug. "I don't know, but toss it out just in case. Now what else?"

"Work clothes—nothing that would work and I need them. Um... flannel shirts, a few t-shirts, jeans, a couple cut tops—"

"Wait. Jeans. Those are sturdy."

Cassie coughed. "Um, sorry to disappoint you but my butt and legs aren't big enough to make it worth it, thank-you-very-much."

"Oh, stuff it. Look, you cut them apart into strips of fabric. Sew those together into one big piece. Then you cut them out into whatever you do to make these bags." Lauren went silent for a minute. "Hey... do you even *have* a pattern or tutorial or something yet?"

"Not yet..." Cassie eyed Think. "But we'll find one. Okay. I've got a few pairs of jeans I keep resisting in my purges. Surely that'll be enough to make a bag or two." She ached to get off the phone but decided being a good friend was better. "Now I didn't hound you about your date... but it's time to spill it. What happened?"

Silence. Cassie chewed her lip as she waited. *This could either mean it went so great she's not ready to share yet, or it was a disaster and she's embarrassed.*

"Can you fall in love with someone on a first date?"

"Oooooh..."

"I didn't say I *did*! I just want to know if you can."

How am I supposed to answer that? Even if you can, would *you? Not likely.* But she tried a neutral approach. "I don't see why not—at least strong attraction-slash-appreciation."

"Well, he didn't *say* anything, and he hasn't been creepy or anything, but I really think Grant fell hard some way or another. I watched it. It was cool and terrifying and amazing—all at once."

"But no pressure on you?" Cassie waited, not realizing that she held her breath.

"Not at all. He didn't say anything, and I could have misread him, but I don't think so. He's kept in touch every day since—just a short text, a call, and today it was a card in the mail—*in the mail*. What guy does that?"

Obviously one who is falling hard. You're right about that. She swallowed down any doubts and asked, "So where did you meet him again?"

"That singles thing in Fairbury. We saw *To Catch a Thief*."

Even as they spoke, Cassie zipped a message to Bentley. "I'm asking Bentley if she knows anything about him."

"Oh, Cass... that's not fair."

To remind or not... that was the dilemma. "Lauren, if he goes through woman after woman, 'falling hard' prematurely, don't you want to know it? I can't imagine it, but just in case. He could be another Chuck Majors."

"That guy is just a legend." When Cassie didn't respond, she added. "Isn't he?"

"I have it on good authority—Joel—he's very real. He's just improved... supposedly."

Bentley's reply came swifter than expected. "Okay, we've got an answer... let me look..." She couldn't hide the grin in her voice. "It's good, Lauren. She says, 'Grant hasn't dated much in a while. He's usually pretty reserved.' Sounds like you might have something genuine." She swallowed a warning and reduced it to mild caution. "Look, I know you don't need to hear me say it, but I'm going to anyway. Still take your time. A guy who thinks you're amazing is an attractive creature. I should know."

Cassie allowed that to sink in for a moment before she said goodbye and disconnected the call. Four pairs of jeans ended up on the literal chopping block. With ruthless abandon, she sliced up the outside seam of one leg and began to slice the inside. "Hmmm... it's a bigger piece of cloth if I don't cut that. It has to be better... doesn't it?" Cassie held them up to show Think. "What do you think?"

Once more, she sliced up the outside leg and stared at what was left. "Maybe I should do the inside next time—not that big thick seam."

Without even cutting off the upper portion, Cassie tossed them aside and started in on the inseams. It proved harder, but the moment she saw the results, she whacked off from the crotch up and grinned. "Perfect." That's great."

Unfortunately, it took less than ten minutes to create fabric to sew. But without thread, pins—basics—she couldn't actually *make* anything. "Tomorrow. At least I'm ready to go. Time for the blog and bed." With that, she dropped her recycled fabric in a heap on the sewing machine case and strolled into the living room.

She gave Think an affectionate pat on the head and pulled out the laptop.

Thinking Ahead

Today—pretty easy at work and everything, but home was another story. You know the problem with this project of mine, right? I'm the convenience queen. I LOVE frozen food. Seriously. It is so good and soooooooooooo much easier than making your own stuff—especially if making stuff comes with shattered bottles of Worcestershire sauce all over your floor. For the record, you can eat off mine right now. It's never been cleaner.

I also have a list—on *paper,* no less—of things I need to make with my nifty new machine. Actually, I think it's a used machine. Pretty sure Joel the amazing got me something used. He's supportive that way. I even got started tonight. Four pairs of jeans are cut into usable pieces of cloth. Here... I even took a picture of them.

Cassie dashed into the kitchen, grabbed the jeans, and laid them out on the floor to show what she'd done. She snapped a picture, zipped it to Dropbox, and tossed the jeans back in the general direction of the machine.

See? Those will soon be my "grocery bags." I'll fill them with delightful things like non-baby spinach (because that stuff comes in bags instead of bunches) and guilt-free bulk rice and beans. Yep. I may have to live on a pauper's diet if I can't find a better way to cook without having all this *stuff.*

Note: I am NOT giving up wrappings of every kind. I cannot hope to have a piece of meat without it being wrapped in something. I'll do butcher paper and burn it so it doesn't end in a landfill—whatever. But I AM eating meat once in a while! (you know, like daily. I'm a carnivore. Sue me).

Also on my list... well, here. Let me snap a picture of that, too.

The picture inserted easily after a moment spinning in Dropbox. "It's crazy to think none of this existed when I was born."

Okay. That's it. That is what I have to make first. If you have any great tutorials or whatever, let me know. I would have tried to make the jean bags tonight, but well... I need things like needles and pins and *thread* for that, first. Gonna borrow from my mom until I can get to a thrift store or estate sale with good supplies. Does thread go bad? Are there expiration dates on this stuff?

Not much exciting happening today. Well, unless you count the disaster of a floor I had. Oh, and dinner—great. You want to make this recipe. I'll link it HERE. Yum!

Until tomorrow... *assuming all this doesn't kill me before then. I make no promises*

By the time Cassie finished brushing her teeth—with a plastic toothbrush impregnated with plastic bristles, no less— Cassie had her first comment.

Joel213: Maybe you should open your presents. Wrappings usually hide things. Oh, and Mom says go to eco-crafty.blog for great ideas.

With a groan and more than a little excitement, Cassie dashed for the sewing machine and jerked it up to the island. Each side unlatched with ease, but nothing could have prepared her for the avalanche of supplies that rained down on the surface of the island, the kitchen floor, and her feet. "Okay, you are seriously the best guy friend a girl could have. I think I need to thank your mom for this." She just found her phone and sent a text.

THANKS, JOEL. After a moment of hesitation, she added, WANNA HELP ME FIGURE THIS OUT TOMORROW?

His reply didn't come until she'd slid under the covers an hour later. WHAT TIME? I'LL BRING PIZZA. IF I BUY IT FOR ME...

Now that's just scary brilliant. She zipped out one more text and turned off her phone. 6:30? I OWE YOU.

Wednesday, January 13—

Joel carried two pizza boxes to the back door and gave it a gentle double kick for a knock. "C'mon, Cassie... the pepperoni is getting icicles!"

The door flung open almost before he finished speaking. "Squeeee! Yes! Pizza to the rescue! Bad—bad day. And you're here which—" She ducked inside, pizza boxes in hand.

I never know if I'm supposed to ignore those things or remind her that I'm not some pathetic idiot that can't differentiate between a friendly compliment and flirtation.

That thought—such a familiar one. Happened at least once every time they spent more than ten minutes together, and this time, he took the risk. "Um... Cass?"

"Yeah?" It came out more like, "Hmpheeeaah?" She turned back to him with a mouthful of pizza, her face turning as red as the sauce dribbling down her chin.

"I don't even know what to say now." Joel's laughter—he couldn't stifle it if he tried. "Did you *eat* today? Take ten seconds to thank the Lord—"

But Cassie interrupted him. "I... I'll do that when I'm done. It's easier to be thankful when you're not half-starved."

Joel pulled a plate from the cabinet and passed it to her. "We can pretend to be civilized, right?" He pulled a chair out for her at her little dinette and gestured for her to sit. "Drink?"

"I wish I could have something super alcoholic." She seated herself, smiled up at him, and once again, started to say something. Once again, she stopped herself.

This time, Joel didn't hesitate. As he filled a plate, poured a glass of milk for each of them, and seated himself, he worked out what he'd say. He pushed one glass toward her and gave her a smirk. "Next best thing to beer with pizza."

"How would you know?"

"Lucky guess?" Joel waited for her to take a bite before he tried explaining. "You know, when I told you how I feel about you, it was to *avoid* that awkwardness when you figure it out and have to pretend you don't know." His first drink of milk slid down smoother than he'd imagined. "But you've got to give me credit for being able to handle you being *you*. I never took your compliments as come-ons before. I'm not going to now."

Protests sputtered forth and died. She stared as the piece of double pepperoni pizza and nodded. "Yeah... I get it. I do that now, don't I?"

It took him until half his first piece of pizza was gone before Joel could say what he knew he needed to say next. "I know you, Cassie. If you change how you feel about me—you'll tell me."

There they were again—protests. Again, they petered out to nothingness. "Thanks, Joel. You know, I think you're the only person who doesn't hate me for not..." She gave him a shrug and jumped up for another piece. "Anyway. You're right. Thanks."

"So..." The moment she seated herself again, he asked the next obvious question. "So just why *are* you so hungry? Are you even chewing?"

For a moment, he regretted the question, confident she'd smack her food to prove it. Instead, she jumped up and carried her favorite leather tote bag over to him. "That's why."

Glass pieces and shards mingled with lettuce, cucumber, tomatoes, carrots, and chicken, of course. "Ouch."

"Note. If you carry glass to work, don't forget and drop your broken, industrial-sized and weight stapler in the bag *before* you eat lunch."

"And why would you…" Joel rolled his eyes at the only thing he could think of. "Steal? Steal a *broken* stapler? Is it vintage?"

If she hadn't already been annoyed with herself, Cassie might have been offended. She just put her feet up on a kitchen stool left over from the fifties and leaned back with her next piece of pizza. "I was going to take it to get fixed. Then I broke my lunch, so I couldn't even eat it on the way. No food equals starving Cassie." She grinned at him. "You couldn't have picked a better night."

They finished their pizza in near silence. When she reached for her sixth piece, Joel pulled the box away and dug another salad from the fridge. "Get something less artery-clogging in you first. Sheesh."

"You brought *two!* I was just helping with the leftovers before they were leftover!"

"They're staying here. So just pace yourself."

Her eyes widened—and widened again. She batted them—in rapid, vapid, obnoxious flutters. "My hero!"

I remember the first time you did that. I thought you were obnoxious and shallow.

"So, I found a tutorial…"

"I'll put the pizza in a Zip—um… *container* and then you can show me."

Her whisper reached him from across the room and lodged in his heart. "I hate this, Joel."

"Hate what?"

"All of it… no water bottles, no ordering pizza because it comes in a box, sending my friend all over town to find me ice cream that doesn't come in packaging I'm not allowed to do. No *Ziplocs* or even buying something to replace them. Because that's just contributing to the excess manufacturing."

With pizza in the fridge, Joel seated himself beside her once more and listened as she ranted, near tears, about the pervasiveness of plastic. "It's everywhere—like soy and high fructose corn syrup! You can't buy anything without plastic being involved somehow—even if it's just the debit card you used to pay for stuff."

Some things you can't argue with—truth, truth should be one of them. Joel sat listening, hoping to find something she'd overlooked She didn't. "And everything's more work. I can't just be hungry like today and go, "I'll grab a taco from the truck or a burger from the drive-thru. No... why? Because it comes with paper or plastic packaging—all of it. And you know the worst of it?"

He shook his head, but his heart argued. *Just give it up, then. Or go for only the non-essential stuff. It doesn't have to be this extreme, does it?*

"There's also a certain satisfaction in it. I mean, what's with that? I hate this. Every morning I wake up and x out another day on my stupid calendar. I'm so done with it all. But when I add up how much stuff I haven't wasted..."

"Well, we'll make it a bit easier. We'll think ahead, plan ahead. We'll go to HearthLand this weekend and see what they can save you."

She gave him an odd look and then pulled her phone from her pocket. Another glance turned into a stare before Cassie slid her fingers along the surface and passed it to him. "I'm thinking about doing a list of exceptions..."

Finally. Reason. I knew you had it in you.

"So, like food stuff—you know, if I need... *ground beef*. I have to choose the least packagey stuff, but I can have it. I don't have to go vegetarian just because you can't get meat without a bunch of stuff wrapped around it, you know?"

Her words sparked a new thought. "So... you'll buy flour and salt and... sugar for pancakes, but not say Bisquick because those things are staples and that's just a lot of packaging for convenience?"

Cassie's face fell. "I didn't think of that. I just thought making them myself would be better than metal *and* paper packaging from canned."

"Don't over-think it, Cassie. Just let yourself make natural changes." Her lips formed a protest that he could have predicted—likely word-for-word. "No... you're going to burn yourself out. You already hate this. You need to make it fun—a challenge."

"I don't know how to do that."

A new idea sent him down the hall. "Where are your checks?"

"Top drawer of the desk... why?"

Joel bolted for the check box, snagged the untouched register, and hurried back down the hall before she could decide to follow him. Just in time, too. Cassie dropped back in her seat and eyed him with curious suspicion. "So..."

He dropped the checkbook on the table. "Every time you save more than a dollar doing something "green," record it. Every time you have to buy something—like the tote bags last night. If you just bought them instead, deduct it."

"But..." Despite her automatic protest, he saw something shift in her.

C'mon. Your natural competitiveness will keep you enjoying it if you can be playing against yourself.

Cassie's green eyes seemed to grow more vivid with each second as she flipped her eyes between the register and his face. A slow nod began, and relief relaxed her features. "I—I could use it for new underwear!" She flushed a deep red. "Sorry, but it's true. I don't mind used clothes, but some things..."

"We all wear 'em." Joel disguised an uncomfortable

swallow with a sip of his now lukewarm milk. *There, that sounded nonchalant, didn't it? Your thoughts can't go there, Hudson. Do. Not. Think. About. It.*

"So..." Cassie stared at the register and pulled it closer. "Can I add up last week's potential savings?"

"Sure. Make it your starting balance."

She dug through her purse for a pen and clicked it. "Um... I estimated at least thirty dollars last week."

When she hesitated again, Joel relieved her of register and pen and wrote $30.00 on the top line of her register. "There. Now where are these tote bags? Let's get you set for your next shopping trip. Where's the machine?"

"Don't you want to read the instructions, first?"

"I'm a man, Cassie. We don't read instructions until forced by failure to concede that there might be another way..." Shock washed over her. Cassie stammered something about not having enough jeans to ruin what little cloth she had, before Joel's laughter filled the kitchen. "I was just joking! Get the tutorial set up. I'll see if I can figure out how to thread that thing. Surely there's an..." He grinned at her. "*Instruction book.*"

She didn't have tissue paper or even paper grocery bags. But Cassie did manage to find her newspaper from the previous week. "I had to cancel my subscription, you know. I'm all digital now."

Something in her tone—it sounded as though she'd exchanged a pet poodle for a "Webkinz" or something. "Well... that's good, though, right? And you still have these!"

"Only because the recycling doesn't go out this week. That's next week." Before she could wax eloquent again, her phone rang.

The pink in her cheeks sent his heart plummeting. *It's that guy. Bet you anything it's that guy.*

"Be right back."

Five, four, three...

"... Evan, how are you adjusting...?" Her voice faded as she reached her room and closed the door, but the tone... the tone said it all.

And you're interested in him. I shouldn't be surprised... not really. He pulled the machine from the case and set it on the dinette. *But really, Lord? Did he have to call while I'm here?* The whine in his mental tone—it nauseated him. *Okay, that was just pathetic. How about this, instead? Can you help me keep from showing that it hurts?*

She appeared in less than five minutes. Just as Joel re-threaded the machine for the fifth time. "I think I've got it this time." But try as he might, he couldn't make the thread go through the needle. "Not sure what I'm doing wrong. Every time I get to this point, it *won't* go through the needle."

"Perhaps..." She shrugged and pulled out her phone. "Let's try Google. Maybe there's a trick." Thirty seconds later, she said, "Trim the end of the thread. If there's a tiny piece that isn't cut smoothly, it says it can make it impossible to go through. Otherwise..." Her finger scrolled up a couple of times. "Otherwise, it says the needle could be backwards... no wait. I think that's for the kind you use to sew a button—just regular needles. Not for sewing machines," Cassie added as if she hadn't made it abundantly clear what she meant.

"Got it. Must have been that thread thing." He pointed to her laptop on her coffee table. "Gonna get that thing? The phone would be kind of small for directions."

They made it halfway through the basic steps—improvising at almost every turn—before Joel mustered the courage to ask about the date. "So, you going out with Evan on Saturday?"

"Friday." She whipped her head around and stared at him. "How'd you know?"

"Um... you said, 'Hi, Evan' and then disappeared for a couple of minutes. I could only imagine that if you didn't want me to hear what you expected to hear, then you expected a date."

With a slow shake of her head, Cassie measured the fabric for the straps again. "I am an inch too short."

"Who cares? They're for holding groceries from cart to car and car to house. You aren't going to use them to carry the stuff around the store!"

Joel decided that she'd agreed when she began whacking the fabric into two long strips. He waited until they'd double-stitched around the top to prevent fraying—something about how she couldn't hem to save her life—and had begun to sew the straps down the side of the bag before he spoke again. "So... if you don't have a date on Saturday night, want to get a few people together for pool? It's been since before Christmas." When she hesitated, against his better judgment, he added, "You could always bring Evan if the date goes well."

Her head snapped up and she stared at him. "Um, Joel?"

"Yeah?"

"I may not be the person you want me to be, but I'm not that callous. C'mon... we can shoot pool without *him* there, surely."

A slow smile formed before he could prevent it. "I won't complain."

The finished tote, the *single* finished bag—the one that took ninety-three minutes to make—lay on the table before them. Cassie shook her head. "Saturday, it is. Assuming I get the others done before then." Then it happened—the first time since he'd told her how he felt. Cassie jumped up, wrapped her arms around him as he sat fingering the bag, and whispered, "Thanks. You're..." The hesitation still cut, but Joel couldn't help but relax just a little as she finished. "—the best. Really."

"We try...."

<hr />

Think pondered the deeper things in life—probably whether world peace or green peace was more easily obtained—as Cassie Swiffered her floors and tried not to imagine life without those blessed little pads. "Bet there's a hack for that, too—like washable Swiffer pads. I'm going to spend every spare minute making substitutes for things I already have. This is so frustrating!"

But the memory of that check register still languishing on the table sent her for it. "I made a tote bag. Cheap ones are a dollar. I don't know how much canvas ones are, but surely..."

It took ten minutes of price comparisons before she decided on an equivalent. "Okay, Think, here's my thoughts. These on Etsy kind of look like mine, but I doubt mine are as nice. So, I think fourteen dollars each is too much. The plain canvas ones are between two and six, but mine is a bit bigger. So, I'm gonna cut that fourteen in half. I get seven dollars for this bag. I mean, I'd have to *pay* that fourteen to buy them, so..." Before she could talk herself out of it, Cassie added seven dollars to her total.

That simple total—$37.00—sent such a strong feeling of personal satisfaction through her, that she thrust the register in Think's face. "Look at *that*! Thirty-seven bucks. Man, if I keep this—" She closed her eyes and took a slow, cleansing breath. "Oh. Brother. I just got played. Royally played."

Cassie snatched up her phone and zipped a text to Joel. YOU GOT ME. I JUST FIGURED OUT YOUR PLAN WITH THE REGISTER. WELL PLAYED, MY FRIEND. WELL PLAYED.

She opened up a new page and began her next blog post. Several ideas flitted through her, but Cassie couldn't help but contrast her earlier feelings with her current ones. So, ignoring Joel's reply of, WONDERED HOW LONG IT WOULD TAKE YOU TO FIGURE IT OUT. YOU GOT THIS, Cassie went to work on a title.

Green Living: The Love/Hate Relationship

I need to get a few things out of the way before I get into tonight's blog post. First? A PLASTIC recycle bin. Oxymoron much? I'm dying

120

to know if it has any post-consumer waste plastic at all in it. Wanna bet the answer is no? For that matter, I doubt there's even *any* recycled plastic in it—other than the things I have dropped there until next week's pick up.

Also... if anything beats me at this green game, it'll be Ziplocs. Seriously. Every day I reach for one. Every day, I want to cry— seriously. (did I mention I'm serious?) I'm not talking about exaggerated words like 'I didn't get to finish chewing the last bit of flavor from that gum. I just wanted to cry." No, I seriously mean I wanted to CRY. Like crocodile tears but sincere ones—just great big tears. I've been Googling eco-friendly alternatives. I've got some plans. We'll see. But you know what? Wanna know the worst part of it all? I don't WANT an alternative. I. Want. The. Bag. Some people wash them out and reuse. I can—for organizing stuff. But for leftovers—ew. I tried it. Just... ew.

I wanted chicken nuggets today. I mean, serious craving here—you know, the kind people only tolerate in pregnant women? Yeah. That kind. Except I'm not pregnant. But man... I wanted them SO BAD.

total random aside. To those who complain about me YELLING AT YOU... I'm not. If the whole post was like that, I'd totally get it. But if there's just a word or two in all caps, pretend they're italics. I'm on a roll when I write this stuff, and I don't want to stop to switch out every emphasized word. That's just dumb. So, sorry.

Where was I? Oh. Chicken nuggets. I can't buy them. Fast food. I think I'm going to carry containers with me and BEG the places to put my food in MY containers. Maybe then I can get away with fast food now and then, because you know what? I don't think I can make it eleven and a half more months without any fast food. Maybe I should... but I can't.

So that brings me to tonight's revelations and what this post is really about. If I wasn't the competitive person that I am. If I didn't HATE quitting even more than continuing, I would be done with this. As I confessed to a friend tonight, I hate it. What I can't tell is if I hate it because it's inconvenient or if it's because it's just restricting what I love and who I am. And if it is, should those things matter more than trying to conceive of a life that is less detrimental to the long-term health of our planet?

And that brings up another little problem. You see, I don't actually believe we CAN destroy this planet as easily as we think we can. I really don't. I think we can affect the quality of life on it, which is why I took this challenge. I want to see if I can get used to making choices that are less selfish.

Look, I agree with my friend. The choices I made for my party were, in one way, anyway, very selfish. It was all about my comfort and convenience. And if I never did those things any other time, maybe I wouldn't have taken her gentle rebuke so seriously. But my whole life has been about ME. What makes ME comfortable. What makes MY life easier. And if that doesn't have any effect on anyone else, there's nothing wrong with that. But what if it does? What if me choosing to do something means that later it DOES make an impact—either because of my behavior or because of my example?

So, like I told my friend. I hate this. I don't want to do it. I want it over. I want to wake up tomorrow and know I finished. But I don't actually want to DO it. I usually want the satisfaction of a job well done. This time, I just want it DONE.

Except... there is a certain satisfaction in seeing that I really have made a difference. I only had one bag of trash this week. ONE! At least THREE didn't go to the landfill. THREE BAGS! I mean, if I wanted to, I could totally share the trash service with my neighbor. That would save the landlord a bundle, right?

And my friend? He knows me so well. He gave me a way to compete against myself. And man... that's just exactly what I needed.

Look. I was so discouraged tonight—seriously discouraged. Now... Now I'm ready to beat this thing. It'll be fun. Not every minute of it, no. I'm not quite that Pollyanna-like. But the thing as a whole? I'm gonna win it. I've got it. I can DO this.

Goodnight.

Thursday, January 14—

The second Thursday—often Cassie's favorite day of the month. Occasionally... her least. And Marla Wren knew it. So when Cassie asked if they could meet at Olive Garden instead of their usual fish market, Marla decided *not* to make a big deal of it.

But seated across from her daughter, listening to her talk about all the things she had to do without, Marla couldn't help but ask if she wouldn't regret it. "Don't you think you're being just a little...?"

"Obsessed? Ridiculous? Insane?" Cassie's eyes looked a

122

little half-crazed as she spoke. Then her features relaxed and her gaze softened. "Probably. But I'm also determined. Oh!" Before Marla could reply, Cassie pulled out a rolled-up piece of denim. "Look what Joel and I did last night."

No one would ever call Marla a proficient with the sewing machine, but the jumbled mess of stitching lines and unhemmed edges would make any grocery bagger quake. "You did it out of old jeans. Clever."

"Yeah. It's ugly." Cassie laughed as Marla tried to protest. "Mom, I'm not stupid! I can see it's ugly. But it's a start. And now that I have my own machine, I can absolutely learn to hem."

"I keep telling you, learn to press it first."

"Because that's what *you* do..." Cassie laughed at her chagrin. "Look. You've got to hear about Mrs. Morrison and Mr. Chao. They came to my house this morning."

Marla tore a breadstick in half in a futile attempt to convince herself she'd only eat half. "Together?"

"Right? I knew you'd get it. I told Lauren and she just said, 'Oh, how cute.'"

"That's not cute, that's potentially lethal. Who spoke first?"

Again, Cassie's laughter rang out. "That's just the best part. I let them in—cold out there, you know—and they said together, 'I can help with this green thing.'" She rolled her eyes in that way she'd used as a teenager when Marla had said something particularly uncool. "Then, of course, they started arguing. Mr. Chao says that she doesn't know how to be green. She says that being wise is smart, but we've got modern advances and shouldn't be afraid to use them."

"What does that even mean?"

With a shrug, Cassie waited for their server to pass their plates and dump a flurry of cheese atop them before she asked, "Did you know they were both born in 1930? I thought Mrs. Morrison was like sixty. She's eighty-six! She lived through the depression. So, did he!"

123

"So, they know how to do the whole make it up or use it over thing?" Marla tried not to wince at how snide her words sounded. "I never do get that saying right."

"Close enough for me. She thinks we shouldn't even try. She 'lived through that once' and is glad she doesn't have to worry about it anymore. But Mr. Chao says, 'If we take care of the earth, it will take care of us.'"

Protest welled up in her throat and fizzled there. Instead, she tried asking questions instead of lecturing. *Now I know what Mama meant when she told me to ask, not talk.* "Um… so how does he suggest you do that?"

"He says cooking as much as I can from whole foods— shop the outside aisles, like they always say—I'll use less packaging, therefore, less waste. If I buy used—only when I have to buy, of course—and if I am conscious of how I use my energy, I can 'reduce my carbon footprint by eighty-percent.'"

"That's… impressive." Marla twirled her straw in her glass. "If everyone did that…"

"Our economy would tank."

Marla blinked. Twice. And then coughed. "Say, what?"

"Well, think about it. If every American decided to shop the outer aisle, that means that 80% of the inner aisles wouldn't get sold. So, what would happen? Those companies would lose massive amounts of money. People would lose their jobs. The stock market—I doubt it could recover. First, we had the savings and loan thing. Then we bailed out the car companies. Then the bank mortgage bailout…" She twirled pasta onto her fork. "Next, we'll have the cereal bailout."

"Or the canned soup." Marla grinned. "Can you imagine your father without his Progresso?"

"He's like that writer in that movie about the girl on the island!" Their laughter filled their corner of the restaurant, and Marla grinned as Cassie sighed. "Oh, that would be funny."

"Well, just don't stress yourself out. It's a lot of work to change your life so drastically."

For the better part of a minute or two, Marla almost feared she'd gone too far. But then Cassie set down her fork and sank back against the booth. "You know... I think just knowing that this is only for a year is going to help more than anything. I mean. It's only fifty-two different new things for fifty-two weeks."

Marla gave her a non-committal look. "Well..."

"When you look at it like that, it's not so bad. And I'm already thinking differently. Maybe I'll find that I don't *want* to go back later. Maybe I won't like how salad tastes from the deli down from the office, or I'll learn to hate the rancid greasiness of fast food." A skeptical expression flashed across her face, but Cassie wiped it off again. "No... it could happen. I doubt it, but it could. I'm open to it. I think."

"Well, anytime you want a good burger from The Moo Shack, you just call me. I'll deliver it on a plate."

"And *that's* why you're the best mom ever." Cassie winked. "I'm so going to make sure you get to prove it a time or twenty, too!"

⅃⅃ ⅃⅃ ⅃⅃

As she changed, brushed her teeth, washed her face, and otherwise readied herself for bed, Cassie rambled to Think. "Mom was great about it. I kept expecting one of her famous lectures, but she just talked *with* me instead of *to* me. And offering to bring me burgers on a plate. Awesome! I shouldn't do it, of course. You know it. But..."

Still remembering the neighbors' assurances of being "there for her" during this time of upheaval, Cassie turned out the lights, pulled the covers over her head, and snuggled down into her bed. The night sounds grew louder and louder in her ear, and no matter how hard she tried, nothing she did would calm her nerves. *I didn't even drink Coke! I had Sprite!*

Five minutes later, she bolted from bed and stumbled down the hall to the living room. As she snapped on the light,

125

she glared at Think. "I blame you for this. Don't ask why. But it's totally your fault. Why couldn't I just post it tomorrow? Why tonight? Huh?" Think didn't respond.

With the laptop booting, and her feet now freezing, Cassie tucked a lap blanket around her and tried *not* to drum her fingers. "Ugh! Updates! They're evil!"

She could have sworn Think nodded. "Okay... you're forgiven.

But, at last, the screen shifted from green to dark to her browser. She clicked on her bookmark, still trying to decide exactly what she'd write. Saying her mom was great might be nice, but it wasn't like anyone who knew her didn't already believe that. Then it hit her—the day's biggest triumph. "Oh, man! Think! I almost forgot!

A Paradigm Shift

Or at least, I'd like to think so. So, I met my mom for dinner tonight. We do that, you know—every second Thursday. If you don't have a regular date with your mom, start. That's all I'm sayin' on that.

But you know, on the way home, I decided to stop by Target. Look, I haven't been shopping for anything but groceries since December 30th. That's... a long time for me. So, I went into the store and didn't even *look* at the Dollar Spot. They have the best notepads there sometimes—super cute. I didn't look. After all, I can't buy paper. I almost went to see if they had any of those adorable metal pails they have sometimes. After all, it's not metal week yet. But I didn't.

I flipped through the clothes—nothing tempting. Purses. Nope. Movies? Nope (which is huge, because they come wrapped in plastic, and I bet the disc is plastic, too). They had Valentine's candy out. I didn't even buy a single tiny box of conversation hearts—my fave.

Bedding—c'mon. I buy the good stuff at sales. We all know this.

So, I was feeling pretty good—amazing, really, when I saw it—this adorable cellphone case. It had an *elephant* on it. Well, two, actually. Facing each other. Trunks intertwined. Cutest thing I've ever seen, and let's face it. ELEPHANTS! AAAAK!

Right then and there, I began this huge, elaborate point system in my head. If I denied myself this much, I got that many points, and points were one tenth of a dollar. Even with that, I figured out I had earned it. I could even do a double-whammy with myself and my register. Make myself pull out double dollars for non-essentials like that if I'd earned it. I mean, c'mon!

So picture it. I'm standing there in the checkout line, positively giddy about this ten-dollar elephant phone case. So, ready to buy it. It's plastic, and I don't even care. I just handed it to the gal and pulled out my debit card. Then it hit me. Was I really going to cheat that much this soon? Really? For a *phone case* just because I have this thing for elephants? I like the one I have! So why would I do this?"

The checker looked at me like I was crazy. I mean I swiped the card and hit delete. Told her to void it. I think I said, "I can't cheat on my plastic diet." Hmmm... you know what? I bet she thought I have huge credit card debt.

And that makes me wonder. Should I *use* plastic to pay for things? I mean, isn't that cheating?

JUST KIDDING!

Anyway, I thought I'd share my success story, too. I keep telling you how awful this is, so it's only fair to tell you when I had a breakthrough and was actually happy I did it. I am not missing that phone case at all. And for the naysayers, I WANTED THAT CASE. I really did. If I'd bought it, it'd be on my phone and I'd be stroking it right now. Love. It. But I love not having it even more. Wow.

Now if I can only keep that up.

Post published, Cassie turned out the light, said goodnight to Think, and shuffled back to her room. Just as she started to fall asleep, her phone signaled a notification. "Forgot to turn it down. Drat."

But temptation overrode her need to sleep, and Cassie snatched it up. As she suspected, a comment.

HermionesTwin: Oh, great. You're going to become THAT person. Another fanatic. Watch out, everyone. Cassie's going to be one of those people who preaches at you for using a straw or a cup lid at a restaurant. Everywhere we go it'll be about how stupid we are for not being "better stewards of the planet" or something.

The first words sent Cassie into education mode. "All that

paper and plastic! Okay, the paper is thin—probably biodegrades fast enough. But the straw itself! I've read about how many we use a day and it's a ton." But even as she was ready to get the statistics out and prove her point, Cassie's eyes slid over the next words and stopped cold.

"Oh, great. I'm *already* that person. I hate it when people do that—become so passionate about something that everyone avoids them to get away from their latest obsession. It's like I've become a direct-sales 'consultant' for green living, and I'm only on week two!

But despite her outburst, Cassie resisted, too. "So, I can't even share my triumphs? I mean, it might be a little thing to her, but it's a big thing to me?"

Her fingers flew over the keys as she tapped out a quick protest.

TheVintageWren: If I ever start doing that face-to-face, I want people to tell me. I don't want to be that person who can't shut up about her new obsession. BUT… here on MY BLOG… I'm not going to feel guilty about sharing what I'm doing and how well it is or isn't going. If you don't like it, maybe you shouldn't read it.

She turned down her phone volume to almost off, pulled up the covers, and once more, tried to sleep. But instead of dreams of a garbage-free planet or a hunky guy who just happened to be crazy supportive of her new venture, she dreamed of elephants with intertwined trunks standing in her living room arguing with Think.

Week 3: Glass

Friday, January 15—

Four outfits lay spread out across her bed, each having its own advantages and disadvantages. But try as she might, Cassie couldn't whittle down her choices any further. "I got rid of six others. That has to count for something." Her eyes shifted to the doorway. "Right, Think?"

When her "pet" didn't respond, Cassie marched out into the living room, retrieved the thoughtful gentleman, and returned to prop him up against her pillows. "Okay... which one?"

His gaze seemed trained on the dressiest of her options. "Too much, eh?" Cassie snatched up the dress—the one she'd just *had* to have and still hadn't found a decent place to wear it—and rehung it next to three others she'd hardly worn. "Fine. So now which?"

Think thought.

When he didn't answer to her satisfaction, Cassie, feeling utterly ridiculous, snatched him off the pillow, closed her eyes, and sent him spinning onto the bed. "Closest one to you touching wins. If it's a tie, the one your *head* is touching wins."

It landed on the dressier of the two remaining outfits. Cassie stared at the Windsor green heathered sweater, the gray jeans, and nodded. "With that new scarf I got for Christmas, and my boots... good choice, Think! Thanks!" She kissed the top of the bald little guy's head and set him on the dresser as she dashed to change.

The next question came as she stared at her hair. Dark ringlets—spiraled out over her head. "Maybe it's time for another blowout. The last one really did work well... I kind of miss waves."

Had Think chosen the dress, Cassie absolutely would have gone for a semi-messy up-do. However, the sweater seemed to call for something down...casual but put together. Cassie added just a bit more curl-defining crème to her hair, combed through, and scrunched her curls back into place. "So glad I learned how to get rid of those frizzies. But still..." Lip-gloss, a few swipes with darker eyeshadow, and Cassie stared at the results with a critical eye.

"Think? Watcha think about this?" As Cassie retrieved her friend and replaced him, she talked out her nervousness about the date. "And you know, I'm crazier than ever now that I'm talking to you. I swear I should have stuck to talking to myself. But, you're here now, and I named you. They say never name a stray or you're stuck with it. Well... Just sayin'."

The doorbell rang before she could feel any stupider. Cassie dashed for it, boots in hand, and opened it. A blast of cold air made her toss a glance of gratitude Thinks direction before she welcomed him in. "Hi! Get in before you freeze. I swear it's dropped twenty degrees since I got home!"

"Weather guy said something similar." Evan pushed the door shut behind him and grinned at her. "Wow, you look great."

"Well, then I'm either overdressed or I lucked out. Which is it?"

"I was thinking BJs and the skating rink?"

Cassie wrestled her foot into a boot and nodded. "Sounds great. I'll grab my skates." With the other boot on, she dashed down the hall, grabbed gloves and her ice skates, and tried to act cool walking back out again. If it hadn't been for quick moves on Evan's part, she'd have face-planted into her coffee table.

"Wow. You okay?"

"Only thing bruised is my ego, as my dad always says."

Inwardly, Cassie groaned. Outwardly, she glared at Think as if he alone were responsible for her gaffe. *Seriously? Why do I always throw Dad's stupid line out there at embarrassing times like that? It just makes it worse.*

"My Dad says that, too. And I always quote him and then feel stupid for doing it."

Cassie's head whipped up as she stared at him. "No way. I was just thinking about how stupid it is that I always do that!"

The drive to the restaurant—delightfully awkward. Waiting to be seated—not so delightful, but definitely still awkward. However, with menus in hand, the date really began. It started with Evan. "Eat here much?"

"Now and then... not this year, yet."

He eyed her with exaggerated dismay. "Oh, a wise guy. Just what I needed."

"Watch it, buddy. I am suffering from withdrawal. You do not want to mess with a woman who has endured fifteen days of paper reduction. Just sayin'." She pointed to the menu. "And I'm having the fresh Atlantic salmon. Their lemon sauce is awesome. I forgot about this!"

"I was thinking about the Parmesan chicken, but..." Evan's eyes met hers over the top of his menu. "I don't suppose you'd split plates..."

If you're wanting to share a meal, I'm going to have to offer to pay for my half. I need food. Cassie shrugged. "If you're not that hungry—"

"I'm starving, but not enough to order both. I just want to try it. But if you don't like the Parmesan—"

"Oh! Sorry. I thought you wanted to split that fish between us, and fish is never filling enough for me. I couldn't figure out how you'd make it through ice skating on half a salmon fillet."

His eyes twinkled at her. "And you wondered what kind of cheap date you'd found yourself on?"

"Well..." Cassie tried to think of something that didn't sound quite that censorious and failed. "I was prepared to pay for my own meal as long as I got to *eat* it all."

As soon as the server took their orders and brought their drinks, Evan leaned back in the booth and eyed her. "So, you work as a legal assistant? Are you a law student?"

"Nope. Didn't want to be. I took business classes and loved the legal stuff, but..." Cassie shrugged. "I'm not interested in more than helping out Mr. Sylmer with the kinds of stuff he wanted to."

"So, you have a BS in Business... Administration?"

"A.S... same degree." Cassie tried not to allow herself to sound defensive. "I went to Rockland Community College, got my A.S. and called it good. I just wanted to *work*."

But Evan didn't blink. "Sounds smart to me. If you ever want to go back, you're half-done, but if not, you have enough that with your experience, you'll be highly sought-after."

"Tell my mom that. She thinks I'll get beat out by a recent grad willing to take any salary to pay student loans. Well, I don't *have* student loans, so at least I don't have to make as much as I would if I'd have gone to Rockland U. Man, that would have been expensive." She smiled at him. "So, what do you do? I don't know if Lauren said."

Evan played with the straw in his drink—the very straw Cassie wanted to rip from it and plunge into her own glass. *How is it that I miss something so ridiculously unnecessary! I want my straw back!*

"—ion rep for the Transportation Employees Union."

Oh, dear. Lord, please don't let me have to tell my father what he does. Or maybe, it would just be easier to end it now. There's no hope here.

"Your face just fell. Not a big fan of unions?"

Cassie's throat went dry. "Um... I am pretty ambivalent. I'm of the, 'to each his own' philosophy. If people want 'em, more power to 'em. But my *father* is about as anti-union as they come. We lost everything when I was a kid because his machine shop unionized and..."

"Ouch." He stared into his glass for a few seconds. "Well, if I ever meet him, perhaps I should tell him I'm a negotiator."

Her eyes narrowed. "Creative truth-telling. That's either genius or scary."

"Or both? I can hear it. 'Mr. Wren, I think you would be most comfortable knowing that I'm a negotiator.' Your dad stares at me. 'Police?' I say, 'Well, they've been known to get involved, yes...'" Evan laughed. "Maybe it would make him feel better to know that my dad hates my job, too."

"Yep!" Cassie beamed. "That absolutely would do it. At least there's hope for a prodigal." She dropped her voice. "'A man can work with that, but an idiot...'" Her eyes widened. She covered her mouth, closed her eyes, and shook her head. "I think we should change subjects. How about something neutral... like nuclear power or toilet paper—up or down?"

"Lauren said I'd like you. She wasn't joking." He gave her a suspicious look before adding, "And who cares about over and under. Toilet lid—*up!*"

Cassie folded her arms over her chest. "This date just officially ended."

They laced their skates in silence. Evan watched her in his peripheral vision, trying to decide if he should pretend not to know anything about skating. *It's cheating, but...*

"You ready?" Cassie examined his skates. "Did you get them snug up on your ankles?"

"I think so. Want to check?" As much as he was *sure* she wouldn't take him up on it, Cassie knelt down and felt his boot. "Looks good! Great job!" She beamed up at him. "So... you do a lot of roller blading on the beach or something?"

He tried *not* to fake a stumble on the blades as they made their way to the ice. "Um, how do people roller blade *on the beach?* All that sand..."

"You know what I mean. I've seen pictures. Sidewalks

running along the beach in Southern California…"

Evan choked. "You do know I'm from Arizona—Tucson."

The pink in her cheeks only made a fresh, pretty face even lovelier. Cassie rolled her eyes. "That's your cousin, Ethan, isn't it? The one who lives in a beach house somewhere?"

"Not quite a beach house—just a block from the beach in Ventura. But yeah. Great rollerblading down there. We'd take off from his house, up this street—Pier-something—and there's this cool park at the end. A marina—everything. Loved going to see him as a kid. He's in Chicago now, though. Doing a residency at some big hospital there."

The moment they stepped onto the ice, Cassie grabbed his hand. "Okay, so what you do is…"

He couldn't do it. As much as Evan *wanted* to skate around the rink hand-in-hand with Cassie, lying by action wasn't the way to accomplish it. So, he spun backwards and folded his arms over his chest. "What was that?"

"You can skate!"

He nodded. "And I can do axels, Salchows, and Y-spins, too." Evan held out his hand. "Nine years of figure-skating competitions."

Cassie absently took his hand, her eyes never leaving his. "You're joking."

"Nope. If we get a bit of open ice and I can warm up, I'll show you."

"Lauren never said—"

His laughter cut off her words. "Good. My threats paid off. I swore to tell all her deepest, darkest secrets if she told when we were kids. I guess she still fears the wrath of Evan."

One second they were skating along hand-in-hand, and the next her arms crossed over her chest. "You'd tell people about the bed wetting?"

"Until she was a whole two-and-a-half." Evan shook his head. "You won't trip me up. I'm not telling you, and you can't quiz me without risking telling me. Just ask Laur—"

He hadn't finished before she pulled out her phone and zipped a text to Lauren. The suspicion in her eyes was drowned out only by her growl. "Don't you dare touch your phone or…" Hers beeped before she could finish her threat. Her eyes widened. "She told you about her *baptism*? She refused to go to church for *weeks*."

"Not very spiritual of her, is it? Bury yourself in baptism— *into* Christ—and then forsake the assembling—"

"Well, I don't know if I *ever* would have gone back to that church as long as that guy was the youth pastor. Talk about mortifying."

Well, who wears a dress and forgets a change of underwear on baptism day?

"—is why I wore shorts and a t-shirt as *well* as a baptismal robe. If she hadn't had that experience…"

"Mom said the robes had been removed. Still, I would have tried something else. I mean—"

But Cassie's legendary loyalty rose. She almost plowed into the couple in front of them as she took off in a huff. Evan caught up at the next turn. "Cassie, I wasn't criticizing. I was thinking aloud. Sorry."

The fire in her eyes died almost instantaneously. "Sorry myself. She trusted you with the story. You've gotta be okay."

He held out his hand once more. "Forgive me? I just wanted a nice skate for a while. I didn't mean to turn it into a challenge."

He didn't expect it, but Cassie grabbed it again and adjusted her stride to match his. "Fine… but you have to teach me a basic spin. I've always tried and *always* failed."

⟨⟨⟨⟩⟩⟩

Fuzzy sleep pants, baggy t-shirt, sloppy braid. Cassie made herself comfortable on the couch, pulled out her trusty laptop and stared at it. Her eyes slid over to Think. "What do I do if this thing dies? I'm a laptop junkie! I *need* my laptop!" His thoughtful contemplation reached her by ESP and she nodded. "Of course. Used—*refurbished*. Cheaper and saving the planet one lithium battery at a time. Woot."

A Facebook request greeted her as she clicked open her account. "I can confirm that." She eyed her thoughtful friend. "He's really a nice guy. He totally could have played up the ignorant guy—had his hands all over me 'trying not to fall.' So that's cool. Especially after the negotiator thing. I guess this puts that in context. I wasn't sure what to think of that."

The blog cursor blinked as she stared at the title bar and waited for inspiration. "Think..." But he gave her nothing. For all she knew, he slept over there with his head resting on his fist. Cassie stared at the bar once more and typed the first thing that came to mind.

Underwhelming

Look. For those who know I had a date tonight, that's not what I'm talking about, so let's just get that out of the way right now. And, for the curious—it was nice. There. That's all you are getting out of me on that front.
No... I'm talking about GLASS. I've done this big photo purge each first day of a new thing to reduce in my life. But you know what? Look at this!

Cassie zipped over to Dropbox to retrieve the pathetic picture of her great glass...non-purge. With the photo of a dozen glass jars on the island inserted, she returned to her explanation.

See that? That's all I found in my whole apartment. Nothing is made out of glass anymore. Juice jars—remember those? The funny little pyramiddy (yes, that's a word! Or it is now) tops and stuff? Nope. All plastic now. The pimento jars and mushroom jars are there. Little things, but hey. I'll take 'em. I can use them for organizing things when we're done.
And that brings me to the coolest part of this week. I don't have to

find a way to pack more stuff in my overloaded shed!!! This week it's going to be about trying to find glass containers over plastic. Because they're better for us, the planet, and I read this article that the more recycled glass is in a bottle, the cheaper it is to make that bottle. Sterilizing is even BETTER! But for once it's going to be about buying real maple syrup in a glass bottle instead of cheap stuff in plastic. I don't have to quit! I can just CHANGE. That's awesome.

Well, there probably won't be many estate sales tomorrow, but I'm determined to go anyway. I already killed my subscription to the paper. *insert wails of despair here* But tomorrow I'll work from the Internet. It's going to be great. I know it. Here's to finding fabulous stuff that will fill a few shops around the city and my bank account—all at the same time! G'night world!

Saturday, January 16—

The sign to HearthLand filled her windshield as Cassie followed Joel's directions and turned onto Hearthfield Way. "A bit into this hearth thing, aren't they? Isn't that the name of the store? The Hearth Something?"

"Hearth & Pantry, yeah. I think the other streets are a bit more original. There's Market Square and Candlewood Lane. I can't remember the rest." Joel pointed out cows as they whizzed past. "Look at them out there. Does the milk come out half-frozen already?"

"Ha. Ha." Cassie slowed and stared. "Why do they have baby cows out in the *snow*? Kind of mean, don't you think?"

But before Joel could comment—likely with the ever-brilliant, "How am I supposed to know?" retort, the handmade stop sign loomed ahead. To the right—a snow-covered road. To the left, a field. But straight ahead, a few buildings loomed around a town square too large for the number of buildings. "Optimistic, much?"

"They're new! They've done a ton of building in a really short time—like two years? Or something like that. It's insane how much they've gotten done. Mom keeps trying to talk Dad into retiring out here, but he says, 'I didn't work for thirty-five years at the same job just so I could quit and work *harder.*'"

"I'm with him." Cassie pulled up in front of the Hearth & Pantry, but her eyes slid sideways. "No way. They have a Confectionary here! It's misspelled. It *has* to be the same one as Fairbury."

Joel hopped out and waited for her at the hood of her car. "Yep. Same gal, same stuff, but she actually lives *here* now. So, most of the stuff for both stores is made on site here instead of in Fairbury now."

Cassie sent a longing look in that direction and then surveyed the rest of the town. A building across the street caught her eye. "Ooooh... what's that?"

"Some kind of furniture that doubles as a planter thing. We should go over there. You could grow your baby spinach in your end table or whatever." Joel tugged her arm. "C'mon. Let's look."

As much as she knew she'd regret it, Cassie couldn't help but follow with an eager step. "I didn't realize there was so much stuff here—a restaurant, a gift shop, the general store, this place—oh! Look! That's the Roth studio, isn't it? Man, if I wasn't the vintage queen, I swear I'd decorate my house in his style. Have you seen it?"

Joel's snicker could have meant anything from "You're hopeless" to "Do you think I'm an idiot?" He held open the door to the planter furniture place and urged her inside. "I've been here with Mom. What do you think?"

"Good point. Oh..."

A man stepped forward with a huge grin on his face. "Like that, do you?"

Cassie nodded and drooled over the coffee table growing an entire salad. Two kinds of lettuce, dwarf cucumbers, carrots, spinach, and radishes all in one indoor box lit up with full spectrum lights. "I just can't believe how *pretty* it is. I've seen some PVC type stuff, but nothing like *real* furniture that does this. It's so smart!"

Bookcases with towers on each side, end and couch tables, a dining table, and even a desk—the store had it all. "We're working on a way to have headboards and foot boards that have planters in them, but people aren't always careful about picking off insects, and…"

"I can see that. But, really. That's their problem." Cassie ran her fingers along an end table and sighed. "I need a catalog— one with prices." She smiled at the man and stuck out her hand. "Cassie Wren. I'll probably end up buying, but not until I save up. And I can't save up if I don't know how much I'll need."

"Derek Remmer." The man shook both their hands and waited for Joel to introduce himself.

"Oh, sorry. This is my friend, Joel. He brought me in here. I should make him pay half."

"I'll do it—just as soon as you make it through your year of green." Joel smiled at her. "You get through this thing without quitting, and I'll pay for half of anything you decide to buy— even retroactively."

Cassie whipped out her phone and tapped the voice recorder. "Say that again…"

It took less than ten minutes to get a good idea of the prices of things, be added to a mailing list, and hurry back outside with a catalog in hand. "I can't believe I didn't even *try* to finagle a bargain." She grabbed his arm and pulled. "C'mon! It's cold!"

As natural as if they did it every day, Joel grabbed her hand and ran with her. It felt good—natural—as if the awkward confession of his feelings for her hadn't happened. But as they reached the door, Cassie dropped it again. A glance at his face showed the faintest trace of disappointment, but he smiled. "Ready to buy food in bulk—like, for *real?*"

"Because Costco is fake food?"

Joel growled and led her to the dairy case first. "You know what I mean. Now look at that."

Giant gallon jars of milk sat on the bottom shelves. Butter sat on covered dishes in blocks and sticks—unwrapped. Eggs sat in baskets ready to be placed in her container and taken home again. "Wow."

A young woman stepped forward. "Hi! I'm Susannah Vega. Welcome to HearthLand. May I help you?"

She'd ordered herself not to tell her new life's story. She'd decided that it wasn't anyone's business why she wanted to buy from this place. But as she asked about flour, sugar, oil, the whole frustrating challenge tumbled out. "I heard you have meat?"

Susannah nodded, confusion in her eyes. "But it comes wrapped in butcher paper. I guess you could burn it..."

"That's it. I want one of those fire pits for my carport. I'm going to burn what I can't avoid buying. And, then I'll put some potted plants or trees or something nearby. They can convert the burned air into oxygen or whatever plants do."

Joel snickered. "I think it's a good thing you didn't go into forest science or something like that."

"I'd have learned!" Cassie turned to Susannah. Okay, so I need to make a list of everything I can get from you that I can use my own packaging for."

Soap—it had paper sleeves. Candles in mason jars were wrapped in paper sleeves as well. Homemade loaves of bread and rolls came wrapped in plastic bags. Cassie's heart sank. *How am I supposed to do this stuff if even the eco-gang has excess packaging?*

Joel's voice broke through her thoughts. "Um, if she buys say... three bars of soap, would you keep the wrappers and put them on another bar or would you throw them away?"

"Oh, no way would we toss those. Do you know how much work they put into that stuff? Those are hand stamped, hand cut, hand wrapped—every bit of that is made by hand. If you don't want the labels, we'd keep them for future batches. And..." She dashed for a laptop and returned. "If you made an

140

order before you came..." A web page showed up with a shopping list. "See? If you just pick out what you want and put 'no packaging' in the notes, it could be all ready for you when you come. You can even leave extra containers with your name on them so next time it's ready to go in your stuff." She gave Cassie a weak smile. "You did bring containers..."

"I did!" Cassie dug out her keys. "Joel, can you—"

"And this is why she brings me. It's not my brilliant conversation on the way here? Nope. Not at all. It's my—"

Cassie shoved him toward the door. "The bribery, if I recall correctly, included me buying you lunch. Go earn it!"

The moment he stepped through the door, Susannah broke out laughing. "That was great. He looked so ready to argue, but I think he believed you wouldn't actually *feed* him." She pulled up a fresh screen and set the laptop on the counter. "Why don't you make out your order here? I'll start gathering what you put in."

"Great! Thanks. And shopping from home—that's going to be great!"

Empty egg cartons—Cassie had finagled half a dozen from several people. "I could leave three here for next time?"

"Exactly. If you don't need all your other containers, leave them as well." Susannah hesitated on her way back to the cold case. "Did you already have plans for lunch?"

"We were just going to eat in Dolman."

"I recommend the restaurant. Mama Vega is doing lunch today—tacos and burritos. Best Mexican food you'll ever eat."

From the doorway, on his third trip through, Joel shouted, "Sold! I've earned it."

———

"—nothing! Joel! I can't do this. What if every week is like that? I'll be out of business!"

Joel aimed for a stop shot, took a slow, deep inhale, and shot on the exhale. "Gotcha." He turned to Cassie. "Okay, so I'll send you screen shots of Mom's paper each week."

Cassie glared at him. "Like you driving halfway across town is any better than me buying a paper. I can't believe the stupid online classifieds are incomplete! I found *nothing* today."

"Okay. So, you got to go back to bed. That's got to count for something."

Before Cassie could answer, Lauren arrived with her new boyfriend. "Hi! Sorry we're la—aaaand where are Amy and Jeremy?"

Cassie shrugged. "Not here yet. And you're interrupting my personal crisis! It's a good thing I don't want Grant to hate me before he gets to know me or I'd totally go off on you right now." Cassie grinned at Grant and stuck out her hand. "I'm Cassie, that's Joel."

"So, I can hate you *after* I get to know you?" Grant grinned and shook her hand and turned to Joel. "Nice to meet you, too." The air sucked out of the room with Grant's next words. "Lauren, I thought you said Cassie was going out with your cousin. Is this another cousin?"

Silence—awkward, miserable silence. Not for the first time, Joel questioned his sanity in talking to Cassie at all, and shook his head. "Nope. Just a friend. Haven't convinced her how great I am yet, but I'm workin' on it... "

Again, silence. *So much for that idea. Now what?*

Lauren found her voice first. "And this is why trying *not* to gossip sometimes just makes things work. Cassie went out with Evan last night, but it's their first, and for all I know, last date." Under her breath she hissed, "He was there when Evan called to run his plans by me. Sorry."

Cassie nodded and looked like she choked down half an elephant in one swallow. Grant looked ready to bolt. He had to do something and fast. "Okay, okay. We all know I think Cassie's great and she's not there yet. We're good. Sheesh. Shall we rerack 'em or wait for—" The appearance of Jeremy and Amy provided the perfect diversion. "Oh, there they are."

His heart flopped as Cassie nudged him and whispered, "Look! They're holding hands! It took them long enough."

And how pathetic is it that all I can think of is that it'll take us twice as long—if ever. But Joel cut those thoughts off before things got any worse. "Jeremy will take forever to kiss her. How much you wanna bet?"

Cassie's eyes lit up and stuck out her hand. "Deal. Ten bucks."

Without even shaking it, he pulled out his wallet and slapped ten on the pool table. "I forgot New Year's. You're good..."

She eyed the bill with a dubious expression on her face. "I'll give you a shot. You win the game; you keep it. If anyone else wins, including me, it's mine."

Joel grinned. "You are so on."

The game—never had he played with such intense concentration. Ten dollars? Who cared? Beating Cassie—priceless. But as he planned out each shot, Cassie rambled about their day. Anyone listening just to the tone of her voice, would have assumed she monopolized the conversation, but he heard it—that crazy ability she had to talk about random stuff and pull information out of other people at the same time. Grant paid half a dozen compliments to Lauren—all compliments of her carefully chosen words. Amy kissed Jeremy's cheek. Again, Cassie's doing.

"—HearthLand, this guy and his wife come in. I mean, at first I just assumed it was his daughter. He was affectionate—arm draped around her shoulder kind of thing. But then, right there in the restaurant in front of everyone, he kisses her when she jumps up to go get something. I couldn't believe it."

Joel's heart wrung in the sigh that followed. Cassie glanced his way and asked, "Have you ever seen someone so in love? It was so beautiful I forgot to be creeped out about it until halfway home! He has to be twice her age or really close to it."

"Who cares?" Lauren aimed her shot, missed, and

shrugged. "They're adults! What business is it of ours?"

He started to agree, but Cassie preempted him. "That's what I told Think. I said, 'Look. It may be unusual, but it's not like he's forty and she's fifteen.' I mean, she looked easily in her thirties."

Grant's forehead furrowed. Jeremy stared. But Lauren just nodded. "Exactly. But again, even if she was fifteen and he was forty, as long as they waited three years..."

"What's a Think? I missed something."

Joel laughed and dropped an arm around Cassie's shoulder. "Cassie has a new pet. You know 'The Thinker' she had under her coffee table?"

Jeremy nodded.

"That's him. Think. She talks about him like he's her dog or her cat. I say, it's just another part of her eco-consciousness. Pets require food that has to be packaged in stuff she's not supposed to buy. Think just needs to be dusted and he's good to go." Cassie's indignant expression prompted him to add, "Tell them about the store."

It worked. Cassie forgot about challenging him to a duel of pool cues and shifted right into the vintage store Ralph Myner had tried to talk her into. *You've got to do it, Cass. It's so you.*

Clueless in Rockland

Yep. That's me. Today was a total bust in so many ways. It started with my first weekend of sale-ing without a newspaper. For the record, it stinks. Like the dump. Or the road to Wallup. Oh, those cattle ranches are nasty. Ugh. I have to find a better way to do it. I just don't quite know how. The stupid online version of the paper doesn't have all the classifieds in it. It's like they stop at X number of pages and if what you wanted comes after that, tough toodles. I need to find a neighbor who gets the paper and will let me take photos of those pages before they read it. What are the odds?

I had a date last night. I mentioned that, right? Well, I spent a lot of today thinking about it. Dates are going to be tough things in this eco-year of mine. They're *not* eco-friendly. Let's start with the pick-up. So, this great guy drives across town to pick me up. Takes me another direction. And then drives me back before going the other direction home. Total waste of gas. Maybe I should make oil products week number 51 or 52. Otherwise, I may have to give up dates this year. And that just stinks.

There's another problem. So, let's just say we meet at a restaurant after work and it's on BOTH of our ways home. There goes one problem, right? Well, I've got another. So, the server was this really nice guy. He took our order and hardly gave me a second glance when I asked for no straw. Of course, he also FORGOT and left one on the table for me when he returned. I had to hand it back to him and pray that he wouldn't throw it away when he came back later. So that would seem to be it all, right? Everything is perfect? No. I sat there ENVYING my date's straw. Who knew you could miss a plastic tube??!! On the upside, I'd almost come to the decision that I'd have to give up all soda. And c'mon. That just stinks. My dentist has been demanding I do it for years. I've been ignoring her. Well, with the whole no plastic and the upcoming no cans, that left glass for bottles. I did research. Know what I found?

They don't sanitize bottles anymore. They should. It's CRAZY cheap. But it's all about having bottles with "a uniform feel." Customers supposedly demand it. So, I decided I can buy an occasional single bottle of soda or I can get glasses of soda at restaurants. But otherwise, it's gone.

Look, everyone I know has gone on the "Coke is evil. Down with all sodas" kick. Well, I fought it. It just felt too "trendy" to me. I thought about one of those Soda Streams, but you have to buy bottles of stuff to use in it. So, we're right back where I started. Those bottles are plastic. Can I just say, right now, if you EVER decide to do what I'm doing, start with lesser-used things like... appliances? Save paper and plastic for the end. Trust me.

But I found the coolest thing in HearthLand today—this store that sells FURNITURE that you can grow food in. How amazing is that? Not only that, but Joel says if I stick this out for a year, he'll pay for half of any piece I want. I might even let him do it.

The best part of HearthLand, though, is how accommodating they are. They didn't even look at me funny when I left my packaging on the counter. They just folded it up and put it in a box to use again. Now THAT is how you do packaging. So smart! I have cute little bars of soap on my shelf in the closet just WAITING for me to run out of liquid soap in the bathroom. I have a recipe for dish soap to try, too. I also have a fridge of the freshest food you'll ever see. I only want to go once a month, and I was afraid the eggs wouldn't make it, but if what I read online is true, they'll STILL be fresher than stuff from the store. How gross is that?

Look, I really had fun today. I bought things in bulk with no or packaging. The food is fresh and hormone-free. I have vegetables that like they should. Tomatoes in January that are deep, vivid red. I ate one an apple. It was SO GOOD.

But, there's a down side to all this. I feel like a slave to the earth right now. Everything I do is about best for the earth. What about the person impact? Why don't people count, too?

Sunday, January 17—

"I'm in love with Grant."

Cassie stared at the phone, tapped the screen a couple of times, and stared again.

"Cassie?"

"I'm sorry. I think my phone is cutting out. You won't believe what I just heard you say."

"Not funny, Cassie."

Her eyes darted toward Think but it wasn't the time. "No, really. It sounded like you said—"

"I'm in love with Grant. I did, and I don't appreciate your attitude."

This time she heard it—raw pain in Lauren's voice. *Oh, help, Lord. She thinks she means it. Now what do I do? Will she get her heart broken if she just rides it along and figures it out or…?*

"Cassie!"

"Sorry." She swallowed hard and tried again. "I guess I'm just surprised. It's not what I expected, okay? I want to ask how you know, but I don't want to sound like I doubt you. I've just never been in love."

Laughter pierced her ear and rang through her head. "Ha! You've been in love more than all of us combined."

The words stung. She tried to smooth the tremors in her voice as she tried again to respond. "I meant *real* love.

146

Obviously, I've been infatuated a few times..."

"A few *dozen*. And now you're keeping every good guy at arm's length to try to rebrand yourself."

Cassie tossed Think a "Can you believe she said that?" look and cleared her throat. "Rebrand myself as *what* exactly?"

"Just... *not* the easily-infatuated teenager you used to be."

"I wasn't easily infatuated! I had a soft spot for underdogs. Tell me one guy that I fell for before he fell for me. One."

Silence pressed in on the conversation until it felt like they'd both implode. Lauren spoke first. "Okay... you've got a point. How did I not notice that before? I could have saved you and a couple dozen guys from heartache."

"Yeah, well..." Cassie swallowed back a lump of pain that tried to escape from her heart and strangle her. "Anyway. You've gone out with Grant twice? I'm not trying to dump on your hearts and flowers, but you aren't the impulsive type. How do you know?"

"Actually, we went out to lunch today after church. Four times now, but it's not that. It's the notes, the phone conversations until two in the morning, the way he looks at me." Cassie heard her swallow and sigh. "You know how I said I thought he was falling in love with me?"

"Yeah..."

"Today at lunch he asked me if I've ever been in love. I had just realized how much I really like him and I almost said, 'Not yet, but I'm almost there.'" Lauren wailed. "This isn't *me!* Forgive me, Cass, but this is your territory. What do I do?"

Of every thought that flitted through her mind, only *one* wasn't what not to do. "Look. I can't answer that. Not really. What I can tell you is to take your time in telling him. If you're wrong. If he's not falling hard—"

"Cassie?"

Her heart sank. *Don't do it. Don't get your heart broken. You're too sweet for that.* But she had to answer something. "Yeah?"

"When he asked if I'd ever been in love, I told him I didn't think so. I mean, it's true—or it was at the time. I wasn't sure still. You know what he said?"

Why do I suddenly feel like Mr. Bennett? "You want to tell me and I have no objection to hearing it." I hate that book! How do I even remember that?

"Cassie?"

"Sorry. Something distracted me. So, what did he say?"

The faintest wisp of a sigh whispered a hint just before Lauren answered. "He said, 'I thought I had been—once. You're teaching me that I wasn't. Not really.' Then he said, 'I wasn't going to say anything for weeks—even months. I didn't want to scare you off, but I feel like I'm being disingenuous.'" Lauren sighed again. "Cassie, who even says that? Disingenuous?"

"You do. That sounds just like you—and the guy for you. So, that was it?" Cassie felt as though she could *hear* Lauren shaking her head. Then it hit her. *Your earrings are hitting the phone.*

"He said, 'But I've never felt like this about anyone before. It has to be love, but how can it be?'"

"Okay... make me swoon. Go ahead. Next I'll be reading from the romance section of the Christian bookstore just to feed the pitter-pattering of my—"

"Oh, stop!" Lauren's giggle belied the irritation in her tone. "You're terrible. But yeah. It was crazy romantic. The way he looked at me, and oh man. Did you see his Adam's apple? He's got this adorable—"

Rude or not, Cassie couldn't help but interrupt. "I don't believe it. Practical Lauren is swooning over a guy's throat. Oh, you are... something. If it's not in love then I don't know what it is. Smitten? Do people say that anymore? Whatever it is, you're it."

"I know! You know what else he said? You're either going to love this or hate it."

Warning bells danced in Cassie's ears. "Um... okay..."

"He wants to talk to a minister—about us. He wants guidance because he feels that since we're both experiencing uncharacteristically intense feelings so early..."

"But you didn't tell—oh." She swallowed hard. "You did."

Another explanation followed—long, detailed, beautiful. Cassie's throat ached just hearing how Lauren had been praying over a guy who had already captured her heart. "I agreed to go. Am I nuts?"

"Will he talk to anyone? Does it have to be *his* minister?"

Once more, silence answered her question. But Lauren spoke first—just as Cassie had started to press her for more information. "Sorry. I zipped him a text to ask. And he said as long as it's a married minister with a wife who will join us and will use the Bible as the basis of everything we discuss, he's all for it."

"Does he have a brother? Cousin? Best friend who is so like him people *think* they're brothers?"

"You'll break Evan's heart with talk like that." Lauren cleared her throat. "So, would you go—if you were me?"

Who wouldn't? This guy sounds perfect. And he was great last night—obviously... smitten with you... "Lauren, if you don't, I'm going to try to get you an intervention. I think it's brilliant. Remember when Amy first met Ryan Grossman? They thought they were crazy in love. Now her one dating regret is him because she let her emotions take her to places she'd always sworn she wouldn't go until she got married. If they'd had—"

"I'm not going to *sleep* with him!"

"Yeah, and Amy would have said the same thing, right? I mean she's the one of all of us who was so adamant about keeping her virginity. And who fell first? Talking about this stuff—having that kind of accountability when the attraction is already so strong... sounds smart to me!"

As had become the rhythm of the conversation, Cassie waited for Lauren to process the idea and respond. It took longer than ever. "I always wondered if Amy didn't put her confidence in her decision rather than in the Lord. If she'd kept her eyes on *Jesus* instead of on her determination to remain pure, she might not have those regrets today."

"That's a good point. And it backs up my present decision."

"What's that?"

Cassie swallowed the rising panic in her and took a deep, cleansing breath. "I'm not letting myself go there with Evan—if it even 'goes there' so to speak. I'm just not doing it. It'll be harder to get swept up in emotions if I'm not holding some guy's hand and kissing him goodnight."

"From what I heard, you were already holding hands..."

Great. He kisses and tells. Or touches—ew. That doesn't work. Anyway, he's a teller.

"And before you think he just rushed home and spilled every bit of the date, I had to drag it out of him. It was lie or say it." Lauren giggled again. "He was so cute. He likes you. He's not falling for you like Grant is for me, so take a deep breath and stop panicking."

"You know me too well. Anyway, I've always thought it was natural to be at least modestly affectionate with a guy you're dating, but then someone gets hurt. So, I'm not doing that this time." A though sent her mind spinning, and Cassie panicked. "*Don't* tell Evan it's not normal. I don't want him to think it's because I like him more than I do—or less. I just want to focus on building a friendship and seeing where it goes instead of all the other stuff that just leads to regret when it doesn't work out."

Lauren promised to keep Cassie's past relationships out of conversations with her cousin. "I would have anyway. So, you haven't talked about week three here. So... what are you doing again? Glass? Isn't it? I saw that puny picture. Kind of anticlimactic, isn't it?"

"Right? I scoured this house. Kept trying to put *containers* up there, but that would totally skew results, because Mom bought me all those containers with the plastic lids on Black Friday. And I didn't do pictures of all my plastic containers."

The statement sent her reeling as it did *every* time she considered it. What Lauren said, she never heard. Instead, Cassie interrupted her. "Lauren?"

"I knew you weren't listening. What's wrong, now?"

"My vintage Tupperware collection. I don't have to give that up, right? I mean, it was made decades ago, and because of it, I don't have to buy stuff now. Or, should I get rid of it to be consistent? I mean, I could sell it on eBay. I'd make a fortune. But..."

Lauren's answer came almost the second she stopped speaking. "Keep it. Really. You get a lot of pleasure out of that stuff, and it's the *one* thing you've always done that's green. I don't think you've ever bought a plastic Rubbermaid or new Tupperware container—ever."

"Mom did—the batter bowl, remember?" A decision formed as she pondered it. "And I'm not giving that up either. I used it to make cookies this afternoon."

"Wait, *you* made cookies? What about Oreos?"

The rant began. Cassie made it about five sentences in before Lauren stopped her. "Don't. Go write it. Now. While you still feel it. Those are your best posts. I swear, I was rolling at the one about of you in the gas station. Now write. And thanks for not making fun of me for being crazy silly about Grant."

The phone went dead. Cassie stared at Think for a moment and then grabbed her laptop. "My best friend is in love. Why do I feel like a mom who just found out her only daughter is getting married or something? Eeep! I have *got* to warn my mom in plenty of time. She'll be crazy."

Hidden Ecological Dangers

I'm sure you're sick of hearing it by now. But I just have to point a few things out. Number one. Canned food. Why am I asking about that on glass week? I'm not to metal yet! We should be sitting pretty, right? Yeah. That's what I thought. Until I went to make my eggplant Parmesan tonight. That's right. I cooked. I'll sit and wait while everyone picks their jaws up off the floor. Okay... get ready. And it was delicious. I'll wait again...

But let me tell you what had MY jaw on the floor. That's right. ME. The can of tomato sauce? Yeah. Plastic inside. That's right. I opened it up, enjoying each blissful moment of knowing that I didn't have to make my own from scratch-scratch. You know... like smashing up tomatoes from the produce department to do it! That's right. I was all set. And then I got lulled into a false sense of security.

Confession: I had planned to buy a case of the stuff this week—to tide me over until the end of the year. I thought it would be easy enough. It may be cheating, but I was going to do it. Of course, now that I'm thinking about it, I realize that the stupid cans are covered in paper, too. You know, that stuff I am supposed to be good at spotting and avoiding now. Ooops!

The other thing I did today was make cookies. Not buy. Make. You see, I decided I wanted cookies in my lunch after the crazy lady at the sandwich shop refused to use her little tongs and hand me the cookie without a paper wrapper or a napkin. She REFUSED. So, I can't even buy favorite macadamia nut white chocolate chip cookie anymore—you know, with the dried cherries that are SO GOOD. So, I went to the store. I was going to buy my favorite store cookies. Oreos. You know how I love Oreos. And if you don't, you do now. Just sayin', if love were a cookie, it would be an Oreo. Sweet gooshiness squeezed between two strong arms—or discs. Same smell.

But Oreos come in plastic. Double plastic. I went for Milanos. They come in paper and metal. Every stinkin' thing—whether boxed, bagged, or plastic-wrapped comes in something I can't have! There are NO cookies that come in glass jars. I should have stocked up on those Christmas tins of butter cookies. At least those things are useful for storage or something. I feel like I've been put on the world's cruelest diet. If I die, I'm gonna give St. Peter what for.

As usual, when I went to get the ingredients, I reached for a box of parchment paper—for the cookie sheet, you know? So, they don't stick? I do that every time. I bet I have five hundred—okay. No. I can't. Why can't I? Because we ALL know I've never made five hundred batches of cookies. But I bet I had ten before I purged half. And I would have added another box today if it weren't for the fact that I'm not allowed.

So, my question is: What did people do before they could buy parchment paper How do you keep the cookies from sticking? Grease? Like Crisco or something? Maybe? I don't know. Seems like the probable reason a lot of people's cookie sheets look awful. All that grease. Ugh.

So all of this to say, people who claim that life is EASIER when you don't have all that "excess stuff" are full of their own toilet filler. It's hard work. I mean, I've kind of gotten into a groove, okay? Like today at the store. I went to grab "my" brand of spaghetti sauce and had to change to a different one because mine comes in plastic. And it was so automatic now. And really, as long as I can find glass alternatives, I'll be good.

I pack my food for work now because most of the places close by don't serve without disposable stuff. And while I would like to make allowances for things like work meals, I know I'll justify it for EVERYTHING if I do anything. So, If I can't eat out, I have to take food. If I have to take food, it has to be in appropriate containers. And it becomes this endless cycle.

And don't let anyone fool you. Most "eco-friendly" things are more expensive. I have to look for alternatives where I can, and I do without a lot. I'll be honest. Most of what I do without I don't miss. I miss Oreos. My birthday is in April. I thought I wanted paper towels. But if I have to choose between those and Oreos... well... not even a contest. Gimme the cookies. Oh, and if one person dares to mention Girl Scout Cookies to me, I think I'll end up in jail. So, I won't be going to any stores in whatever month those are. February? Good. No shopping in February. I'll save enough right there to buy me a fire pit to burn my trash.

Did anyone EVER think that Cassie Wren would be open to the charge of being "crunchy?" Me EITHER.

She pushed publish, winked at Think, and slid the laptop under the couch. "Goodnight, Think. Try to get some sleep. You look like you have the weight of the world on your shoulders. Just remember. You're Think—not Atlas."

Monday, January 18—

<u>Mondays Are Evil</u>

That is all.

Cassie gave Think the stink eye. "I am not doing it. I don't need to humiliate myself further."

For half a second, Cassie would have sworn that Think's head dropped further.

"I disagree. I think personal humiliation trumps empathy."

When her "roommate" refused to nod in agreement, Cassie tossed her scarf over his head. She hit publish and jumped up to make a cup of coffee. A new book—one brought home from the church library, no less—beckoned to her. "That's perfect! I'll read and drink my coffee and forget about the day from places that shall not be named."

But she hadn't made it more than a page or two before Think's relentless stare worked its magic. "Fine! Whatever. You—"

A comment sent her temper flaring.

HermionesTwin: Um, this is like the blog equivalent of Vaguebook. Seriously. Either post a post or don't. This is just annoying, Cass.

As much as she hated to admit it, the commenter had a point. "Who do you think Hermione is, anyway? I haven't figured it out yet."

Think shrugged.

"Too bad you *aren't* Atlas. You'd be the perfect personification of that stupid book my Uncle Greg tried to get me to read. You know, the one that is like six inches thick and all about how being selfish is a virtue or something like that."

But with that thought in mind, she returned to writing.

Edited to add:

My new roommate complained that I can't just drop a statement like that. Me, I was going for discretion and brevity. After all, there are articles all over the Internet about how people share too much on social media and blogs. Be concise, they say. Well, I did. But yeah, I have to agree with Hermione up there. It probably opened up more questions than it answered. It's true, okay? Totally true. It's enough right there. I would have said, "Monday's suck" but then my mom would have posted and embarrassed me, so in case anyone just thinks I'm being lazy or whatever, um not really. Just self-preservation and the pathetic attempt to be discreet in the midst of my indiscretion.

So why are Mondays evil? Could it be because I dropped an entire quart of delicious, whole, hormone-free milk all over my floor? It went the way of the Worcestershire sauce. Major mess without paper towels. Need I say more? Right. I don't.

But wait! There's more! I knocked my jar of salad to the floor in the cafeteria at work today. The maintenance guy said, "We'd prefer it if you didn't bring glass. It's a safety hazard."

Yeah. So now, my attempts at being eco-friendly are a safety issue for others. That didn't surprise me. Not really. I always thought it would be. But I thought it would be because I throttled someone who tried to take my last remaining paper towel or something.

So, if you see me at work with Tupperware, just know that it is vintage, purchased used, and used at work under duress. It is more eco-friendly than buying plastic containers from the store but LESS than just bringing the jar, because now I have to use twice the water—one for the jar that I have to dump in the plastic container, and once for said container. Just sayin'.

And, if you read right now, you'll get the bonus misery! That's right, for only 65.32 seconds, you'll get to hear about how I had the cops called on me today. That's right. I bought a bottle of root beer at a convenience store. I wanted carbonation, and they had that fabulous root beer that tastes like the nectar of the gods. I downed that thing in like half a dozen gulps. I should have savored it. First, it would have lasted longer and the temptation to buy another one would have been a moot point. Second, I would have been down the road before disaster could possibly strike. Well, it struck.

So, I was going to toss it into the trashcan by the front door, but there's this pillar there? Yeah. Depth perception issues or something. Don't know what to tell you. I tossed, it hit the pillar. It broke. Perfectly in half, no less. The thing was just lying on the ground looking all weird.

And this is where it got complicated. So, I picked up the pieces and dropped one into the can, but the woman at the register was looking at me. So, I waved the top half over my head to show that I was cleaning up my mess.

It's winter. It's cold. The door was shut. I said, "I've got it!"

Apparently, she thought I said, "I got him."

If you ever need a cop, call from a convenience store. I swear, they m
have been sitting around the corner, waiting. Watching.

I made it to my car, got in, put my wallet away—the works. I started
engine, flipped on my lights (yeah, I drive an old car that doesn't do that
you. I'm smart. I can pull a switch. Woot for me), and put the car in g
Spotlight blinded me right then. Three cops had guns on me.

No. Joke.

The one with the radio told me to get out of the car—both hands first. I
have to take a moment here and ask, "Who thought of that???" Seriou
Do you have any idea how hard it is to get out of a car without falling on y
face? If I listened to my dad and didn't drive with my steering wheel in
chest, it would probably have been easier. But I like the security of that th
close. I would have shifted the seat back, but that means I have to put
hands under the seat to move it. I can't do that without getting my he
blown off. So, instead, I ended up stumbling forward.

Guess what they thought THEN? Yep. One breathalizer test and finge
nose walking, balance test later, they decided it was the ROOT beer th
claimed it was.

Then they asked who I hurt.

Since I can't be any more humiliated than I am right now, I'll just confess
burst into tears. I was so tired, so hungry, so confused, and couldn't s
burping every other minute because of inhaling so much carbonation in su
a short time. They gave me another breathalizer.

Finally, one cop grew a brain. It was a woman. Just sayin'. She managed
translate my blubbering into semi-comprehensible English or somethi
because she went to the trashcan. Pulled out the bottle halves. Read
label. Told me I could go. With a warning.

Yes, a cop let me off an assault and disorderly or whatever you call it wit
warning. "Don't drink root beer that fast again. And next time you brea
bottle, throw it away without making a big deal out of it."

I didn't even try to explain. Some things defy explanation.

So... like I said.

Mondays are evil.

Goodnight.

Cassie snapped the laptop shut and stared at Think, tears welling in her eyes. "I wish you were plush."

Another thought occurred to her and she zipped a message to Lauren. CHANGED MY MIND. AS MUCH AS I WANT

156

THIN MINTS FOR MY BIRTHDAY, I WANT A STUFFED "THINKER" MORE. IT WOULD BE NICE TO BE ABLE TO CUDDLE WITH MY PET.

Tuesday, January 19—

Beverly Morrison shivered at Cassie's back door, a bundle in her arms. How long she'd been there, Cassie could only wonder. So, as her car dieseled for a moment before coming to a shuddering stop, Cassie zipped a few prayers heavenward and snatched her purse from the passenger seat. Cold air bit through her pants and send shivers up and down her spine.

I'd rather get that from looking at a cute guy who acts like I'm the greatest thing since... whatever the latest, greatest thing is this week. Getting it from arctic wind that got lost on its way to a polar cap—not so fun.

"Mrs. Morrison? What are you doing out here?"

"Just doing my daily fanny freeze. It's how I eat a dozen cookies and keep my girlish figure."

Cassie choked on her laughter in a desperate attempt to *hide* her amusement. Instead, she stammered something about needing water and bolted into the duplex in a weak attempt to mask her embarrassment. She downed half a glass of water, dumped her purse on the counter—in that order, no less—and turned to her neighbor with an apologetic smile. "Sorry."

"I'm not. And for the record, this..." Her hands waved up and down over her body as if trying to sell it in a showroom. "This is *half* what it was as a girl. I might not be skinny, but I'm not nearly as big as I was when the mean girls called me 'Beverly Lardley.'"

She blinked. "Wait. They had 'mean girls' back then? I thought the 'good old days' were all about peace, and joy, and rose-smelling farts or something."

"Well, that's what you get for throwing that word 'old' in

there. By associating me with it, you've called me old, and that'll get you in trouble every time." At the jaw to floor connection Cassie couldn't quite prevent, Mrs. Morrison winked. "Gotcha." She shoved the parcel in Cassie's hands and said, "I got you something. My sister in Topeka makes all these amazing things out of stuff that would otherwise go in the landfill—tote bags, scrubbers for dishes—everything you can imagine. So, I told her I wanted a sample of everything. If you don't like them, throw it away give it to someone—whatever. If you want more, I've got her email, and you know how to use it."

"Wow! That is so cool of you! Thanks!" Without even looking at the parcel, Cassie dumped it on the island and threw her arms around the older woman. "Thank you so much!"

"You're welcome. I know how hard you're trying, and I thought it might make things easier." She gave Cassie a stern look. "Now don't tell her I know how to use the computer, or I'll never hear her voice again. I'm warning you. If you use my name and computer in the same sentence, you *will* live to regret it— just before you disappear into Lake Danube with concrete shoes."

Cassie pointed to the container on the counter that held her cookie masterpieces. "You should take home a few cookies. I baked, and they're good."

A grin burst over her face as she snipped the tape and unfolded the brown paper wrapping. Inside, printed on the paper was a logo for a Topeka grocer. "Look! She recycled the grocery bag. That's so cool."

"It still jars to hear you say things like that. The Cassie I know would have said, 'She should ship everything USPS Priority. They give brand new boxes for every shipment. It's perfect!'"

"Well, is it awful to admit that it was my first thought? But the other one came right on the heels of it, so I thought that was pretty cool."

Mrs. Morrison waved her cookie. "This is one of the best

cookies I've had in a long time. May I take one to Thomas?"

The words sounded normal enough, but coming out of Beverly Morrison, something was off. "Really?"

"Thomas doesn't think you'll stick to your commitment. When he hears you *made* cookies instead of buying them..."

"He reads my blog, Mrs. M. I got a comment from him the other day when I made them. I was complaining that the woman at the store wouldn't give me one without paper, and that's just not what I signed up for, so I made my own. He said, 'Take the napkin the first time. Then offer it back to her every other time. You'll just have to save it, but you can do that.'"

Mrs. Morrison waved the cookie over her head as she shuffled to the door. "Don't listen to him. Make your own. There's no way that cookie you wanted to buy was anywhere near this good."

Cassie, for the second time in as many weeks, squeezed the woman in a bear hug and thanked her for the encouragement. "I can't tell you how much it means to me."

"Well, I think you're nuts. We *had* to do all this stuff in the thirties and forties. In the fifties, we started getting more convenience stuff, but a lot of it was more complicated than it was worth. But now it's all so easy. I can't imagine why you'd *want* to go back to the old ways. I'm grateful they're gone."

"And I will be too—in three hundred forty-six days. Until then, I want to prove I *can* do it—even if just to myself."

The call came just as Cassie dried her hands after washing her dishes—hence the wet hands. She ordered Siri to answer it. Her mother's voice burst through the airwaves and ripped a hole in her heart. "They just took Dad to the hospital. Heart attack, I think. I'm on my way there now, but—"

"Coming!" She didn't even say goodbye. Cassie snatched up the phone, grabbed her coat and purse, and dashed out the door. Her heart slammed against her ribcage, with rhythmic force that threatened an attack of her own. Hands shaking, she tried to insert the key into the ignition, but it refused to go. She stopped, prayed, and tried again. Fail.

"C'mooooon… I need to go!"

Her phone rang just as she slammed her fist against the steering wheel and fumbled once more. "Evan! Go away. I need—" That thought sent her into overdrive. "Okay, Siri, call Joel." Even as she spoke, her fingers shook, trying to wedge the key into the ignition. "Just work. Pleaaaase!"

"What'd I do?"

"Joel! I can't make my key fit into the ignition! Dad's on the way to the hospital—heart attack—and I can't make my stupid car go! The key. Won't." She growled as she tried to wedge it in again. "Fit!"

"Cassie?"

Something in his tone turned her screams of frustration into tears of fear. "Joel!"

"Shhh… listen to me. Take a deep breath."

"I can't! My *da*—"

"Your dad. I know. I'm on my way. But you have to get there, too. So, this is what you're going to do. Turn on the dome light."

The words made no sense, but Cassie punched the button overhead. "Okay… now what?"

"Take your keys and look at them."

Frustration welled up in her once more, but Cassie jerked the keys into her palm and stared. "Wait—these are to my storage…"

"That's what I figured. Get your *car* keys and try again."

A wave of nausea washed through her, tumbling her thoughts over and over until she felt ready to lose her dinner. "They're on the table. I didn't hang them up when I got home, because Bev—"

"So, go get them."

"My house key—"

Joel interrupted once more. "Is with them, yes. But Mrs. Morrison—"

"Has a spare! Thanks! See you there. Can you tell Lauren to pray?" Cassie didn't even wait for an answer. She dashed from the car and raced across the road. Spare key in hand, she dashed back, burst into her kitchen, and snatched the keys from her table. Her heart said she didn't have time to return the spare key. Her mind insisted she didn't have time *not* to. *If I'd done that last time, it would be inside, and then what would I do?*

Responsibility won out over her heart, but inside twenty minutes, she burst through the emergency room doors and began the frantic search for her mother. Joel met her outside the double doors that led to the cubicles where her father likely laid half-dead on a table masquerading as a bed. "Where—"

"They took him back. Your mom said to text her when you get here. If there's anything to tell you, she'll come out. Otherwise, she'll just zip a text back."

"Why wouldn't—" Cassie found the nearest chair and sank into it. "She expects it to be bad, doesn't she?"

The pained look in Joel's eyes answered without him needing to speak. He just took her hand, held it, and sat there. Only when the overwhelming desire to bean him with her purse made her look at him closer did Cassie get it.

He's praying. Lord, I wanted to kill him for just playing boyfriend or something, but instead, he's over there praying. Like I should have been.

Her phone buzzed—a text from Lauren asking her for an update when there was one. I SENT THIS TO THE PRAYERBOOK. JOEL'S REALLY WORRIED. HE IS COMING TO YOU.

A sidelong glance showed him deep—*lost*—in prayer. Cassie started to reply, but a text came through from her mother. HOOKED UP TO AN EKG. BE OUT AS SOON AS WE KNOW SOMETHING.

Cassie zipped back a reply, assuring her mother that all would be well. DAD'S STRONG. LAUREN PUT IT ON THE

PRAYERBOOK.

And the wait began. First, she paced. Then she took a brisk walk around the outside of the building. She paced again. Joel tried to get her to relax, but Cassie couldn't do it. Every few minutes he'd find her and show her yet another prayer or comment on the church's Facebook prayer page. Some promised to pray. Others typed out their prayers—sometimes several in a row.

When he brought one from the sweetest old man in the church—ninety-eight if he was a day—Cassie burst into tears. "Why can't *I* pray? Why is this so hard for me?"

"We're praying *for* you. Let us love you this way. It's what the church does." Joel tried to lead her back to the chairs near the double doors, but Cassie wrested herself away from him. "I can't sit. I'm going crazy."

And time ticked past again. One long minute after another. Five. Ten. Thirty. An hour. Two. Still Joel sat and prayed. Still Cassie paced. Still no word from her mother. The prayers continued, dwindling in number but not in frequency. Cassie read every single one. Some several times. She couldn't respond, couldn't pray herself, but her thumb should have grown arthritic with the number of times it hit "like."

Joel found a mini-mart that carried glass bottles of iced tea and brought her three. He added a banana and orange to the mix. "Sorry. Couldn't find a cookie that wasn't pre-wrapped. And everything else came wrapped in paper, plastic, or both."

At that point, Cassie wrapped her arms around him and wept. "It's taking too long. He's going to die, isn't he?" Her eyes widened. "Unless you think he—"

"Shh... that's crazy talk. If he were that bad, I don't think they'd let her back there."

Still the tears flowed as Cassie tried to cling to Joel's words. He shook her a moment later. "Cassie—"

"Oh, don't. I just—"

"Your—"

A familiar voice filled her ears. "Cassandra Marie Wren. What are you bawling about?"

She whirled in place, staring at her father as he stood there grinning with a sheepish expression on his face. "Dad?"

"Indigestion."

How she managed not to bean him with her purse has been submitted to *Ripley's Believe It or Not.* "I can't believe—"

But Joel's voice near her ear stopped her. "He's embarrassed enough already. Wait a few days, Cass."

"They gave him some great medication to kill it and told him to follow up with Dr. Hellman." Marla gave Cassie a hug before turning to Joel. "Thank you both—for everything. I need to get him home and in bed. Then I need to go explain to the world that heart attacks and indigestion can look a lot alike. The good news?"

Cassie's eyes flitted back and forth between her parents. "Yeah?"

"Your father, aside from not handling coffee after a dinner of chili and jalapeno cornbread, has a nice, strong heart."

Perhaps it was overkill—she didn't discount the possibility—but Cassie held her father a little tighter and longer than usual before kissing his cheek and shoving him off. "Go home, Peter."

"Peter?" Adrian Wren stared at his daughter for a moment. "I don't get it."

A slow smile crept over her face. "Isn't that the name of the boy who cried wolf?"

⟁ ⟁ ⟁

Exhaustion and adrenaline warred within her as Cassie tossed and turned in bed. She'd opted *not* to write her blog post in favor of more than five hours of sleep, but when forty minutes passed and she still wasn't any closer to slumber, Cassie dragged herself out of bed, retrieved the laptop, and snuggled back under the covers.

By screen light, she tried to write an account of a day full of successes and failures in her quest to avoid adding to the planet's overloaded landfills. After three tries, she scrapped yet another jumble of nonsensical words. Perhaps writing from the heart...

<u>Wake-Up Call</u>

We all get them. Sometimes it's a shock when we step on the scale and see ten pounds more than we thought we weighed. Other times, it's our bank balance or a note from a friend who has found peace and happiness telling inner city kids about Jesus. Whatever causes them, we all need them now and then.

I got mine tonight—and it was a literal call. From my mom. "They just took Dad to the hospital."

The good news? It wasn't a heart attack. Indigestion is real, but I don't think it's life threatening. And please, if I'm wrong, let me be in ignorance right now. That little tidbit of truth isn't something I'm ready to handle. If indigestion is lethal, then tell me in a month or a year. Just not today, okay?

So, is that my wakeup call? Take care of my heart while it's still healthy?

Nope.

No, my wakeup call is that we get so caught up in things like my quest for greenness that we miss the important stuff—like calling our parents and inviting them out to dinner, or bringing dinner *to* them. I remember when I got my first cellphone. I called my dad every day. Without fail. If he didn't answer, I left a voice message and tried again later.

I don't do that anymore. Nowadays, I call when I need something or on his birthday. Oh! And I called when he got that promotion. Yeah.

Look, before anyone says, "You're just saying that because you were at the hospital for hours so you probably drank water from plastic cups or bottles or something." Well, I didn't. Nope. I drank tea from glass bottles that my friend brought me. Why? Because he likes to support me. Would I have chosen plastic bottles if I had to? Yeah. If staying perfectly green meant I had to leave the hospital when my father could be dying from a heart attack, I would choose plastic without blinking an eye. Dad comes first.

My competitive side says, "Just keep going. You can do this. You're under three hundred fifty days now!" And that side of me is right. I can and will keep going. But here I am, unable to sleep, still dealing with the fallout of a long night in an ER worried sick about my dad. And I have one thing to say.

Everyone loves someone. I don't care who you are; you love someone. They may be dead even, but you still love them. It may be a dog, a snake, or a secret. You may only have one friend or a cousin. You may have a huge extended family and a list of friends a mile long. Doesn't matter. Everyone loves someone. Tonight taught me that you can't take that for granted.

Tell that someone—even if they're in heaven or you don't know where they are. Tell them. I'll be calling more now. I'll be saying, "I love you" more. And after seeing a wall full of prayers for my father, I'll be saying thank you a lot more, too. I can't imagine ever regretting that.

But tonight, I almost regretted not saying it—*showing it*—enough to my father. I never want to let that happen again.

So, goodnight. Joel and Lauren? Thank you. I love you. Westside Assembly? I love you guys, too. Thank you for praying.

Cassie closed the laptop, and as she did, her eyes drooped lower and lower as well. She snuggled back under the blankets, and finally the prayers she had ached to pray while at the hospital filled her heart and overflowed her lips. When she shifted from prayerfulness to sleep, she didn't know. But somewhere in the depths of sub-consciousness, the Lord wove her pleas into a mantle of comfort around her heart.

Wednesday, January 20—

"Took you long enough."

Cassie rolled her eyes and stared at the salad that she suddenly despised. She shifted her attention to the phone in her hand and tried again. "It's my lunch break. Aren't you eating now? I didn't want to interrupt you while you were working."

"I'm in my recliner." Adrian Wren's voice dropped. "You've got to save me. Your mother is hovering. I'm now married to a helicopter wife."

Her giggles sent a few curious glances her way, but Cassie didn't care. "I'll ask her to help me find a new-to-me dress for my date."

"Oooh... she has a date? With Joel or Evan?"

Irritation welled up in her but Cassie stamped it back down again and tried to remember that she'd still been terrified of losing him about twelve hours earlier. "If I ever date Joel, you'll be the first to know. But I'm telling you now. It ain't happenin'. Period. Exclamation point."

"Every time you say that, you end up doing it. Might want to rethink your trademarked emphatic denial."

He had a point—a big one. "Fine. I regret to inform you that I see no reason to ever date Joel, despite the great guy he is, but if I do, I'll let you know about it first. Okay?"

"Deal. So, where's Evan taking you?"

She swallowed hard and tried not to sound as pathetic as she felt. "Don't know. Haven't asked him to take me out yet. I'll let you know that, too. Love you. Take care. Sneak out for a walk when she's not looking. Bye!"

"Wait! Cassandra!"

Oh, great. Nothing good happens when he calls me by my full name. At least he didn't say "Marie." She tried to steady herself before speaking. "Yeah?"

"I just want to ask one question."

Do I even bother pretending I don't know what it is? Or does he want to ask more than I want the question over? Cassie sighed. "Yeah?"

"Why won't you date Joel? Of all the young men you've ever brought around, he's been my favorite and you're not even interested."

"That's why. I'm not interested. I just think he is such a great guy that he should have someone who feels about him the way he feels about her."

"But you might... if you focused on a relationship. Relationships take work, Cassie-rie. Maybe if... "

She gave him a couple of seconds to finish, but when he didn't, Cassie decided to end it all before it became too much of a dream of his. "Dad... and what happens if I don't? Okay? Then he's hurt, I've lost a great friend, and for what? Trying to make something happen between us because I feel bad for him."

"True..." Adrian blinked three times and shrugged. Cassie didn't need to be in the room to see it. Eyes closed, she "watched" him in her mind's eye, a smile spreading across her lips. But his next words ripped the breath from her. "Sometimes, I wish arranged marriages were still in style. I'd set one up with his parents and sit back and gloat when you guys had the best marriage of everyone in your little circle of friends."

She choked back a groan and tried a different tactic. "Or, you'd meet Evan or one of a million other guys, and wonder if you made the right decision for my life." Before he led the conversation into another rabbit trail, Cassie reminded him that she had a date to set up to save him from Marla overload. "Love you, Dad."

"Love you too, little girlie."

Of course, getting *off the phone* only meant a more difficult task. Her eyes bored into the screen, but her thumb refused to tap Evan's name. Instead, it slid up the screen and landed on Lauren. "Help."

"If my boss says one word..."

"Sorry! I need to ask Evan out. Is he going to be totally ticked off that I'm not only asking him out but I'm totally using it as a way to manipulate my mom?"

Dead air. Cassie nearly disconnected and tried again. Eventually, Lauren coughed. "And why would you tell him this?"

"Dad wants Mom to stop hovering. I said I'd get her to take me out shopping for something to wear—"

"Got it. Okay. How about this? Let me get Evan to call you."

Protest welled up in her heart. She ached to say no, but if she'd heard it once, she'd heard it a few hundred thousand

167

times. Beggars can't be choosers. Instead, she sighed and agreed. "I so owe you. And I'm warning you. I'll probably confess."

"I know. That's what makes you, you. Gotta go."

She waited until the very last second before any hope of arriving in the office on time had dissolved. Her phone sat open on her desk. Waiting. Watching. It didn't ring. Two o'clock. Three. Four. Mr. Sylmer called her in to confer about an important client the next day. He sent her down to pick up something from a courier. He left early for a business dinner. Still she waited. Worked. Wondered.

He's probably one of those guys who doesn't do stuff during a workday. Or Lauren couldn't call until now... or soon. Maybe when I get home.

"It's driving me crazy! Does this mean he doesn't *want* to ask me out again? Is Lauren over there scrambling, trying to figure out what to do—how to tell me that her cousin isn't interested? Aaak! Think! What do I do?"

As her little friend pondered the tougher questions of life—love, friendship, and a cure for indigestion—Cassie glared at the grilled cheese sandwich and tomato soup she'd made for herself. "Oh, and don't ever let me forget to turn on the crockpot again. That's just sick. A cow died so I could throw part of his butt in the trash. What kind of jerk *am* I?"

Three bites into her sandwich, the doorbell rang. Cassie growled and bolted for the door, hoping she'd manage to get back before it became a semi-re-congealed mess on her plate. Before her soup turned into a bowl of lukewarm catsup instead of the delicious, steaming bowl of deliciousness she'd finally reconciled herself to. Before discouragement and despair became evident.

Bet it's Mr. Chao. It's gotta be. But as she flung open the door and a large bouquet of mixed flowers filled the space between her and whoever hid behind them, Cassie rethought that idea. *Dad?*

"Cassie? Can I come in? Kind of cold out here..."

"Evan!" She jumped back and waved him inside. "Sorry. Couldn't see you there behind—are those for me?" Inwardly she groaned. *Dumb question. Totally dumb. He's going to think you're an idiot.*

"Well, unless you think your new *roommate* would like them..."

It took a moment—a very long, dragged-out, confusing moment—but she laughed. "I didn't know you read my blog." With a flourish, she presented her new pet. "This is Think. I moved him from the table basement down there to a prime spot up here. He's my new pet, my new friend, and my new roommate all in one." She grinned as she accepted the flowers. "He doesn't leave his clothes lying all over the place—"

"That might be because he doesn't *wear* any."

"Right? He also doesn't use the last of the toilet paper and not replace it or leave the cap off the toothpaste." Cassie fumbled through a cabinet for a vase until Evan came and pulled it down for her. "But that might be because I buy the kind with the cap attached... for now anyway."

"But does he pay his rent on time?" Evan gestured around him. "Kitchen shears? My mom insists that flowers last twice as long if you cut the stems off before putting them into the vase."

Smart mom... but what does it say about you for listening? Smart guy or mama's boy? I guess time will tell. Cassie dug the scissors out of the drawer next to the silverware and shrugged. "That's what I've always heard."

Evan interrupted before she could thank him. His hand swept the table. "I interrupted your dinner. I'm sorry."

"And I'm even sorrier, because I'm going to finish it before it gets disgusting. Do you want one? I'll be happy to make you a sandwich as soon as I finish mine, but I like my cheese *melted* not 'softened by lingering heat.'" She pointed to the stove. "But

I can get you some soup now... there's some left in the pan."

He nudged her toward the chair. "I can do it—both. And thanks. I was going to stop by McDonald's on the way home, but I really didn't want to. Tomato soup and grilled cheese—comfort food if I've ever seen them."

"Right? I ruined my roast so..."

"Ruined?" He sent her a curious glance. "Burned?"

A snort escaped before she could stop it. "Don't I wish? I could have eaten parts of it. Note for the culinary deficient—i.e. me. You can't cook beef without heat of some kind."

His head whipped around from where he poured the remaining soup into a bowl. "Wait. The case of the unplugged in crockpot?"

"Plugged in, but not on, yeah."

"My empathetic sympathies. Let's just say I have a note stickied to my back door that says, 'Did you turn on the crockpot?' Otherwise, half my meals would feed the landfill—not really a recommendation for a budding environmentalist, but I believe in honesty in all relationships, so there you have it."

Relationships? Do you mean like with your neighbor, your best friend, and the girl you like, or do you just mean all romantic relationships? And how does this fit in with me having to confess— That'll do it. Cassie nodded. "Yep. I agree with you there, but you won't get judgment from me. After all, I'm the one tossing a fifteen-dollar piece of beef tonight." She pointed to the cupboard to the right of the stove. "Bread's in there. Sourdough or seven grain. Take your pick. And speaking of honesty in relationships..."

His laughter startled her. "Sorry... Lauren said you'd confess—probably before the date that I haven't asked you on yet, but we both know I will, because it was your idea in the first place... something about saving your dad?"

"Yep. That's it. He needs a break from Mom so..."

"So, what kind of date do I need to ask you on so you can go shopping with her, and why does that not sound very eco-unfriendly? Aren't you supposed to wear what you own until it falls off and gets you arrested for indecent exposure?" His forehead wrinkled as he whipped back to face the stove. "Um, that came out wrong."

Ya think? But Cassie stifled a snicker and tried to explain. "I was going to hit consignment shops or thrift stores. It's just what you gotta do." She waited until he went to retrieve cheese and added, "Note to the wise: don't challenge yourself to do something you know you'll hate. Only the fact that tomorrow I get to tally my savings is keeping me from losing my senses."

Questions, answers, a long explanation of how she'd turned it into a competition against herself—Cassie rattled off her plan. "I'm determined to end this year knowing what kind of impact one extreme person can make *and* translate that to a realistic plan of action. I know I'm selfish about this stuff, but I know I don't want to live like this forever."

"So why do it at all? Note that you need to lower your 'carbon footprint' or whatever they're calling it this week, and then make a few changes to that effect. Why stress yourself like this?"

"Because I tend to be extreme by nature. I'll learn more if it affects me in a realistic way." Cassie remembered a few comments she'd received and hastened to add, "But I'm not over here judging everyone who isn't doing it. It's just what *I* need. And one year isn't going to kill me."

She felt it—an instant cooling in the conversation. Evan plopped his sandwich in the frying pan, ate a bite or three of soup, and flipped it over. By the time he seated himself opposite her, his soup was almost gone, and her sandwich languished in the exact place she hated it most. The microwave, however, fixed that.

"You never answered the question."

Cassie plopped in her chair and stared at him. "I didn't? What question?"

"What kind of date do I need to ask you on so you can

rescue your father from smothering?" His eyes narrowed. "Is there some kind of hint or deeper meaning to that? You know—how mother seems to be the root word to ssssmother?"

"Very funny." Cassie sighed. "The problem is, I don't *need* anything. But if we were going somewhere... ethnic or cultural, I could justify wanting something new. You know like if we went to a rodeo, I could say I wanted a western shirt or something." She stared at her plate, gathered her wits and a bit of courage, and looked back up at him. "I'll totally take *you* out if you'll just let me indulge my dad. You don't have to pay for this. I can do something like..." Her brain scrambled to think of something *other* than a western or country themed date and failed.

"Do you have anything that would work for say the forties? There's this restaurant I found that teaches swing dancing on Saturday nights. Maybe..."

"That'll work. Do you like to dance?"

He took a bite of his sandwich and chewed—long, slow movements designed to take as long as humanly possible. Cassie, with admirable self-restraint—or so she thought—didn't throw her plate at his head. Evan's laughter bubbled over and he shook his head. "I have no idea, but it looks fun. I like ice dancing, so..."

"What about school dances?"

Evan shrugged. "We didn't have those—homeschooled."

Cassie growled. "Okay. Need to write that in the 'things I must not forget. No homeschooling. My kids should have to suffer the character-building process known as public humiliation on the dance floor of junior high dances."

"I told my mom you were different." Evan popped the last of the first sandwich half in his mouth and grinned as well as he could while chewing a mouthful of food.

"I don't get it."

Evan jumped up, dug her unbroken jar of milk out of the fridge, and gestured for permission to have a glass. Sandwich washed down, he explained. "Most women I know *want* to homeschool to *avoid* their little darlings enduring public humiliation. You're ready to throw your non-existent progeny to the junior high wolves."

Some things, Cassie refused to dignify with a response. She watched him inhale the rest of his food, rinse his dishes, and lean against the sink, arms folded over his chest—watched and waited. *Are we actually going or not?*

"Well... I hate to eat and run, but you have a mom to call in a rehearsed panic because you have nothing to wear on this date you instigated." To her astonishment and dismay, her stomach flopped at the wink he gave her. "Meanwhile, I need to get a reservation. And, I need to thank you."

The retort she'd rehearsed as he spoke disappeared with those last two words. "Thank *me?* You're the one saving my dad fro—"

"You made it easy to ask you out sooner. I was trying to figure out when, where, what—and you just made it so much easier." Again, a wink. Another stomach flop. A stifled sigh. But Evan spoke before she could. "Of course, this means that next time I get to ask whenever I want, and unless you hate me, you have to remember that you totally owe me."

With that, he grinned, waved, and disappeared out the front door. Cassie jumped up to see if he'd grabbed his coat—it didn't seem possible—but it too was gone. "Okay... that was weird. Kind of nice, but weird..." Her eyes slid to Think. "So... what do you think? Nice guy? I think so, but..."

Think's opinion rang throughout her duplex—loud and clear. *Don't over-think this. Just enjoy it.*

Surprises

Okay, so not everyone is going to get this. Every day I learn just how many people don't get what I'm doing at all, so when I say that, I mean it. But for those who are already in touch with their eco-conscious side, this really won't make sense. I don't care.

So, what's the great big surprise? Well, it's that I've been sitting here fo
hour, staring at the screen. I have absolutely nothing to say about g
today. Glass is easy. You avoid it if you can, and reuse it if you can't.
really an amazing thing. I did a Pinterest search on how to repurpose
out of glass vs. out of plastic, and you know what? Plastic has ten tir
more options. It does. But glass options are ten times nicer. I can't believe
the cool things you can do with a glass jar. It's just... well, not to
redundant or put too fine a point on it. COOL!
I wanted to tell you how I searched all afternoon for a glass bottle of wate
how I wish tomato soup came in jars. But then I want to Todd's Market
there was this nice jar of tomato soup. JAR. How cool is that? I bought it
because I could. Bought chicken noodle and vegetable beef, too. Then I
the tomato tonight.
And that's where all this just flops. Like, huge big, belly flop into a swimm
pool. My stomach is still red and raw. Or at least the rump roast I v
SUPPOSED to have for dinner is. Still. It's languishing in my trash
because I didn't turn on the stupid crockpot.
Just what's the point of going all eco-friendly if I'm going to toss a cow's
in the garbage because I'm too messed up to do anything right these day:
So that brings me to my little rant. It's small, but I have to share it. I w
looking up how much the average American wastes on food. Wanna gue
Thirty-five TONS of food a year. That works out to 165 BILLION dollar:
food. How much per household? A measly 2,200 dollars. One book s
something like forty percent of all food is wasted here! Now, if they're talk
2,200 per family of four, then it stands to reason people like me are wast
550 every year. That works out to OVER ten dollars a week just in fc
waste. I tossed fifteen bucks tonight.
A lot of people have told me that they could never do what I'm doing. It's
much. They don't have time. They can't give up this or that. And I'm v
you, okay? I'm only doing it because I'm one of those gluttons
punishment. But you know what you can do? Buy less food. Eat every b
it. Learn how to use leftovers more efficiently. Learn how to make bre
ends into tasty croutons. And really. Turning on a crockpot. I swear it's
new motto.
Save a butt. Turn on the crock.

Thursday, January 21—

Three text messages filed in one after another. Cassie was
still reading Lauren's when the second—from her mother—

arrived.

EVAN LOVES THAT YOU WERE GOING TO TELL HIM ABOUT WANTING TO ASK HIM OUT. AND HE LOVES THAT YOU WERE GOING TO ASK, TOO. HE SAYS YOU'RE GOING DANCING. HINT. BUY SOMETHING THAT WILL LOOK GOOD WITH VOLLEYBALL SPANDEX. TRUST ME. YOU'RE GOING TO WANT SOMETHING TO COVER THOSE LEGS. EVAN CAN SPIN, LIFT, THE WORKS. HAVE FUN. BUY SOMETHING SUPER CUTE. YOU DESERVE IT.

The text warmed her heart. *She's right. I've worked hard. And I'm buying used.* Her denim tote bag stuffed with two sweaters, a top, and a pair of dress pants she'd decided she hated that morning waited in the backseat of her car. She'd give them to the shop owner. Maybe it would earn her a discount. If not, it would earn her closet space. *And that's a win, too.*

Her mom's text proved a little less interesting but more urgent. I FOUND FOUR GOOD PLACES. ONE HAS THE PERFECT DRESS. IT'S THAT DARK PEACOCK THAT LOOKS SO GOOD ON YOU. I'M GOING TO CHECK OUT A COUPLE MORE. MEET ME AT TWELVE-THIRTY AT REFRESH IN BOUTIQUE ROW. GREAT STORE.

Cassie zipped a text back over the airwaves and pulled up the third message—from Evan. IN CASE I DIDN'T MAKE IT OBVIOUS, I'M REALLY LOOKING FORWARD TO ANOTHER DATE. AND I WANT TO HIRE YOU. CALL WHEN YOU CAN.

"Hire…" A glance at the clock told her there wasn't much time to get the inbox cleared out before she left to meet her mother. "I'll call on the subway."

"What was that?"

Cassie swallowed hard and tried not to grimace as she looked up at her boss. "Sorry. Just talking to myself."

"I thought you drove to work—that car that always looks ready to fall apart if you stop too quickly."

"I do. But I'm supposed to meet my mom—to find a dress." The words tumbled from her lips before she could hope to stop them. "For this date, I have. Because my dad needs

Mom out of the house. So, I needed an excuse. And I didn't think of things like how I'm going to need better produce bags for the store. So, no, I get this guy to ask me out..." She closed her mouth and her eyes. "Sorry. I'm just crazy nervous. I've got the inbox almost—"

But Mr. Sylmer shook his head and punched off the monitor. "Get out of here. If I see you before two, I'll fire you."

"Wha—"

"If your dad needs a break from a hovering wife, then you need to keep her busy for more than an hour."

She rushed to explain—to assure him her mother had been shopping, but when his arms folded over his chest, Cassie shook her head and grabbed her purse. "Yes sir. Need anything while I'm out? Coffee? Paper clips? Zoot Suit?"

Mr. Sylmer's laughter echoed throughout the office until he closed his door behind him. Then, only his repeated, "Get out of here" could be heard through the thick door of his nearly soundproof office. *Must have shouted that for me to hear it.*

⊐ɹɹ ɹɹ ɹɹ⊏

Cassie's text arrived just as Marla stepped out of yet another "bust." She tapped out an answer and hurried back to Refresh. "If this Evan would just take her to a speakeasy, I could get her outfitted in a minute. The twenties stuff is amazing."

A man gave her a wide berth and an even wider-eyed expression, but Marla ignored him. "People who don't think aloud probably don't think much at all. Yeah. That sounds intelligent enough."

To her amusement, Cassie passed her walking at a brisk pace and talking on the phone. Marla hurried to keep up and couldn't help but overhear half the conversation. "—hire me to find a Bonanza lunch pail? Really?"

Oooh... that might be a fun side business during the cold months when her sales are hit and miss.

"Um... okay. Is there just one lunch box like that, or were

there a lot of varieties? I mean, wasn't there kind of a big cast?"

Kind of? Sure. There was kind of a big cast. And do you want a box for a boy or a girl? There's a lot you're not asking, little girl.

"—kay. Well, I'll do an Internet search of the ones that were available and you can tell me which one, then."

And that's why I shouldn't underestimate you. Way to go.

As she reached Refresh, Cassie held the door. Amused that *still* her daughter hadn't noticed her, Marla thanked Cassie and stepped inside. "You're—Mom!"

"Yes, I am Mom. Glad you noticed. Who wants the lunch box?"

"Evan. For his dad. For his birthday—the dad, not Evan." Cassie's eyes narrowed. "How long have you been behind me?"

"You passed me back when you confirmed that Evan wants to hire you." At that moment, Marla saw the hideous tote bag slung over one of Cassie's shoulders. "Oh, dear. Tell me that's not your—"

A glare that anyone would understand in any language stopped her short. Cassie swept the room with eagerness. "So, what'd you find?"

"It has this hint of iridescence. It's not quite, but..." Marla dragged her to the mannequin where the dress hung displayed with a pair of chunky beads around the neckline. "I'm not sure about the accessories. I thought maybe a silk scarf tied in a knot—the short ones, you know? Lucy Ricardo style."

"If we can find one in like gold or silver... maybe a print with this color in it..."

A saleswoman appeared at their side as if teleported. "I didn't actually think you'd bring her back. Most people say that but they're just using it as an excuse to leave without buying anything."

Marla's throat went dry, and she struggled to find a response that wouldn't make an awkward moment worse. Cassie blinked. "What?"

The woman shrugged. "I'm Barb, by the way. I just don't

know why people are so embarrassed to leave without buying something." Barb turned to Marla. "But you were right. That color will look *great* on her."

"Can I try it on? Oh!" Cassie passed the tote bag. "Ignore the horrible sewing, but I was going to take these to the thrift store, but they're good quality. I thought maybe someone down here might like them."

"I don't buy—"

Cassie's head shook at the first word. "I'm not trying to sell. I was going to donate, and I still can." She reached for the bag again. "I just thought maybe you'd like to have—"

"Oh! Thank you. That's so nice."

Marla tried signaling—anything to stop Cassie. *Someone else might buy them!* But Cassie just beamed and wrestled the dress from the mannequin.

"Can you find a scarf, Mom? I'm going to go try this on. Where…"

Barb pointed to the back corner. "There's better lighting up front, but I couldn't find a good way to set them up there, so…"

"I'll come out. Thanks."

The wait began. Marla had almost decided to buy four blouses for herself before Cassie finally stepped through the door. The dress—made for her. No one could deny it. It lacked only something to add a bit of sparkle, but Cassie didn't go to the wall of scarves to one side of the room. She found a rack of belts and tried a dozen. None worked, but she turned to Barb and smoothed her hands over it. "I'll take it. I just have to find a belt. Or a scarf for around my waist…" Her eyes sought Marla. "What do you think?"

"Great idea!"

"A simple string of pearls would be classic and authentic…" Barb glanced around the store as if trying to make them materialize. "I don't think I have anything small enough, but…"

Marla started to agree. The words hovered on her lips, but Cassie shook her head. "We'll be dancing. I wouldn't want to worry about them or worse, have them swing around. That could be awkward."

Three stores It took three before Cassie found what she wanted—a slim little silver chain belt with a clamshell buckle. Marla expected to see her daughter dash off down the road, but Cassie tugged her into a sandwich shop and pleaded with her to order. "Just make sure I don't see paper or plastic. Please. I am starving. I think they use real plates here, but..."

A server appeared at the table next to theirs carrying plates *without* paper liners. Cassie pulled a fresh napkin out of her purse and waited for the woman to bring menus. "Okay. We're good. I remembered correctly. I've only been here once—just to get out of the rain one day. I only ordered coffee, but..."

"I'm impressed that you remembered. I still can't believe you're doing this. We're three weeks in!"

"*We're*? You mean *I'm* three weeks in. I haven't called for help since—"

But Marla couldn't help but admit her secret. "I keep trying to do it with you—smaller scale, but still. I've been reducing everything I can. I thought you were nuts when you said paper and plastic are on and in everything, but they are!"

Of all the replies she could have received, Cassie's confession was the last she'd have expected. "Well, while we're admitting things, I should tell you that I actually convinced Evan to take me out so I could ask you to go shopping."

"Huh?"

"Eloquent, Mom. Way eloquent." Cassie stared at the menu before her and didn't answer for several seconds. "Dad's feeling a bit... suffocated. So I said I'd get you out of the house for a bit. But you know me. I can't hide this stuff." She reached across the table and squeezed Marla's hand. "But I can't decide if I should hint that he needs a break, or thank you for hovering so I could get that great dress."

"The latter. Definitely." Marla grinned. "And I got the two-by-four hint."

⫯⫯ ⫯⫯ ⫯⫯

Evan flipped through Facebook as he waited for Cassie's nightly post to appear in his feed. The clock on his phone rolled over number after number but nothing. He pulled up a browser and typed in the blog name. www.365daysofgreen.blog. Wednesday's offering remained at the top.

Though tempted to zip a text message urging her to hurry, Evan hadn't planned to let her know just how much he read them. *She'll probably take it as silent support.*

A new idea prompted him to pull up a text message. DO YOU THINK CASSIE IS DOING A BLOG POST TONIGHT? I'M TIRED. BUT IF SHE'S GOING TO GIVE ME A LAUGH BEFORE BED... Evan zipped it to Lauren and waited.

Of course, this means she'll probably tell Cassie that I'm waiting. I should have told her not to say.

Another refresh left nothing but six cat videos and three cat memes—all posted by his great aunt, Mary. Much to his disgust, he watched every single one. Cats attacking boxes as if delectable prey, cats swinging from a slow-moving ceiling fan—refusing to get down. One cat sat on a mini snowboard and slid along the snow-capped hills of some snow-covered country where they spoke a language Evan couldn't hope to recognize.

His phone buzzed. Lauren's smiling face appeared on the screen just as he tapped it. I DOUBT SHE'LL SLEEP WITHOUT POSTING. I TAKE IT YOU DON'T WANT HER TO KNOW YOU READ OR YOU'D ASK HER YOURSELF?

"Should have known you'd be on to me." His reply whizzed its way across town and hers came back almost immediately. Evan grinned. "Yeah, I do like her, but I'm not telling you that. You'll make more of it than there is. I'm not in any rush."

When another ten minutes passed, he went back to the

blog and set up a notification to come to his phone. Teeth brushed. Sleep pants. Lights out through the half-empty apartment. His phone plugged into the charger. Evan did everything he could think of to delay crawling into that bed, but when he couldn't think of anything else, he flipped back the covers and climbed in.

Minutes ticked by once more—minutes in which he ordered himself to sleep and couldn't. The phone lay silent. His eyes stared at the black hole of his ceiling as he waited for sleep or the buzzing of the phone to win out. *Why am I doing this again?*

The need to answer dissolved as his phone skittered across the nightstand. He snatched it up and stared at his newsfeed. A picture of a row of jars filled the top of the screen. The title prompted a chuckle.

Habits Are for Nuns

I just ended the first twenty-one days of this craziness that has become my life. I am now, officially, in the habit of avoiding excess paper—or so the habit experts (no, not nuns, the other kind) tell me. And, I have to say, I pause before even TOUCHING a piece of paper. I swear, people think I'm some kind of germophobe. They offer me a magazine on the subway, and I shake my head.
Do I think it's evil to read magazines? Nope. But if I take it to read, then I'll feel like I should get one the next day and share—that pay it forward thing.
So, what is the hardest part of paper reduction? Notes. Just putting it out there now. I had no idea how dependent I was on paper for notes to myself. A guy I know says he has a sticky note on his back door to remind him to turn on the crockpot. I have one now, too. It's an old cookie sheet that I scrubbed up and painted with this chalkboard paint I had left over from a piece of furniture I updated. I have these cool liquid chalk pens that I'm going to use with it. At least I won't throw away another roast because I forgot to turn it on.
But can I say it would have been SO MUCH EASIER just to slap a sticky note on the door? Do you know how hard it was to find something that would fit in that small space? If I hadn't had that toaster-oven cookie sheet that I used once and ruined because I

forgot the PARCHMENT PAPER, I couldn't have done it. Maybe a piece of cardboard would have fit in that space, but how tacky!

But I miss my notepads. I didn't realize how much paper I used until I couldn't. I mean, I probably OWN enough paper to last me for a YEAR. I probably don't NEED to reduce the paper load. But if I don't do it, I'm not really making much of a PAPER REDUCTION change. I'm making a shopping change. That's not the same thing.

So, I'll be using my chalkboard now. I have a Boogie Board by my bed, and I use my phone, too. I need to buy more of those Boogie Boards, so again, if you have one you want to sell me, let me know. I'm dead serious.

And, I learned something about myself in all of this. Paper is my thing. Shocker, right? I mean, I just said that up there. But I'm saying it again. I miss my paper planner. I don't use my phone like some people do. Google calendars are great, but paper is better—for me. I have a nice notebook I bought for habits I wanted to develop this year, for bucket type lists, and stuff. I'm using that to record what I will and won't change next year as well. Tonight, I wrote down one more thing. This is what it said:

Next year's paper usage:

I'm going back to paper planners, paper notebooks, and paper journals. I might keep up the blog, but I miss handwriting stuff. It's just how my brain works, and I'm reading all these studies on how analog stuff really makes a bigger impact on the brain. So, I'm doing it.

But I am going to keep my paper usage down. There's no reason to use a sticky note for EVERYTHING. There's no reason not to avoid wasteful paper. I'll probably stick to cloth napkins and not as many paper towels as I used to. But I think I'll want SOME paper towels. Still gotta figure out wrapping paper. Maybe gift bags. They can be reused. Sigh.

Yep. I'm already panicking over Christmas and birthdays. I mean, who wouldn't? I really need a wood-burning stove. I thought fire pit, but it would be nice not to have to freeze off my butt to try to get rid of some of this stuff, and if it helped with keeping my apartment warmer, well that's got to be better for the environment, too. So, I'm in the market for one. If anyone has one in their garage or something, let me know. It just can't be new, of course. Especially since "metal" starts in like thirty-two minutes. That's scary. I'm getting nervous. What am I gonna do if I crash my car? I'd say, "buy a Corvette" because don't they have like fiberglass bodies or something? But there's a problem. Still pretty sure the engine is metal. Then again, a car is a necessity, and I wouldn't be buying brand new—kind of like the dress I bought today. Not brand new, so it counted as following the plan.

Ick. That sounds like some kind of diet. Is that what I'm on? A diet? AAAAK!

So, week three tallies are as follows:

I reduced:

Eating out waste
The contents of my closet
Cans (yeah, it was glass week, but I swapped them out!)
More paper. I didn't print things at work I usually would. I sent more emails to my boss. Oh! And I didn't take the store bag offered when I bought that dress. Instead, I stuffed it in my hideously ugly tote bag, much to my mother's mortification, and "Barb's" befuddlement. I didn't even bother to explain.
Gasoline usage. I didn't go sale-ing so I probably saved a good three or four gallons. Add to that the fact that I'm not shopping on Amazon, so I'm saving UPS trips and …
Plastic trash bags. I replaced them with the eco-friendly ones. The verdict is out on those.
Junk Mail. I put myself on several opt out lists. So I shouldn't be getting pre-screened credit card offers, phone calls, and other direct mail stuff. It only lasts for like five years, but hey! Maybe by then I'll have moved and they can't find me! Off grid! I could go to like HearthLand or something!

I increased:

Food waste. A nice rump roast is fertilizing a landfill right about now. So sad.
Glass consumption. Is it consumption if I'm not eating it? Whatever. I bought more stuff with glass in it.
A bit of unnecessary clothing spending. But it was used so…

Neutral:

Not sure about this. Part of me thinks glass should have gone here. Because let's face it. I bought more glass stuff, but I reduced other stuff in the process. I just have one question. Why do they have to put paper labels on glass jars?!

Speaking of glass jars. Here's a picture of them. This is just from this week. I'm getting a bit nervous. Yeah, they're better. But um... what am I going to do with all of these? Does anyone need glass jars? They make great containers. I promise.

Oh, and one more thing. I have over a hundred dollars in my "bank book" of savings. Even with buying that dress and a matching belt. I'm so excited.

So, that's this week. It's a wrap. All is well. And things are looking up for the weekend. One of my neighbors read this blog, found another neighbor who doesn't read the classifieds, so I get to have theirs. I just have to come get it and reassemble the paper when I'm done. YES! Great neighbors are awesome! Goodnight world.

Week 4: Metal

Friday, January 22—

Just as Cassie reached the parking garage, an alarm on her phone sent her nerves tingling. *What? So help me if I forgot something, I'll scream. It's the* weekend! *I need a* break!

The note: a reminder of a meeting at the library for tips on simple ways to be more "eco-conscious." She stood in the middle of a row, car doors slamming shut and motors starting all around her, and stared at the screen. *To go or not to go... Where's Think when I need him?*

A horn blared, nearly sending her phone flying into a concrete pillar. "I'm going. I'm going...."

Eyes darting back and forth between the screen and the few feet of concrete before her, Cassie made a note to add Think to her phone plan and fumbled out a text message to Joel. WHY DID I WANT TO GO TO THIS STUPID MEETING?

The reply came before she could insert the key in the ignition. JUST DO IT. I'D GO WITH YOU, BUT IT WOULD BE OVER BY THE TIME I GOT OUT OF HERE AND GOT THERE. NEXT TIME, THOUGH. IF YOU NEED MORAL OR ECO OR SOMETHING SUPPORT.

Her duct-taped phone dock—the one that refused to stick to her crumbling dashboard without the aid of adhesive wonders like duct tape—held the phone for her as Cassie backed out of her semi-usual parking spot and headed to the east exit. She waited for a call, a text, *anything* that would release her from the self-imposed obligation to go to this meeting. "Take a note."

Her phone assured her that it would take the requested

note. "Remind yourself later that you went to this meeting for ideas—not because you have to become some pseudo-hippie."

Those words haunted Cassie all the way to the library. The discomfort intensified as she stepped from the car, flung her leather purse strap over one shoulder, adjusted her polyester-wool blend skirt, and tried to forget that she wore "leatherette" boots. *Not a bit of natural fibers on me—unless you count the cow I killed to get my purse. And the three ounces of wool in this skirt so they can jack up the price. Nylon and polyester underwear with a bit of spandex in my bra band. Yeah. That's eco-friendly. My makeup probably qualifies me as a walking petroleum plant sample kit. Maybe I should consider mineral makeup. That's probably next in my growing list of ways I'm ruining my life.*

Cassie fumbled for her phone and told the app to take another note. "No more dares without two weeks of prayerful contemplation—even if it's a dare to smile at a cute guy!"

The 10th Street library boasted the most diverse programs in the city. If it wasn't hand-lettering lessons on glorious paper with fabulous fountain pens—not that Cassie had grown bitter or anything—she could learn square foot gardening, join a book club on almost any genre, watch championship chess, cribbage, and dominoes matches, or attend a "Dating for Wishful Luddites" mixer. *Maybe I shouldn't have skipped the depression support group. Perhaps I could learn preventative maintenance. Feels like I'm going to need it.*

A white board "sandwich sign" stood outside one of the many meeting rooms on the second floor and read "Conscientious Objectors." *Clever, but it makes it sound a bit like they object to eco-consciousness rather than the other way around.* Her hand pressed against the cool corner of the sign. Cassie couldn't help but smile. *At least the sign isn't a burlap sack stenciled with coffee dye or something like that.*

She took a deep cleansing breath, hitched her purse straps up onto her shoulders, glanced back over the railing at the rows of books her new "club" probably decried, and stepped into the room. Her eyes swept the floor. *Not a pair of Birkenstocks in sight. Then again, it is still January.*

A prematurely balding man—scrawny with John Lennon glasses—stepped forward and introduced himself. "Are you here for the eco meeting?"

She nodded—didn't seem capable of anything else.

"I'm Aaron. Nice to meet you."

"Cassie—Wren." The moment she spoke her surname, Cassie groaned inwardly. *Why did you do that? He didn't give his last name!*

Aaron urged her to the center of the room where people milled about, chatting. Business suits, jeans and t-shirts, a girl who looked like she expected the paparazzi at any moment—everything in between. Just no peasant tops with broomstick skirts and macramed belts. No body odor. Not a single stereotypical thing that she'd spent the last week dreading. *It's almost anticlimactic.*

"Hey, this is Cassie... Wren. She's here for the meeting."

Way to state the obvious, bud.

African-American, young, athletic—any guy would pronounce her *hot*—the woman stepped forward with a bright smile and proof that the eco-conscious come in all shapes, sizes, and economic backgrounds. This woman was *loaded.* "Hey! Nice to meet you. I'm Maya. What brought you to our meeting?"

"Long story." The two words dropped on the floor and rolled to the center of the room—hand grenade style.

"Okay, we're going to get started. Tonight's topic, why Cassie Wren came tonight—if we can talk her into it, of course."

Against her better judgment, Cassie shrugged and agreed. "You'll so regret this. I'm not exactly a willing convert."

If she had expected those words would put the others off, Cassie would have been disappointed. Unfortunately, the moment she spoke, she realized if anything, she'd only increased curiosity and interest. Maya urged her to get a plate of snacks and refill her water bottle before sitting. "If you don't have a bottle, we have one you can use. I always bring a spare."

"Got it right here." Without even a glance at the table Maya had indicated, Cassie brushed off the notion of food. *It's probably tofu, soy nuts, and kale chips or something. No thanks.* Aloud she just shook her head and gave a moderately realistic sigh. "I've got dinner in the crock-pot. If I snack here, it'll go to waste—not exactly eco-friendly."

Of course, when Aaron passed with a brownie that looked beyond delicious, Cassie instantly regretted her attempt at subterfuge. Maya gave her a knowing smile. "You sure? No one makes better brownies than Mabel." Her eyes slid to where a woman who had to be ninety beamed at them. "Maybe just half?"

A confession tumbled from her before Cassie could stop herself. "I thought it'd all be health stuff or..." She lowered her voice. "Don't hate me—recycled from like a restaurant dumpster."

Maya's laughter rang out in the room. "Oh, yeah. I like you already. Come tell us this long story."

Since she'd gotten herself into it, Cassie decided to make it good. She tried to describe the shopping trip, her friends mocking her idea, and the first days. "I *so* didn't know what I'd gotten myself into until I tried making those napkins. I mean how do you decide which is worse? Is it paper that comes from a renewable source like *trees* or petroleum because it's only a onetime thing to save a *lot* of paper processing that probably has its own environmental impact aside from deforestation— which I don't even know is a problem here in the States. Which? I don't know. But it just got worse from there."

Aaron choked back a guffaw or two and leaned forward. "Did you really count TP squares?"

She leveled a deadpan expression on him, crossed her arms over her chest, and hesitated before answering. "I use the Subway bathrooms now because they have TP that doesn't *have* squares. If I get too much, well, it's not my fault. They didn't measure it."

Mini explosions of laughter rang out in the room in bursts reminiscent of Independence Day fireworks. Tears streamed down Mabel's cheeks, and Maya pumped her fist. "Told you it would be gold. I've got a sixth sense. Be sure to let me know how you keep from getting grossed out in those restrooms."

Cassie tossed a wicked grin. "I know the cleaning schedule, and I'm not afraid to wait."

Mabel spoke up before Cassie could explain what had brought her to the meeting. "Did I miss where you said why you're here?"

"Nope. I just need help. I have to come up with fifty-two things to change, and I'm feeling like I'm going to fail. I'd also love to know how to be able to decide between the lesser of two evils. I'm so lost on this stuff."

Maya stepped up and pulled an overstuffed Composition Notebook from the canvas tote bag at her feet. "Well, you can start by flipping through there. It might help." She addressed the room. "So, what would you all do next? She's done plastic, paper, um... glass? Yeah. Too many jars. So, what's this week?"

Cassie almost whimpered. "Metal. For the record, I love canned tuna in summer. It's like an addiction. I have to limit myself—the mercury and stuff. What am I going to do? Can you buy tuna in jars? And is there *any* way to like... create something people would *buy* out of jars or leftover cans or something? I feel like I'm going to have to turn my garbage into boutique quality *tchotchkes* to be able to survive until December." At the dubious expressions on the faces around her, she shrugged. "Sorry. A girl's gotta eat."

Once more, laughter filled the room.

⸺ ᴉᴉ ᴉᴉ ᴉᴉ ⸺

With a plate of over-cooked crock-pot mac-n-cheese and ham, Cassie curled up on the couch next to Think and regaled him with stories from the meeting. "Everyone there is so different. I did figure out that Miss Society chick is probably a journalist in disguise. The way she asked questions—almost screamed with excitement when I mentioned my blog—I'm telling you…"

The memory of her blurting out her surprise at the lack of body odor sent a groan through her. "When will I learn to think before I speak? I should be more like you. You never blurt out whatever's in your head without considering how it'll come out."

A call from Evan interrupted her confession. With just a little trepidation, she answered. "Hey…"

"I just wanted to see how your thing at the library went."

Okay, maybe you're more supportive than I gave you credit for.

"Cassie?"

"Sorry." She swallowed a mouthful of mac-n-cheese almost whole and washed it down. "Too big of a bite."

Disappointment? Was it? She heard *something* in his tone that sounded suspiciously like disappointment. "I can call back…."

"No! Sorry. I just am starving. Decided not to eat the great food they had there because I thought it would all be fake stuff or whatever. Yeah. Not so much. But I'd already told them I had food waiting, so I had to stick to it."

How he heard the last words, Cassie couldn't imagine. Evan's laughter filled the room. Cassie, on the other hand, shot Think a look that said, "Do you believe this guy?"

She imagined a frown on the pensive "man's" face.

"Sorry. You confessed, didn't you?"

"How—" Eyes rolling and self-disgust growing, Cassie sank back against the cushions and sighed. "Yeah. I did. Maya—she's kind of the leader—thought it was funny at least. They're all so weird."

Rustling over the phone hinted that he must be doing

190

paperwork while they spoke. "Nut jobs or…"

"That's just it. That's what is so weird. They're so *normal* that it's weird. I mean, I'm weird now. Instead of researching makeup tips or Depression glass, now I research ways to reduce my impact on the environment—*me!*" It was a test and not a nice one, if she was honest, but Cassie heard herself telling the story of McDonald's restaurants in Hong Kong. "They have no-straw Tuesdays! It's like our taco Tuesday! Crazy. I can't remember if it's every week or if it's just once a month now."

"And…"

That he didn't laugh seemed to mean something but what, she couldn't say. Cassie, to the contrary, did. Her giggle sounded strangled, even to her ears. "I know this! How is it that I know this and I care about it? I'm not an environmentalist! But I think it's so cool that people do this as a matter of course."

"Sounds like a blog post to me."

Her eyes slid toward the laptop.

"And I haven't seen your metal pile." Evan chuckled. "There's no way you can give up metal. It's your car, your—"

"That's not—" But Cassie stopped herself. "Okay, I'm gonna go write it. See you tomorrow. And thanks again for being my excuse. Mom gets it now, but I got three texts today asking if I'm going to get someone to record me dancing."

"I'll see what I can do," Evan promised. "I mean, gotta make the mom happy, right?"

"Not on your life. You do and it'll be the *last* time I trust you with an important errand."

With a promise to pick her up at six-thirty, Evan said goodnight. "Write fast, okay? I have an early meeting."

"You'll get it when I'm done. Pictures were dark, so I've got to play with them a bit."

Chuckles… "And that is one of my favorite things about you. Night, Cassie."

She stared at Think. "What is? What's he talking about? I can't even ask! How full of myself! 'So, what is one of your favorite things?' Stupid. Jerk." A smile and a wink at Think later, she sighed. "But a nice jerk, right?"

A glance at congealed cheese and noodles prompted her to shove the half-eaten dish aside and grab her laptop. "Still, wouldn't want him to stick it to the wrong people tomorrow because I kept him up forever. He did get me out with Mom...."

Browser, dashboard, new post—all ready to go. Her fingers hovered over the title bar as Cassie fought to create a clever ditty. Nothing came to mind. She did a search on blog post titles and learned she'd been doing everything wrong. Fifteen minutes later, she gave up and wrote a sub-standard title that her recent research assured her would flop if she were trying to make a living from her blogging attempts.

A Metal Dilemma

Okay, so plays on words—or is it play on words—I think it's plays. Like more than one. Yeah. Kind of like mothers-in-law. People always say, "Tell your mother-in-laws" this or that. It's wrong. I remember that much, anyway. MotherS-in-law. There. Now that we've solved that riddle, let's talk metal, dilemmas, and even the morality of consumption.

Here's the picture of every metal thing I could find in the house aside from pans or dishes and stuff. Canned food, aluminum foil, disposable roasting pans and baking pans—had NO idea that there were so many of those. I mean, who has a stack of pans like that when she almost never cooks? Well, okay, I USED to almost never cook. Now I cook. But still. Sheesh. I look like I'm trying to take a month's worth of food to a MegaFamily or something.

Oh. Yeah. I know what it is. Every month we have a potluck at church. And for the past three years, every stupid month, I've tried to convince myself I was going to make something. So, I buy a pan while I'm shopping. Because, you know, I don't know if I kept the last dozen I didn't use, right? I also buy all the food to make something amazing. Because that's how I roll. Then, I grab a couple of pies on the way to church because I didn't bother actually cooking the stuff.

Okay. In the interest of full disclosure, because I've not humiliated myself enough, yeah. I also ended up tossing most of the food I bought. Seriously, when you consider the twenty bucks I spent on wasted food each month, I could have just donated that to the church and claimed it on my taxes! Sheesh! Sorry, but the IRS isn't going to take a twenty dollar a month "donation" to the landfill off my tax burden. Jerks.

See all that canned food? How am I supposed to replace that stuff? I need to eat, you know. I like canned chili. I hate my chili. It's gross. Okay, it's not. It's good. But if you want a chili dog—which, I probably can't buy anymore because they and their lovely spongy buns come wrapped in evil plastic—that stuff that's the scourge of the planet. Maybe from a butcher and a bakery? Anyway. If you want a chili dog, you need cheap, disgusting chili to make it perfect. Oh, and lots of onions and cheese.

See the canned air? How am I going to survive without canned air? And hair spray? I don't use it often, but I DO use it. Then mousse. C'mon. I can use handmade deodorant and not use aerosol. I'll live. But MOUSSE. Have you SEEN my curls? Sometimes I need help taming them. It works when I go off my Brazilian Blowout kicks.

Okay, most of this stuff wasn't a big surprise. I've had three full weeks to dread today. But then, then today I noticed that my bathtub needed a clean. So out I pull the "scrubbing bubbles" and seriously. No pride left here, folks. I totally bawled. Sat on the toilet, the one I can't clean with a disposable scrubber anymore, and wailed. I pulled stuff out from under the sink. I found…

o   Lysol—seriously? I am NOT giving up this stuff. Flu—gag. Yeah. Not happening.

o   Air freshener. At first, I was like, "No biggie." Um, I like my lemon-lavender stuff!

o   Glass polish. My aunt gives me this stuff from Amway. GREAT stuff. Didn't cry, but I wanted to.

o   Pre-wash. Again, great Amway stuff. I have to find something else. Because everything else in the store comes in plastic, so it's not like I can use that stuff, either.

That was just the bathroom. I found frozen concentrate orange juice that didn't make the cut. So, what, now I have to squeeze my own juice on those weekend mornings when I feel like having a Pinterest-inspired life and make a fancy breakfast? Well, that'll save more burned crepes, and failed clotted cream experiments. I just don't have the patience for twelve hours of baking at eight in the morning. Some would put it in before they went to bed, but I like to live dangerously—or stupidly. Or something.

Now, see the steel wool? So not going to miss that. Stuff shreds my fingers and if I use gloves, I put too much pressure, so I can't use gloves. Vicious cycle that leaves me looking like I tried to grab a metal cable as I slid off a roof or something.

I've already cut out cans of soda and stuff, but still. See what's left? More than I expected. Dig through your cupboards and it's amazing what you find.

So, my metal dilemma—will I or will I not give up canned chili and tuna? Will I give up Lysol? Or will I make my own vodka/eucalyptus/lavender/orange/rosemary concoction to spray when I need to de-germify the house. I suppose if it doesn't work, I can always drown my sorrows in it. Can't taste any worse than most alcohol does. Yeah.

I'm dying to tell you about tonight's utter embarrassment, but I'm tired. So, I'll do that tomorrow. After all, I've got a date that could be a huge flop—not the guy's fault, I mean. After all, we're going to try learning swing dancing. A flop means I land on my butt or fall flat on my face. And anyone who knows me…

Cassie stared at the blinking cursor. "Well, is that enough? Can I go to bed now? Gotta be up at four…." She scowled at the pasta that would become rock hard if she didn't rinse it out at least. "I should do the dishes." A glance at Think answered everything. "You're right. Soak the dish, wash tomorrow. There won't be more than two or three sales anyway. Plenty of time to scrub later." A wave of foolishness washed over her as she kissed the top of Think's head and snapped off the light. "Try to get some sleep. I hear counting sheep works."

Saturday, January 23—

Six sales—a record for January it seemed. Cassie sat out in front of the first, half an hour before it opened, waiting for the sale sign to go up in the yard. With Gayle the liquidator in charge, she'd get in fifteen minutes early. "I'll have to listen to her whine the whole time, but it could be worth it."

As she muttered her early morning complaints and sipped coffee from her Starbucks mug—refillable, of course—Cassie

194

scrolled through comments on her blog post.

Joel2:13— Can't wait to hear more about the meeting. I have a feeling it's a good one. Be sure to get a video of you dancing. If you like it, we all know how obsessive you are. You'll be an expert in no time, and you'll want that comparison video. Trust me. Have fun.

Cassie's heart constricted as she read the words. "That must have cost you to write. Seriously, if Lauren weren't already my best friend, you would be."

A flick of the thumb brought her face to face with another jab from Hermione squared.

HermionesTwin—See. This is what I mean. You're doing it again. You're turning everything into a VagueBook thing. "Ooooohhhh... I'm all dramatic—got a huge thing to tell you, but I won't. I'll make you wait." Just tell it or don't, already. And seriously? Your dates? I thought this was about 365 Days of GREEN. Or is this just proof that you're trying to do the whole "Make your friends green with envy" thing." You think you have some superior boyfriend or something?

"Harsh! What is with you? I didn't know I had anyone who hated me this much. Wow." Her words sounded overly loud in the enclosed car. A glance over the steering wheel showed no sign of life at the house, so Cassie took a deep, cleansing breath, closed her eyes, and flipped her thumb upward again. "You can just go out of sight and hopefully out of mind."

Her eyes slid to the empty seat beside her. "Would it be totally bizarre to bring Think along for these things? If he were a dog or a guy, I would. Why not a sculpture."

That thought shook her. "That's it. I'm officially losing it. I'll take a picture of him like people do of their plants and bird feeders and... yesterday's *lunch*. That'll count. Then I can pretend I'm talking to it instead of an empty seat."

The next comment wiped away the sting from green Hermione.

Sonofabird— Looking forward to it, both the dancing and the story about your library adventures. And Joel is right. We should video it. I'll bribe the server. Thanks for the update. I will never look at store shelves the same again.

Tapping on her window sent Cassie's phone flying and crashing against the dashboard with a thud. "Wha— Gayle!"

"No use sitting out her burning gas or freezing your butt off. Get in here. I've got some stuff you're going to *die* over."

"Great," Cassie muttered as she grabbed her phone from the passenger floorboard and scrambled for the door handle. "She's already killin' me."

Cold, snow-threatening wind bit her as Cassie climbed from the car. Gayle plowed—in heels, no less—through the driveway snow "banks" and to the walk. "I heard that. And you'll pay... oh, yeah. You'll pay."

"Not a dime more than I should!" Her words—defensive, and she knew it. Still, Cassie felt better for uttering them—right up to the moment when an arctic blast hit her and eked its way up the back of her parka. "Eeep!"

Not until she stepped inside the mid-century modern did Cassie realize what Gayle had alluded to. The place—amazing. It looked like a magazine ad in House Beautiful circa 1945. "Check out this game cupboard—in the totally authentic storage unit. Did they ever *play* these games?"

Okay, so Gayle had a point. The games looked like they should be wrapped in plastic to be so pristine. Only slight bowing in a few of the tops from the weight of the games above it marred assembly line perfection. She didn't even look through the boxes. Even if pieces were missing, incongruous as an idea as that might be, the boxes and boards would be worth a fortune. "I'll take them all if you're being reasonable."

"I knew you would." Gayle flipped a card over from the shelf above it read "Reserved for Cassie Wren." At Cassie's glare, the woman shrugged. "Look, it's time. This is perfect stock for that store you're always dreaming of. Now you have

196

prime stuff to stock it with. I even dropped the price a bit just because I wanted you to have them for it." She leaned closer at the sounds of a car pulling up. "Just don't put them all out at once. Get some more that don't look as good. You'll set unrealistic expectations. Now hurry."

Never, had Gayle been so accommodating. She led Cassie through room after room and pointed at things she knew Cassie liked. Aprons—did the woman ever cook? Fondue set—never opened from the original box. A well-loved set of melamine stacked right next to what looked like an untouched set of Franciscan ware—Coronado, no less. "You know I want it-all of it. And that pie safe in the garage. Why is all that old, great stuff in the garage?"

"They were up in the rafters and down in the basement. Looks like the wife went all modern—seventy years ago—and didn't bother to get rid of the old stuff." At the sound of screaming kids, Gayle inched her way to the front. "Look, if anyone is looking at something you think you want, just cough. I'll say it's sold until you decide."

"Why the sudden niceness?" The hiss came out before she could stop herself.

"Leave your card if you have to go! We'll talk later! Dot's by the back door."

She shouldn't have done it, but Cassie couldn't stand it. She hurried to the back door with a fistful of tags and got her started on a tab. "I'm either going to have to write a check, or I'm going to have to go get more money. This sale—I won't have money left for any others."

"But so worth it, right? Gayle has been dancing since she got the call. Apparently, this was some vacation home—only here for a couple of months a year. The people bought it to have for the grandkids to visit." Dot dropped her voice. "They never came. Kids didn't speak to the parents or something."

She *needed* to go before she lost something big, but Cassie couldn't help but ask, "So what's with Gayle?"

"She has a business proposition. Don't tell her I told you, but she'd give you great prices to sweeten you up. You should listen."

All through the house, as Cassie slapped sticky notes on everything she wanted, Dot's words danced in the periphery of her mind. She missed a sculpture that she could have sworn was George Aarons. Someone walked past with coral Pyrex, and Cassie almost cried, but Gayle jerked her head toward a doorway. "In there. I marked a few. Hurry!"

Pink—Gayle had reserved pink and... could it be? Cassie almost swooned. *I swear, this is like the thrifting version of wining and dining. Sheesh! Cloverberry Pyrex? Whoa...* She reached for the tag and a woman behind her snapped. "That's reserved."

"For me." She turned and tried to give the woman a genuine smile, but it proved difficult with venom and blood dripping from fangs.... *Okay, not fangs. But come on!*

"You know, they didn't advertise this as a pre-sale. I would have liked the same opportunity as others—namely you."

Cassie tore off the tag of the Cloverberry, the tag of an Eames—or at least, inspired—set of cannisters, and of a Peugeot coffee grinder as she spoke. "Look, if you have a problem with how Gayle runs her business, I suggest you take it up with her. I have *not* gotten everything I wanted, which, I believe, is proof that she did not offer a pre-sale. Now if you'll excuse me, I'd like to try to avoid missing anything else. Have a nice day."

But the woman wouldn't leave her alone. From room to room, she hovered like a helicopter mama. But rather than try to prevent catastrophe, she worked to create it at every turn. If Cassie even *looked* half interested, the woman snatched it up.

Fine. Two can play at this game. You watch where I'm going. Psyche! A grin spread. *How eighties of me.*

She took one step to the left—no clue what was over there, and the woman dashed past and went for a bowling ball.

Really? What kind of ridiculousness is that? Bowling ball? Unless it belonged to Don Carter or something. Sheesh. As she enjoyed mental triumphs, Cassie grabbed a lamp, clock, and double peacock chenille bedspread. "Have a nice day. Oh, and you might want to look at that set of fishing flies. Looks good!"

It worked—until she reached the basement. The woman, hot on her heels again, ramped her complaints up a few decibels. Cassie's ears thundered as the woman, too infuriated to interfere much with Cassie's shopping, screeched her objections in the form of obscenities. Gayle arrived within seconds.

"I'm sorry, ma'am. But if you can't lower your voice and tone down your language, I'll have to ask you to leave. You're interfering with the other shoppers' experience."

"And you interfered with *mine!* I wanted that Cloverberry. I've been looking for one since long before it got popular again." Tears—were they genuine? Cassie couldn't tell. "Mama had one."

She'd been ready to relent—to offer the thing up as a peacemaking sacrifice. But the unfamiliar way "Mama" *didn't* roll off the woman's tongue gave her away. "Yeah. You almost had me." Cassie inched a tad closer and dropped her voice. "Hint. If you're going to tell a sob story, put as much truth in it as you can. Mom, Mother, Mommy—whatever. Use the real thing."

It worked. The woman—embarrassed or infuriated, no one knew—stormed from the building, the tags for items she'd tried to best Cassie out of with her. Gayle rolled her eyes. "This is why I *always* pay the extra dollar or 'reserve the right to refuse sale' on *all* of my ads." She pulled a handful of tags from her pocket. "What did she have that you wanted?"

A sick feeling washed over her as Cassie named off half a dozen items. "Um, Gayle?"

"Yeah? Is that it?"

Business demanded she name it all. "Just a few random

pieces of furniture—gotta call Joel for those—that I want to desecrate since they aren't worth restoring."

Gayle pulled her toward a side entrance. "I've got the basement key. We'll go in this way—faster. Now what did you want?"

"Are there strings attached to your helpfulness today?" As much as her inner self screamed for her to stuff it, Cassie wrestled the words from herself. "Because if there are, I'd just better go now."

"Strings?" Gayle jiggled the key and grinned as the lock turned. "No. Buttered up—definitely. I think I have a proposition you're going to love, and I decided to make considering it worth your while. That's it. If you say no, we're good."

Cassie couldn't help but flash her a smile. "And you'll go back to being the same, old shyster who tries to charge me double what anything is worth?"

"I promise." Gayle stuck out her hand. "Deal?"

Hesitation—she couldn't help it. "Deal that we'll go back to normal, or unknown business deal?"

Laughter echoed in the basement. How, with its wall-to wall boxes and furnishings, Cassie didn't know. "You're quick—paranoid, but quick." Gayle took note of the items Cassie wanted and shook her head. "He's going to have to make two or three trips. Do you have *room* for all this?"

"That storage unit is getting, full, but I can't *not* do this." Cassie stared at a wrought-iron washstand. She'd seen them converted into gorgeous planters—perfect for the non-existent shop. "Need that, too."

And with that addition, Cassie officially lost her mind. "Okay. I'm just going for it—probably spending my whole savings, but I don't care. I need this stuff. Maybe Ralph at HearthLand will let me consign stuff in the gift shop there."

"Great idea. Can I make a suggestion?" Gayle pointed to a few things as she spoke. "Call Joel, get him to rent a small moving truck, and come—one trip. Then call 'Ralph at HearthLand' and ask if you can take the stuff right there. If you can, spend today emptying out that storage unit into whatever place Ralph lets you use. Trust me."

She couldn't argue the point, but two things held her back. *First, if I do that, I can't go back. I'm stuck with a store I still am not ready to open. Two, you just clinched a deal that I don't even know about yet. Scary.*

Still, she pulled open her phone and swiped across her contacts. Joel popped up. "I'll make you a deal, Gayle. I'll take you to lunch on Tuesday and discuss your proposition *if...*" She paused for dramatic effect and waited until Gayle squirmed before continuing. "You don't try to bump prices until *after* I tell you no and *if* Joel agrees." With that, she tapped his name. Gayle nodded. Joel answered.

"Hey, Joel, got a proposition for you."

"I knew this day would come!" Only the faintest trace of exaggeration told her he knew what she meant.

"You know that store I've always talked about?" Her eyes met Gayle's and a smile formed. Gayle gave her a thumbs-up. "Well, I think I just bought it. Feel like renting a moving truck for me—small but not *too* tiny."

"Sure thing. Where'm I going?"

"First to the unit. Fill it up. Then..." Cassie fumbled for her phone notes. "You'll need to come here. I'll text you."

Just as she was about to hang up, Joel's voice came through. "Hey, Cass?"

"Yeah?"

"I'm proud of you—finally doing this. Where's the store?"

A lump the size of her fist tried to form in her throat, but Cassie choked it back down. "I... well... um... I'm about to call Ralph."

"Yesss!!!!"

201

Music—Louis Jordan's, "Caldonia"—pulsated around them. Spent from several minutes trying to mimic the movements of the Lindy Hop, Evan called for refills and grinned at her. "You did *great.*"

"You can say that because I followed you." Cassie folded her hands over her chest and frowned. "Why didn't you tell me you could swing?"

"Can't—never done it before. But...." He grinned. "Dancing is dancing at its barest form. It's like cooking maybe—different cuisines but still a blend of harmonious flavors."

She blinked at him, arms still folded over her chest, smile tugging at the corners of her lips, eyes bright and laughing at him. *Okay, so do you even* know *how gorgeous you are?* Unsure what else to do, he shrugged and reached for the watered-down remnants of his former soda. "What?"

"Did you just use poetical language to compare food and *dancing?*" Cassie threw back her head and laughed. "This is too cool!"

All building panic fizzled. "Well, cool is better than pathetic, so I'll take it. Now tell me about the library."

"Nope. That's tonight's blog post. I was saving it for tomorrow, but I haven't heard back from Ralph yet on his business proposition, so I'll do that tonight and business tomorrow."

Great. More of this eco-stuff. I don't get it. If you are going to be Ellie Environmentalist, then do it. Why the resistance?

"—ays he'll probably have a building ready for me by the end of March or the beginning of May at the latest. Meanwhile, he's letting me store it in one of the building shells—*free!*"

"Nothing is ever free, Cassie. So, what does *he* get out of it."

The way she fiddled with the edge of the tablecloth told him it had to be big. Her foot, in heels too high for much more comfortable dancing, bopped in time to the music. Arms still over her chest, posture screaming, "You won't shake me",

Cassie grinned. "My promise to give the shop a full chance through Christmas before moving it elsewhere."

"Starting when?" As soon as he asked, Evan groaned. "End of March to beginning of May—somewhere in there. Duh." He started to sit forward and talk business but the arrival of drinks stopped him, and from the disappointed look on her face, just in time. *She doesn't want this date to be about business. Reasonable expectation there.* Only one thing would reassure her that he'd only been showing an interest in *her* with his questions. "So, metal. Did you buy any today?"

"Tons!" The brightness of her eyes, the way she lit up as she began describing her purchases—it all pointed to one thing.

"That's your true passion, you know. Finding old things that were once cherished and finding people to cherish them again—that's it. That's what you love."

Everything changed—from the way Cassie leaned forward and engaged with him to the subtle flirting he didn't think she knew she'd assumed. "You know, this is all recycling. You're probably the greenest person in the whole of the Rockland area. I mean, c'mon! Look at you."

"Not hardly, but thanks." Cassie eyed her shoes and gave him an apprising glance. "I've got enough in me for one more if someone wanted to ask me to dance or something."

The band leader called for a foxtrot just as the set ended. Professional dancers took the middle of the floor and demonstrated the slow-step, slow-step, quick-side-together movements. Cassie shrugged at him and held out her arms. "Looks easy enough. I just don't see how everyone isn't going to be bumping into each other."

"There's a turn, I'm sure. All dances have them. I'll figure it out if they don't show us."

Not every dance had been a success. They'd enjoyed it, sure, but Cassie's dancing skills lent themselves more to improvisation than cultured steps. Evan led well—when she managed *not* to take over— but despite her best efforts, no one would say she was a "natural." Despite the kinks, she'd managed a fairly strong Lindy Hop, and when one of the professionals stopped and murmured, "Allow him to *lead*. Don't think about where you're going. Just trust that he'll guide you," everything shifted.

Cassie stepped a little closer than the dance required, closed her eyes, and waited. "Fair warning: if you lead me into another couple, I'll kick you."

How can something that would annoy me in so many people be endearing in her? First the environmentalist wacko stuff, and then a statement like that. She knows as well as I do that if we plow into someone, it would be their problem—or hers.

They moved. Evan concentrated on following the steps of the professional leading their side of the room and used the pressure of his hands to warn which way they'd go next. She followed—right up to the moment she opened her eyes. She backed away and right into the man behind them. "Argh!" She apologized profusely before turning back to him. "That's it. I'm just going to keep 'em closed and do what the gal said—*let* you lead and trust you won't guide me into everyone else. Clearly you can't trust *me* not to botch it."

And she did—for the better part of the song. But at some point, and Evan doubted she knew when, Cassie slipped her arms up around his neck, rested her cheek on his shirt, and swayed. He ducked them out of the dance line and tried to keep his heart from racing at her nearness. *There is something about her, isn't there?*

"Ruined it again, didn't I?"

Eyes closed, swaying to the music in time with the heartbeat of the music, Evan just murmured a simple, "Hmmm-mmm. Pretty much perfect."

⚏ ⚏ ⚏

What about this guy inspires such perfect dates? The thought had barely formed when they reached her door. She fumbled with the key, grumbling at the ridiculous Hollywood notion of a leisurely goodbye at a front door. "Seriously? You can so tell that Hollywood is in California just by that ridiculous nonsense!" She wrenched open the door and nearly fell inside. "Here, you'd either freeze to death before you got the word 'night' out of your mouth, or you'd be eaten alive by mosquitoes."

She reached for the door, but Evan pushed it shut behind him and leaned against it. "I had fun. Maybe springtime will let me stand under a porch light and give your neighbors a show." His forehead wrinkled and his lips pursed. "Beverly and... Timothy?"

"Thomas—and they're not a couple. Thought you should know. They might get testy about that if you ever meet them and hint at it."

In one of those obnoxious out-of-body moments, Cassie watched Evan reach out to touch her face—to pull her closer. She watched his expression change from conversational to kiss-er-sational. Something she'd never felt welled up inside as her resolve *not* to kiss him recharged itself. Cassie jerked back and whacked her head into the fridge. "I—"

"I'm sorry." Evan stood there, fists plunged into pockets and eyes filled with confusion.

"You have no idea how much—" Her wiser-self stuffed an imaginary sock down her throat before she made it worse. "I—" Frustration welled up and overflowed. She grabbed his hand and dragged him through the kitchen to the living room, nudged him into a chair, and plopped down next to Think. Habit? The need for comfort? Who knows for sure, but her hand began rubbing his head as if for comfort.

"Okay, what just happened there? One second I was going to kiss you and the next you're over there fondling that thing like it's a talisman against what seemed to me very much wanted kisses."

"Yeah. They are. That's the problem. So, I thought we

should talk."

In the thirteen seconds she expended trying to word her explanation, Evan came to his own conclusion. "Oh, wait. I get it. You have convictions against unmarried affection." He leaned forward, smiled, and shook his head. "You could have told me, Cassie. Just tell me where the line is, and I won't go near it."

Even as a groan escaped, Cassie's mind complained. *If I groan one more time, he's gonna rush me to the ER for appendicitis or something!* With a roll of her eyes and a smile she hoped didn't look as pained as it felt, Cassie tried to explain—again. "Look, I don't know how to tell you this without coming off as a total hypocrite, but here goes."

Cassie stared at her hands as if somehow they'd make everything sound more reasonable. "Look, I'm always affectionate with guys I go out with. I mean, if there's more than just a date or two, I'll hold hands or whatever. I kiss guys. I do." Her eyes rose to meet his. "And look where that has gotten me? Mild make-outs with half the guys of our acquaintance for what? Where did that go? Nowhere. I date the wrong people and go about it all the wrong way. So, I'm not doing it anymore."

"You're not dating—so you're 'breaking up' so to speak. I mean, we're—"

"No!" The giggles started before she could hope to stop them. Evan flashed a grin. "I'm just keeping some things, obvious ones and now kissing for sure, for more committed relationships—maybe engagement or—"

The moment she used the E word, Cassie threw a malevolent look at Think. *Why didn't you stop me! How embarrassing!*

"I can respect that. Yeah. Okay. It'll make us focus on each other rather than just emotions, too."

When a blink showed him still there, Cassie blinked again. "I'm waiting for words like, 'pathetic' or 'loser.' Where are they?"

"If that's what you want, wait for a guy with no morals or scruples or sincere interest in getting to know you."

She drew her knees to her chest, wrapped her arms around them and glared at him. "Way to say just the right thing so I don't know if I should trust you or not."

In answer, Evan stood, squeezed her clasped hands, and thanked her for asking him to ask her out. "Want to do a picnic tomorrow?"

"In the snow?"

He inched toward the door. "Not what I had in mind, no."

"If I don't have to do HearthLand talks, you're on."

The duplex reverberated with the rattle of the door as Evan pulled it closed. Cassie grinned at Think and pulled him into her arms. "Did you hear that?! He *totally* gets it! I can't believe this! Wow! And he's thoughtful. I bet this picnic is cool."

Then like a toddler with a shiny new toy, she almost flung him back onto the end table, dinging her lamp in the process, and scrambled for her laptop.

Support

Yeah. That's what we're talking about today. It started with the group I went to last night. It might just be a meeting about being eco-conscious, but to me it felt like a support group. Like "Consumer's Anonymous." I mean, I did get up and practically say, "Hi. I'm Cassie Wren and it's been six hours since I last looked longingly at a plastic bottle."

Did you know that eco-consciousness knows no political, social, or financial bounds? Except maybe hippies. There wasn't a single one there last night. I was relieved. Gotta confess, tonight I'm kind of disappointed. Apparently, they usually talk about things they've learned how to do without, how to substitute, or that something they assumed was bad for the planet wasn't.

Gotta confess. I thought it would be all about planting "woolly lamb's ear" to use instead of toilet paper. Yeah. It's a thing. I was trying to justify my consumption. Do you know I use two rolls a week? I didn't. Yeah. Two. I go through a twenty-four pack every quarter. So, I thought, "Well, I'm not doing the washable TP wipes thing, but maybe…" So, I looked it up. Yeah. It's a thing. Plant this stuff, wipe your butt, and flush, baby! Totally biodegradable. Not degrading my bio that way. Just sayin'.

But when I whined that I can't bring veggies home without the denim bags getting all soggy, one old gramma—bless her soul—said, "Just get some of those old white kitchen towels—everyone has some—and a sheer shower or living room curtain. Sew one side of each together and voila! Instant produce bags that won't raise your produce weight costs."

Guess what I'll be doing next week?

Also, moral support. You've seen the comments. Joel and Evan—Lauren. They're great. They really have backed me up on this, even though I know Evan thinks I'm nuts. By the way, if you want video of my pathetic dancing, you'll have to get him to share it with me. I didn't think to do it on my phone too. This support group at the library? They just might help keep my friends sane! I won't have to call Lauren fifty times a week going, "What about produce? Everything is all icky wet by the time I get home!" I've got Ima Jean over there to save my butt on that one.

You know, something happened at dancing tonight. I kept messing us up. We all know how I am. Total jump in with both feet, flounder, and make a mess but have a blast. Okay. It's me. Those of you who remember my first furniture refinish job. I rest my case. The rest of you, trust me. The fact that I'm alive and with fingerprints still is a test to God's goodness.

Which, once again brings me back to tonight's dancing. Here I was not so foxy at the foxtrot when one of the professional dancers came over and said, "Allow him to *lead*. Don't think about where you're going. Just trust that he'll guide you."

Isn't that profound? Forget DANCING. What about GOD??? That's a total GOD thing. We're talking totally awesomely cool. Change a couple of those H's to capitals and whoa. Profound. And that's when it hit me. I have my friends. I have my eco-group. But you know what? I have a one-deity support group. It's all I NEED. I have JESUS. He's there. He's got my back. We do these things like we're in it alone. But I think God cares about my project. I think He cares that I want to learn from it. I think He knows it's not "me" but what IS me is learning through my craziness.

So today? Go out and be YOU. Just lean on your greatest support group Leader when you do it. Lean on Jesus.

Sunday, January 24—

Cassie's car whizzed down the Dolman Highway. Okay, it whined every inch of the way. That whine warned against any rash decisions about opening stores in out-of-the-way towns like HearthLand. "But I bought all that stuff! I have two thousand dollars' worth of stuff from Saturday's sale alone. By March, I could have my entire car budget blown on stuff for the store—a store I don't even have."

The sign for HearthLand—simple but inviting. Cassie flipped her blinker and held it in place until she rounded the corner. A glare at it nearly sent her into a ditch, but the car whined down Hearthfield Way despite her malevolent thoughts.

Small dots grew into long, tall buildings—a block of them. Houses surrounded by snow painted a charming, almost Rockwellian landscape with their whirling windmills and diminutive but distinctive trails of chimney smoke. "There's even cows over there."

Ralph met her on his porch, his eyes crinkling in a welcoming smile. Even as she shivered from the car and ran across the yard to his porch, he beckoned. "Annie's making brownie a la mode—and they're almost out of the oven."

"Okay, that's just not fair. If you're going to brownie me up, I'm helpless to resist."

"That was the idea! C'mon in."

The house—everything she'd ever hoped for but without the vintage touches she would have added. *Oh, if I could just have a couple of hours with my stuff and this room. Man, that quilt I got last June—perfect over the back of that couch. And that card catalog would make a great entry table. Wow.*

"Cassie?"

She jerked out of her reverie. "Sorry, just admiring your house. This is seriously awesome. Man, someday."

"Could be sooner than you think if I can just talk you into a store."

Doubt I'd make it do that *well.* "You're optimistic."

As he led her into the kitchen—that alone, nearly created a salivary gland overload—Ralph protested. "I've been researching."

"Oh, leave her alone." Ralph's wife—his *bride,* Annie—rolled her eyes at Cassie. "Let the brownies do their job."

Cassie slid onto a barstool at the island and propped her chin on her hands. "So, basically, resistance is futile. Drink the Kool-Aid?"

"Basically." Annie pulled a covered glass bowl from the freezer and dug an ice cream scoop from a nearby drawer. "It probably sounds intimidating, but Ralph can be very persuasive. After all, he convinced me to marry him."

Ralph just cleared his throat.

Her eyes darted back and forth, heart aching to see the love there and so curious about their enormous age gap. "Have you been married long?"

"Three weeks." Annie grinned. "Barely."

The faint scent of baking brownies became a heady perfume as the door opened and the heat billowed out into the room. Annie's movements—already swift and comfortable in what had to be a new kitchen. So many questions bubbled up inside her, but Cassie waited until the bowl of ice cream-topped brownie slid in front of her. She picked up the proffered spoon and dug into the bowl with relish. "So, how'd you meet?"

"I was homeless, and he shared a beefsteak sandwich with me."

All rational thought, all hope of a response disappeared as she listened to the story. They spoke in tandem, each adding a different nuance to the same tale. Something in the interweaving of the tale reminded her of the Regency dances in Austen movie adaptations. *Stupid movies aren't any better than the books. But the way they move in and out, never quite connecting on a full level—that's what it sounds like.*

"—about you. Got a boyfriend?" Annie dug into her brownie with enough relish that Cassie couldn't help but appreciate.

"I guess I do." She shrugged at their odd expressions. "I mean, I just started going out with this guy—only a couple of times—but considering he didn't walk when I told him I wasn't doing the whole kissing thing." With her mind screaming for her mouth to stop, Cassie spilled the entire encounter. "So, I'd say he's a boyfriend. I think."

"Sounds like one to me," Ralph agreed. "And a good one." He gave Annie a wink before he turned back to her. "Smart move on the kissing. I think it's a good thing we pretended not to be interested until she gave up and asked me to marry her or the three week wait from engaged to married might have felt like three years."

Annie shoved him. "Speak for yourself." To Cassie she added, "It *did* feel like three years. At *least*."

"Well, I've not been so smart in the past—with guys, I mean. I don't think I'd care so much about knowing I'd kissed someone I broke up with if the relationship had ever had a real chance. It's just knowing that I treated all of them as if they were permanent even when I knew they couldn't be—that's what gets to me." Anxious to avoid further questions, Cassie dropped her spoon into the bowl and folded her arms. "I am going on a brownie strike unless you tell me what I want to know."

Ralph snickered and reached for her bowl. Cassie, had she had one, would have given anything to stab him with a fork—gently, of course. Instead, she snatched it from his grasp and glared. "I *said*, '*Unless* you tell me.' Is this your way of informing me that you *aren't* going to tell me?"

"Ralph, don't antagonize the girl you're trying to get to do what you want." Annie gave Cassie a 'What can you do?' expression. "It's like he never left elementary school or something."

An iPad slid in front of her, and with a few taps and swipes, a floor layout appeared. "And here I thought I was trying to give her what *she* wants."

"What am I looking at?"

"This is the space we can offer you. Now, if you decided you wanted to establish yourself here, we could work on considering a building designed to your specifications. This is what is being built now—or will be. We have the shell up. They're working on the inside."

A swipe showed demographics. Cassie studied the information about their shoppers, about their residents, and about themselves. He showed previous projections and how those had played out. He showed current projections and how on track they were with those. "As you can see, so far we've exceeded every projection we've made. We're conservative that way."

Ralph pointed to one line. "That's from a survey we conducted with every single person we've been in contact with since you arrived." The next line showed drastically higher numbers for the same questions. "Those are website survey results."

Annie swept a brownie mix box into a trash can. "People are eager to find a store that carries a wide variety of top-quality retro, vintage, and antique goods."

"But are they willing to pay for it?" Cassie leaned back, arm curled around her warm brownie bowl, and eyed the numbers. "My stuff won't be cheap."

And with that, Ralph jumped off the chair. "Finish your brownie. I'll go get the keys. There are a few things you should see."

Cassie watched as he strode from the room, excitement and what seemed like confidence oozing from him. She turned to Annie. "Is he always so self-assured?"

"Nope. Just when he knows he has a good thing." Her voice dropped to almost a whisper. "I shouldn't tell you this, but he wants this badly enough that you have bargaining room. Use it."

⚟⚟⚟

Her hinge-lidded, step-open garbage can lay on a towel on the kitchen floor. With a rolling pin, Joel worked to smooth the front, but it only served to create a crepe paper look to the stainless finish. "I don't know, Cassie. I feel like it looks worse now than it did before I started."

Deep breath. Don't freak. He's helping. Cassie moved closer and asked to see. "Maybe it's just your light."

It wasn't. The pebbled section looked like it'd been hammered by hailstones. Joel sat back on his heels and shook his head. "I think the dent would have been better."

"Not after I almost tore the metal trying to pop it back." A new idea sent Cassie searching for her tiny upholstery hammer. Joel tried to stop her, but she refused to listen. "It can't be worse. Maybe if—" *bang!* "The—" *bang!* "Whole thing—" *Bang! Bang! Bang!* "Looks the same, it'll look cool—unique, even."

Five minutes later, the mangled garbage can stood in its usual place, looking like it had lost a battle. "Yeah. It did," Cassie muttered as she gripped the hammer and resisted the urge to hurl it through the window. "With a *hammer!*"

"Well, it is more uniform. Maybe it'll grow on you."

"Meanwhile, what do I do? It's horrible!" Cassie sank into a chair and covered her head with her arms. "It's *metal.* I can't even replace it!"

Joel said nothing. Anger—delightfully irrational anger—welled up in her. She jerked her head up and found him texting something to someone. "Having a laugh at my expense? Of all the people—"

"No, I was putting up an ISO post for a nice used one on the Facebook sale page."

In half a second she'd flung herself from her chair and wrapped her arms around him. "You are the best best guy friend *ever*."

Joel held her, murmured another apology, and then stepped away from her with the kind of deliberation that hinted at difficulty. "I should have been able to do *something*."

You've got to stop—

"And if you beat yourself up for hugging me, so help me I'm going to grab you, hug you, and refuse to let go until you get that I can take it. It's *you*, Cass! I mean, it's just one of the many things that make up who you are." Joel gathered up the mess on the floor and began putting it all away. "I was thinking about Evan there, okay? He wouldn't like it. Respect for you guys—that's all it was, okay?"

Way to make me feel like an idiot while trying to make me feel better. A glance at Think earned her what she felt sure was a censorious glare. *Okay, that's not fair.*

When Joel grabbed his coat, Cassie did the only thing she could think of. "Hey, Joel?"

"Yeah?"

"One, will you forgive me? I'm just learning how to do the non-loser guy thing. Okay?"

Joel dropped his coat on a chair and moved to her side. If she *hadn't* been dating Evan, he'd have cupped her chin or pulled her close. The desire showed in every look, every movement. Instead, he folded his arms over his chest in a direct but likely unconscious imitation of her usual stance and shook his head. "Dave wasn't a loser. He wasn't right for *you*, but he wasn't a loser. Trevor, Franco, Jan, and Roger—all not losers. All wrong for you, yes. But not *losers*."

"Works out to about the same thing."

"No…" Joel's head swung from side to side as he argued. "They were good guys. Your judgment skills aren't lacking. You didn't choose criminals and commitment phobic idiots. You just have a heart for people that sometimes overrides reality. There's something great about that—even if it isn't what you need for *yourself*." As she stood there, considering his words, he searched her face. "What was two?"

"Could you go get ice cream? I need to drown my sorrows." She eyed his phone. "Maybe add an ice cream freezer to your ISO post?"

Once more, he snatched up his coat and left. Cassie stared at the offensive garbage can and pulled out her own phone. With a quick snap, she started to post a "Free" ad on the Facebook page, but a moment later, she uploaded it to her blog and pulled out her laptop.

Warped

That's what my life has become. Seriously. So, let's pretend this is DECEMBER 24 instead of January 24—just suspend reality for a moment. C'mon, let me dream a bit, okay? I kind of need it right now. I've never been so beaten down—pun totally intended—by something so pathetic. What is it?
Trash.
Okay, maybe that's a bit simplistic. It's really my trash CAN. I got mad tonight and kicked it. And it dented. So, I tried to pop out the dent and well, I almost TORE the stupid metal doing it. Seriously? I could see it trying to rip—kind of like paper! So, bizarre. So, Joel to the rescue. He came over and tried to help me roll it into place. He got it all hot with this tool of his mom's—something for making pretty cards. It got that metal HOT and then we rolled the rolling pin—bet you didn't think I had one—over it. It still stayed bumpy everywhere he rolled it. No. Joke. So, I took a hammer to the inside—to make it ALL bumpy. I thought it would look cool—like hammered copper or something. Yeah. Not hardly. It looked like I was hammered and... you can fill in the rest.
So here it is. Look at this thing. Isn't it ugly? I need a new trash can. Could I have done this last week when I could have justified replacing it? Noooooooo. I have to do it this week when I'm supposed to start eradicating the excess metal from my life.
Look. This thing works. It is a perfectly functional trash can. I just hate it. And well, hate isn't sufficient excuse to buy "off plan" so to speak. I want a "new" one (someone's undented cast-off). So, I'm giving this to anyone in the Rockland area who wants one. I'll deliver. And I'll survive without one until I find the one I want that doesn't come from a big box store or Amazon. Because that's the challenge I

accepted.

I fully accept that my vision is skewed—WARPED, if you will—by my world. In my world, when you want something new, you buy it. If you have a perfectly good one, you give it to the thrift store knowing that someone else will get it at a price THEY can afford. Some charity gets the proceeds. We all win. And part of me says, "What's wrong with that?"

But there's a new, emerging part of me that says, "What's RIGHT about being so discontent with a stupid TRASH CAN that you have to do without one until you get a new one?" I don't know. I don't think there is. I think that this "green" endeavor of mine is really tearing off new blinders every day and making me see just who I am?

I mean, I sent Joel to the store for ice cream. I forgot to give him a jar. It's okay, because he'll pay for it so it's not on me. He'll take home the container. Why? He's that kind of supportive friend. But I did it knowing all this. I did it knowing that I was going to take a situation and exploit it. And that's the worst part of all.

I had decided to tell you about something cool that happened Saturday and yesterday. But well, it's late, I hear Joel's car in the drive, and I want ice cream. So, goodnight. Have a chuckle at my stupidity. And if you want a "hammered" stainless steel trash can, just let me know. I'm happy to get it out of my life. I don't need reminders of my patheticness.

⚏ ⚏ ⚏

The phone rang just as she crawled in bed. Evan's smile on the screen caused her to jump back up and shuffle down the hall to the living room as she answered. "Hey! How was your day?"

"Great. Sounds like you had a bit of a frustrating evening."

"You aren't kidding! Want a trash can?"

Something in the way Evan demurred sent her senses on alert. Cassie threw a, "Oh, help" look at Think as she snapped on the lamp and waited for him to continue. He didn't. "Evan?"

"I guess I just called to tell you that I don't get this eco thing of yours—"

"Yeah. You've made that abundantly clear. So you had to call and make sure I know? Really, Evan?" Her "oh help" look morphed into a, "Can you believe this jerk" scowl in half a second flat.

Think—Cassie was certain he rolled his eyes.

Amen, Think. Amen.

"That's actually the opposite of what I was going to say. I called to tell you that *while I don't get it*, I can help. I know a thing or two about metal."

Being helpful or jealous? Both? It's cute.... Cassie gave Think a questioning glance and threw all caution to the wind. "Does it bother you that Joel came? I mean, he's been one of my best friends for years. I—"

"I'm not jealous of *him*...." Evan cleared his throat. "But I am a bit jealous of the ease with which you call him to join you in your little adventures. I just wanted you to know I'm always willing to help, too."

It was a sacrifice—a *big* one, actually—but Cassie decided it was also a good test of the future of their relationship, such as it was. "Well, I am going to be making produce bags this week. You could join me."

Brownie points in the guy's favor, he didn't even hesitate. "Just tell me when and where and what to bring. I've never sewed more than a button or..."

Cassie snickered. "Admit it. You had to sew sequins back on, didn't you?"

"Yeah. By hand. So if you need hand sewing, I might be okay. But machines... maybe I could read directions or cut... whatever it is you cut."

That right there—that's cool romance. Pretty cool stuff. She rang off and stared out into the room. One hand pulled her throw blanket from the back of the couch. The other grabbed another pillow. In seconds, with lights blaring and Think watching with a parental eye, Cassie drifted into sleep.

Monday, January 25—

217

She sat at her desk, the jar of salad mocking her. Mr. Sylmer stepped out to leave for his twelve-thirty lunch appointment and stared at her. "Um, Cassie?"

"I brought glass again."

"Um, okay, and that's bad because..."

She raised her eyes to meet the half-concerned, half-annoyed expression on her employer's face. "That's why I'm up here. They don't want glass downstairs."

"Again, I do not see the problem. You are here. I haven't asked you not to bring glass." He paused. "Unless you plan to break it and use it as a weapon to coerce me into giving you a raise..."

Jaw-to-desk collision followed by a snicker. Cassie shook her head and glared at the jar again. "You get me every time. I always forget that you have a sense of humor." In one of those odd moments when her life played out before her like a Looney Tunes cartoon, Cassie felt her face drain of color. "I mean—"

Mr. Sylmer snickered. "And this is why you have job security around here. You keep me young and laughing." He paused as he opened the door. "Well, that and my wife would divorce me if I fired you."

"Well, you wouldn't have to find a lawyer...."

"That's what you think." Sylmer waited the perfect number of seconds for best impact and then quipped, "Except she'd hire Fahir."

Cassie, having lost what remained of her senses, tossed another loaded one after him. "Remind me to send her a box of those chocolates she likes. Gotta keep her on my good side."

Once the door shut behind him, she groaned. "Learn to keep your mouth shut. Seriously, he's your *boss!*

The salad continued to mock her, taunt her. Cassie glared. Still it sat as her stomach rumbled its protest at the delay in nutritional gratification. The office door opened again, Sylmer's voice greeting her before she could even look up. "—got my scarf. It's probably still windy—" He stopped halfway across the

218

room and shook his head. "Okay, what else is it? Clearly it's not just the glass."

Never had she felt more foolish than when she admitted her latest chagrin. "It's the rings. They're almost disposable. They rust, so you have to buy new ones. What am I going to do when they rust? Wha—"

"Buy the stupid rings. They're recyclable."

"But isn't that just chea—" She couldn't continue—not with the look of incredulity on the man's face. *I think he just decided to risk that divorce.*

Sylmer stared until Cassie couldn't help but squirm. "You have a brain, Cassie. A fine one, if you must know. So use it. This experiment of yours will fail if you decide to fall victim to the eco equivalent of being 'penny wise and pound foolish.'"

With that, he retrieved his scarf and disappeared, leaving Cassie still staring at the offending metal ring. Slow, methodic movements followed. She dropped the ring to the desk and spun it. Fork. Bite by bite, it speared the salad, but not until she'd finished did Cassie realize she hadn't added her dressing. "Oh brother."

Her phone buzzed—Joel. Cassie tapped the screen and read the message, her heart sinking with each word.

SO, WANT TO MAKE THOSE PRODUCE BAGS TONIGHT?

"Great. Where's Think when I need him? I forgot I mentioned it to Joel. Now what do I do?"

The office walls closed in on her as she held her phone in both hands and waited for direction from the Lord.

⸻ ⸻ ⸻

The freezer boasted two burritos, a box of frozen mac-n-cheese, and meat from HearthLand—none of it defrosted, of course. Cassie spun in a circle hoping for some inspiration, but nothing came to her. The jar of spaghetti sauce *might* have enough for *one* plate—if she were lucky. "And I'm not, Think. We both know this. So, what do I do?"

That's all it took. Cassie whipped out her phone and dialed her mother's number. "Help!"

"Hang up and call 9-1-1."

"Mom!" Her giggle—Cassie could have sworn Think snickered in perfect unison. *I'm losing my mind.*

"What was I supposed to think? You do this. You call and act like the sky is falling, but it's really that you wanted a picture of a fluffy white cloud, and it's too small or something."

She's got a point. Still... Before she lost her determination, Cassie laid out her problem. "Evan is coming over. I didn't shop to feed him. So now what do I do? I have two burritos, frozen mac-n-cheese, and hunks of meat. Frozen."

"No spaghetti sauce? You can brown ground beef from frozen, you know."

No, I didn't know, but I do now. Still, there's not enough sauce. Cassie stared into her fridge as if it would magically sprout more than the half dozen mushrooms left in a plastic bag she still hadn't stopped repenting for using. *No more after tonight! Yeah, baby!*

"—ssie!"

"Sorry, what?"

"I said, what's in your fridge?"

She began with the mostly empty jar of spaghetti sauce. "And there are a few mushrooms. Um, I have baloney that I found in the back of the freezer—must have bought it on sale. Um, there's turkey breast for salad chunks and condiments. Oh, and milk. I still have milk, eggs, and butter that I brought home yesterday. Maybe a tomato..."

"Any cheese?"

"Provolone slices. I think." Cassie pulled out the deli drawer and stared into it. "Yeah, there are three slices—no, four slices of provolone. I could do sandwiches, but I don't have b—"

"Pizza. You need flour, oil, salt, yeast—"

Cassie cut her off there. "Um, no yeast, Mom. You—"

"Have neighbors. Go talk to Bev Morrison. She'll have some. And actually, she might have better cheese—maybe mozzarella. Provolone will work, but…"

As much as she didn't want to do it, Cassie began assembling the aforementioned ingredients. "Can you send me a recipe? How long does the dough have to rise?" Cassie grabbed her coat. "And—"

"Sending now. It's easy. It doesn't have to rise at all. You're fine. It'll make a nice yeasty crust—just like you like it."

Cassie dumped the phone on the table next to Think and bolted from her front door. The air warned of an impending snowstorm. "Like we even *need* more snow. It's crazy!"

The doorbell reached even her ears, but Bev never appeared. Cassie tried the doorknob and when it opened, she called out, "Bev? Are you in here?"

"In the bathroom!"

Oh, how embarrassing. A few awkward seconds passed until she found her voice. "I can go. I just wanted to borrow some yeast."

"Little jar in the fridge. Help yourself to anything. Sorry. Upset stomach."

I can't believe I'm borrowing yeast instead of ordering a stupid pizza. This is ridicu— The sight of a bell pepper stopped her. *Oooh, that would be good. I wonder….*

All pride dissolved at the sight of a little ball of mozzarella cheese. Cassie inched toward the hallway, yeast jar in hand. "Um, do you need your cheese and your bell pepper before I get home tomorrow night? Or even before tonight? I could totally go get them after Evan—

"Take anything you need. I have plenty. Tomorrow is fine, and right now, cooking sounds horrible."

"Do you need anything? I've got Pepto—" Her heart sank. *If I give that to her, what'll I use? Does it count if stuff is medicinal? I mean, a person has to get well.*

But Beverly demurred, assuring Cassie that she had

everything she needed. "Cut your baloney into small pieces. It'll sizzle like pepperoni. I promise."

Just as Cassie opened her mouth to agree, realization struck. "Wait. How did you know I have baloney—and what I'm using it for?"

"Marla called. I just used the last of my salami, or I would have sent that."

Before any more embarrassing moments hit, Cassie thanked the older woman and dashed out the front door, arms full of supplies. Her antique clock chimed as she stepped into her duplex. "Great. Evan'll be here in like ten minutes."

Think commiserated.

In seconds, she had her phone open on her little island and the process begun. "Call Mom."

"Hey, sweetie!" Marla's voice came through the speaker in seconds. "Did you find everything? Was Bev out of the ba—"

"Mom! That's just gross, okay? And no. She's still sick. I offered my Pepto—a huge concession, if you ask me. I mean, I haven't even considered if I can buy stuff like that or not. Now tell me how to make this up to Joel. I know he expected to help me make these bags, and then Evan offered last night, so I told him *he* could, and now I feel guilty."

"Didn't you just use Joel to take stuff to HearthLand?"

Understanding didn't bother to take the time to dawn. It blinded her with instant full-glare sun. "Gotcha. Love you! Bye!"

Two minutes later, she called back. Marla answered and said, without waiting to hear the question, "Cookie sheet. Pizzas don't *have* to be circular. Or use one of those million disposable pans you have."

Even as she disconnected the call, Cassie shook her head. "Only a Mom."

But it worked. Her little cookie sheet would make exactly the perfect sized pizza. Cassie pressed the dough into it and stared at enough left to make another one. *But I don't need another one. So, then what?*

This time, her phone buzzed with a text before she could even open her mouth. FREEZE THE REST OF THE DOUGH UNCOOKED. YOU CAN HAVE PIZZA LATER. HOPE YOU STILL HAVE PLASTIC WRAP.

"That answer's that." Cassie folded it into a small Tupperware freezer container and ignored the plastic wrap remark. "It's inside plastic. That's basically the same thing, right, Think?"

Think didn't have a chance to answer. A knock on her front door announced Evan's arrival. Cassie stared at the cookie sheet mortified that it took so long. "I just wanted it in the oven before he saw the baloney!" Her hiss did little to engender Think's sympathy. The statue sat there, unmovable, uncaring.

Evan stood there with several plastic containers. "I started to go to the store for chips and salsa, but I knew you couldn't do that, so I dumped them in here. We wash. I take home. Is that okay?"

If she hadn't already announced her no-kiss policy, she might have done it right then and there. "Well, first, get in here. I'm freezing, and Think over there isn't wearing much, so icicles are probably forming...."

"I would... if you'd just take a step back..."

"Ha! Funny." Cassie beckoned him to follow and hurried back to the kitchen. "We're having 'Refrigerator Scrounge' topped with 'Neighbor Donations' for dinner."

Evan swept the kitchen with a nervous glance. "Pizza?"

"Yep. Sorry, you get baloney for meat." Cassie growled inwardly. *Can't you just keep your mouth shut!* "—and mushrooms and bell pepper. You were getting provolone cheese, but Bev had mozzarella, and I took it."

"Well," Evan piled up his containers and turned to examine the pizza. "You know, I bet it would be pretty good if you actually put it in a hot oven and baked it. Might want to try that sometime."

Cassie leaned against the sink, folded her arms over her

chest, and scowled at him. "Seriously? You just lost all brownie points for that."

Sheer white fabric with little dots embroidered at four inch intervals skittered all over the table as he tried to cut it. "I can't make this stay in one place. You need pins!"

"Then use them. They're in that thing somewhere."

If Evan thought his cutting skills were a problem, just watching Cassie wrestle the layers of fabric together destroyed his self-pity. "Let's start with pinning your bag. That's got to be a nightmare."

"But it'll just slip when I take out the pins anyway. So what's the point?" Cassie sank back against the chair and shot fiery darts of hatred at the contorted pieces of the bag.

He ignored her. Instead, he fumbled for pins, grabbed a piece of sheer fabric and the old towel she'd cut up and pinned them together. An extra bit of sheer at the top mocked his attempts, but scissors straightened the edge nicely. *I can do this. Can't look stupid now.* "Mind if I try?"

Cassie slid off the chair and reached for the scissors. "I'll cut more."

The fabric slid all over the place. Evan jerked the threads out, snipped them, and turned it over. The cotton didn't slip and slide half as much as the sheers. "Looks like if you put the towel down against the machine, it's a little easier to control."

She moved to his side, one hand resting on his shoulder, hovering. His senses zipped into high gear as he tried to ignore the nearness of her and stitched down the long side of a bag. He jumped, nearly elbowing her in the gut as Cassie's scream ripped through his eardrum.

"Watch! Wait. How—" She stood back, arms folded over her chest, and eyed him with suspicion. "You know how to sew! You little—"

"Never used a machine in my life." Evan held up two

fingers. "Spock's honor."

Without giving his words time to register, Cassie quipped, "Wrong fingers." With super-human effort, Evan repressed a smile just in time. She growled in frustration. "Don't try to put one over on me."

Do you have any idea how cute you are? He watched as she tried to read him. *No, I don't think you do.* Evan stared down at the machine. "So, what'd I do?"

"You sewed *right over* those pins. Like nothing! They didn't break and send pieces of needles flying all over the place."

"I take it you've had that happen."

She snatched up the scissors and began cutting. "Almost lost an eye once. Mom always takes them out first. I know it." She stopped mid-slice. "You said Spock! Oh, brother."

"Gotcha." Something in Cassie's face hinted she might not be as amused as he'd intended. As a face-saving measure, he directed the conversation back to needling her with his pin-dependence. "My mom sews over them, so I just did it. I wonder why your needle broke. Mine just slid right over that pin like nothing."

Cassie lunged as the fabric tried to slip off the table and managed not to impale her chin on the open scissors in her hand. "Maybe the machine likes guys better. After all, Joel gave it to me."

And that's what I wanted to hear. Just how close are you two?

"—helped me get those tote bags made. I got the thing threaded easier than him, though. So..."

Do you know how he feels about you? Everyone else does. Do you know they think I'm some kind of relationship killer? They try not to show it, but even Lauren, as excited as she is for us, is still a bit iffy when Joel is around.

"—lled to ask me out that night, actually. Joel invited you to go play pool with us, but I didn't want to....."

Whatever else she said, Evan missed. He tied off the

corners and started to turn the bag right side out, but the way the fabric raveled unnerved him. "Hey, Cassie?"

"Sorry." Her eyes met his. "I'm so used to him being comfortable—"

"It's not that. He's your friend. I get that. I'm not messing up old friendships out of some stupid petty jealousy." *Even if I want to sometimes.* "But this is going to ravel like crazy. There'll be holes in it in no time."

The answer came almost before he finished speaking. "Since I don't have those zig-zag scissors, we just have to stitch around the edges a few times. That's what I did on my napkins."

Evan whipped out his phone. "I'm calling Mom. I feel like you've hit on something with zig-zags. Pretty sure that's what she does."

"But I don't *have*—"

His mom answered before she could finish. "Hey, Mom. Look, I'm at Cassie's house and we're making these produce bags for her to take when she's shopping? So, they have…"

Step by step, he described the fabric, cutting them out. From pins to ravels, he tried to explain the issue, and nodded as she suggested a zig-zag stitch. "I knew it. So, we don't need the scissors? That stitch will work? I see it on the machine here. How do…?"

In seconds, he had a nice, neat wide zig zag stitched down a folded over piece of toweling. Evan passed it to Cassie. "How about that around the edge?"

"Tell your mom she's my hero. Then sew it. I'm cutting these." Just as her scissors sliced through a bit of toweling, she added, "Did I ask you to tell her thanks?"

"Got it. Thank you, hero Mom. I have to sew now."

"Ha." Cassie and his mother spoke in unison. "Very funny."

Okay… that was scary.

It's In the Bag

My boyfriend came over tonight. There. I typed it. I tried to word it a million ways, and it didn't do any good. Just a friend sounds like I'm ashamed of him. Boyfriend sounds like I'm presuming too much. Well, he's a guy and he's a friend and we've been on a few dates, and we've talked about a few important boyfriend/girlfriend things, so here we are. I had my boyfriend over for dinner tonight and we made "throw together" pizza and bags.

Produce bags. Remember how I talked about them? Sheers+towels=produce bag when mixed with threads that hold it all together. I was making a mess of them, so he just went over there, pinned them and sewed them up. Then he got input on how to keep them from falling apart and did that too.

Why do all the men in my life have better luck with sewing than me? It's a little sexist if you ask me. Whatever. I have bags! Don't they look cool? All right, so they look hideous, but they'll work. I even tested one in water. Got it wet, rubbed it until it should have produced a genie or something, and BAM! It's still intact. I'm actually looking forward to going to HearthLand on Saturday. Yeah. I'm going back. Again.

Okay. So HearthLand. I've talked a lot about opening my own store someday So I went there and talked to the head guy. Ralph is amazing. He really wants the kinds of things I have for his town.

Okay. Is it just me, or is it weird to call some town "his" like a person can own a town? Weird, right? Still, he wants my stuff. So, we're talking about it. I'd say it's still up in the air, but like the produce I plan to bring back from his monster-sized greenhouses, I think you can safely say that it's "in the bag," too.

Meanwhile, on the metal front, I had a bit of a meltdown today. Does anyone know if you can buy metal lids for mason jars that DON'T rust? I just realized that these things are going to rust. Has anyone ever seen an old lid that WASN'T rusted? Yeah. Me either.

Think says that he agrees with my boss. Just recycle the metal and buy more. But you know, it seems like there has to be an easier way. Buying is still contributing to consumerism which leads to further negative environmental impacts. So, I need something balanced there. I just don't know what. What would you do? Mason jars are a given. I NEED them. So, what about the lids?

Well, tomorrow I talk to someone else about this store idea. I think. I'll let you know what's going on there. Meanwhile, Think and I say, "Goodnight, world!"

Tuesday, January 26—

Mexican food had sounded amazing—right up until Cassie entered the sandwich counter-style restaurant and discovered metal—not plastic or paper, no *metal*—containers. *I think I'm with O'Reilly on this one. Murphy was an optimist. Can I win—just once. Or at least, can I not fail?*

An overly chipper, and definitely out of character, "Hi!" nearly helped Cassie shed her winter skin. "I thought that was your car!"

"Gayle, if I get thrown out of here for loss of bladder control, I'm firing you."

"So, are we in business?"

Okay, she couldn't help but laugh. "Good try, Gayle. You forget I know you well. You've tried to squeeze every dime you wanted from me for five years. You can't get me that easily."

"Well, let's get food first. I know how much you love a good burrito."

And how do you know that? Kind of... The answer to the question shadowed over her thoughts. "You stalked my social media, didn't you?"

"Research, Cassie. Just research." She pointed to the menu board. "I recommend the *carne asada*. It's amazing."

With no reason *not* to order it Cassie half-choked out her request and almost shook as she pulled out her wallet. Gayle pushed past her and held out a twenty for the guy behind the register. "I've got this."

"You're showing your hand way too soon, Gayle."

Without even a second of thought, Gayle quipped back, "Or that's what I want you to think."

Okay... This is just weird. She's never this... this... normal. *What's up?*

Oh, the mortification of staring at a plastic—washable, at least—tray with a paper liner, plastic cup, plastic fork, and a metal container. *Should've thought this out better.*

At the table, she snapped a picture of her confession, and Gayle pounced. "Seriously? I had no idea you were one of those 'document every bite' types. Do you take a picture of your car thermometer, too?"

And that is the Gayle I know. Cassie zipped the picture to Lauren with the text, F- IN THE NO METAL/PAPER/PLASTIC DEPT. A+ ON NO GLASS.

Cassie took her time doctoring the taco with rice, beans, *pico de gallo*, and lime. Then, just before taking a bite, she raised her eyes to Gayle and shook her head. "My car doesn't have one."

"And I know how you can afford a new car."

It's not about thrifting after all! She joined some MLM direct-sales thing! She wants me to sell tote bags or vitamins or... Cassie blanched. *Tupperware. Plastic goodness. Is she insane?!*

"—eard about your trip to HearthLand."

"Read my blog, you mean." Cassie couldn't stand the suspense. "Just tell me now. Are you doing home parties now? Like scrapbook stuff or purses—no!" Her eyes caught the perfectly matching and clearly *new* earrings and necklace set. "You're selling jewelry! Well, I—"

The little restaurant rang out with Gayle's hilarity. "I'm not selling anything, Cassie. You are. Or you want to be."

The store. It is about the store. Okay... keep cool. Cassie stirred her beans with the plastic fork and tried not to let her conscience's screams of, "Hypocrite!" drown out the rest of Gayle's words.

"—have the way to keep you stocked with a little less stress on both of us."

"Let's hear it."

The plan unfolded as Gayle's lunch grew cold. The woman didn't even seem to notice. She pulled out a notebook—oh, how Cassie ached to stroke the paper just for the pure joy of it—and passed it across the table. "I shouldn't be showing you these. I mean, if we're not in business, you know what's coming. It gives you an edge over the others. But I'm doing it because I think you'll see that what I'm offering is a huge deal."

"Why the big plan? Why not just call in advance and tell me what's there? I look at pictures, tell you what I want, and show up on sale day to pay. Why all this...?" Cassie swept her hand over the table.

"Because I want the guarantee. I know what you buy. I know the prices you are willing to pay. I'm willing to take a bit of a cut if you're willing to come up with more standardized prices. For your store, you won't need to get it as low. You won't be having to make a profit and *still* sell it at a wholesale price."

Um, wholesale? For second-hand goods? Really? But the idea grew on her as she considered it. "What would I be agreeing to exactly? And what do you get out of it?"

"I get an easier sale day. We do all our transactions prior to sale day. Either you come to the site and pick out what you want, or I send you pictures if it's just a few big pieces. You can come to sales, too, but it would save you so much time. No more staking mine out for half an hour before, in case I get the sign out earlier. No trying to beat Bob Bolowski to a pair of pie birds or egg cups!"

Shopping pre-sale. It would save time on Saturdays. And if she did well enough from Gayle's pre-sales, she could skip a Saturday now and then. That alone would be huge. "I suppose if it was a home that didn't have enough to make it worth your while, you could accept a few like that if you said, 'I can't do a full sale for you, but I can bring someone in who will buy such-and-such.'"

"Exactly." Gayle finally took a bite of her taco, oblivious to the congealed grease on the meat. "I don't want to do retail. I don't want to hassle with storefronts and things. And at sales, no one is going to pay top prices. But you with your HearthLand connection..." She wiped her mouth, took a swig of her soda, and readied for another bite. "You can get twice the price for stuff there than you can in most Rockland shops. It's the equivalent of Boutique Row and Fairbury! Top dollar, Cassie. And you've got the in."

It still didn't make sense. Cassie stared at the notebook, looking for something to explain it all. "What's the catch?"

"There's no catch. I want to increase my business. I can only do that if I have someone I know needs volume. Bob will do it. And if you don't want it, I'll give it to him. But we both know he's going to put everything up on eBay and there's no *soul* in that."

I didn't know you had *a soul, Gayle.* Cassie's face flamed as she realized how catty she sounded. "Okay, but what's it going to cost *me*? I can't believe you're going to do this *just* to get more sales. There has to be more."

Several minutes passed as Gayle ate in silence. She waited, watching over the top of her cup, her taco, her fork. She waited as Gayle ignored pointed looks and more than one exasperated sigh. And no matter how tempting it was, Cassie even managed to avoid asking. But Gayle didn't hold out indefinitely.

"Okay. Here it is. You know that I always get first dibs on things. I don't take much—maybe one or two items per sale at most."

Cassie thought she knew where the "agreement" was going. "Consignment over at The Hidden Cottage, right?"

"Right. Well, sometimes I want things and can't do it. Lynda only allows me so many pieces at a time, and I am not paying to store them. My apartment can't hold anything else. I keep a very minimal place and I like it that way."

"You want consignment privileges?"

"At a reduced rate." With those four words, Gayle's entire tone changed. It went from almost courting her to all business in the shift of the conversation. "I want up to ten percent of the store space at twenty percent consignment. You can put things wherever you want as long as they aren't hidden."

Ten percent. That's a hundred square feet out of a thousand.

So, a ten by ten space if the store is a thousand square feet. That's a lot. Cassie pushed her tray aside and leaned against the table. "I don't know if I can promise ten percent."

"I said *up to.* I don't know that I'd need that much. I just want the ability to buy a few big pieces and know they won't be in a back room for six months before making it out on the floor."

"Five/twenty-five." The words flew from her mouth before Cassie could stop them. *What are you doing? You can't make an agreement like this! You don't even have the space yet! You haven't signed anything with Ralph.* At that thought, Cassie added, "Assuming the store goes through. Otherwise, I have no obligation."

Gayle's laughter—quieter this time and almost sinister— sent shivers up her spine. "Cassie..." Seriously, the woman actually tisked. "You just bought a houseful of stuff. You took it all out to HearthLand. You *have* a store. Either there or elsewhere, but otherwise, just what do you plan to *do* with all of it? You'd spend more on rent for a unit than you'd make on the stuff."

She couldn't help it. Cassie reiterated the offer. "Five/twenty-five if the store goes through. I can't give you store space if I don't *have* store space. And I have veto power. If you bring me something that doesn't work with my merchandise, I can say no."

"I can get prior approval?"

She's going to take it? No counter? Still, it was a good offer—a great idea. Cassie nodded. "Yep. I can't imagine needing to use it—veto power, I mean. I just need it in the contract."

Gayle pulled the notebook to her and scribbled a few things down. Once finished, she slid it across the table again. Cassie read. The final line made her shake her head. "Fine. Seven/twenty-two."

Gayle swore. "You'd have gone for eight."

As she stood to dump her trash—trash that almost suffocated her—Cassie shrugged. "I'm not saying you can't have *ten* sometimes. I just won't *promise* more than seven. It's a lot of floor space." She pointed to the third item while balancing the tray on one hand. "And I want that stricken. I reserve the right to haggle if you think something is worth more than I do. Value is based on demand. I don't care if the stupid antique resource guide tells you a milk glass pitcher is worth fifty bucks. If I can only sell it for thirty, I'm not giving you twenty-five. I get to haggle."

Satisfaction washed through her as she strode to the garbage cans. The metal container taunted her. She set it on the tray rack, dumped the rest, dumped the contents, and carried the thing to the restroom. Rinsed, she folded it as tiny as she could and stuffed it into her plastic makeup bag with a dirty napkin. Purse zipped, she stared at her reflection in the mirror. "I just became *that* person. I'm taking home *trash*. This is what happens when you make rash challenges for yourself, Cassandra Wren. Be careful in the future. Be very careful."

⫩⫩ ⫩⫩ ⫩⫩

The front basket of her shopping cart—the place where mothers of small children strapped their little charges for safety—now held her purse, half a dozen denim bags, and another half a dozen white "produce" bags. Once more, the feeling of having become "that" person washed over her. "It's sick. It's totally sick."

"Excuse me?" An overweight man, larger than any man she'd ever seen, stood in front of the marshmallow crème and put several jars in his cart. He glared at her. "What business is it of yours?"

"Sorry. I was talking to myself." She pointed to the bags and began rattling off an explanation that she neither owed him nor would help the situation.

The man glared. "Lame. Mind your own business."

Before he decided to lob one of the jars at her, Cassie took off for the produce. A head of romaine lettuce, a bunch of spinach—her eyes slid longingly to the cold case where clear plastic tubs of baby spinach beckoned her—two cucumbers, four tomatoes, a bunch of celery, and three bell peppers slid into perfectly imperfect produce bags. A man, cuter than any guy she'd seen in the produce department before, paused by her cart and eyed her bags. "Cool bags. Where'd you get 'em?"

"I made them last night. They're ugly, but they'll get the job done."

He started to protest, but as she held it up for closer inspection, the guy shrugged. "Okay. They're ugly. But they're cool. Wonder if you can buy them anywhere. Maybe FreshMart would have them. They'd be good for the bulk stuff, too. Except maybe flour."

For just a split second, Cassie thought she knew what it felt like to have a split personality. Excitement at the idea of bulk food in a store clashed with her usual opinion of "designer food" stores. "They have bulk? Like what?"

"Nuts, dried fruit, pasta, soup mix, coffee, tea, cereals, grains..." With his phone out, the guy began reading off an impressive list. "I usually shop there, but this is closer to home, and I just needed a couple of things."

"Wow!" Cassie stared at her bags realizing she'd probably have to make more. *If I had just the towels, I could fold them in half and put drawstrings there. Yeah....*

Four steps away, chuckles stopped her in her tracks. She glanced back and saw the guy watching her. Smiling at her. And yes, *chuckling* at her. Mortified, Cassie zipped her cart around the corner and made a beeline for the dairy case. *Mozzarella cheese. Need that. But I'm good on the rest—except medium cheddar. Need that, too.*

As she rounded the corner, Mr. Chuckles nearly ran into her cart. "Oops! Sorry. Hey, do you know where they keep the coffee in this place?"

"Aisle five." She started toward the bakery and paused. "But FreshMart probably has better coffee."

"Probably, but without it, I won't be coherent enough to drive there tomorrow."

Who could argue with that? Cassie pointed in the direction of aisle five and scuttled to the bakery before the day's paper bagged bread was gone. *I can't wait half an hour for the next load. I need to get home and see what Ralph has for me.*

Cookies in a plastic container called to her. Cassie had them halfway to her cart before she resisted. Deli meat—nope. *Not until I make new packaging. I'm going to do this right. I can do it. I can.* But the second time, cookies called to her, Cassie strode to the baking aisle and stared at what was available. Chocolate chips beckoned, but their plastic wrapper sang an obnoxious, "Neener, neener" as she wrestled against the idea. *I wonder how hard it is to make chocolate chips. Can you do that with cocoa powder? I know I have that.*

Her eyes slid to the cans of cocoa. *Surely, it's better to buy raw ingredients, even if the packaging is there. It's so much less than the cookies, right?*

She zipped a text to Lauren. DO I HAVE TO WAIT 48 WEEKS TO HAVE CHOCOLATE CHIP COOKIES AGAIN OR CAN I BUY CHOCOLATE CHIPS?

And as she waited for a response, Cassie started a Google search on her phone. Cocoa powder, powdered sugar, oil. *That's not too bad. I can get powdered sugar in a box and burn it in that rusted out cast iron Dutch oven I bought.*

Lauren's text dinged. *That's it. If she says I can buy the chips, then I can buy the stuff to make them. There's the fleece, Lord. Stupid as it is, there it is. Here goes.*

BUY THE STUPID CHIPS!

A box of powdered sugar practically flew into the cart. Just in case, Cassie also grabbed a container of cocoa. A voice behind her nearly made her jump from her skin for the second time that day. "If this is about a diet…"

Cassie whirled. Produce guy. "Why? Do I need one?"

"No!" Red stole up his neck. "That's what I meant. If you're hesitating—"

"Because I can't buy plastic, paper, glass, or metal." Her emotions crept to the border of hysterical as she grabbed a bag of chocolate chips. "Plastic. I can't even buy stupid chocolate chips because they come in plastic!"

With a dismissive toss, she flung the chips into the bin and grabbed the can of cocoa. "Plastic and plastic coated paper. It's ridiculous." Cassie shook the box. "Paper. I'll burn it. That'll be a *bit* better." She shoved her cart toward the checkout stands and stopped. Without even turning around, she added, "Don't challenge yourself to eco-consciousness for a year. Trust me. Just don't."

At the end of the aisle, she also tossed back, "And thanks for the thing on bulk at FreshMart. Thanks, and you're evil. Now I have to sew more hideous bags. But thanks. You just made it possible for me to buy chocolate chips most likely."

He might have said "You're welcome." Cassie couldn't be sure. She *was* certain that he said, "See you at FreshMart sometime."

Weird.

Not until she'd unloaded her cart and climbed into her car did the entire encounter hit her. Cassie dropped her phone into its holder and ordered it to call Lauren. Her friend didn't even have a chance to say hello. "I just totally spaced a guy flirting with me. I mean I think he followed me around the *store*. He joked. Hinted. Even said he'd see me at FreshMart—"

"Wait. FreshMart? You." Lauren's laughter filled the car as Cassie pulled out of the parking lot. "You flirted with *him* if you even *hinted* at going to FreshMart."

"Did you know they sell stuff in *bulk?* I can buy noodles! Chocolate chips! Everything. It's going to be awesome." A memory prompted her to amend that statement. "Well, as soon as I make some more bags. Ugh."

"This—this stuff." Lauren giggled. "Grant is dying over here. You should know that. Anyway, this stuff you couldn't make up if you tried. Go write your blog."

A slow smile formed as she turned toward her street. "Yeah. You might want to watch for it. There's something you'll love. Gotta go."

"Hey, Cassie?"

Cassie almost missed the question. "Hmmm?"

"I won't tell Evan you were flirting—this time."

"Wha—" The phone went dead. "Oh, man. You are so dead."

Groceries put away—check! Coat hung—check! Comfy clothes—check, check! Cassie rushed through her evening routine, grabbed one of the frozen burritos, nuked it, and scurried to the couch. With a pat to Think's head, an offer of a bite, and a swig of HearthLand milk, she pulled up her laptop and began typing.

Who Am I?

Seriously. I can't help but wonder anymore. Let's start with today's metal issues. I had a business lunch. The "client" met me at a restaurant of her choice—chosen because she knows I love a good burrito. I ordered tacos. I just realized that. Nicely played, Gayle. Very nicely played.

Anyway. Can you imagine how I felt when I saw them pull out aluminum foil containers to put my food in? Plastic cup. Paper napkin—yes, I used my cloth ones and put them in my makeup bag like a good girl.

And I put the container in there, too.

Seriously! I can't believe it, but I did. I had to toss the plastic cup and fork, the paper liner and an extra napkin my lunch "date" kindly left for me. But that container? I rinsed it out in the bathroom, folded it into a tiny bit of a thing, and stuffed it in that bag.

Cassie reached for her purse and pulled out the folded piece of foil, snapped a picture, and put it back. As the photo

237

uploaded to her blog, she went back to writing.

See? I have become THAT person. And it only got worse when I went to the store. This guy mentioned bulk stuff at FreshMart. How did I not know about this, other than the fact that I don't shop there, of course? I mean, c'mon! Bulk! Packaging is GONE. This is like... GAME CHANGER. And I bought the stuff to make chocolate chips. Yes. Make. Because it's less packaging than buying chips and I wanted cookies.
And that brings me to the whole "got worse" thing. I've always hated the idea of designer food stores—boutique grocers, some people call them. Well, I'll be shopping at one now. Me. And making chocolate chips to save a little plastic? Really? I don't even recognize myself anymore.

Her lip quivered. Feeling an identity crisis emerging, Cassie signed off with promises of more information the next day on her business lunch. She said good night to Think, ignored a clock that insisted it was too early to go to bed, and shut off the lights. "G'night. See you in the morning. I can't take anymore of today."

Think hinted that he understood.

"You're a good friend, Think. Try to get some rest yourself. I may need you tomorrow."

Wednesday, January 27—

In the wee hours of the morning, Cassie stumbled into the bathroom. Seconds later, she fumbled for toilet paper and stared, despite the darkness, at what could only be two or three squares of paper. It took a stretch, but she fumbled for the light switch and stared. Two squares—and a partial. Nothing under the sink. "That'll teach me for not refilling under the sink! Argh!"

Lamb's ear—maybe it wasn't a bad idea after all. It could grow in here and be ready at any given moment—for emergencies.

238

Twenty-four packs of toilet paper didn't fit in her closet—not that it ever stopped her from shoving them under the bottom shelf. Wrestling the package out—nearly impossible. Still, she managed to rip open the package and extricate a roll. Something felt off, but her bed wailed for her return, so Cassie carried it to the bathroom and slid it onto the spring peg. That's when the "off" turned on the lights of her understanding.

She dashed to examine the rest of the rolls and then for her phone. About a minute later, Cassie snapped a picture and started to upload it to Instagram. "Argh! Why do all the good ideas come at midnight? It took less than two minutes to do it, but at two-thirty, it felt like two hours. 365Green was born. She uploaded the picture with a caption. *"I can't believe it. This roll is half the size of the others. Part of me is ticked. I paid for a whole roll. The other part can't help but wonder if maybe I can save TP this way."*

Toilet paper bizarreness recorded for posterity, Cassie climbed back in bed and drifted into dreams of giant toilet paper rolls, cut in half, of course, rolling after her. Eventually, each one tumbled over her, half-crushing her with their downy softness

⚡⚡⚡

Half-frozen, Cassie scrambled onto the bus half a mile from her house. "Stupid car."

"Excuse me?"

She passed him two dollars and three quarters. "My dumb car won't start. Sorry."

"Subway on Holden?"

Cassie swung behind him and nodded. "Can you just yell at me when we get close? I didn't get much sleep last night."

"Insomnia? My wife's got that." The bus lurched forward. "I've got the opposite. I sleep enough for both of us. Always tired."

"Nope. Might get that checked out. Could be something

medical."

"Yeah." The guy, for someone who claimed to be tired all the time sure had enough energy to chat. "So what? Nightmares?"

All hope for a short nap on the way to the subway stop dissolved. Cassie sighed. "Of a sort. Ran out of TP, and when I went to get a roll—it was half-sized. No joke."

"No way. How would it roll? It would fall off—"

Cassie coughed to cover a snicker. "The other way. It's like a skinny roll or something. So weird." The bus pulled up to another stop, so Cassie whipped out her phone. "See… right… there!" Cassie shoved the phone around the barrier.

"That's—that's just wrong. You got gypped."

"Yep. But my brain kept going after that."

Once more the bus lurched forward. What the driver said, Cassie didn't hear. Her mind still swirled, wondering if she'd notice the difference. *I should. I mean, it's like using half the number of squares, but maybe it would wad differently. Maybe. I should pay attention. It could save a ton of paper in a year. Like…* Her mind spun. *Probably fifty rolls!*

"Hey, girl!" The driver's eyes met hers in the mirror. "Your stop ahead. Don't know where you were, but you weren't here."

"Sorry. Trying to figure out if I could save on TP."

All the way down the street to the subway station, Cassie worked out her thoughts—right up until she nearly bumped into a man with a huge bouquet of flowers. "Sorry. Just—"

"No worries."

The voice—familiar. Even the man's coat as he jogged down the steps looked familiar. Hair… then it hit her. *Grant! Oh, I wonder if he's going to surprise Lauren on the way to work.*

Her thoughts propelled her after him. *Maybe he'll let me watch.*

But just as she started to call out, Grant turned toward the transportation hub train. This time his profile showed him perfectly. Cassie scuttled after him, but dug for her phone as she wove in and out of the throng heading that way.

As they waited, Cassie scuttled around a pillar and flipped through messages until she found the one Lauren had sent of her and Grant just days before. *You are so my Lauren's Grant. No doubt about it. I hoped, but no way....*

The train whizzed into the station, and Grant inched forward. Cassie tapped out a text message to her boss and waited. She entered the car next to his and hid behind a pole. *Guys don't usually remember faces, do they? Then again, we talked a lot that night....* The doors closed. The train zipped down the tracks and in the opposite direction from Cassie's office. She hit send.

GOT ON THE WRONG TRAIN. CAR BROKEN. GONNA BE LATE. TAKING ME TO THE TRANS HUB.

The reply came seconds later. GET OFF AT THE NEXT STATION?

She ignored it. Ignored and watched. Grant offered his seat to a teenaged girl with spikes coming from anywhere the body could possibly support them. *I'd be impressed if you weren't heading somewhere with a giant bunch of flowers—roses mostly, it looks like. Maybe grandma's coming in on a train or on a plane. That could be.*

Hey, she tried. All the way there, Cassie thought of every scenario she could imagine. She even zipped a text to Lauren asking when their next date was. The reply came almost immediately. TOMORROW NIGHT. HE SAYS HE HAS SOMETHING TO TALK TO ME ABOUT. PRAY, CASS. HE CAN'T PROPOSE ALREADY. HE JUST CAN'T.

And what if he's breaking up with you. I'll make him regret it. Jerk.

She sent back a one-word text. PRAYING.

A reply, from Mr. Sylmer, appeared almost immediately. PRAYING FOR ANOTHER STATION OR...?

"Oh, brother."

"Excuse me?" An elderly gentleman with a bow tie, mustache, and the cutest fedora stared at her.

"Sorry. I just mixed up text messages. Sent my message for my friend to my boss. Now I *have* to come clean about how I deliberately got on the wrong train." Cassie sighed.

Curiosity mingled with amusement in the man's eyes. "Sounds like *some* story there."

She pointed. "See the guy with the flowers?"

Mr. Fedora nodded. "Going to ask him to dinner? A man who brings flowers…"

"He's my best friend's boyfriend. She's at work. This train isn't going anywhere near her work."

"Maybe his mother's coming in from Des Moines."

Something in the way the man spoke spoke of courtesy and grace that didn't seem to exist anymore. Cassie listened to it with a sigh in her heart and hope for a revitalization of masculine chivalry. "I was just thinking maybe a grandmother."

"You'll have to introduce me. I could use a lovely evening out with a lady from Des Moines."

"Why are you going there?" The question slipped through her lips before she could stop herself.

"To the airport?" Mr. Fedora smiled and patted a fat messenger bag slung over one shoulder. "I bring sandwiches to the homeless. We talk. Sometimes they ask about Jesus. Those are the best times."

She asked about tracts. He shook his head. She asked about Bible studies. Again, a quiet, "No."

"So, how do you talk about Jesus?"

Over three stops he described his visits with the homeless who wandered around the transportation hub on a daily basis. "They just want someone to listen—to care. The missions do, but they run on almost a tit-for-tat system. And homeless people are homeless, not stupid. But if you listen long enough, they become curious. They ask questions."

"And you use that time to tell them about Jesus?"

Again, he shook his head. "Little lady, I tell them about Jesus when they ask about Him. Eventually, they do. And when they do, I tell them." His eyes met hers and held for a moment. "I've found people curious about Jesus once they trust you not to ram Him down their throats."

That, she couldn't argue—didn't even want to. "You got that right. Sometimes..." She glanced around to be sure no one heard her. "Seriously, sometimes when friends start in on people who don't believe, it makes me want to 'pull a Peter' as my grandma says. I'm sure people have come to Christ through that kind of aggressive evangelism, but wouldn't they likely have come with less obnoxiousness? And with less obnoxiousness, maybe we wouldn't have turned away a dozen more?"

"Paul preached with boldness. So, it probably is the best way sometimes," the man conceded. "But it isn't the best way for me." He pointed at the door to the next car. "Your young man is angling to get off."

It was true. Cassie fished for her wallet, pulled out a twenty, and shoved it into the man's hands. "Buy someone lunch for me. Tell them one of the cool stories about your childhood that I'd give anything to hear."

Before he could argue, Cassie squeezed past a couple of other people and prepared to bolt from the car. Protests filled her ears, but Cassie ignored them. *Gotta see what this guy is up to.*

Grant took the platform almost at a run. With shorter legs and boots with a decent sized heel, Cassie *did* have to run after him. Twice he stopped to adjust his flowers and check his phone. He crossed to the tram for terminal four. Cassie barely slipped in behind. She shuffled down by the other door, weaving in and out of passengers with suitcases and hoping she didn't *look* as conspicuous as she felt. The four-minute ride gave her time to zip her boss another text.

REMIND ME TO CONFESS ABOUT MY WRONG TRAIN.

A reply came seconds later.

I WON. HELEN WILL BE BUMMED. PIZZA INSTEAD OF THE OAKES. REMIND ME TO GIVE YOU A BIGGER CHRISTMAS BONUS.

Am I that predictable?

Cassie watched all the way to terminal four, but nothing exciting happened. Grant watched his phone, the doors, and the state of his flowers. But as they neared the stop for baggage claim, everything about him changed.

He grew tense—excited. His feet tapped—eyes swept the tram as if somehow it would get them there swifter. Twice she felt his eyes on her, but with her side to him, Cassie felt sure he couldn't see enough to recognize her.

At baggage claim, she prepared to bolt—even if it meant leaping over the mini roll-on of the flight attendant at the front. "Hey!"

"Sorry!" She strode as quickly as possible, overtaking Grant and passing him at nearly a run. But once she reached the carousels, Cassie didn't know where to go—where to hide. Every time she thought she'd situated herself, something would give away her position—a glass window, a wide mirror.

Passengers strolled down from the upper floor. Old women embraced middle-aged daughters. Young men found and connected with apparent magnetic force to their wives or girlfriends. Businessmen looked for drivers holding placards. Grant waited, passenger by passenger, until a woman flew down the ramp and into his arms. "Grant!"

Cassie snapped a picture. With super-human, or so she thought, self-restraint, she resisted the urge to run up to him, snatch up the flowers, and pulverize the embracing couple with them. *Jerk! Bentley has lost her touch. He's a creep. And Lauren is afraid of a proposal. He's going to break up with her! Jerk! Squared!*

So wrapped up in her thoughts was she that Cassie didn't notice them turning and moving her way until they faced her.

Cassie gulped, scowled, and stormed past. *Please don't have recognized me.*

"Hey Cassie! Cassie!"

She turned and gave him her best, "You'd better not annoy me" look. "Yeah?"

"Don't tell Lauren you saw me here, okay?"

Eyes bugging, jaw hanging, Cassie folded her arms over her chest and strode back to face him. "You—seriously? I thought I liked you. But you're—ugh!"

Twice he called after her. Both times she ignored it. Instead, she jumped back on the tram. Rode it to the station. Climbed aboard the mid-town train, and continued to work as if she hadn't taken a heartbreaking detour. She stormed into the office, hung her coat, dumped her tote bag on the floor, and sank into the chair. As Cassie reached for the phone, the office door opened. "Everything okay?"

Why she did it, why she risked the unprofessionalism, Cassie couldn't have hoped to explain. She slid the phone across the desk, fumbled with it, and leaned back, arms folded over her chest. "That's Lauren's boyfriend. As you'll remember her from the Christmas party, that is not Lauren."

Mr. Sylmer picked up the phone, stared, zoomed in, and pushed it back across the desk. "They look an awful lot alike."

Cassie snatched up the phone and stared. "Oh, no..."

⚏ ⚏ ⚏

"—so, I had to call Bentley, tell her everything, and get Grant's number. I had to call *Grant* and ask his forgiveness. It was crazy. So, at lunch, I was feeling like three feet high, so I call my mom. You do that when you need to feel better about yourself. So, what does my mom say?"

Think gave her a thoughtful expression and waited.

"She says, 'Oh, dear. That sounds like one of your Great Aunt Essie's escapades! My mom used to tell me...'" and of course, then I had to hear about the time Aunt Essie caught a maid stealing the silver and followed her to the pawn shop to prove it."

Her little metal buddy's silence proved eloquent.

"Don't say it. Don't even *think* it." A giggle escaped before she could stop it. "Oh, man. That was bad. Funny, but bad."

Did his eyes go to the laptop? Cassie chose to assume they did and decided to go fess up about her day's purchases. "You rest, Think. It seems like you've had a tough day, too."

Metal Fail

Remember when I said I wasn't looking forward to running out of mousse? Yeah. I did this morning. I haven't been paying attention, or maybe I've been in denial. Yeah. Probably that. So, all day I thought about it. Researched recipes. Yeah. Recipes. Did you know you can make your own mousse? Did you know that it takes *oils* to make mousse? Supposedly if you whip shea butter, coconut and olive oils with some essential oils for like fifteen minutes, BAM! It's mousse.

So, I decided to do it. Went to FreshMart. Bought the stuff. Bought a few bulk things in my veggie bags, too. Anyway. And twenty-three bucks later, I was ready to make this stuff. I mean, it's a lot, but I can make a lot with it, too. Still. CHA-CHING! Talk about messing up this week's tally. I need to find a good used stand mixer. Supposedly that's better. So, I wanted one. But well, yeah.

Full disclosure people. I stopped at Walgreens on the way home and bought a can of my usual stuff. I hang my head in shame. I bought metal and plastic. And probably aerosol. Isn't that what canned mousse is? Isn't that stuff like instant death to ozone or whatever? Yeah. Shoot me. I don't even care. I just wanted my mousse. I will feel bad tomorrow, but tonight I felt relief. If I hate my new mousse, I have a can of the real thing, baby! YEAH!

Okay, guys? Fair warning. I'm gonna get REAL girlie here. So, scroll on down to the second to last paragraph if you don't want to read about stuff I doubt you want to read about. And with that bit of ambiguity, here we go. (Hey, Lauren! I used ambiguity. I apologize for flipping out on you the last time you did that. It's a good word).

You know that stupid monthly visitor? Some people call it "Aunt Flo." I think that's gross. Others call it "TOM" (for time of month) or Fabio (just to be weird or whatever). Well, whatever. It arrived. I counted tampons. Um, yeah. Not gonna make it. I needed more. But c'mon.

Paper and plastic. I HAVE to have these things. They're essential. But PLASTIC and PAPER. *insert whimper here*

I did a bunch of research on that today, too. Did you know people sew and crochet tampons and pads? Yeah. They do. They also make these "cup" things to catch it all. EW. But I have to do something. Can I really justify a year's worth of "sanitary supplies"? Especially after I just bought MOUSSE?

I can't help but feel like metal week was a big, fat failure. So many things interrupted it. And most of the metal stuff I use are things that I don't have to replace THAT often. It is going to catch me off guard again. I know it. So, tell me. How do I plan ahead better? Do I really have to examine every bit of my life and put calendar notes in my phone or something? Isn't that overkill?

See you tomorrow for the week's tally. I'm already bummed. It's not going to be good. And after last week's thrifting tally, I could have used a pick me up. Sigh.

Thursday, January 28—

Whew!

So many things to tell you today. I can't believe it. Do you see that picture? That's from lunch today. Why is my lunch sitting on a produce bag, you ask? I'll tell you. Because I got DESPERATE for a good burrito. And there's this taco truck around the corner. Seriously amazing stuff. So, what did I do? I went over there and begged the guy to wrap my burrito in that thing. He said no. I got in the back of the line and tried again. Said no again. The third time a string of Spanish that I'd give ANYTHING to understand erupted from somewhere in the truck. Seriously. It sounded like the truck was ten times deeper than it is. The guy took my bag and my money. From the malevolent (there you go, Lauren. Just for you) look he gave me, I suspect he wrapped my burrito in aluminum foil paper and THEN put it in my bag. Just so he could do it "right."

Who cares? It's pure supposition. Meanwhile, I did not walk away with anything but my food. I've decided to become persistent. It's obnoxious, maybe, but a girl needs her burrito!

And you know, this finishes off the end of week four. I have to admit something. I don't know what I'm going to do next week. There are so many things I could decide. Chemicals, petroleum products, electricity… it could be a million things. Synthetics? Water? I mean, do you KNOW how much water I waste? And the idea of Navy showers in winter? I don't think so. I'll save that for summer if I can manage.

But there's another problem. You can't just stick to the little bits you've started. On week one, I was already thinking about plastic. By the end of week two, I was resisting metal and glass already. I feel guilty if I waste gas in the car or forget to turn off a light. It's ALREADY taking over my life. I'm not supposed to even have to think of this stuff yet. But I do. Because when you make changes based on principles, it changes who you are, and then you do more than is required. Wow. That kind of sounds like the Bible. I mean, isn't that what we do as Christians? We read the Bible because it's what you're supposed to do. But the next thing you know, you're making all these changes, not because you planned to change, but because who you are is changing.

And that's kind of scary for me. Call me self-centered, but I like who I am. I don't want to become Ellie Eco-Freak. I don't WANT to ask food vendors to give me special privileges. It feels rude.

Biggest surprise for the week? I don't use as much metal as I thought I would and I use a whole lot more than I ever knew. That doesn't make sense. I know it. But it's true. Really. I buy a lot of things that are metal and consumable. But what I don't do is buy them often. Canned air isn't something you use every day. Even my mousse. I don't go through a can a week or anything! Aluminum foil—if I used it to replace plastic wrap? Yeah, then maybe I'd use a lot. And I've had people argue that it's recyclable. It is.

But do you know how much stuff is taken to recycling centers that ultimately ends up in landfills? Just because it is recycleABLE, and just because the place gave you the money for it, doesn't mean they actually recycle it all. And recycling, while better, still uses resources. I keep trying to find ways to avoid buying things that NEED to be recycled. If you can avoid it in the first place, that has to be better. Well, it would be if everyone did it. I know that just ME… I'm not making that big of an impact. Not on the environment. But this environmental experiment is making an impact on me. And that's kind of cool. Scary, but cool.

There are only three days left in January, so I'm keeping this week's summary ONLY on metal. I'll do a month summary on everything on Sunday night.

I reduced:
Aluminum foil usage.

248

I increased:
Aluminum container usage. One time.
Mousse can.

Neutral:
I'm also putting the aluminum container here as well as the mousse can. Why? Because I did bring home the container to recycle (even though it was kind of gross. Just sayin'.) And the mousse can is going here because I have everything to make the mousse. If it works, I can take that can back. So, I'm calling it both until I make a decision. If it goes back, I get to "write it down" in my ledger. Right now, I have very little to add to this week's. I mean, I am giving myself that half a roll of TP savings. But I shouldn't. They charged me for the whole thing. But because it might be a saver, I'll let me have that half a roll. I'll do the math later.

Now, if you don't mind, I have a date. Think and I have decided to try playing chess. It's been a long time and I want to challenge my new boyfriend to a game. So, I need practice, and if I can beat Think, I bet I can beat anyone.

Why yes, I have gone half-crazy. I'll finish the other half when I'm an old lady. It'll make things interesting. See you tomorrow. I know this week's summary was a bit anticlimactic. And that's good, I think.

She hit publish and closed the laptop. It took a couple of minutes to set up the chess game, but at last Think sat opposite her on the coffee table and considered his first move. Her phone blipped with a notification. At the commenter's name, she almost turned off the phone, but curiosity overrode sense.

HermoinesTwin: Maybe you should just marry Think. He sounds like the perfect guy for you. He won't argue, won't complain, and he won't care if you throw away his stuff. Because he doesn't HAVE any. He's even naked, isn't he? Or did you crochet a leisure suit for him? Seriously, Cassie. Who are you?

"Think, I have an enemy. I've never had one before. But this gal really hates me. And she knows me." His answer came in a flash. Cassie nodded. "You're right. Lauren will know."

Cowardice sent her fingers flying over the phone, tapping

out a text message instead of hitting the contact button. DO YOU KNOW WHO HERMOINESTWIN IS? SHE REALLY HATES ME. DO YOU KNOW WHY?

Lauren's response came minutes later. I'LL DO SOME RESEARCH. TRY NOT TO LET IT BUG YOU. I HAVE A THEORY, BUT I CAN'T REALLY BELIEVE IT'S TRUE. NOT SAYING ANYTHING UNTIL I KNOW. MEANWHILE, JUST READ YOUR POST. GIVE THINK WHAT FOR.

Her laughter rang out as Cassie moved her first pawn. "Okay, Think. She said to beat you. And I'm gonna."

Week 5: Uncertain

Friday, January 29—

Another day on the bus, then the subway. The press of people suffocated her. Gordo from the cleaning crew waved as she swarmed from the train with the rest of Rockland's workforce. "When you ride the train?"

"Since my car broke down. See you at ten-thirty!"

Out on the street, Cassie wove through crowds with a recklessness that would likely get her knocked to the ground. Her phone buzzed. Joel. No hesitation—Cassie tapped the screen. "Hey! What's up?"

"Do you need a ride tomorrow? Will your car be done?"

"Don't know yet. They haven't called. I'm going crazy."

Cassie knew what he'd say before he spoke again. "Well, if you need a ride or to use my truck or anything…"

"Sure! That'd be great. I'll let you know. If they don't call by five-thirty, it's not going to happen."

"What about tonight?"

That question hovered between them for what seemed like an age. Cassie's mind whirled with possibilities. *What if Evan calls? He might be making plans or—* Mid-thought, Cassie stopped herself. *Oh, no you don't! You've been her for too long. You're not miss, "I'll wait around for you to make time for me" anymore.* Joel started to reassure her that he understood if she was busy, but Cassie cut him off.

"What did you have in mind? If it involves freezing my butt off, it ain't gonna happen. I don't get a nice, long shower tonight, so—"

"Why—no! You said you weren't doing water until

251

summer! What made you change your mind?"

Cassie waited until she wrestled the large glass doors open and squeezed in before answering. "Snow."

Who could blame him for his confused response? "Huh?"

"There's all this snow out there—in the *gutter*. I can be so stinkin' conservative with it that it's not even funny! I can bring it all up to my yard and save it—let it melt into a cistern."

"You don't *have* a cistern!"

"Well, I thought metal trash cans would work. Just keep them close to the house and the heat would melt enough that I could pack it down. Then I could use it to water plants or a garden or something."

She waited for his laughter, but it didn't come. Instead, he sounded excited—pleased. "You're so going to fit in at HearthLand. I bet you end up moving there when your shop takes off."

"Um, not happening. I can't afford to lose my job. I'm barely making it right now as it is."

"Whatever. I just want ten bucks on you moving to HearthLand inside three years."

The idea sent a ripple of the queasies through her. "So, what did you have in mind for tonight?"

"Well, are you in the mood for casual or a bit nicer? Just us or see who has time to do something?"

And this is why I've got to find you someone else to fall for. You're seriously one of the sweetest guys on the planet. Joel's silence reminded her that he'd asked a question. "Well... I don't know. Do you have any more cheesy old movies your mom thinks we should watch? I could make popcorn. I actually saw some in FreshMart. No packaging! With my non-packaged butter and my deli-packaged hand-grated Parmesan, you'll get gourmet popcorn that doesn't contribute to the landfill—" Just listening to herself turned queasies into full-fledged nausea. "Oh, Joel. I'm sorry. That—"

"Is just a joke. I know. Don't let sss-tupid people make you doubt yourself."

"Yeah, well it is easier than I thought, okay? I find myself thinking it even though I hate it at the same time. It's pervasive and intrusive and... a bunch of other 'ives' that I can't even think of right now."

A courier slammed into her and drowned out Joel's next words with his apologies. Not until she got into the elevator was Cassie able to explain, but Joel stopped her. "I'll tell you about it later. How about I make dinner?"

"That would be great. I slept through my alarm—nuttin' in the crockpot." The elevator dinged. "Okay, time to get to work. If you need—"

"I got this. If you want me to invite anyone, just send me a text. Have a great day and don't sue anyone."

Ha. Very. Very. Funny.

❦ ❦ ❦

The scent of onions and peppers greeted her as she shoved open the door. Without ceremony, Cassie dumped her stuff on the kitchen table and shrugged out of her snow-dusted coat. "It. Is. Cold."

Without turning from the stove, Joel muttered, "You should have let me come get you."

"Yeah. Well..." Cassie shrugged. "Yeah. Whatever."

"Go take a hot shower."

"I *can't*." Despite her best efforts, the word escaped in a wail. "I'm not supposed to waste water." Cassie hadn't finished her sentence before she snatched up her jacket and zipped it again. "I forgot to go get snow. Be right back."

Joel called out to her, but Cassie let the door bang shut behind her. An icy step sent her sliding with a jar to her backside and a sprawl on the carport. With ginger movements, she managed to right herself. "Ugh."

A five-gallon bucket sat waiting by the back step. Cassie grabbed it and her snow shovel on her way to the curb. *This is going to be great. All the stuff that ends up in storm drains or the river will now water my house plants.* She couldn't help but feel a bit ridiculous about it as she packed the bucket. "All two of them."

Carrying a loaded bucket of wet snow *and* an unwieldy snow shovel proved more difficult than she'd expected, but when she leaned on it for a moment, a smile grew. "Walking stick. That'll work."

The warmth of the kitchen greeted her as Cassie, once again, burst through the kitchen door. She dropped the bucket on the mat and shivered. Sizzling steak and peppers greeted her along with the invigorating aroma of fresh cilantro. "Fajitas?"

"Can I cook anything else?"

"Don't care." Cassie almost kicked herself in the face in an attempt to stop her chattering teeth. "I'm starved."

Joel turned to face her. With one look, he moved the skillet from the stove and leaned back against the counter. "Um... Yeah. About that. I'm not finishing these until you take a hot shower. You're going to freeze."

"But I don't *need* one."

"Surely, you just saved the equivalent of..." A sigh. "Okay, maybe not. But really?" At that moment, Cassie knew she'd lost. Some vulnerability must have shown, because Joel flicked a finger at the doorway. "C'mon. Just go. I can't stand hearing you abuse your teeth like that. My dad would pitch a fit."

Resistance—futile. Cassie grinned at him and bolted from the room. In less than a minute, hot water beat against her, driving out the cold and the aches that come with tumbles on ice. But she showered quickly. The minute Cassie felt warmed through, she finished rinsing the conditioner out of her hair and shut off the water. Fuzzy sleep pants, two long-sleeved t-shirts, and a fresh towel for her hair.

It might not be glamorous, but that's the great thing about friends like Joel. They don't care and neither do I. If it was Evan...

A plate of fajitas sat at the table. One of her mason jar

candles from HearthLand flickered cheerfully in the dim kitchen light. Joel grinned at her questioning glance. "Mom says nothing feels warmer than candlelight, so, I figured mason jars are even homier and warmer."

"Nothing is homier and warmer than a plate of fajitas. Did you put jalapenos in?"

"Just a couple."

Cassie grinned. "Wuss."

"Guilty as charged."

A bowl of freshly heated chips tempted her. "Lime?"

"Is there any other way?" He grinned. "And I got the salsa from El Sarape—*in an empty spaghetti sauce jar.* You're welcome."

"Okay, that's impressive." Cassie held out her hand and almost snatched it back again. "Pray?"

Joel didn't seem to notice her awkwardness. He took her hand, waited a moment, and thanked the Lord for food. "And wisdom. I think Cassie could use wisdom on this water thing."

Her foot shot out and kicked him before Cassie could stop herself. A giggle escaped—a chuckle. Their moment of prayer dissolved into nervous hilarity. "You. Are so bad." Cassie sent her eyes heavenward. "Sorry, Lord. And thanks for friends who know how to make me laugh at myself. Amen."

<hr>

Rebecca. The title appeared as music shifted from suspenseful and dramatic to the sweet notes of violin strings. On the opposite corner of her small couch, Cassie pulled her legs up under her and jumped as Joan Fontaine jumped and shouted, "No! Stop!"

A smile formed before he could prevent it. Fortunately for his shin, Cassie didn't notice. So, while Laurence Olivier insulted a busybody, Joel watched Cassie and tried to discern what about her snow scheme bothered him. *It's a good idea—using snow to water houseplants. I can't see it'll save much. Maybe if she had a greenhouse full or something.*

The unsettled idea wouldn't leave his mind. It nudged him scene after scene. At one point, Cassie grabbed the remote and punched pause. "Okay, why is this so riveting?"

"We don't have—"

"That wasn't sarcasm. I'm serious." Cassie shifted to face him. "I mean, right now there's just a girl riding around in a car with a guy. So why is anyone even watching it? I don't get it."

Joel hadn't ever considered it, but the answer came in a flash. "Because deWinter just doesn't do anything that should interest her. And she's obviously in love. So, you want to know why?"

"Maybe..." As she reached for the remote, Joel stopped her.

"So, did you get the idea for the snow thing from Ralph or come up with it yourself, or..."

With pink cheeks that deepened with each passing second, Cassie fiddled with the remote. "I get this email every day—green tips, you know?" When he nodded, she sighed. "I couldn't decide what to do for this week, so when it showed up this morning and the thing said, 'Use snow to water houseplants' I decided to start my indoor garden now. I mean, for two house plants, I doubt it'll be worth it, but if I do the container thing I was telling you about, it'll be worth it, right? I'm even thinking about melting the snow and then pouring it into the trash cans. That way they'd be full in spring—ice at first, but full."

Cassie punched the play button and lost herself in the world's most unremarkable proposal. He made it three and a half seconds before Joel pulled out his phone and searched for snow to water houseplants. An article—probably the one she'd received if the pop-up sign-up box meant anything—promised to help her go green with a few buckets of snow a week. He read. On the third paragraph, he grabbed for the remote again.

"Hey! This was your idea!"

"Actually, it was yours." Joel waited for her to

acknowledge it before he passed her the phone. "Did you *read* this?"

A flush, more pink cheeks. Cassie shrugged. "I only read the title. Most of them are stupid. This one…"

"Read paragraph three." As her eyes widened, Joel cleared his throat. "Didn't you tell me you were going to use the pile up by the curb?"

"Yeah." She stared at the phone before tossing it back at him and grabbing the remote. "Fine. Whatever. I won't use the street stuff. Stupid salt."

Just as the screen filled with life again, Joel offered his suggestion. "I think you should consider waiting until summer for water. Fill your trash cans, but otherwise…"

"I would, but…" All attention to the conversation faded as Cassie watched Olivier purchase an enormous bouquet of roses. Her sigh reached into his heart and twisted his heartstrings.

I hope Evan recognizes and touches that sensitive, sentimental side of yours.

The deWinters of Manderly hadn't been "home" for more than a day when Cassie punched the pause button with great frustration. "What did she ever do to them? Where's her backbone? Sheesh!"

"They considered it more suspenseful if she was a mouse. A girl with innate spunk lessened the suspense." Joel winked. "Or something like that."

"Well, then I won't be suspenseful, because no one is going to make me feel like I don't belong in my own home. And he treats her like a child!"

Um, Cassie, compared to him she is a child. And if you watch her, she acts like she likes it. How's he supposed to know? The thoughts came, one after another, but in Cassie's agitated state, he knew better than to voice them. "Yeah. I can't see treating my wife that way."

She whirled to face him again. "Don't. You. Dare. So help me, if she doesn't beat you up for it, I will."

"Gotcha." A kick told him he'd amused her. *Strange how that works. She can kick me if she's teasing, kick me if she's annoyed—and I know which one it is every time. Kind of like when I tell her she's being stupid. Sometimes it's because she is, and sometimes it's because she's brilliant. And she always knows which it is.*

"—did you hear me?"

Joel jerked his head her way and made a show of swallowing hard. "Sorry. Lost in thought."

"I asked if *Rebecca* was a Gothic novel."

"Well, yeah. Isn't it?" He fumbled for his phone as rambling thoughts spilled forth as he scrambled to look it up. "It's all about setting and mystery, right? Isn't that what Gothic is?"

A Spark Notes citation filled his screen. "Yeah. That and stuff about it having a dark undertone. You know, a bit of terror and something supernatural. Well, I don't know about the supernatural in this one, but it makes you want to think there is, anyway."

As if a punctuation to his words, the moment she turned the screen back on, terror filled Joan Fontaine's face and sucked her right back into the movie. *Good choice, Mom. Thanks.* He watched her relax and kick her fuzzy-socked feet up onto the coffee table. Every doubt and disappointment fizzled as the movie accelerated to the climax.

"She does get some spunk when she needs it, doesn't she?" All of her relaxation vanished and Joel...? He kicked back and watched the show.

The house collapsed, and Cassie pumped her fist. "Yes! You totally got what you deserved, you evil... evil... *person.*"

Heart pounding, squeezing, breaking, Joel stuffed down his emotions and punched the remote to turn off the TV. He nudged her knee with his foot and tried to sound as normal as possible. "So, I had an idea for your week five goal."

"Since I failed so miserably on water, you mean?"

"No, you changed your mind. You're a woman. You're

allowed."

She shouldn't have taken that drink just as he spoke. She snorted Coke not intended for nasal consumption and spewed it all over her pants and the coffee table. "You are so dead." She wiped tears from her eyes. "Ow! That actually hurts!" A glare, a grin, another glare—Cassie sighed and jumped up for a towel.

You shouldn't have done that.

In seconds, she was back, mopping up the mess and demanding answers. "Okay, what's your idea?"

"Let the readers vote. It's a way to get them engaged on the blog, right? People like to tell other people what to do, so..."

Hesitation, a slow nod. Cassie pulled her laptop from beneath the couch and flipped open the lid. *Aaand... you forgot I'm even here.* Without a word, he squeezed her elbow, stood, and went to grab his coat. But a kitchen full of his dinner mess ordered him to clean it up. *She'll be tired and won't want to do it tonight. Tomorrow...*

A sigh built up in his heart, but Joel stuffed it down again and grabbed her "compost pail." *Stupid idea in winter. They just freeze out there.*

The frustration that threatened to turn his attitude sour fizzled at the sight of Cassie hunched over her laptop, pouring her heart out onto the screen. He grabbed the plastic store bag he'd used, stuffed Styrofoam meat tray, plastic wrap and bags, and seasoning packets into it. With that hung on the door, Joel rinsed and racked the dirty dishes in the dishwasher, and as he did, his heart settled back into his preferred position. *My job is to love her and leave everything else to You. Help me remember that. Some days...*

Undecided

As my friend, Joel, said. I'm a woman and allowed to change my mind. That was half a second before I spewed Coke through my nose and across my coffee table. Guess who needs to learn how to make eco-friendly glass cleaner if he's going to hang around?

What was he talking about? Well, you see, I had decided that despite my aversion to Navy showers in winter, I was going to do water. You see, I read about this gal who uses melted snow for things like watering house plants and stuff. I had these cool ideas of using the plow pile-up to water plants and start an indoor garden. I'll wait while you laugh at me.

For those like me who don't "get" this stuff, I'll spell it out for ya. They salt the roads. They plow the roads. Salt + plants= death. So, instead of doing water this week, I'm gonna add a "freebie" to my routine. Bring in snow from the yards and let them melt. Then I'll pour 'em in trash cans. They'll freeze, but come spring, I'll have some free water for my upcoming container garden. No, it won't be as good as I wanted it to be, but it helps. Everything helps, right? I just wanted to save stuff from the gutter, but no, they have to use that environment-destroying stuff.

Yeah. I'm grateful for it—or I am when my car is running. Note to all: I still don't have it back. Something about knock sensors and bad fuel pump. Ahem. There are only four of these sensors in the country, and mine is taking an eco-not-so-friendly trip here from some dealer in Seattle.

But of course, we all know what this means. I have no plan for the week. And my brain is frozen. Joel's suggestion? Let you guys decide. So, while I tell you about my day of water reduction, be thinking of what I should reduce or implement, or whatever.

Water isn't easy. I am not looking forward to "take two." But here's what I did today. I considered things I *have* to use water for. Those are:

    ○   Drinking. It's kind of essential for life, and I am not going so "green" that I kill myself off for the sake of the planet.

    ○   Cleaning self. But, I don't need four-hour hot showers in winter. Or even twenty-minute ones after struggling to fill buckets with snow using a snow shovel. Not that I'd ever do something so ecologically irresponsible. Nah…

    ○   Cleaning my living space. I guarantee I use twice as much as necessary. I tend to let the water run while I brush my teeth or scrub potatoes or even wash out the sink. I do half loads of laundry and dishes. So, at water time, I'll work on that.

Well, this morning I turned off the water while I brushed my teeth (1 gallon according to a government website). I took a shorter shower (6-8 gallons—same website). I didn't do a small load of laundry so I could have my favorite jeans and my dad's flannel shirt for tomorrow (10-15 gallons). I also made a reminder note for by the kitchen sink. It says, "Use a bowl of water to clean the veggies." I guess I can take that down. All in all, I think I saved about twenty-five gallons today.

So, folks, what's it gonna be? Am I going to cut back fuel usage? That feels like cheating since I haven't driven half the week and won't be able to until Tuesday. Maybe chemicals? What about electricity or...something?

Cassie looked up to ask Joel a question and found him closing the dishwasher. *Oh, man. That's just wrong. He cooked.* She jumped up, snapped a picture of the bucket of snow, and uploaded it. A dash for the laptop—uploaded. She typed a few words for a caption and hit submit.

"Okay, sorry. I just zoned out on you." Even as she spoke, Cassie dashed for the kitchen. She snatched the towel from his hand and popped him with it. "Hey, you cooked. I'll clean up."

Joel turned and leaned against the counter as he watched her. "Cassie?"

"Yeah?"

He waited until she faced him before offering a weak smile. "I'm allowed to clean up after myself—even at your house, even if I made you dinner, even if some unwritten social rule says it isn't fair."

"But—"

"You were in the zone." He almost strained as he swallowed. "Yeah, I wasn't excited about it—at first. But..." Joel snatched the towel. "Now I just want to finish and let you go to bed."

By the time he left, self-loathing nearly smothered Cassie. She turned and glared at Think. "Why didn't you tell me to hug him or something. It's ridiculous. He's such a good friend, and I just keep hurting him. He tried to hide it, but this time I really think I did."

Think refused to speak to her—to look at her. She felt the

cold shoulder keenly. So, in a huff, Cassie snatched up her laptop and her phone. Once ensconced in bed, she zipped a text to Lauren. PLEASE WEIGH IN ON THE BLOG. ALSO, I HAVE A CONFESSION. CALL ME.

That done, she opened her laptop and refreshed her blog. Joel's comment brought a smile to her face. "You posted before you drove away, didn't you?

Joel213: I think you should have "preparedness" week. You make all the canvas and mesh bags you need. You look at your napkin stash, your kitchen towel stash (hint: you need more), and stuff like that and you spend all week making them. Or at least that's my idea.

He had a point. She couldn't ignore it, but two other comments were pending—waiting for her to approve them. "Ooooh, New commenters. Cool!"

EcoMaya: You are doing such amazing things for the planet. Every little bit does make a difference. You're the butterfly wings that cause a tsunami. BWWAAHAHAHAHA. I know you were rolling your eyes and swearing you'd never come back to a meeting. No really. Don't ever feel like your efforts don't matter. They do. Meanwhile, I think you should consider reducing chemicals in your home. You wouldn't believe how many things that seem so innocent are so toxic. Look up the toxic properties of nail polish. Just nail polish! Keep it up! And let's have dinner some night!

Cassie punched "approve" and scrolled down to the next.

MarlaNAdrian: Sweetie, haven't you done enough? I mean, just keeping up with all the plastic, glass, metal, and paper—that's a lot to deal with. I'm worried that you'll burn yourself out. If you insist on doing more, maybe just go for something simple like take the bus once a week or something.

"Oh, Mom. You're worried about nothing. It's just a challenge. This isn't any different than not buying new shoes until I wear out my Toms." The memory of that challenge sent a shiver through her. "Then again, who knew I'd be stuck with that one pair of shoes for *six* months?!"

SonofaBird: I think you should spend less time working on a new item and more working on personal relationships. That's a great way to improve the planet, don't you think?

Something about Evan's comment rankled, but despite mental wrangling that almost created a headache, Cassie couldn't determine what. "How can something so complimentary feel so backhanded?" A glance at her nightstand showed no Think to answer her. "Fine. Going to sleep. I'll decide tomorrow, I guess."

Exhaustion nearly won out over prudence. She held tight to her laptop until it almost slipped from her arms and crashed to the floor. Cassie startled and fumbled, catching it within inches of destruction. "G'night, Think. You should've seen that."

Think alone in the living room, didn't bother to respond.

Saturday, January 30—

Her phone blared at her until she snatched it up and demanded, "What?" With eyes refusing to open, she couldn't see the caller's face, but she heard him—right outside her bedroom door. Instantly, fully awake, Cassie sat up in bed and stared at Joel leaning against the doorjamb.

"You said to make you get up." He pulled his arm from behind his back and produced a mason jar of snow. "So, get up and go figure out where I'm chauffeuring you, or face the consequences."

In reply, Cassie threw her pillow at him before stumbling from bed and into the bathroom. Clothes. Teeth, necessities. She reached for her wide-toothed comb and groaned. "There's no hope for it." Pride mocked her as she pulled it into a ridiculously messy bun. *And wasn't that a gorgeous sight for poor Joel. That'll cure him of whatever infatuation he's suffering under.*

The scent of coffee greeted her in the kitchen. Joel handed her the Starbucks mug she *knew* had been in her bag the night before and shoved the neighbor's papers in her hands. "You figure out what we're doing."

"Where's the Starbuck's cup?"

"In your hand."

Cassie folded her arms over her chest. "I meant the one that *this*," Cassie held up her refillable mug. "—came in." Another thought hit her and churned her stomach a time or two. "Please tell me you at least rinsed it out."

"I did. Washed it, too. And your mug is still with you. I decided to get one for me to use later, but you can use it this morning. That way your drink is still 'on plan.'"

Every time she swore she wouldn't do it again. And yet every time she did. Without thinking about it, Cassie hugged him. "Thanks for putting up with my silliness."

"It's not silly, Cassie. It's not. Not everyone can or will go to the…"

"I think the word you want is *extreme*."

But even as she spoke, he protested. "No, I was trying for extent, but it wasn't working with my sentence. Anyway, we can't all do everything you're doing, but we can do some. And I decided to start with refillable cups at places like Starbucks and RB Burgers."

"Only you would not only know that RB has them, but also eat there enough to make it worth buying one." She waved a finger in the direction of her small bank of cabinets. "I bought bagels and muffins. You can have one, both, neither if you'll smear a bunch of cream cheese on one."

"Oh! I wanted to try that HearthLand cream cheese. Is it good?"

"It's *amazing!* Seriously, who knew that homemade cream cheese could be so incredible. *And* it's easy to make. I read up on it. I'm totally trying my own."

A yawn cut off her next words—and any idea of what those words might have been. Newspapers in her hand hinted at what she should do next, but by the time she climbed up onto the couch, Cassie's eyes slid shut. *Just for a minute.*

⫴ ⫴ ⫴

Plates in hand, Joel sauntered to the couch and stared at sleeping Cassie. The newspapers had spilled from her hand and slid across the floor. Her nose flared with each gentle snore, and at the thundering gallop of his heart, Joel questioned his sanity. *Cassie would say, "Really? You're attracted to my snore? Get a life!" And she'd be right. But man... Is anything more attractive than a girl who is completely herself with you?*

Visions of her awaking, smiling, taking his hand filled his mind until he snapped himself out of it. *Quit fantasizing like a girl. She'd never let you live it down.*

With each bite of bagel, he watched her and fought within himself—let her sleep or wake her? She'd kill him if he let her sleep. Torture him if he woke her—again. The bagel disappeared faster than he'd ever eaten one before, and to delay the inevitable again, Joel carried the plate to the sink and reached into the freezer for the jar of snow.

"Well... The threat worked last time." He took a deep breath and hunkered down on his heels. "Cassie..." She didn't even stir. Against every protest from his heart he brushed hair from her face and smiled as Cassie snorted, sighed, and sank back into snore-ful slumber. "Aaahhh... Cassie. You make it so hard sometimes."

She didn't move. So, without further ceremony, Joel dumped the jar of snow on her head and jumped back. Cassie squealed as she flung herself off the couch. One look at her is all it took for Joel to bolt from her clutches. Three steps into the hall, he recognized his mistake. Locking the bathroom door would only mean a full-on attack when he capitulated.

He tried to dash past again, but it didn't help. The four self-defense classes she'd taken were all she needed to pin him to the wall, her arm at his throat. Could he have escaped? Sure. But *who wants to hurt a friend?*

265

Joel began with the basics. "Um, I'm sorry?"

"Fail."

A hard swallow followed by the best apologetic look he could manufacture did little to soften the glare in her eyes. Still, he might have had a fighting chance... had a drop of water not dangled from a curl and fell to her nose. "No, really. I'm sorry you're wet." Even to his own ears, he sounded a bit desperate—panicked, even.

The arm pressed deeper into his neck. As he swallowed, Joel winced. *She felt that, for sure.* Triumph gleamed in her eyes. *Yep.*

"But not that you dumped *snow* on me."

"You wouldn't wake up. I tried."

"Sure, you did."

Through half-strangled vocal cords, Joel assured her of his vain attempts to arouse her gently. Her arm relaxed as he spoke. Relief washed over him as he plotted his escape—just in case. "You were so out of it you barely stopped snoring!"

Ooops! Wrong words. Joel bolted. Cassie followed. He grabbed his coat and scrambled for the back door. She reached for him and almost fell as he leapt out the door, over the steps, and nearly flattened himself against his truck. "I know better than to insinuate that you snore."

"No insinuation about it." Cassie shivered, narrowed her eyes, and slammed the door shut.

Left alone outside, Joel climbed in his truck for some semblance of warmth, and pulled on his coat. Already the wonderful heat had succumbed to the frigidity of the icy morning. For five minutes he waited, each one growing colder than the last, until he knew it was time to pull out his only weapon.

He shoved his key into the ignition and started the engine. With an affectionate pat to the dashboard, Joel murmured, "I give her five minutes, tops, old girl."

Lauren's text message came as Joel whizzed down Hearthfield Way. Two words: CALL ME.

"Oh, boy. Lauren is finally speaking to me about her date on Thursday."

"What happened?"

Heat filled Cassie's cheeks as she tapped Lauren's contact button and waited for it to dial. "Just listen. You'll hear."

Lauren's voice filled the phone. "Okay. Spill it."

Oh, great. Cassie took a deep breath and a sneak glance at Joel. "So, what'd Grant tell you?"

"Well, when Grant arrived with Kayla and I squealed, he laughed and said, 'That's not what Cassie did when she saw Kayla.' So I asked what he meant and all he said, 'Ask Cassie.'"

Eeep! I said to let me tell her, but isn't that a bit excessive? Joel nudged her as Cassie sat scrambling for words. "Sorry. Well, you see, I didn't have my car, so I took the subway on Wednesday, remember?"

All through the story, she tried to play it up with as much suspense as she could interject. "I just didn't have any idea why he'd be going the wrong way with flowers. And then when he met a gorgeous gal, all hugs and kisses, handing her flowers— what was I *supposed* to think? Then he told me not to *tell* you! Seriously, Lauren, I was ready to call you and show you proof with pictures and everything."

"If anyone else told me this story, I'd be incredulous, but you..."

"Only you would throw a word like incredulous into this conversation!"

Even Joel snickered in almost perfect sync with Lauren. "Okay, so why didn't I get pictures of my cheating boyfriend's philan—um, *cheating?*"

"I showed Mr. Sylmer and he said, 'They sure look a lot alike.' What else could I do? I called Grant and asked who the girl was. He begged me not to tell you about it until after you'd met her. I guess she was concerned about his sudden declarations of love for some Rockland chick and decided to visit... something about making him promise *not* to tell you she was coming?"

Lauren didn't answer—*couldn't* from the sound of her laughter. Cassie put the phone on speaker and warned Lauren of it. "Joel's listening to your cackling."

"I do *not* cackle!"

"Like a witch! Ha! Does Grant know it?"

Silence. Cassie glanced at Joel and nodded a warning. A sigh, a shrug, and capitulation—beautiful. Joel sounded a bit hen-pecked as he muttered, "You do sometimes sound a bit... cackly...."

"Oh, Joel..." Lauren didn't bother continuing. They all knew exactly what she thought.

"So, what did you think of Grant's sister... Kaylee?"

"Kayla. She's great." Before Cassie could ask for elaboration, Lauren went off on an uncharacteristic download of their evening. Cassie switched out of speakerphone mode—just in case. "—great. I mean it. She is a lot like you, actually. We laughed so hard. By the time we left the restaurant, she said, 'I came here to tell you not to hurt my brother, but so help me if he hurts you...'"

The sign-less storefront loomed before them. *When did we stop? How long have we been here?* Telepathing the questions to Joel failed to give her the answers she wanted. Lauren called her name—twice. "Sorry, what?"

"I asked if you were busy tonight. Grant wanted to take you and Evan out with us." She swallowed hard. "Who can we get to be a sort-of date for Kayla? I'd ask Joel, but—"

Without hesitating, Cassie covered the phone speaker and asked. "So, Grant and Lauren want to take Evan and me out tonight, but Grant's sister..."

The flash of pain—it barely showed, but she caught it. However, despite her assurances that he didn't have to, Joel nodded. "She's not moving here, right?"

Even as she shook her head no, Cassie decided to ask. "Hey, Joel seems willing, but wants to make sure Kayla isn't moving here or anything."

"Nope. She's happy in Chicago thank-you-very much. Tell Joel I owe him. Meet at Vivaldi's at… seven? I think that's what time the reservations are for."

"Sure." A second thought hit her. "Well, assuming Evan wants to go."

Once more, Lauren's laughter filled the phone. "Cassie, just mention Joel. That's all it'll take. He has no idea how jealous he is of Joel."

A glance Joel's way showed him growing antsy. She grabbed her purse and reached for the door handle. "I'll do that. But he doesn't have anything to worry about."

❦ ❦ ❦

She burst through the door at six fifteen, covered in dust, grime, and drenched in snow and sweat. Joel's truck roared away from the house with finality that, if Bev and Mr. Chao had observed, would certainly mean a call to her mother, "concerned" about the "fight" she must have had with her "nice boyfriend."

"Think, people should mind their own business!" With each word, came another tug of her clothing—tugs that left a shirt in the living room, a bra in the hallway, and jeans—how she managed not to fall flat on her face struggling to run *and* remove them, she didn't know—half in her room, half in the bathroom. The shower came on, and not until she'd managed to step into the already steaming spray did Cassie realize how disappointed she would have been had she not changed her goal for the week. "That had to be You, Lord. Thanks. Like, a million or something."

The clock read six twenty-five as she began the closet "flipple." "What do I wear, Think?" No answer. "Pants or skirt?"

269

Again, silence.

With each flip of her fingers over the hangers, Cassie grumbled more. "—use is having a roommate if he won't help me get ready! Evan is going to be here in five minutes, and I am *so* not going to be ready."

The doorbell rang.

"Think, will you get that?!" She couldn't help but grin. One foot kicked the door shut before she dove for her jeans and the phone she hoped she'd stashed in the pocket. "Score!" The doorbell rang again just as Cassie finished typing a text. COME IN. JUST GOT HOME. SORRY.

Once more, the closet loomed with unhelpful selections. Her favorites—too cool or too warm. The ones that looked best on her? Too casual or too dressy. The rest? Too boring. So, with hair dripping down her shoulders, soaking the towel wrapped around her body, Cassie called out to him. "Evan?"

His voice grew louder with each step. "Yeah? Where are you?"

"In my room. I can't decide what to—" The doorknob turned as a gentle knock filled the room. Cassie dove for the bathroom. "Eeep! Come... in!" Even as she spoke, the door swung mostly shut. Cassie peered around the edge and through the crack. "Can you pick something out for me? Anything? Fast! Vivaldi's is good for mildly casual to moderately dressy so just don't go too far either way. I can't decide."

A pink sweater—too warm, of course—and a muted turquoise skirt appeared. "Got black boots anywhere?"

"Other room. Closet. Top shelf. Wide green box. And thanks. Can you shut my door behind you? I need a few... *other* things."

A solid *whap!* filled the silence. Cassie peered around the door again and stepped through. *I cannot believe I did that. How weird is that?* "Hey, I'm like six and can't make up my mind about what to wear, so will you do it for me?" *Oh, grow up, Cassie.*

Despite her grumbling, she saw the effect in the mirror and

almost squealed her excitement. *Good eye for color. I wouldn't have put these two together.*

A second once-over showed her dressed. Cassie flung open her door and hurried to the bathroom. She reached for the tub of "mousse" and hesitated. *This is not the time for experimental stuff. It worked yesterday, but still…*

Without a second thought, she grabbed her can and squirted the perfect dollop into her hand. An unexpected thrill filled her as she pulled out her hair dryer and, with diffuser in place, began drying her hair. Evan appeared at the door, box in hand. "These?"

"Yep. Can you set them on the bed?" Evan reappeared seconds later, and when he tried to take a furtive glance at his phone, Cassie took pity on him. "Can you time me? Five minutes. The drier my hair is, the less likely it is to create icicles as we wait to get into the restaurant."

Her heart slowed into an almost non-existent beat as she waited for his response. There it was—disbelief. Evan shook his head. "Tell me that's not possible…." Her manufactured blank expression—it couldn't have been more perfect. "Wow… ice in your *hair?* Dry it all the way!"

As Cassie flipped the dryer to the other side of her head, Cassie winked at him in the mirror. "Gotcha."

"I guess I'll go wait in there with Think. Maybe he'll give up some of your secrets."

A snicker escaped before she could stop it. "Waste of your time, Robinson. Waste of your time. He's 'as silent as the grave,' as they used to say." A thought prompted her to call out. "How many minutes are left?"

Evan waved her back to her hair drying as he leaned against the doorjamb once more. One hand held his phone, the other slipped into his pocket. That one movement changed everything. Just as Cassie flipped her head over to get the under layers, she saw him—truly—for the first time. *Whoa, Lord! I knew he was attractive, but wow. That is a seriously great look on* him. *Who wears vests like that? I mean, hipster types, sure. But he's not a hipster! And it works for him.* Cassie flipped her hair back once more and swallowed. *Man does it work for him.*

"Time."

Disappointment—she couldn't hide it. Cassie turned off the dryer, scrunched her curls once more, and reached for her makeup. "Thanks. I needed it as dry as possible."

"If you need to finish, I could always call Lauren—"

"No, she hates it when people are late." She reached for a foam makeup sponge and froze. "Oh. Nooo... no, no, no, no..."

"What!" Evan stepped forward just a bit." Cassie watched, with unsuppressed amusement as his eyes darted about, looking for some critter ready to jump at her. "I don't see anything."

She wriggled the sponge. "That's because this doesn't attack, but I just realized that eventually I'll *have* to switch makeup types. I can't keep using these, and I know there aren't *that* many left in the bag. Drat!"

"Isn't that taking things a bit far? I mean, when a girl has to mess with her makeup—" He choked back the words. "I mean, not that you *need* it...."

"You can stop there. No use digging a hole. I know what you mean. But surely mineral stuff is better for me, the planet, and who knows who else. A brush isn't disposable and isn't made of petroleum products." She glared at the offensive foam "sponge." "This, on the other hand, probably is."

Cassie's fingers shook as she reached for her blush. "Um, can you go grab my dark gray coat? It's in the same closet where you found the boots. I'll be right out."

The smile he gave her sent her stomach flopping in delightful ways it hadn't for a very long time. *And you thought he was attractive* before. *Ha!*

A swipe of one eye brush—another. Eyeliner, mascara— careful attention to the shape of her lips with a pencil and a quick coat of lipstick. *There. That'll have to do.* Cassie grabbed a scarf she often wore with the pink sweater and marveled that it happened to have the same muted turquoise in the pattern. *How did I never notice that?*

One step into the hall sent her heart racing, her face flaming, her mind reeling. *No, no, no, nooooooo...* She snatched up her bra and hurried to the hamper. In the living room, with Evan's back to her, Cassie dove for the shirt and tried to stuff it behind a couch cushion before he turned around.

She failed.

The twinkle in Evan's eye, the smirk on his lips. He tossed a look at Think and shoved both hands in his pockets before leveling a look on her. "Lose something back there? Maybe you should check the hall."

"You're so dead. I can't—oh, man." Cassie snatched her coat from the back of the couch and fumbled with it in a futile attempt to dress herself. *You clearly had no trouble with the reverse—just like a toddler!*

Evan's hands appeared in her peripheral vision as he took the coat and held it for her. Once settled on her shoulders, he leaned forward and murmured, "That's what you get for the icicles. I didn't even have to *try* to get you back. The Lord apparently takes care of *that* kind of 'vengeance', too."

⚞⚞ ⚞⚞ ⚞⚞

Light flipped on, coat tossed in the general direction of a hook—tossed and missed—vaulted couch and flopped against the cushions. Fumble for the remote. TV on. Phone out, feet kicked up on the arm of the couch, and fingers scrolling for the website as the late-night show host interviewed a disgraced actor who narrowly escaped jail.

Evan sighed. No post yet. He scrolled through pictures of the evening. The one he took as Cassie blow-dried her hair with her head upside down. *She didn't get mad that I took it. That has to be a good sign.* Three selfies—ones he'd searched for a fault with so he could ask for another until he realized she didn't mind selfies—with someone else in them. *Missed that nuance when she mentioned hating them. Must pay attention to everything she says. Her words often sound flippant and rambling, but every one is an insight into her. They actually mean something even when it's just "totally" or "seriously."*

Another click on the website showed nothing. But before he could scroll back to his pictures, the phone rang. *Mom*

"Mom! What's wrong? You—"

"Deep breath. We're all fine. I just couldn't sleep and thought you might still be up—being a Saturday night. Did you go out with Cassie again?"

Why did I ever think that moving across the country would possibly give me some relational privacy? When she called his name again, Evan jerked himself out of his thoughts. "Sorry, Mom. Yes, I was out with Cassie—group date. Lauren's boyfriend's sister is in town...." Evan retraced those mental and relational steps to ensure he'd spoken correctly. "Yes. Anyway, so we went out with them. Cassie's friend went as Kayla's date—the boyfriend's sister."

"I thought I was following it. Now I think I'm confused. Lauren is dating Grant whose sister is visiting. The sister is Kayla?"

"Right. And she went out with—"

"Joe. Got it."

Evan tried to avoid rolling his eyes. Somehow, even over the phone, his mother had "eyes in the back of her head." "Actually, it's Joelllll."

"And you're still jealous of him."

"I'm not—" It wasn't worth the argument. She'd always been able to read him and well. "Well, I should say I'm *trying* not to be jealous. Oh, and I have pictures. Hold on." He selected the night's pictures and zipped them over to her. "Even got one of her drying her hair."

Another mistake. He'd lost his mind or something. His mother's voice broke through the stern lecture he began for himself. "—doing in a young woman's *bedroom?* I see her bed in the mirror reflection there. You know better, Evan!"

"I just brought her shoes, she asked me to time her hair drying—she was late and wanted to avoid icicles in her hair— and then I left." A slow smile formed. *I guess I won't mention the trail of clothes from the door to the bedroom. No reason to prejudice you against her.* Evan swallowed hard at the memory.

"And what are you leaving out?"

How do you do that? Desperate to hide that little factoid, Evan blurted out the first thing that came to mind. "She spent all day with him again."

"With Joel? Well, they've been friends a long time, right?"

Too long. He flipped his phone back to the picture of just the two of them. "Yeah. And he's told her how he feels. She's not into it."

"And she went as *your* date. Don't over-think this, Evan. To put it somewhat crassly, if she wanted Joel, she could have him. She went out with *you.*"

If anyone wonders why guys tell their moms things they regret later, this is it. Because despite all the nagging and meddling, they manage to say just what you need to hear when you need to hear it. The thoughts filled his heart, but he didn't speak them. Instead he said the words she wanted to hear most. "I love you, Mom. Thanks."

"Buy her flowers. Girls love flowers."

"If I can find any without cellophane, I just might do it."

"They come in vases, you know—mason jars, even. There are these nice little cold cases in grocery—"

His laughter filled the room, drowned out the comedic monologue on the late-night show, and drowned out the rest of her teasing. "Got it. For the first time, notification of her post actually made it to the phone. "Hey, Mom? I've been waiting for her blog post. She said it was going to be a great one tonight— funny story. I'm going to go read it. I'll call you tomorrow."

"Evan?" His heart clenched at the tone. He knew it—knew

it well, and didn't like it. "What's wrong?"

"Look at the picture of you and Lauren. Buy those flowers—tomorrow. And it might be time to admit you're nervous about being able to compete with someone who knows her so well."

Mouth dry, he choked out a goodbye and flipped to the picture. There, to one side, almost out of view, Joel and Cassie leaned close together in conversation. That wouldn't have bothered him much, but the way she had her hand on his arm, gazed at him, laughed with him. *Oh, great.*

Some things need time to consider—that would be one. Evan flipped back to his notifications, tapped the blog post, and began reading.

It's Not Easy Being Green

No. Seriously. It's not. First, you do stupid things like make bad change choices—no extra hot water in winter? The more I think about it, the more I can't believe what I did! Second, you let everyone decide for you. Since out of fifteen suggestions, nine were "preparedness" for green choices, I'm doing it, but I don't have to like it. That sewing machine is going to become my new best friend. Or, maybe it'll be my new worst enemy. Whatever it is, it's going to be something extreme. That much, I know.

Saturday is thrifting day. I go to estate sales (all two of them today) and garage sales (ha! In January. That's funny) and when there aren't many of either (like today), I scour my favorite thrift stores in search of treasures that have been overlooked. It wasn't a very successful day on any account, but I did get a couple of large pieces of furniture that I'll need for my new store, as well as some great fabric for making reusable bags for shopping at various places and for various things.

Wait. Just so you can fully appreciate how horrible the first part of my day was, I should tell you about how my friend woke me up with coffee—sounds nice, right? And then when I fell asleep again on my couch, he DUMPED SNOW ON ME! That's right! But girls, this is why you take your self-defense classes. I had that guy by the neck in my hall inside thirty seconds. He didn't scream like a baby, but I think he wanted to. *Joel, don't kill my delusions*.

He ran out and into his truck. Cheater. I mean, it got cold. So he turned it on. He KNEW I'd HAVE to come out there or deal with guilt. I capitulated. Bully for me. OR him. Or whatever.

Of course, we had to take the stuff out to HearthLand. Let's just say that I think gas is going to be my last week thing. And I'm closing shop the last week of December. Yeah, it's stacking the deck. I'm all for getting decked out after Christmas. Or something.

As he read, Evan's head wagged like a puppy with a sock. "This is who you are. This carefree, tell it like it is, no pretension at all person is exactly who you are. Lord, I love this about her. She's so real, raw—so... *something*."

He'd have continued praying, but words on the screen beckoned him.

Okay. So, we're at HearthLand. I got the contract to sign. I didn't sign it.

That probably got your attention. Yeah. I didn't. I told him I wanted to read it some more, think about it, look around, see what the store apartments were like, talk to people who might be running my store for me—everything. So first we went on a tour. Look, HearthLand is amazing. If you've ever wanted the freedom to have a lettuce garden instead of a lawn, this is where you want to live! If you've ever wanted a petting zoo for your kids IN YOUR BACKYARD, move here. Look there are pros and cons to this place. There are lots of them, actually, but to making the decision, people seem to get hung up on the idea that you're not actually owning the property. They're right. You technically do not pick up dirt, let it spill from your fist as you raise it over your head, and you can't say, "As God is my witness..." and then insist you'll have the land forever and eternity! But, people don't get all bent out of shape that they don't own the dirt of the land Walmart sits on. They're investors. They have it. But they don't do it. Why? Well, because that's how investing works. You have a financial stake in the success of the enterprise. Think of it as paying rent for life that you can GET BACK if you don't want to live there anymore— maybe get back more than you paid. See, it's just like owning. But not.

So, Ralph and Annie took me around to see the different ways that people live there. There's this cellist. Seriously. From the Rockland Symphony! She has chickens and a couple of indoor planters for herbs and tomatoes. Otherwise, that's it. She doesn't want a bucolic life. She's going to get one, of course. She's marrying a farmer soon. HA! Too funny. Sounds like something that would happen to me. Plan for a nice city penthouse and end up hoeing potatoes on a farm. There's this cool woman who owns a taco truck that is also running the restaurant here on Mexican night Oh. Man. Her tacos are AMAZING. Just sayin'. Get Mama Vega's tacos next time you need a new food addiction. And then buy a Prius. Trust me, you'll save the cost of the car in gas over the course of your addiction.

They took me out to see the community chicken coops, the goat pens—did you know they milk those things?—and the cows. Obviously, they milk the cows. They're such little cows! I mean, they're BIG... but not like a regular cow. They call them Dexter cows and I tried not to visualize vigilante cows out to rid the world of Chick-fil-A chickens or something. Just sayin'.

I begged to milk one. I know. I don't know what I was thinking. It seemed like a good idea at the time. You know, I pictured me being Pa Ingalls on TV. I'd just sit down on a stool, pat the cow's side, squeeze, and bam. Milk. Oh, no. You have to wash those teats, and you can't just sit too close or they'll kick you or the milk pail. Then you go to squeeze and well... Sorry. It's taking a minute to keep this G rated. Let's just say that it feels inappropriate to be man—make that WOMAN—handling anyone's um... PERSONAL parts. Even a cow. I'm waiting for PETA to report me to the APS (animal protective services) for inappropriate contact or something. Please visit me in jail. Do not bring milk or other dairy products. Thank you.

Right there, Evan lost it. Laughter, tears streaming down his face, he fumbled to copy the link and text it to his mom. His message: GET KLEENEX AND READ. YOU'RE WELCOME.

The story drew him back. He could just imagine what might come next.

This is where things got really—awkward. I squeezed. Nothing. They told me to pull and squeeze. I pulled and squeezed. They said "harder." I stared at that hoof and almost gave up. Confession time. If Joel hadn't been standing there doing his best NOT to laugh at me, I probably would have quit. That guy brings out the worst in me. Or the best. Don't know which it is, actually.

Annie suggested I go "faster." Okay, so by this point I have a drop of milk in the pail, aching hands, sore arms, and I'm just pumping and squeezing these teats like chocolate is going to flow or something. I mean, I was going to town. The udder is all saggy, the teats have no life in them, and I'm getting suspicious right about this point. That's when Annie, Ralph, and Joel bust out laughing. Yeah. For the record, you can't milk flaccid teats. If that udder isn't full, don't try. You'll be the butt of a joke about—whatever.

It gets worse. Before I could manage to squat properly enough to rise up off the stool, the cow expelled noxious fumes. Flatulence. Look. I thought I knew farts. I went to middle school. There were middle school boys there. Need I say more? I thought not. Those boys had nothing on this little heifer—cow—bossy—whatever you call milch cows. (See, at least I know that much! Milch, not milk. See! HA!)

So right about then is when I fell over. And right about then is when I also decided to join PETA in the fight against animal products—well, specifically bovine. I couldn't care less if you want to milk a horse or a rabbit. Go for it. Eat 'em for dinner for all I care. But please. If every cow in the world lets out one of those things every day, ozone will be a thing of the past inside a week or two. I'm sure of it.

In case you were wondering, I did eat a lot of Mama Vega's beans after that. And if we needed the truck windows rolled up to keep warm on the way home, well... What can I say? Payback stinks or some saying like that. I just made it literal. *pumps fist*

In other news, I managed to get all that flatulence out in his truck and *not* in my boyfriend's car. WHEW. Or should I say "Peeeewwwwww?" Either works. Score another one for Cassie. HA!

As for the green front, I say I did a lot of green stuff today. Mostly it came in the form of handing my hard-earned green over to people for furniture, and bringing home a contract that'll make it possible for me to make some back, but otherwise...

Hopefully, tomorrow I'll have more for you. Maybe a nice picture of me with a pretty tote bag. Or at least, not an ugly one. That'll work. Meanwhile, here's me and Farty—I mean, Bossy. I actually don't know if she has a name. But here she is. Here I am. Here we are. Is it me or is she gloating?

What I wouldn't have given to see that. Oh. Man. Maybe I should buy a truck when my lease runs out on the Avalon. Just the thought shook him. That's a bit extreme for after a few dates. Maybe I should just offer to drive her around for her stuff. Joel can pick up her stuff like they used to. Yeah.

He pulled up her contact and grinned at the goofy face she made on screen. With a tap, his text message screen opened, and Evan typed.

GREAT POST. WISH I COULD HAVE SEEN THAT. WOULD LOVE TO GO WITH YOU ON YOUR THRIFTING TRIPS SOMETIME. THANKS FOR A GREAT NIGHT. HAD FUN. LAUREN IS FALLING IN LOVE WITH GRANT. ISN'T IT KIND OF SOON? GOODNIGHT. WANT TO MEET UP AFTER CHURCH FOR LUNCH?

His thumb hovered over the send button. He took a deep breath, prayed for favor, and tapped it. The message disappeared into cyberspace. Time for bed.

Evan's teeth foamed with toothpaste as her reply came through. His toothbrush hand froze in place as his free hand tapped the screen. Her eloquent response brought a smile to lips that now looked rabid and maniacal.

SURE.

Sunday, January 31—

The moment their server turned away from the table, Cassie pulled out the contract and passed it to Evan. "You will so regret inviting me out. What do you think of this?"

With that, she kicked back and sipped on her drink, watching him. Evan read every line, or at least he appeared to, with the paper held out away from him. *You're farsighted. Do you know it or is your eyesight changing? How old are you, anyway? I don't even know. Do I? Did Lauren say if you're older or younger than she is? Aaak!*

"This line here…" Evan paused until she looked up at him. "The one about the rent. Is this for real?"

"Right? That's what I said! But he said he wants this store there enough and that it'll be more than he'd get from an empty place that he's willing to risk it. We'll reevaluate actual rent costs later, but I thought ten percent of sales was dirt cheap."

Without another word, Evan kept reading. Their food arrived. Cassie prayed and ate. Evan picked at his fries but left his burger untouched until he'd read the entire document—at least twice, from the looks of it. "Well, it's thorough, but not couched in legalese."

"And…"

He picked up the burger, ready to take a bite and shrugged. "My only concern is that rent clause. Anything that sounds too good to be true, usually is. And well, think about it. There's no telling what price he'll charge for rent once he has you hooked. You might—"

Cassie shoved back from the table, folded her arms over her chest, and scowled. "Seriously? You just decide that a guy is a crook because he gave me an incentive to even give his *remote town* a fighting chance? What is with you?" She grabbed her purse and started to rise, but Evan dropped the burger and leaned back in his chair, confusion filling his eyes and a tight line across his lips.

"What's with *you?*"

Purse in hand, Cassie ordered herself *not* to swing it at him. *You'd probably miss and just make a mess anyway.*

"Well?"

"I can't believe you think I'm so stupid. Um, I'm not the only one who's talked to hi—"

"I know. Joel has vetted him, so everything is just fine. I'm curious, Cassie." Evan leaned forward and planted his palms on the table as if ready to rise. "If *Joel* has approved the project, why ask *my* opinion?"

Before she could stop herself, Cassie sank back into the chair, purse still clutched in her lap. "Really? This boils down to your jealousy of Joel?"

He blustered, argued, laid out an explanation that couldn't have been more eloquent if he tried. And at the end of it, with set jaw and eyes that hinted at anger or pain—though she couldn't tell which—Evan pulled out his wallet, threw cash on the table, and turned to go. "I'll be in the car."

The sounds around her—dishes clinking, laughter, a baby's cry—pressed in on her until she thought she'd go mad. Cassie whipped out her phone and zipped a text message to Lauren, Silvie, Amy and Joel. IS ANYONE NEAR FARGO'S? I THINK I NEED A RIDE.

That done, she bolted from the table. Each step toward the bathroom added another coal to her rapidly flaming ire. Cassie stood before the sink, glaring into the mirror. "What is *wrong* with him? Jerk!"

A voice from one of the stalls jerked her from her not-so-internal tirade. "Dump his sorry butt."

"If even his *butt* was sorry, I might be able to handle it, but I think he's seething in the car—aaaand... why am I talking to a stranger in a restaurant bathroom stall about my now non-existent love life? Sorry. Bye."

With that she strode from the bathroom and to the front of the restaurant. Two steps from the coat rack, she plowed into Evan. "Sorry—oh."

"That's my line—the sorry part. I owe you a big one."

"Yeah, you do." Cassie sagged. "And I probably owe you one, too. Let's go." Without another word, she pushed through the entrance door and pulled her phone from her pocket. Hardly watching where she was going, and irrationally irritated at Evan's careful propelling of her out of the path of oncoming vehicles, Cassie sent out another group text. CRISIS AVERTED. RIDE NO LONGER NEEDED. EXPLAIN LATER.

The car—warm. *Bet he ran the engine so I wouldn't be cold. Can't he even fight fair on that one? Jerk.* But despite her mental grousing, Cassie smiled.

"Does that smile mean you'll consider forgiving me, or should I begin the groveling process?"

"You grovel, we're through. I don't do the grovel thing—from either side." Cassie let out a long, slow exhale. "Evan, if Joel is going to be a problem for you, then we won't work.

Maybe you should take some time to think—"

Evan gripped the steering wheel and glared at the painted brick wall before them. "He'll be a problem for me. Yes. Always. But letting your friendship come between us is a bigger one for me. I've never been jealous before. I convinced myself I wasn't really. Talk about dumb."

"If you stick around, you can't blame me for doing exactly what I warned you I'd do. You can't change the rules. I don't play those games—not anymore."

Slow-motion movies had nothing on Evan's snail-like speedlessness as he reached for her hand and squeezed it. "I never promised not to hold your hand—just that I wouldn't try to kiss you. So here we go. Take two." He stared at their intertwined fingers until Cassie wondered if he'd changed his mind. But his eyes met hers. "So... Did I tell you I asked Lauren to bring me to your party because she'd talked so much about you that I couldn't wait to meet you?"

Focused on half a letter obliterated by time and scrubbed off graffiti, Cassie didn't even look his way when she murmured, "And he redeems himself in one endearing question. I'm toast."

The chuckles that filled the car *and* her heart sent conflicted emotions through her. *Kind of regret that whole no kissing thing now, Lord. I mean... wow. Then again, it's probably for the best. Eeep!*

‖ ‖ ‖

Think and Cassie sat side by side—him on the end table, her on the couch. Laptop open, bank register open, Boogie Board waiting, she began her final blog post of the month. "Here goes nothing, Think. We did it. A whole month. Only eleven to go."

State of the Eco-ness Address

January 31. I made it a whole month. I started this process with no clue of what I'd committed to. I've wanted to quit every. single. day. And frankly, I'm going to want to quit tomorrow. Something always happens. But when I look back on changes that really are just second-nature now, I can't help but think, "Wow! It's not so bad!"

And it's not, okay? I grumble, I complain, I throw mini tantrums that only Think sees and will never tell—he's loyal that way—but at the end of the day, most of what I've started doing isn't so bad.

Take my salads. I've always taken them to work. So that hasn't changed. Now I make them fresh instead of buying bags. Now I take them in jars instead of plastic bowls. Why? Because it's so cool to see all those jars lined up in my fridge!

Shopping? It's no longer a recreational hobby. Gotta admit, I don't even miss it. I was SURE I would. But seriously, it's not fun to go into a store and stare at a million things you can't even hope to purchase and be "on plan" as my friend called it. Almost everything in stores is wrapped in paper or plastic. Most things are made of one of those two. And you know what is really scary? The things I've wanted most, I managed to get second-hand. I wanted a Silver Settings CD. Guess what I found yesterday at the thrift store. It was just released LAST MONTH. There. Unused. Someone must have gotten Christmas present they didn't want. And thanks to that unfortunate gift, I have one of the few things I've had to do without that really mattered to me.

I made new friends this month—first a boyfriend and then people at the eco-group. Maya and I are going out this week. I think I'll invite Aaron to lunch, too. He was fun. How about it, Aaron? Want to grab a hot dog from that vendor on 34th? He said he'd serve me on a cloth napkin if I insisted. Still haven't won over a pasty vendor, but hey. I'm working on it.

Restaurants can still be a problem. I mean, you ask for a drink without a straw. They comply without a problem. But they bring a refill, and when there's no straw in the old glass, they plop one on the table unless you're fast enough to stop them. Once it touches the table—land-filler. These poor servers are just doing their jobs, but it's stressful to me.

My garbage has morphed into almost nothing. No joke. I've considered getting a small dog to eat my meat scraps so I can use the same trash bag for a month. I BET it would take that long for the thing to fill up. I am WASTING my expensive trash bags on meat scraps. They're the only things that make me have to dump it. Sigh.

But the biggest thing that's happened is the effect this has had on my bank account. I've written down every single thing I would normally buy but didn't. Subtracted the things I did. And in one month—you will not believe this—even with several things I chose to buy, I've saved almost four hundred dollars. In one month!

Look, I'm not going to save that much every month. But that I did at all is huge! Just the fact that I made instead of bought things like the napkins, tote bags, produce bags, etc. Saved a huge amount. I saved a ton on gas this week. Had to pay to fill up Joel's truck yesterday, and that was more, but even then, I came out twenty bucks ahead just by having my car in the shop.

What's up next? Well, this week I'm making some cool stuff. On my list are...

- ○   Tote bags for groceries
- ○   Mesh bags for fruits and vegetables
- ○   Something washable for meats
- ○   Washable Ziploc style bags

I'm trying to figure out a better laundry bag/basket. You see, my stupid laundry basket is almost dead. I tripped over it and snapped a couple of the lattice pieces. Half a dozen already were goners. No comments from the peanut gallery on my weight or clumsiness. Hey, just what IS a peanut gallery, and why do we care? You've gotta help me out here, folks. Think is ignoring me tonight. I think he's jealous of the other men in my life.

Cassie snickered at that. "Bet Joel and Evan both groan at that one thinking it's about him when it's both. HA! Her eyes grew heavy as she typed. "Gotta finish this, Think. I need sleep. Tomorrow is another month, and I have to learn to hem. Somehow. May the Lord have mercy on my stitches—or something like that."

I'll admit to a bit of nervousness. I have so many big things ahead of me. I mean, this week I discovered something I'd missed all along. Makeup. I have to change mine. I need something I can apply with a brush. My liquid stuff—not so much. So... Well... Yeah. Guys, close your eyes and scroll up a couple. There. Girls, I have to come to grips with sanitary products. Right now, my options are crocheted tampons, flannel cloth pads (which sound both comfy and miserable at the same time), or these rubber cup things. BLECH. Okay? Just blech.

I need to toss the chemicals. I need to increase what I grow in my house. I need to plan for less petroleum products and do PRO-active things instead of reactive. I mean, the whole eco mantra is "reduce..." CHECK! "Reuse..." Somewhat. Not great. And "recycle." Haven't done much of that yet. It's hard to recycle much when you're avoiding purchasing things you're supposed to recycle.

Would it be awful to have a "cheat day" a couple of times a year? I think I'll need one. I want to take my boyfriend to StoryLand. I want to buy sodas there. Funnel cakes. Cotton candy. I want to do it all without GUILT. And my birthday. Shouldn't a gal be able to go to her favorite bakery and eat a cupcake without the guilt of the stupid paper wrapping? I think so. I'm just trying to figure out how many is reasonable. My guess is five. What do you think?

Well, I have a long day tomorrow. I'm going to get up early and try to cut out some of those things. I also have a contract to sign and fax over to Ralph. Yeah. I'm going to sign it. That's another thing that happened in one month. I HAVE A BUSINESS! Time to start planning a logo. Does anyone know a graphic designer? I know just what I want, but not how to make it work without being "too much" or worse, "too blah!"

OH! I almost forgot. My messed up Dutch oven that I bought to burn little papery things so I don't have to throw them away? It worked! And I read that if I don't use too much, I can add the ashes to my compost stuff. Considering they were talking about people using fireplace ashes, I doubt my dusting of stuff in that pan can mess stuff up too much. I also learned that you can save up those ashes to make lye. Then you use the lye to make soap. And in the soap making process, the lye disappears or something. I didn't get it, but supposedly there's no lye by the time you actually USE the soap. So ashes to soap. That's pretty amazing. I want to try it, at least. I also sent in a letter to my landlord asking if I can use a wood stove. I read about this brand that has like almost no smoke! It traps it into soot or something like that. I didn't quite get how it worked, but it was cool. They're expensive, but I think it would be worth it—planet-wise.

Well, that's it for the month. See you in February.

An enormous sense of satisfaction filled her as Cassie pushed publish and closed the laptop. With feet up on the coffee table, hands laced behind her head, and eyes closed, she allowed herself a long, slow sigh. "It's been rough, Think. I got and almost lost a new boyfriend. I started a business. *Me!* A business! Wow."

Her phone buzzed. Joel. Cassie tapped the screen and

smiled at the message: SO PROUD OF YOU. CAN'T WAIT TO SEE WHAT YOU DO WITH THAT STORE.

Feeling foolish for *not* feeling foolish about it, Cassie held up the phone for Think to read. "See? I've got people who have my back. It's gonna be a great year."

Lost in thought, Think didn't appear to have heard a word she said.

"Some roomie you are."

to be continued...

Chautona Havig's Books

The Rockland Chronicles

Aggie's Inheritance Series

- Ready or Not
- For Keeps
- Here We Come
- Ante Up!

Past Forward: A Serial Novel (Six Volumes)

- Volume One
- Volume Two
- Volume Three
- Volume Four
- Volume Five
- Volume Six

HearthLand Series: A Serial Novel (Six Volumes)

- Volume One
- Volume Two
- Volume Three
- Volume Four
- Volume Five
- Volume Six

The Hartfield Mysteries

- Manuscript for Murder
- Crime of Fashion
- Two o'Clock Slump
- Front Window (coming 2016)

Noble Pursuits
Argosy Junction
Discovering Hope
Not a Word
Speak Now
A Bird Died
Thirty Days Hath…
Confessions of a De-cluttering Junkie
Corner Booth
Rockland Chronicles Collection One
(Available only on Kindle: Contains *Noble Pursuits*, *Argosy Junction*, and *Discovering Hope*)

The Agency Files

- Justified Means
- Mismatched
- Effective Immediately
- A Forgotten Truth

The Vintage Wren (A serial novel beginning 2016)

- January (Vol 1.)

Sight Unseen Series

- None So Blind

Christmas Fiction

- Advent
- 31 Kisses
- Tarnished Silver
- The Matchmakers of Holly Circle
- Carol and the Belles

* * *

Meddlin' Madeline Mysteries

- Sweet on You (Book1)

* * *

Ballads from the Hearth

- Jack

* * *

Legacy of the Vines

- Deepest Roots of the Heart

* * *

Journey of Dreams Series

- Prairie
- Highlands

* * *

Heart of Warwickshire Series

- Allerednic

* * *

The Annals of Wynnewood

- Shadows & Secrets

- Cloaked in Secrets
- Beneath the Cloak

* * *

Not-So-Fairy Tales

- Princess Paisley
- Everard

* * *

Legends of the Vengeance

The First Adventure

Made in the USA
Lexington, KY
14 July 2017